DUDLEY PUBLIC LIBRARIES

The loan of this book may be renewed if not required by other readers, by contacting the library from which it was borrowed.

...ance from her hom... ...active in local affairs and ...rite the script for the annual .... Her eldest son is a hospital manager ...in all her medical research. As part of a ...ose-knit family, she treasures having two of her sons living close by and the third one not too far away. This also gives her the added pleasure of being able to watch her delightful grandchildren growing up.

Connie Cox used to think authors were sophisticated creatures who lived in NYC, went to glitzy parties and wrote as the muse dictated. Then she met one. The writer looked a lot like her – jeans, a few extra pounds, a love of books and a quirky imagination. With the encouragement of that writer and many like her, Connie now lives the dream, writing big stories from her little desk in her little town. Even as you read this, she is working on a new story and living happily ever after.

A Surprise Family

July 2020
Against the Odds

January 2021
Written in the Stars

August 2020
Proving Their Love

February 2021
The Perfect Family

September 2020
Their Perfect Surprise

March 2021
Baby Makes Three

Their Perfect Surprise

LUCY GORDON

ABIGAIL GORDON

CONNIE COX

MIX
Paper from
responsible sources
FSC
FSC C007454

This book is produced from independently certified FSC™ paper
to ensure responsible forest management.

For more information visit: www.harpercollins.co.uk/green

Printed and bound in Spain

MILLS & BOON

First Published in Great Britain 2020
By Mills & Boon, an imprint of HarperCollins*Publishers*
1 London Bridge Street, London, SE1 9GF

A SURPRISE FAMILY: THEIR PERFECT SURPRISE © 2020
Harlequin Books S.A.

The Secret That Changed Everything © 2012 Harlequin Books S.A.
The Village Nurse's Happy-Ever-After © 2010 Abigail Gordon
The Baby Who Saved Dr Cynical © 2012 Connie Cox

Special thanks and acknowledgement are given to Lucy Gordon
for her contribution to *The Larkville Legacy* series.

ISBN: 978-0-263-28206-1

THE SECRET
THAT CHANGED
EVERYTHING

LUCY GORDON

PROLOGUE

HE WAS there!

After such an anxious search it was hard to be sure at first; aged about thirty, tall, lean, fit, with black hair. Was it really him? But then he made a quick movement and Charlotte knew.

This was the man she'd come to find.

He'd looked different last time, elegantly dressed, smooth, sophisticated, perfectly at home in one of the most fashionable bars in Rome. Now, in the Tuscan countryside, he was equally at home in jeans and casual shirt, absorbed in the vines that streamed in long lines under the setting sun. So absorbed that he didn't look up to see her watching him from a distance.

Lucio Constello.

Quickly she pulled out a scrap of paper and checked his name. At the back of her mind a wry voice murmured that if you'd sought out a man to tell him devastating news it was useful to get his name right. On the other hand, if you'd only exchanged first names, and he'd left while you were still asleep, who could he blame but himself?

She tried to silence that voice. It spoke to her too often these days.

She began to walk the long path between the vines, trying to calm her thoughts. But they refused to be calmed.

They lingered rebelliously on the memory of his naked body against hers, the heat of his breath, the way he'd murmured her name.

There had been almost a question in his voice, as though he was asking her if she were certain. But there was no certainty left in her life. Her family, her boyfriend—these were the things she had clung to. But her boyfriend had rejected her and the foundations of her family had been shaken. So she'd invited Lucio to her bed because—what did it matter? What did anything matter?

He was looking up, suddenly very still as he saw her. What did that stillness mean? That he recognised her and guessed why she was here? Or that he'd forgotten a woman he'd known for a few hours several weeks ago?

When Lucio first looked up the sun was in his eyes, blinding him, so that for a moment he could make out no details. A woman was approaching him down the long avenue of vines, her attention fixed on him as though only he mattered in all the world.

That had happened so many times before. So often he'd seen Maria coming towards him from a great distance.

But Maria was dead.

The woman approaching him now was a stranger and yet mysteriously familiar. Her eyes were fixed on him even at a distance.

And he knew that nothing in the world was ever going to be the same again.

CHAPTER ONE

GOING to Italy had seemed a brilliant move for a language expert. She could improve her Italian, study the country and generally avoid recognising that she wasn't just leaving New York; she was fleeing it.

But the truth was still the truth. Charlotte knew she had to flee memories of an emotion that had once felt like love, but which had revealed itself as disappointingly hollow, casting a negative light on almost everything in her life. It was like wandering in a desert. She belonged to nobody and nobody belonged to her. Perhaps it was this thought that made her leave her laptop computer behind. It pleased her to be beyond the reach of anyone unless she herself decided otherwise.

For two months she wandered around Italy, seeking something she couldn't define. She made a point of visiting Naples, fascinated by the legendary Mount Vesuvius, whose eruptions had destroyed cities in the past. Disappointingly it was now considered so safe that she could wander up to the summit and stand there listening hopefully for a growl.

Silence.

Which was a bit like her life, she thought wryly. Waiting for something significant to happen. But nothing did. At twenty-seven, an age when many people had chosen their path in life, she still had no clue where hers was leading.

On the train from Naples to Rome she thought of Don, the man she'd briefly thought she loved. She'd wanted commitment and when Don didn't offer it she'd demanded to know where they were headed. His helpless shrug had told her the worst, and she'd hastened to put distance between them.

She had no regrets. Briefly she'd wondered if she might have been cleverer and perhaps drawn him closer instead of driving him away. But in her heart she knew things had never been quite right between them. It was time to move on.

But where?

As the train pulled into Roma Termini she reckoned it might be interesting to find the answer to that question.

She took a taxi to the Hotel Geranno on the Via Vittorio Veneto, one of the most elegant and expensive streets in Rome. The hotel boasted every facility, including its own internet café. She found it easily and slipped into a booth, full of plans to contact family and friends. She might even get in touch with Don on her social networking site, just to let him know there were no hard feelings, and they could be friends.

But the words that greeted her on Don's page were 'Thanks to everyone for your kind wishes on my engagement. Jenny and I want our wedding to be—'

She shut the file down.

Jenny! Charlotte remembered her always hanging around making eyes at Don. And he'd noticed her. Pretty, sexy, slightly voluptuous—she was made to be noticed.

Not like me, she thought.

Some women would have envied Charlotte's appearance. Tall, slender, dark-haired, dark-eyed; she wasn't a woman who faded into the background. She'd always had her share of male admiration; not the kind of gawping leer that Jenny could inspire, but satisfying enough. Or so she'd thought.

But Don hadn't wasted any time mourning her and that was just fine. The past was the past.

She touched a few more keys to access her email, and immediately saw one from her sister Alex, headlined, You'll never believe this!

Alex liked to make things sound exciting so, although mildly intrigued, Charlotte wasn't alarmed. But, reading the email, she grew still again as a family catastrophe unfolded before her eyes.

'Mom—' she murmured. 'You couldn't have—*it's not possible!*'

She had always known that her father, Cedric Patterson, was her mother's second husband. Before him Fenella had been married to Clay Calhoun, a Texas rancher. Only after their divorce had she married Cedric and lived with him in New York. There she'd borne four children—the twins Matt and Ellie, Charlotte and her younger sister Alexandra. Now it seems that Mom was already carrying Matt and Ellie when she left Clay, Alex wrote. She wrote and told him she was pregnant, but by that time he was with Sandra, who seems to have hidden the letter but, oddly enough, kept it. Nobody knew about it until both she and Clay were dead. He died last year, and the letter was found unopened, so I guess he never knew about Matt and Ellie.

What do you think of that? All these years we've thought they were our brother and sister, but now it seems we're only half-siblings! Same mother, different father. When Ellie told me what had happened I couldn't get my head around it, and I'm still in a spin.

Quickly Charlotte ran through her other emails, seeking one from Ellie that she was sure would be there. But she found nothing. Disbelieving, she ran through them again, but there was no word from Ellie.

Which meant that everyone in the family knew except her. Ellie hadn't bothered to tell her something so momentous. It had been left to Alex to send her the news as an afterthought, as though she was no more than a fringe member of the family. Which, right now, was how she felt.

Returning to the lobby she again knew the sensation of being lost in a desert. But this desert had doors, one leading to a restaurant known for its haute cuisine, the other leading to a bar. Right this minute a drink was what she needed.

The barman smiled as she approached. 'What can I get you?'

'A tequila,' she told him.

When it was served she looked around for a place to sit, but could see only one seat free, at the far end of the bar. She slipped into it and found that she could lean back comfortably against the wall, surveying her surroundings.

The room was divided into alcoves, some small, some large. The small ones were all taken up by couples, gazing at each other, revelling in the illusion of privacy. The larger ones were crowded with 'beautiful people' as though the cream of Roman society had gathered here tonight.

In the nearest alcove six people focused their attention on one man. He was king of all he surveyed, Charlotte thought with a touch of amusement. And with reason. In his early thirties, handsome, lean, athletic, he held centre-stage without effort. When he laughed, they laughed. When he spoke they listened.

Nice if you can get it, Charlotte thought with a little sigh. *I'll bet his volcano never falls silent.*

Just then he glanced up and saw her watching him. For the briefest moment he turned his head to one side, a question in his eyes. Then one of the women claimed his attention and he turned to her with a perfectly calculated smile.

An expert, she thought. He knows exactly what he's doing to them, and what they can do for him.

Such certainly seemed enviable. Her own future looked depressing. Returning to New York smacked of defeat. She could stay in Italy for the year she'd promised herself, but that was less inviting now that things were happening at home; things from which she was excluded.

She thought of Don and Jenny, revelling in their love. All around her she saw people happy in each other's company, smiling, reaching out. And suddenly it seemed unbearable that there was nobody reaching out to her. She finished her drink and sat staring at the empty glass.

'Excuse me, can I just—?'

It was the man from the alcove, easing himself into the slight space between her and the next bar stool. She leaned back to make space for him but a slight unevenness in the floor made him wobble and slew to the side, colliding with her.

'Mi dispiace,' he apologised in Italian, steadying her with his hand.

'Va tutto bene,' she reassured him. 'Niente di male.' All is well. No harm done.

Still in Italian he said, 'But you'll let me buy you a drink to say sorry.'

'Thank you.'

'Another tequila?' asked the barman.

'Certainly not,' said the newcomer. 'Serve this lady a glass of the very best Chianti, then bring another round of drinks to me and my friends over there.'

He retreated and the barman placed a glass of red wine

in front of Charlotte. It was the most delicious she had ever tasted. Sipping it she glanced over at him, and it was no surprise to find him watching her. She raised her glass in salute and he raised his back. This seemed to disconcert the women sitting on either side of him, who asserted themselves to reclaim him, Charlotte was amused to notice.

Despite being in the heart of Rome they were speaking English. She was sitting close enough to overhear some of the remarks passing back and forth, half sentences, words that floated into the distance, but all telling the tale of people who lived expensive lives.

'You were on that cruise, weren't you? Wasn't it a gorgeous ship? Everything you wanted on demand...'

'I knew I'd met you before...you were at the opening of that new...'

'Look at her. If she's not wearing the latest fashion she thinks...'

Leaning back, Charlotte observed the little gathering with eyes that saw everything. Two of the women were watching Lucio like lions studying prey, but they were in alliance. She could have sworn that one murmured to the other, 'Me first'. She couldn't hear the words, but she could read their expressions: watchful, confident that each would have their turn with him.

She could understand their desires. It wasn't merely his striking looks and costly clothes, but his air of being in charge, directing his own life and that of others. This was a man who'd never known doubt or fear.

She envied him. It must be good to know so certainly who you were, what you were, how others saw you and where you belonged in the world, instead of being that saddest of creatures—a woman who drank alone.

As if to emphasise the point the seat beside her was occupied by a woman gazing devotedly at her male companion, who returned the compliment with interest, then slid an arm about her shoulders, drew her close and said fervently, 'Let's go now.'

'Yes, let's,' she breathed. And they were gone.

At once the man in the alcove rose, excused himself to his companions and swiftly claimed the empty seat before anyone else could try.

'Can I get you another drink?' he asked Charlotte.

'Well, just a small one. I should be leaving.'

'Going somewhere special?'

'No,' she said softly. 'Nowhere special.'

After a moment he said, 'Are you alone?'

'Yes.'

He grinned. 'Perhaps you'd be better off with someone to protect you from clumsy guys like me.'

'No need. I can protect myself.'

'I see. No man necessary, eh?'

'Absolutely.'

A voice called, 'Hey, Lucio! Let's get going!'

His companions in the alcove were preparing to leave, beckoning him towards the door.

'Afraid I can't,' he said. 'I'm meeting someone here in half an hour. It was nice to meet you.'

Reluctantly they bid him goodbye and drifted away. When the door was safely closed he breathed out in obvious relief.

'Hey, your friends are crazy about you,' she reproved him lightly. 'You might at least return the compliment.'

'They're not my friends. I only know them casually, and two I never met before today.'

'But you were dousing them with charm.'

'Of course. I'm planning to make money out of them.'

'Ah! Hence the charm!'

'What else is charm for?'

'So now you're girding up for your next "victim" in half an hour.'

He gave a slow smile. 'There's no one coming. That was just to get rid of them.'

She looked down into her glass, lest her face reveal how much this pleased her. He would be a welcome companion for a little while.

He read her exactly, offering his hand and saying, 'Lucio—'

His last name was drowned by a merry shout from further along the bar. She raised her voice to say, 'Charlotte.'

'*Buona sera,* Charlotte.'

'*Buona sera,* Lucio.'

'Are you really Italian?' he asked, his head slightly to one side.

'Why do you ask?'

'Because I can't quite pinpoint your accent. Venice? No, I don't think so. Milan? Hmm. Rome—Naples?'

'Sicily?' Charlotte teased.

'No, not Sicily. You sound nothing like.'

'You said that very quickly. You must know Sicily well.'

'Fairly well. But we were talking about you. Where do you come from?'

His bright smile was like a visor behind which he'd retreated at the mention of Sicily. Though intrigued, she was too wise to pursue the matter just yet. Later would be more interesting.

'I'm not Italian at all,' she said. 'I'm American.'

'You're kidding me!'

'No, I'm not. I come from New York.'

'And you speak my language like a native. I'm impressed.' Someone squeezed by them, forcing them to draw back uncomfortably. 'There's no room for us here,' he said, taking her arm and drawing her towards the door.

Several pairs of female eyes regarded her with frank envy. It was clear that the watching women had their own ideas about how the evening would end.

Well, you're wrong, Charlotte thought, slightly irritated. *He's a nice guy and I'll enjoy talking to him, but that's all. Not everything has to end in* amore, *even in Italy. OK, so he's suave, sophisticated, expensively dressed and fantastically good-looking, but I won't hold that against him.*

'So why Italian?' he asked as they began to stroll along the Via Vittorio Veneto.

'I was always fascinated by foreign languages. I studied several at school, but somehow it was always Italian that stood out and attracted me more than the others. So I learned it through and through. It's such a lovely language.'

'And in the end you got a job here, probably working at the U.S. Embassy, just up the street.'

'No, I don't work here. I'm a translator in New York. I do Italian editions of books, sometimes universities hire me to look over old manuscripts. And I suddenly thought, it's about time I actually saw the country and drank in what it's really like. So I caught the next plane out.'

'Literally?'

'Well, it took a couple of days to make arrangements, but that's all. Then I was free to go.'

'No ties? Family?'

'I've got parents, siblings, but nobody who can constrain my freedom.'

'Freedom,' he mused. 'That's what it's really about, huh?'

'One of the things. I've done some mad, stupid things in my life, and most of them have been about staying free.' She gave a wry laugh. 'It's practically my family nickname. Ellie's the beautiful one, Alex is the lovable one and I'm the crazy one.'

'That sounds fascinating. I'd really like to hear about your craziness.'

'Well, there's the time I set my heart on marrying this guy and my parents said no. We were only seventeen, which they thought was too young.'

He considered this with an air of seriousness that had a touch of humour. 'They could have had a point.'

'The way I saw it they were denying me my own way. Hell would freeze over before I admitted they could be right. So we eloped.'

'You married at seventeen?'

'No way. By the time we'd covered a few miles I could see what a juvenile twerp he was. To be fair I think he'd spotted the same about me. Anyway, I got all set to make a run for it, and bumped into him because *he* was making a run for it, too.'

Lucio roared with laughter. 'What happened when you got home?'

'My mother's a very clever woman. She knew better than to make a fuss. When she caught me sidling in she glanced up and said, "Oh, there you are. Don't make a noise, your father's asleep." We had a talk later but there were no hysterics. By then she was used to me doing stupid things.'

'But would getting married be the path to freedom? Husbands can be very restrictive.'

She chuckled. 'I didn't think of that at the time. I just pictured him doing things my way. Luckily I saw the truth before too late.'

'Yes, husbands have this maddening habit of wanting their own way.'

'Oh, I learnt the lesson.'

'So you still don't have a husband?'

'No husband, no nothing.' She added casually, 'These days it's the way to be.'

'You're a true woman of your age. At one time an unmarried girl would wonder why no man wanted her. Now she wonders what's the best way to keep them off.'

'Right,' she responded in the same teasing voice. 'Sometimes you have to be really ingenious. And sometimes just ruthless.'

'You talk like an expert. Or like a woman who's been kicked in the teeth and is going to do some kicking back.' He saw her wry face and said quickly, 'I'm sorry, I had no right to say that. None of my business.'

'It's all right. If we all minded our own business there'd be precious little of interest to talk about.'

'I've got a feeling I should be nervous about what you're going to say next.'

'I could ask about Sicily, couldn't I? Is that where you keep a secret wife, or perhaps two secret wives? Now that would really be interesting.'

'Sorry to disappoint you but there's no wife, secret or otherwise. I was born in Sicily, but I left it years ago, and I've never been back. The life just didn't suit me. Like you, I went exploring the world, and I ended up with a family who owned vineyards. Vines, wine-making, I loved it from the start. They were wonderful to me, practically adopted me, and finally left the vineyards to me.'

And he'd turned them into a top money-making business, she thought. That was clear from the way he dressed and the way others reacted to him.

They were reaching the end of the street. As they turned the corner Charlotte stopped, astonished and thrilled by the sight that met her eyes.

'The Trevi Fountain,' she breathed. 'I've always wanted to see it. It's so huge, so magnificent….'

This was no mere fountain. A highly decorated palace wall rose behind it, at the centre of which was a triumphal arch, framing the magnificent, half-naked figure of Oceanus, mythical god of water, ruling over the showers that cascaded into the pool below. Everywhere was flooded with light, giving the water a dazzling glitter against the night.

'I've read about it,' she murmured, 'and seen pictures, but—'

'But nothing prepares you,' he agreed. 'Some things have to be experienced before they become real.'

Nearby was a café with tables out on the street. Here they could sit and watch the humming life about them.

'Nice to see people having a good time,' she murmured.

'Does that mean your life is unhappy now?'

'Oh, no,' she said quickly. 'But it does tend to be a bit too serious. Legal documents, history books. Not exactly filled with fun. And sometimes you need to remind yourself about fun.'

He regarded her curiously, thinking that a woman with her looks could have all the fun she wanted with all the men she wanted. So there was a mystery here. But he was too astute to voice the thought.

'But Italy should remind you of fun,' he said. 'It's not all cathedrals and sober history.'

'I know. You've only got to stroll the streets of Rome in the twilight, and see—well, lots of things.'

His grin and the way he nodded spoke volumes about his own life. Doubtless it was full of 'twilight activities', she thought. And they would be fun. She didn't doubt that either.

'Anyway,' she went on, 'my favourite Italian was—'

She named a historical character with a legendary reputation for wickedness.

'He wasn't as bad as people think,' Lucio observed. 'He was actually quite a serious man who—'

'Don't say that,' she interrupted him quickly. 'You'll spoil him for me. If he's not wicked he's not interesting.'

He regarded her curiously. 'There aren't many people who'd see it that way.'

'But it's true.'

'Certainly it's true, but we're not supposed to say so.'

'Well, I'm always doing things I'm not supposed to. That's why I'm the black sheep of the family.'

'Because you eloped at seventeen?'

She chuckled. 'There were a few more things than that. There was the politician who came to hold a meeting in New York, all virtue and pomposity, except that he'd spent the previous night in a place where he shouldn't have been. I'd seen him leaving and I couldn't resist getting up at the meeting and asking him about it.'

'Shame on you!' he said theatrically.

'Yes, I have no sense of propriety, so I'm told.'

'So you're wicked and interesting, eh?'

'Certainly wicked. You know, everyone has their own talents. My sister Ellie is a talented dancer, my sister Alex is a talented vet—'

'And you're a talented linguist.'

'Oh, that! That's just earning a living. No, my real talent, the thing at which I'm practically a genius, is getting my own way.'

'Now you really interest me.'

'It can always be done, if you know how to go about it.'

'Cunning?'

'Certainly. Cunning, devious, manipulative, wicked— whatever it takes.'

'Is that the real reason you broke off your career to go travelling?'

'In one sense. I wanted to find another world, and I'm finding it. That's the way to live. Know what you want, and don't stop until you get it.' She raised her glass to him. 'I guess there's probably a lot of interesting wickedness in your own life.'

He assumed a shocked air.

'Me? No time for it. I'm far too busy earning a respectable living, I assure you.'

'Right. I'll believe you. Thousands wouldn't.'

He grinned. 'You do me an injustice.'

'No, I don't. Any man who proclaims himself respectable needs to be treated with suspicion.'

'I protest—'

'Don't bother because I won't believe a word you say.'

They plunged into a light-hearted argument with much vigour on both sides, but also much laughter. When she looked at her watch she was amazed to see how much time had passed. She had a strange sense of being mentally at one with him. Almost like a brother.

But the next moment he turned his head so that she saw his profile against the glittering light from the fountain. Not brotherly, she thought. Disconcertingly attractive in a way that eclipsed other men, even Don. Or perhaps especially Don. But definitely not brotherly.

She remembered the first time she and Don had ventured beyond kisses, both eager to explore. But something had been missing, she knew that now.

'Are you all right?' Lucio asked.

'Yes, fine.'

'Sure? You seemed as if something had disturbed you.'

'No, I guess I'm just a bit hungry.'

'They do great snacks here. I'll get the menu.'

'I'll just have whatever you're having.'

He ordered spicy rolls and they sat eating contentedly.

'Why are you looking at me like that?' she asked.

'Just trying to solve the mystery. You don't strike me as the kind of woman who goes along with whatever the man orders.'

'Dead right, I'm not. But this is new territory for me, and I'm learning something fresh all the time.'

'So I'm part of the exploration?'

'Definitely. I like to find something unexpected. Don't you?'

'I sometimes think my life has had too much that's unexpected. You need time to get used to things.'

She hoped he would expand on that. She was beginning to be intrigued by everything he said. But before she could speak there was an excited cry as more crowds surged into the piazza, eager to toss coins into the water. For a while they both sat watching them.

'It's the age of science,' she reflected. 'We're all supposed to be so reasonable. Yet people still come here to toss coins and make wishes.'

'Perhaps they're right,' he said. 'Being too reasonable can be dangerous. Making a wish might free you from that danger.'

'But there are always other dangers lurking,' she mused. 'What to do about them?'

'Then you have to decide which ones to confront and which to flee,' he said.

She nodded. 'That way lies wisdom. And freedom.'

'And freedom matters to you more than anything, doesn't it?' he asked.

'Yes, but you must know what it really means. You think you're free, but then something happens, and suddenly it looks more like isolation.'

A sudden bleakness in her voice on the last word caught his attention.

'Tell me,' he said gently.

'I thought I knew my family. An older brother and sister who were twins, a younger sister, but then it turns out that there's been a big family secret all along. It began to come out and—' she gave a sigh '—I was the last one to know. I've always been closest to Matt, even though he can be so distant sometimes, but now it's like I'm not really part of the family. Just an outsider, in nobody's confidence.'

'You spoke of nobody caring. Nobody at all? What about outside the family?'

She grimaced. 'Yes, there was someone. We were moving slowly but I thought we'd get there in time. Well, I'm an outsider there, too. It feels like wandering in a desert.'

She checked herself there. She hadn't meant to confide her desert fantasy, for fear of sounding paranoid, but he seemed to understand so much that it had come out naturally.

'I know the feeling,' he said, 'but a desert can be a friendly place. There's no one there to hurt you.'

'It's true there are no enemies there,' she said. 'But no friends either, nobody who cares about you.'

'You wouldn't want to be there for ever,' he agreed. 'But for a while it can be a place to rest and recruit your strength. Then one day you can come back and sock 'em on the jaw.'

She longed to ask him what events and instincts lay behind that thought. All around her doors and windows seemed to be flying open, revealing mysterious roads leading to mists and beyond, to more mysteries, tempting her forward.

But could it be right to indulge her confusions with a stranger?

Then she saw him looking at her, and something in his eyes was like a hand held out in understanding.

Why not?

What harm could come of it?

'I guess my real problem is that I'm no longer quite sure who I am,' she said.

He nodded. 'That can happen easily, and it's scary.'

'Yes, it is. With Don I always felt that I was the one in charge of our relationship, but then I found I wasn't. Oh, dear, I suppose that makes me sound like a managing female.'

'Sometimes that's what a man needs to bring out the best of him,' he said.

'Did that happen to you?'

'No, she wasn't "managing" enough. If she had been, she might have bound me to her in time to save us both.' He added quickly, 'Go on telling me about you.'

Now a connection had been established it was easy to talk. Neither of them went into much detail, but the sense of being two souls adrift was a bond. It was a good feeling and she was happy to yield to it.

'What happened to your gift for getting your own way?' he asked at last.

'I guess it failed me. I didn't say it worked all the time. You have to seize the chance, but sometimes the chance can't be seized.'

A cheer that went up from the fountain made them both look there.

'More coins, more wishes,' he said.

'Aren't they supposed to wish for a return to Rome?' she asked.

'Yes, but they always add another one, usually about a lover.'

'I'd like to go closer.'

As they neared the water they could see a man tossing

in coins by the dozen, then closing his eyes and muttering fiercely.

'What's he wishing for?' Charlotte asked.

'My guess is he wants his lady-love to appear out of the blue, and tell him he's forgiven. When a guy's as desperate as that it's pretty bad.'

Then the incredible happened. A female hand tapped the young man on the shoulder, he turned, gave a shout of joy and embraced her.

'You came,' he bellowed. 'She came, everyone. She's here.'

'You see, it works,' someone shouted. 'Everyone toss a coin and make a wish.'

Laughing, Charlotte took two coins from her bag and threw one in, crying, 'Bring me back to Rome.'

'That's not enough,' Lucio said. 'Now you must wish that Don will come back.'

'Too late for that. We're not right for each other. I know that now. But what about you? Your lady might arrive and decide to "manage" you, after all, since it's so obviously what you want.'

But he shook his head. 'She's gone to a place from which she'll never return.'

'Oh, I'm so sorry. Did it happen very recently?'

'No,' he said softly. 'It was a hundred thousand years ago.'

She nodded, understanding that time, whether long or short, could make no difference to some situations. But another thought danced through her mind so fleetingly that she was barely aware of it. Another woman had stood between them, but no longer. Suddenly she had vanished, leaving only questions behind.

Impulsively she reached out and laid a hand on his cheek.

'Hey, you two, that's not good enough,' came an exultant cry from nearby. 'This is the fountain of love. Look around you.'

Everywhere couples were in each other's arms, some hugging fondly, some kissing passionately. Lucio gazed into her face for only a moment before drawing her close.

'I guess they feel we're letting the side down,' he said.

'And we can't have that, can we?' she agreed.

The feel of his lips on hers was passionate yet comforting, confirming her sensation that she was in the right place with the right person.

'I'm glad I met you,' he whispered against her mouth.

'I'm glad, too.'

They walked slowly back along the Via Vittorio Veneto. Neither spoke until they reached the hotel and he said, 'Let me take you up to your room.'

She could have bid him goodnight there and then, but she didn't. She knew now that as the evening passed the decision had been slowly building inside her. What she was going to do was right, and whatever might come of it, she was resolved.

When they reached her room he waited while she opened the door. Then he took a step back, allowing her time to change her mind. But she had passed that point, and so had he. When she held out her hand he took it, followed her inside and closed the door, shutting out the world.

In the morning she awoke to find herself alone. By her bed was a scrap of paper, on which was written, 'Thank you with all my heart. Lucio.'

At breakfast she looked around but didn't see him. She realised that she didn't even know his last name.

Strangely the situation did not distress her. They had been ships that passed in the night because that was what both of them had chosen, both of them needed. He'd been passionate and at the same time a gentle, considerate lover, with a mysterious gift for making her feel as though her troubles were falling away. She could go on to whatever the future held, stronger and more confident.

But gradually, a few weeks later, she discovered what the future did hold, and she realised that nothing would ever be the same. Now it mattered that she didn't know his full name. It took several hours' online research to discover that he was Lucio Constello, one of the most notable men in the business, with vineyards all over the country. But the most famous one was in Tuscany.

She'd set out to confront him, wondering how this business could possibly end, and soon she would know.

There he was, far ahead. The moment of truth had arrived, and she had no choice but to go forward.

CHAPTER TWO

'I'M NOT imagining this, am I?' he asked slowly. 'It's really you?'

'Sure it's me,' she said lightly.

'You…here? In Tuscany? It's great but I can hardly believe it.'

'Why? There was always a chance we'd bump into each other again.'

The reference to chance was deliberate. She was determined to play it casual. There must be no hint of how frantically she'd searched for him, how much it mattered. She, who prided herself on fearing nothing, had been dreading this meeting, dreading the sight of his face when she told him her news.

She covered her feelings with a smile, a cheerful shrug. He mustn't suspect before she was ready.

'I'm flattered you even remember me,' she said.

'Oh, yes,' he murmured. 'I remember. We had a great evening. You made me laugh.'

She stayed calm, although it was hard. Was laughter all he remembered about that night?

'As you did me,' she returned brightly.

'Yes, we had a wonderful time. I'm sorry I had to leave so suddenly the next morning. You were deeply asleep and I didn't want to awaken you.'

That wasn't quite the truth. He'd been overtaken by a desire to keep that perfect night apart, separate from all other contacts, like a picture in a frame. It had made him slip silently out of the room, leaving behind only the note that gave no clue to his identity or whereabouts. Perhaps he should be ashamed of that, but he couldn't think of it now.

The sight of her approaching had filled him with an overwhelming gladness. The awareness of that night was there again, spectacular, intense. She was even more beautiful than he remembered, and for a moment he felt nothing but pleasure.

Then she destroyed it.

'I had to find you,' she said. 'There's something you need to know.' She took a deep breath. 'I'm pregnant.'

'Wh-what?'

'I'm pregnant. I'm carrying your child.'

To his own horror his mind went blank. The pleasure at seeing her, the joy at the beautiful memories, everything vanished. He had the sensation of being punched in the face.

'Are you…sure?' he asked, barely knowing what he said.

'Quite sure. And in case you're wondering, I don't make a habit of doing what I did that night, so there hasn't been anyone else. You're the father.'

'Look, I didn't mean…'

He could have cursed himself for his clumsiness but he couldn't help it. He didn't mean—what? And what *did* he mean? If anything.

Watching him intently, Charlotte saw the last thing in the world she'd wanted to see. Confusion. Blank. Nothing. A desert.

In a blinding flash her courage collapsed. Don had rejected her, and although her heart hadn't been broken, rejection was still rejection. Now Lucio was working himself up to reject her, and she wasn't going to hang around for it.

'It's OK, it's OK,' she said with a good imitation of a cheerful laugh. 'There's no need to panic.'

'I'm not—'

'Oh, yes, you are. You're on the verge of a panic attack. Oh, poor Lucio! Did you think I was trying to trap you into marriage? Not a chance! You and me? Get real! It would never work. We'd always—well, never mind that. Just don't panic. You're completely safe from me, I promise you. I'm only here because you have the right to know. Fulfilling my citizenly duty. How about that?'

She even managed a teasing note in the last words, and had the bitter satisfaction of seeing uncertainty in his face. He was floundering. Good. Serve him right!

'So there it is,' she said. 'Now you know. If you want to talk about it you'll find me here.' She thrust a piece of paper into his hand. 'But if you don't want to, that's just fine. Goodbye, Lucio. It was nice knowing you.'

Turning on her heel she walked swiftly away, determined to escape before he could insult her with any more blank-faced confusion.

But she gave him a last chance. That was only fair. After hurrying a few hundred yards she looked back, expecting to find him watching her, even perhaps stretching out a hand. That would have made her pause to see if he followed.

But he was frozen where she'd left him, immobile, staring down at the paper in his hand. She waited for him to look up, see her, call her name.

Nothing! Damn him!

There was only one thing to do, and that was vanish. She managed this by moving sideways between the vines so that she slipped into the next alley. This she did again, then again and again until she was several alleys away from the one where she'd started. Then she began to run, and didn't stop until she reached her car. A few moments later she was speeding away from the estate.

As she fled she asked herself ironically what else she'd expected. A man who shared a woman's bed and vanished without a goodbye had sent her an unmistakable message. The woman who chose to ignore that message had nobody to blame but herself if she suffered rejection.

And it certainly was rejection. Lucio hadn't said the actual words, but only because he'd been trying to phrase them tactfully. She wouldn't hear from him again but it didn't matter. She'd told him what he had a right to know and her conscience was clear.

She thought of her family back home in the States. She'd known of her pregnancy for several weeks, but so far hadn't told them. How would they react?

Or did she know the answer, only too well? They would accept it as no more than you'd expect from Charlotte—the difficult one, unpredictable, awkward, never quite fitting in.

And the one-night stand? Well, that was just like her, wasn't it? Always ready to explore new territory, even if it might have been best left unexplored. Not that she was exactly a bad girl…

But then again, maybe she was.

She wished her brother, Matt, was here right now. Strange that they should be so close, when he was Ellie's twin, not hers. But there was something in their natures that clicked. She knew that he, too, sometimes felt adrift in a desert, and he fought it the way she did herself, with humour that was ironic and sometimes bitter. She could almost hear him now. 'Why did you bother finding this guy? He didn't even give you his last name. Doesn't that tell you something?'

Perhaps he did tell me the name, she thought, *I just can't remember it. It didn't matter. It was that sort of evening. All about having fun.*

But it hadn't been fun trying to track him down afterwards. The thought of applying to the hotel for information had made her shiver with shame. Instead she'd gone to an internet café and then ransacked the internet for Italian vintners until she found no less than five of them called 'Lucio.' Luckily there was a photograph that identified him, but the search had made her feel like some abandoned serving girl from a bygone era. Which didn't improve her temper any.

She'd finally identified him as Lucio Constello, one of the most successful men in the business. His wine was famous throughout the world, and he seemed to live a glamorous life, enjoying yacht trips, rubbing shoulders with celebrities, making money at every point. There were pictures of him with beautiful women, one of whom had recently ended a romance with a film producer.

'And perhaps we know why,' enthused the text. 'Just look at the way they're gazing at each other.'

But after that the starlet was never seen with him again.

One article declared that he was 'a man who really knew how to enjoy himself.' Which meant, Charlotte thought wryly, that one-night stands were a normal part of his life. Hence his disappearance and her feeling that he wouldn't be pleased to see her.

His vineyards were many, spread out over Italy, and all subject to his personal supervision. Crisis! He could be anywhere. But an article revealed that he usually spent May in Tuscany at the Vigneto Constanza. There was time to catch him.

At the same time a perverse inner voice argued that there was no need to contact him at all. What did this baby really have to do with Lucio? Forget him. He belonged in the past.

But her mother's voice seemed to flit through her mind. It was weeks since she'd learned the truth of how Fenella had led Cedric Patterson into accepting Clay Calhoun's twins as his own, yet still the deception haunted her. No matter how much she tried to defend her mother she knew that she herself must be honest. So she would write to Lucio.

But somehow the letter wouldn't get itself written. Whatever tone she adopted was the wrong one. Too needy. Too hopeful. Too chilly. Too indifferent.

So she'd headed for Tuscany, checking into a hotel in the picturesque old city of Florence, and hiring a car from the hotel for the rest of the journey. For part of the way a map was useful, but when she grew nearer she asked directions. Everyone could point the way. The Vigneto Constanza was known and respected for miles around, clearly a source of welcome employment which was probably why they called the house a *palazzo*, she thought.

But she changed her mind when she saw the building, which was certainly a palace, rearing up three floors, with an air of magnificence that suggested nobility rather than business.

As she approached a middle-aged woman came out and stood waiting on the step.

'Good morning,' she said as Charlotte got out of the car. 'I'm Elizabetta, the housekeeper. Can I help you?'

'I'm here to see Signor Constello.'

'I'm afraid he's not here,' Elizabetta said.

Charlotte gave a sharp breath. He'd vanished. She'd pursued him for nothing. Suddenly she was in the desert again.

But then Elizabetta added, 'Not just now anyway. He's gone out inspecting the vines on the far side of the estate.'

'But he is…coming back?'

'Well, it's a big estate. He won't be home until very late, and sometimes he stays the night with one of his workers who lives on the far side.'

'I need to see him today. Can you tell me where he'll be?'

A few minutes later she headed off in what she hoped was the right direction. The sheer size of the grape fields was stunning—acre after acre, filled with long straight lines that seemed to stretch into infinity. She wouldn't have been surprised to discover that she'd arrived on a strange planet, and Lucio wasn't here at all.

'Stop being fanciful,' she told herself sternly. 'There he is in the distance. Everything's going to be all right.'

Instead nothing was all right. His response had been so bleak that she'd fled after a few minutes, and was now back in Florence, pacing the floor of her hotel room.

The paper she'd left him had contained both the hotel details and the number of her cell phone. He would call her soon, and they would settle it. But as time passed with no call, she faced the fact that she was alone again.

Another desert.

As the light faded she sat at the window, looking out at the old city. Her room overlooked the beautiful river Arno, with a clear view of the Ponte Vecchio, 'the old bridge,' which had stood there for over a thousand years. It was lined with shops on both sides, at one time a common Italian habit. But that convention had faded, and now the Ponte Vecchio was almost unique in still having them. They were lit up, dazzling and golden against the night air, flooding the water with light.

On impulse she determined to go down and explore the

bridge. She would take her cell phone. Lucio could call that number if he wanted to contact her. But if he didn't, he needn't think she was going to languish here waiting for him to deign to give her his attention.

In a moment she was downstairs and out of the door, heading for the street that ran along the river. Despite the lateness of the hour she was far from alone. Couples strolled slowly, absorbed in each other or leaning over the wall to gaze at the water before turning to meet each other's eyes.

At last she reached the bridge and walked halfway across to where there was a gap in the shops and she could look out over the dazzling water. On either side of her couples murmured, pleading, suggesting, happy.

Happy, she thought. Was it really possible to be happy in love?

And what was love anyway?

Briefly she'd thought she'd discovered the answer with Don, but she knew differently now. Not just because he'd let her down, but because in one devastating night with Lucio she'd discovered something that had reduced all other experiences to nothing.

Gazing down into the shimmering water, she seemed to be back in the hotel room, hearing the sound of the door close, feeling him move close. How warm his breath had been on her face, how gladly she had drawn closer to him, raising her head to receive his kiss.

She could still feel his mouth on hers, silencing the last of her doubts. Until then the voice of reason had whispered that she mustn't do this with a man she'd only just met. It wasn't proper behaviour. But the gentle, skilful movements of his lips had conquered her. Propriety had never meant much to her. In his arms it meant nothing at all.

It was obvious that he was a ladies' man, but he'd undressed her with an air of reverent discovery that made her feel special. Of course this was merely part of his expertise, she'd guessed, but it was hard to be realistic when his eyes on her were full of astonished worship.

He'd removed her dress, but before stripping her completely he'd tossed aside his jacket and shirt. There were no lights on in the room but enough came through the window to reveal his smooth, well-shaped chest and arms. Lying beside her on the bed, he'd drawn away her slip and bra, leaving only her briefs.

Then he'd smiled.

Something in that smile had made her reach for him and begin pulling at his clothes until he wore no more than she did. Now she, too, was smiling. This man was going to prove a skilful lover. Every instinct she had told her that was true.

His body was marvellous, muscular but lean and taut, hinting at strength that could bring a woman joy. Almost tentatively she slipped her fingers beneath the edge of his briefs.

Incredibly there was a question in his eyes, almost as though he was asking her even now if she had any doubts. Her reply was to tighten her grip, silently ordering him to strip naked. He obeyed and did the same for her, then stayed looking down at her, letting his fingertips drift across her breasts.

His caress was so light that he could barely be said to be touching her at all, yet the thunderous pleasure that went through her was like a storm. How could so much result from so little? she wondered frantically. Then all thought was forgotten in the delight that possessed her.

No man touched a woman so subtly without first understanding her, not just her body but traces of her heart and mind. Instinct from deep inside told her so, and everything in her responded to him. She couldn't have prevented that response even if she'd wanted to, but she didn't want to. Nothing was further from her desire than to resist him. In that magical moment she was all his, and all she wanted was to make him all hers.

Afterwards, he kissed her tenderly, stroking her hair as sleep began to claim her, and she felt herself drifting away into the sweet, warm darkness.

At the very last moment he whispered, 'You're wonderful.'

The night descended totally before she could respond, but that soft tribute lingered with her in the mysterious other universe where there was rest, peace and joy.

But when she awoke, he was gone.

The memory of the murmured words tormented her. Had she imagined them, or had he really said such a thing before abandoning her? Again and again she went over the moment, racking her brain to know whether it was true memory or only fantasy born of wishful thinking. The search nearly drove her crazy, but she found no answer.

In the weeks that followed she'd known that she could have loved him if he'd given any sign of wanting her love. Instead he'd rejected her so brutally that she'd come close to hating him.

It was cruelly ironic that her two encounters with Lucio had both been under circumstances that suggested romance. First the Trevi Fountain where lovers laughingly gambled on their love, and where she'd been tempted to gamble beyond the boundaries of both love and sense. Now she was in another city so enchanting that it might have been designed for lovers. But instead of revelling in the company of a chosen man she was alone again. Unwanted. Looking in from the outside, as so many times before in her life.

But enough was enough. This was the last time she would stand outside the magic circle, longing for a signal from within; the last time she would wait for a man to make up his mind. *Her* mind was made up, and he could live with it.

She almost ran back to the hotel. At the desk she stopped just long enough to ask, 'Any message for me? No? Right. I'm checking out in half an hour. Kindly have my bill ready.'

In her room she hurled things into the suitcase, anxious to lose no time now the decision was made. Her next step was vague. A taxi from the hotel to the railway station, and jump on the next train to—? Anywhere would do, as long as it was away from here.

At the desk the bill was ready. It took only a moment to pay it, seize up her baggage and head for the door. Outside she raised her hand to a taxi on the far side of the road, which immediately headed for her.

'Where to?' the driver called.

'Railway station,' she called back.

'No,' said a voice close by. Then a hand came out of the darkness to take her arm, and the same voice said, 'Thank goodness I arrived in time.'

She jerked her head up to see Lucio.

'Let me go,' she demanded.

'Not yet. First we must talk. Charlotte, neither of us should make hasty decisions. Can't you see that?' He laid his other hand on her shoulder. His touch was gentle but firm. 'You're not being fair, vanishing like this,' he said. 'I trusted you. Perhaps I shouldn't have done.'

'Perhaps *I* shouldn't have trusted *you*. I gave you the chance. I told you what had happened. You could have done anything but you chose to do nothing. Fine! I get the message.'

'There's no message. I was confused, that's all. It took me a while to get my head around it, but I thought at least you'd stay one night—give me a few hours to think.'

'What is there to think about?' she demanded passionately. 'The baby's here, inside me, waiting to be born and change everything. You're either for that or against it.'

He made a wry face. 'You really don't understand much about human weakness, do you? I didn't jump to your command at once, so you thought you'd make me sorry.'

'That's nonsense,' she said, but she knew a moment's discomfort at how close he'd come.

'I don't think so. Look, let's put this behind us. We have too much at stake to risk it with a quarrel.' He addressed the driver. 'Leave the bags. Here.'

He held out a wad of cash which the driver pocketed and fled.

'You've got a cheek,' she said indignantly.

'Not really. I'm taking a big gamble. I didn't anticipate you leaving without giving me a fair chance. I thought you'd wait for me to pull my thoughts together.'

'All right, maybe I was a bit hasty,' she said reluctantly.

'I wonder if it will always be like that with us, each of us going in opposite directions.'

'I think that sounds an excellent idea,' she said. 'If I had any sense I'd go in another direction right this minute.'

'But if you had any sense,' he replied wryly, 'you wouldn't have wasted time on me in the first place.'

'I guess you're right.'

'But since you did, and since the world has changed, isn't it time we talked to each other properly. There's a little café just along there where we can have peace. Will you come with me?'

She hesitated only a moment before taking his hand and saying, 'Yes. I think perhaps I will.'

CHAPTER THREE

AFTER dumping her bags in his car Lucio indicated the road that ran along the side of the river. 'It's not far. Just a quiet little place where we can get things sorted.'

But when they reached the café Charlotte backed off. Through the windows she could see tables occupied by couples, all seemingly blissful in each other's company.

Not now, she thought. An air of romance wasn't right for this discussion. She needed a businesslike atmosphere.

'It's a bit crowded,' she said. 'Let's find somewhere else.'

'No, they won't bother us,' he said, which left her with a curious feeling that he'd read her thoughts. 'This way.'

He led her to a table by a window, through which she could see the golden glow of the water, and the little boats all of which seemed to be full of adoring couples.

But this situation demanded efficiency, common sense. The last thing it needed was emotion.

Her mood had calmed. She was even aware of a little shame at how hastily she'd judged him. But it still irked her that he'd taken control. She glanced up and found him studying her with a faint smile.

'If looks could kill, I'd be a dead man,' he observed lightly.

'Unless there was some quicker way,' she replied in the same tone.

'If there was, I'm sure you'd know it.'

'Well, you've got a nerve, just taking over like that.'

'But I asked if you'd come with me. You said yes.'

'And if I'd said no, what would have happened?'

He gave a smile that made her heart turn over. 'I'd probably have taken the advice you offered me in Rome.'

'I gave you advice?'

'As I recall your exact words were, "Know what you want and don't stop until you get it". Impressive advice. I know what I want and, well—' He spread his hands in an expressive gesture.

'So you think you can do what you like and I can't complain because I put you up to it.'

'That's a great way of putting it. I couldn't have done better myself.'

'I—you—'

'Ah, waiter, a bottle of my usual wine, and sparkling water for the lady.'

'And suppose I would have liked wine,' she demanded when they were alone.

'Not for the next few months. It wouldn't be good for you or the person you're carrying.'

His use of the word *person* startled her. How many men saw an unborn child as a person, still less when it had been conceived only a few weeks ago? She knew one woman whose husband referred to 'that thing inside you'. But to Lucio this was already a person. Instinctively she laid a hand over her stomach.

Then she looked up to find him watching her. He nodded. After a moment she nodded back.

Now she'd had a chance to get her thoughts in order

she found her brief hostility dying. She could even appreciate his methods.

When the waiter returned with the drinks Lucio ordered a snack, again without consulting her. But it was hard to take offence when he was ordering the same things she'd enjoyed in the outdoor café at the Trevi Fountain, a few weeks and a thousand lifetimes ago. How had he remembered her taste so perfectly? The discovery made him look slightly different.

Studying him, she discovered another change. The man in Rome had been a flamboyant playboy, handsome, elegantly dressed, ready to relish whatever pleasures came his way. The man in the vineyard that afternoon had worn dark jeans and a sweater, suitable for hard work on the land.

The man sitting here now wore the same clothes but his eyes were tense. His manner was calm, even apparently light-hearted, but there was something else behind it. She sensed apprehension in him, but why was he nervous? Of her? The situation? Himself?

When the waiter had gone he turned back to her.

'I'm sorry for the way this happened, but I never dreamed you'd just leave like that.'

'And I thought my leaving was what you wanted. Your silence seemed rather significant.'

'My silence was the silence of a man who's been knocked sideways and was trying to get his head together. You tell me something earth-shattering, then you vanish into thin air, and I'm supposed to just shrug?'

'I guess I thought you were more sophisticated than this.'

'What you thought was that this kind of thing happened to me every day, didn't you?'

'Nonsense,' she said uncomfortably.

'Be honest, admit it.'

'How can I? I don't know the first thing about you.'

'Nor I about you,' he said wryly. 'That's our problem, isn't it? We've done it all back to front. Most people get to know a little about each other before they—well, anyway, we skipped that bit and now everything's different.

'I didn't contact you earlier because I was in a state of shock. When I'd pulled myself together I picked up the phone. Then I put it down again. I didn't know what to say, but I had to see you. I had to know how you feel about what's happened. Tell me frankly, Charlotte, do you want this baby?'

Aghast, she glared at him. 'What are you saying? Of course I want it. Are you daring to suggest that I get rid of it? I'd never do that.'

'No, I didn't mean—it's just—' He seemed to struggle for the right words. 'Do you really want the child or are you merely making the best of it?'

She drew a slow breath. 'I don't know. I've never thought of it like that. From the moment I knew, it felt inevitable, as though the decision had been taken out of my hands.'

He nodded. 'That can be a strange feeling, sometimes bad but sometimes good. You get used to planning life, but then suddenly life makes the plans and orders you to follow them.'

'Oh, yes,' she murmured. 'I know exactly what you mean.'

'And maybe it can be better that way. It can save a lot of trouble.'

'You'll have me believing that you're a fatalist.'

'Perhaps,' he said quietly. 'Things happen, and when you think you've come to terms with it something else happens and you have to start the whole process again.'

'Yes,' she murmured. 'Nothing is ever really the way we thought it was, is it?'

'No,' he said. 'That's true, and somehow we have to find our way through the maze.'

She turned to meet his eyes and saw in them a confusion that matched her own.

'I can hardly believe you're pregnant,' he said. 'You look as slim as ever.'

'I'm two and a half months gone. That's too early for it to show, but it'll start soon.'

'When did you know?'

'A few weeks ago. I was late, and when I checked—' she shrugged '—that was it.'

She waited for him to demand why she hadn't approached him sooner, but he sat in silence. She was glad. It would have been hard for her to describe the turmoil of emotions that had stormed through her in the first days after the discovery. They had finally calmed, but she'd found herself in limbo, uncertain what to do next.

When she'd discovered his likely location she hadn't headed straight there. Her mind seemed to be in denial, refusing to believe she was really pregnant. Any day now it would turn out to be a mistake. She'd continued her trip around Italy, heading back south but avoiding Rome and going right down to Messina, then crossing the water to the island of Sicily, where she spent a month before returning north.

At last she faced the truth. She was carrying Lucio's child. So she went to find him, telling herself she was ready for anything. But his response, or lack of it, had stunned her. Now here she was, wishing she was anywhere else on earth.

From the river below came the sound of a young woman screaming with laughter. Glancing down Charlotte saw the girl fooling blissfully with her lover before they vanished under the bridge. Lucio watched her, noticing how the glittering yellow burnished her face, so that for a moment she looked not like a woman but like a golden figurine, enticing, mysterious, capable of being all things to all men, or nothing to any man.

'So tell me what you're thinking,' he said. 'Tell me how it looks to you, and where you see the path leading.'

'I can't answer that. I see a dozen paths leading in different directions, and I won't know which one is the right one until we've talked.'

'If I hadn't turned up just now where were you headed?'

She shrugged.

'Home?' he persisted. 'To New York?' He searched her face. 'You don't know, do you?'

'Does it matter?'

'What about your family? How do they feel about it?'

'I haven't told them yet.'

He stared. 'What, nothing?'

'Nothing.'

'I see.' He sat in silence for a moment and when he spoke again his tone was gentle.

'When we talked in Rome you said there was a secret that you'd been the last to know, and you felt as though you weren't really part of the family any more. You still feel like that?'

'I guess so.'

'All these weeks you've had nobody to confide in?'

'It wouldn't be a good time.'

The thought of her family had made her flinch. So much was going on there already—the truth about Matt and Ellie's paternity, her feeling of isolation, her uncertainty about what a family really meant—she couldn't confide in them until she'd made up her own mind. She didn't even tell Matt. She'd always felt close to him before, but not now.

'So there isn't anybody—?' Lucio ventured slowly.

'Don't you dare start feeling sorry for me,' she flashed. 'I can look after myself.'

'Will you stop taking offence at every word? You don't have to defend yourself against me. If you'd just given me a chance this afternoon—'

'All right, I shouldn't have dashed off the way I did,' she admitted. 'But you looked so horrified….'

'Not horrified,' he corrected her gently. 'Just taken by surprise. It's never happened to me before, and it was the last thing I expected.' He made a wry face. 'I just didn't feel I could cope. I guess my cowardly side came to the surface.'

'But there's no need for you to feel like that,' she said. 'You don't have to have anything to do with this baby. I told you because you had a right to know, but I'm not expecting anything from you—'

She stopped, dismayed at his sudden frozen expression.

'Thanks,' he said harshly. 'You couldn't have showed your contempt for me more clearly than that.'

'But I didn't—I don't know what you—'

'You're carrying my child but you don't expect anything from me. That says everything, doesn't it? In your eyes I'm incapable of rising to the occasion, fulfilling my obligations. In other words, a total zero.'

'I didn't mean it like that. I just didn't want you to feel I was putting pressure on you.'

'Doesn't it occur to you that there ought to be a certain amount of pressure on a man who's fathered a child?'

'Well, like you said, we don't know each other very well.'

The words *Except in one way* seemed to vibrate in the air around them.

Seeing this tense, sharp-tempered man, she found it strange to recall the charismatic lover who'd lured her into his arms that night in Rome. How he'd laughed as they stood by the fountain, tossing in coins, challenging her to make two wishes—the conventional one about returning to Rome, and another one from her heart. She'd laughed too, closing her eyes and moving her lips silently, refusing to tell him what she'd asked for.

'Let's see if I can guess,' he'd said.

'You never will.'

That was true, for there had been no second wish. She had so many things to wish for, and no time to think about them. So she'd merely moved her lips without meaning, as part of the game.

She'd teased him all the way into her bedroom and the merriment had lasted as they undressed each other. They didn't switch on the light, needing only the glow that came through the windows, with its mysterious half shadows. His body had been just as she'd expected, slim and vigorous, not heavily muscular but full of taut strength.

Everything about their encounter had been fun: it was scandalous, immoral, something no decent girl would ever do, but she enjoyed it all the more for the sense of thrilling rebellion it gave her. No pretence, no elaborate courtesy, no bowing to convention. Just sheer lusty pleasure.

His admiration had been half the enjoyment. In the glow of success she had soared above the world, but now had come the inevitable crash landing, and the two of them stranded together.

She looked around the café, trying to get her bearings. It was hard because there were lovers everywhere, as though this part of Florence had been made for them and nobody else. Glancing at Lucio she saw him watching the couples with an expression on his face that made her draw a sharp breath. Gone was the irony, the air of control that seemed to permeate everything else that he did. In its place was a haunted look, as though his heart was yearning back to a source of sadness from which he could never be entirely free.

She looked away quickly. Something warned her that he would hate to know she'd seen that revealing expression.

One couple in particular caught her attention. They were deep in conversation, with the girl urgently explaining something to the young man. Suddenly he burst into a loud crow of joy, pointing to her stomach. She nodded, seizing his hand and drawing it against her waist. Then they threw themselves into each other's arms.

That was how it should be, Charlotte thought. Not like this.

'No prizes for guessing what she told him,' Lucio observed wryly.

'I suppose not.'

He seemed to become suddenly decisive. 'All right, let's see if we can agree on something.'

Here it was, she thought. He was going to offer her a financial settlement, and she was going to hate him for it.

'I've been doing a lot of thinking since this afternoon,' he said. 'And one thing's clear to me. You mustn't be alone. I want you to come and stay with me.'

She frowned. 'You mean—?'

'At my home. I think you'll like it there.'

Seeing in her face that she was astonished he added, 'You don't have to decide now. Stay for a while, decide how you feel, then we'll talk and you'll make your decision.'

Dumbfounded, she stared at him. Whatever she'd expected it wasn't this.

'Please, Charlotte. You can't just go off into the distance and vanish. I want you where I can look after you and our child.'

She drew a shaky breath. Of all he'd said, three words stood out.

I want you.

To be wanted, looked after. When had that last happened to her?

'You surely understand that?' Lucio said.

'Yes, I—I guess I'm like you. I need time to get my head round it.'

'But what's difficult? We're having a child together. That makes us a family. At the very least we should give it a try, see if it can be made to work.'

'Well, yes, I suppose so….'

'Good. Then we're agreed. Nice to get it settled. Shall we go?'

'Yes,' she said slowly, taking the hand he held out to her, and letting him draw her to her feet.

The die was cast. She had no intention of leaving him now.

'Are you all right?' he asked as they stepped out into the street.

'Yes—yes, everything's all right.'

He led her to where he'd parked the car and ushered her into the front passenger seat. In a few moments they were heading out of Florence and on the road that led the twenty miles to the estate.

There was a full moon, casting its glow over the hills of Tuscany, and holding her spellbound by the beauty. Lucio didn't speak and she was glad because she needed time to understand what had happened.

I want you.

Three simple words that had made it impossible for

her to leave, at least for the moment. Later, things might be different, but for now she had nowhere else to go, and nobody else who wanted her.

With a few miles to go Lucio pulled in at the side of the road and made a call on his cell phone.

'Mamma? We'll be there in a few minutes…. Fine…. Thank you!'

As he started up the engine and drove on he said, 'Fiorella isn't actually my mother. She and her husband, Roberto, were the owners of the estate when I arrived here twelve years ago. I worked for them, we grew close, and I nearly married their daughter, Maria. But she died, and Roberto followed her soon after, leaving the estate to me.'

'But shouldn't he have left it to his wife?' Charlotte asked.

'Don't worry, I didn't steal her inheritance. He left her a fortune in money. She could go anywhere, do anything, but she chooses to live here because it's where she was happy. She's been like a mother to me, and I'm glad to have her.'

Her head was in a whirl at these revelations. Lucio had been engaged to Fiorella's daughter. How would she feel at the arrival of a woman carrying Lucio's child, a child that in another life would have been her own grandchild? At the very least she would regard Charlotte as an interloper.

'You should have told me this before,' she said.

'Why? She wants to meet you.'

'But it's an impossible situation. Her daughter—you—however can this be happening?'

'Charlotte, please, I know it's difficult, but don't blame me. You've known about this pregnancy for weeks, but you sprang it on me without warning. I had to make decisions very quickly, and if I was clumsy I'm sorry. Don't look daggers at me.'

Since his eyes were fixed on the road he couldn't see the daggers, but he'd known by instinct. She ground her teeth.

What did Fiorella know about her? What had Lucio said? What had Elizabetta, the housekeeper, said after she'd arrived, asking for Lucio, earlier that day?

In the distance she could see a palatial house, standing high on a hill and well lit so that she could recognise it as the one she'd visited. As they neared she could see two women standing just outside the front door. One of them was Elizabetta and the other must be Fiorella.

The two women were totally still as the car drew up. Only when Lucio opened Charlotte's door and handed her out did they come forward.

'This is Charlotte,' he said. 'She's come to stay with us.'

Clearly neither of them needed to ask what he meant. Lucio had prepared the ground well. Elizabetta smiled and nodded, but Fiorella astonished Charlotte by opening her arms

'You are welcome in this house,' she said.

Charlotte's head spun. She'd been prepared for courtesy, but not this show of warmth from a woman whose daughter Lucio had once planned to marry. It was Maria who should have borne his children, which surely made her an interloper.

She managed to thank Fiorella calmly, and the two women ushered her into the house while Lucio returned to the car for her bags.

'A room has been prepared for you,' Fiorella said. 'And some food will be brought to you. Tomorrow we will all eat together, but tonight I think you are tired and need to sleep soon.'

She was right, and Charlotte thanked her for her consideration. Secretly she guessed that there was another reason. Now that she'd set eyes on her, Fiorella wanted to take Lucio aside and demand more answers. And she herself would be glad to talk to him privately.

He led the way up a flight of stairs, so grandiose that they confirmed her impression that this was more of a palace than a farmhouse. Then it was down a wide corridor lined with pictures, until they came to a door.

'This is your room,' Lucio said, leading the way in and standing back for her to see.

It was a splendid place, large and extravagantly furnished, with a double bed that had clearly been freshly made up, and a door that led to a private bathroom.

'This is kept for our most honoured guests,' Lucio said. 'I think you'll be comfortable here.'

'I'm sure I will be,' she said politely.

Fiorella appeared, followed by Elizabetta pushing a table on wheels, laden with a choice of food, fruit juice and coffee.

'Have a good night's sleep,' Fiorella said. 'And we will get to know each other tomorrow. Would you like Elizabetta to unpack your bags?'

'No, thank you,' Charlotte said quickly.

She wasn't sure why she refused. But while she was still learning about this place and the people in it some instinct warned her to stay on guard.

'Right, we'll leave you alone to get settled,' Lucio said. 'Go to bed soon. It's late.'

She would have preferred him to stay, but of course he must sort out final details with Fiorella. He would come to her later.

She ate the supper, which had clearly been created by someone who knew her tastes, meaning that Lucio had been at work here, too. Then she unpacked, hung up her clothes in the elegant wardrobes and took a shower. It felt wonderful. When she stepped out her flesh was singing and she felt better physically than she had for some time.

What to wear to greet Lucio when he came? Nothing seductive. That would send out too obvious a message. The nightdress she chose was silk but not seductively low-cut. Some women would have called it boring. Charlotte called it useful. They could talk again, but this time it would be different. She no longer felt the antagonism he'd provoked in her earlier. Tonight would decide the future, and suddenly that future looked brighter than it had for months.

It was only a few hours since she'd arrived at the estate, a confident woman, certain that she knew who and what she was. She would explain the facts to Lucio, they would make sensible arrangements and that would be that.

But nothing had worked out as she planned, and now here she was, in unknown territory. She knew there was much to make her grateful. Where she might have found hostility she was treated as an 'honoured guest'. Lucio wanted their child, and was set on being a good father, which made him better than many men. But he was focused on the baby, not herself. What would happen between the two of them was something only time would tell.

She threw herself down on the bed, staring into space. One question danced through her mind. How much had Maria meant to him? How much did her memory mean to him now? He'd spoken of her without apparent emotion, but that might have been mere courtesy towards herself. Or perhaps they had planned no more than a marriage of convenience.

Surely that wasn't important. How could it matter to her?

Yet, disconcertingly, it did.

Face it, she thought. *He's attractive. You thought so from the first moment in Rome, otherwise things wouldn't have happened as they did. What was it someone used to say to me? 'When you've made a decision, have the guts to live with the result.' I made a decision, and this is the result. Perhaps even a happy one.*

We could even fall in love. I'm not in love with him now, but I know I could be. But isn't that a kind of love already? Well, it'll be interesting finding out.

She smiled to herself.

And I could win him. Couldn't I?

I'll know when I see him tonight. He'll be here soon.

But hours passed and Lucio did not appear.

CHAPTER FOUR

FROM his bedroom window Lucio could see the window of Charlotte's room. The blinds were drawn but he could make out her shadow moving back and forth against the light, until finally the light was extinguished.

He went to bed, thinking about her, lying alone in the darkness, just as he was himself. Was she struggling with confusion? Did they have that, too, in common?

He wasn't proud of himself. His reaction to her news had been fear so intense that at first it had held him frozen. After she'd left he'd spent hours walking back and forth through the alleys of vines trying to believe it, trying not to believe it, trying to decide how he felt. Failing in everything.

But as the hours passed he'd come to a decision. Life had offered him something to hold on to, something that could have meaning. A drowning man who saw a life belt within his grasp might have felt as he did then.

Looking back to the start of the day he marvelled at how clear and settled his life had seemed, and how quickly that illusion had vanished into nothing.

But that was how it had always been.

His childhood in Sicily had been contented, even sometimes happy, although he'd always sensed that his parents meant more to each other than he meant to either of them.

This troubled him little at the time. It even gave him a sense of freedom. And if there was also a faint sense of loneliness he dealt with that by refusing to admit it.

But at last he became aware that the father he adored inspired fear in others, although Lucio couldn't understand why. Why should anyone be afraid of a lawyer, no matter how successful? But he'd come to realise that Mario Constello's clients were at best dubious, at worst criminal. They were used to getting their own way by threats, if necessary channelled through their lawyer.

The discovery caused something deep in Lucio to rebel in disgust. When he challenged his father, Mario was honestly bewildered. What could possibly be wrong with dishonesty and violence if it made you rich?

After that it was only a matter of time before Lucio fled. He begged his mother to come with him but she refused. She knew the worst of her husband, but even for the sake of her son she couldn't bear to leave him.

'Mamma, he's a monster,' Lucio had protested.

'Not to me, my son. Never to me. You're so young, only seventeen. One day you will understand. You'll learn that love isn't "reasonable". It doesn't obey the commands of the brain, but only of the heart.'

'But if your heart tells you to do something that could injure you?' the boy had demanded fiercely. 'Isn't that time to heed the brain and tell the heart to be silent?'

Her answering smile had contained a world of mysterious knowledge.

'If you can do that,' she said softly, 'then you do not really love. But you will, my darling. I know you will. You are warm-hearted and generous and one day you'll know what it is to love someone beyond reason. It will hit you like a lightning bolt and nothing will be the same again.

And you should be glad, for without it your life would be empty.'

To the last moment Lucio hoped that she would choose him over his father, but she had not. On the night he slipped away she'd watched him go. His last memory of his old home was her standing motionless at the window until he was out of sight.

He'd headed for the port of Messina and took a boat across the straits to the Italian mainland. From there he'd travelled north, taking jobs where he could, not earning much but living in reasonable comfort on the money his mother had given him. In Naples and Rome he spent some time simply enjoying himself, and when he reached Tuscany the last of his money had gone. Someone advised him to seek work in one of the local vineyards, and he slipped away to take a sneaky look at the Vigneto Constanza, to see what kind of work it was.

There he'd collapsed from hunger and exhaustion, and by good fortune had been discovered by Roberto Constanza, who'd taken him home.

He'd spent a week being nursed back to health by Signor Constanza's wife, Fiorella, and sixteen-year-old daughter, Maria. His abiding memory was of opening his eyes to see Maria's anxious face looking down at him.

When he'd recovered he'd gone to work in the vineyard and loved it from the first moment. Unlike the other employees he'd lived in the house, and it had become an open secret that he was regarded as the son the Constanzas had never had.

He stayed in touch with his mother, but his father cut him off. Lucio's departure, with its implied criticism, had offended him, and the only message from him said, 'You are no longer my son.' Lucio's response was, 'That suits me perfectly.'

His connection with his parents had been finally severed three years after he left them. Someone with a grudge against Mario had broken into his home and shot him. His mother, too, had died because, according to a witness, she had thrown herself between her husband and his killer.

'She could have escaped,' the witness had wept. 'Why didn't she do that?'

Because she didn't want to live without him, Lucio thought sadly. *Not even for my sake. In the end he was the one she chose.*

There was no inheritance. Despite his life of luxury Mario had been deeply in debt, and when everything was repaid there was nothing for his son.

'Perhaps that's really why your mother chose to die with him,' Roberto suggested gently. 'She faced a life of poverty.'

'She could have come to me,' Lucio suggested. 'I wouldn't have let my mother starve.'

'But she loved you too well to be a burden on you,' Roberto said.

But the truth, as Lucio knew in some place deep inside himself, was that she had not loved him enough. Life without her adored husband would never be worth living, even if she was cared for by a loving, generous son. For a second time she had rejected Lucio.

After that it was easier to accept Roberto and Fiorella as his parents. Looking back he sensed that that was the moment when his life here had truly begun.

The years that followed were happier than he had dared to hope. Everything about being a vintner appealed to him. He was a willing pupil, eager for whatever Roberto had to teach. From almost the beginning he had 'the eye', the mysterious instinct that told him which vines were outstanding, and which merely good. He sensed every stage of ripening, knew to the hour when the harvest should begin. Roberto, a vintner of long experience, began to listen to him.

Sweetest of all was the presence of Maria, her parents' pride and joy. A daughter so adored might have become spoiled and petulant. She was saved from that fate by the wicked, cheeky humour that infused her life, and which drew him to her.

From the first moment he'd thought her pretty and charming, but at sixteen she seemed little more than a child. For a while they were like brother and sister, scrapping, challenging each other. She was popular with the local young men and never seemed short of an escort.

Lucio, who was also popular with the opposite sex, studied her boyfriends cynically and warned her which ones to be wary of. But there was no emotion in their camaraderie.

He still relived the night when everything changed. Maria was getting ready for an evening out with a young man. He was handsome, exciting, known locally as a catch, and she was triumphant at having secured his attention.

Lucio had come home late after a hard day. He was tired, his clothes were grubby and he was looking forward to collapsing when he walked into the main room downstairs and found Maria preening herself at the mirror. Hearing him approach, she'd swung round.

'What do you think?' she demanded. 'Will I knock him sideways?'

For a moment he couldn't speak. The vision of beauty before him seemed to empty his brain. Gone was the jeans-clad kid sister with whom he shared laughter. Laughter died and enchantment took its place. It was the moment his mother had foreseen, the bolt of lightning, and everything in him rejoiced.

But she was unchanged, he was dismayed to notice. She teased and challenged him just like before, went on dates with other men and generally convinced Lucio that he'd be a fool to speak of his feelings.

And why should she want him? he asked himself bitterly. She was a rich girl and he was just one of her father's labourers, despite the privilege with which he was treated. Her escorts were similarly wealthy, arriving in expensive clothes and sweeping her off to luxurious restaurants.

He tried to cure himself. Why should he love a woman who would never love him? But nothing worked. He believed she was 'the one'.

Then one night, at a party, he'd rescued her from the unwanted attentions of the host's son, and his self-control had died. Seizing her in his arms he'd kissed her fervently, again and again.

When at last he released her he found her gazing at him with ironic amusement.

'I thought you were never going to do that,' she said.

'Maria, do you mean—?'

'Oh, you're so slow on the uptake. Come here.'

This time it was her kiss, full of the fierce urgency of a young woman who'd waited too long for this and had finally lost patience.

This time their embrace was so long that her parents came in and found them. Lucio prepared to beg them to understand, not to dismiss him from the estate. But then he saw that they were smiling with delight. They knew he was the right man for their child. Nothing else mattered.

Now Maria admitted that she'd loved him for months.

The next few months were sweet and gentle as they got to know each other on a new level. Long talks went on late into the night, leaving them both with a sense of a glorious future opening up. Nobody wanted to rush things, but, even without a definite proposal, it was taken for granted that they would be together forever.

One day, while they were guests at a friend's wedding, he said, 'Do you think we could—?'

'Yes,' she said quickly. 'I really think we could.'

They were engaged.

Fiorella and Roberto were overjoyed. They didn't care that he was poor.

'You're a great vintner,' Roberto told him, adding with a wicked chuckle, 'This way I can tie you to the estate. Now I don't have to worry that you'll leave me to work for someone else.'

Then he'd roared with laughter at his own joke, not fearing to be taken seriously. His and his wife's love for their foster son was too well known to be misunderstood. The only person who meant more was Maria, and the fact that they were giving her to him told him everything.

The time that followed was so joyful that, looking back, Lucio wondered why he hadn't guessed it was bound to end terribly. Fate didn't allow anyone to enjoy such happiness for more than a brief moment. He hadn't known it then but he'd learned it since.

The wedding was to take place in autumn, when the harvest was safely in. Maria and her mother had spent a long afternoon in Tuscany choosing a wedding dress, returning home in triumph. Mario had filmed her in it. Lucio had walked in while she was parading up and down for the camera. She'd laughed and displayed herself to him, but Fiorella had screamed.

'You mustn't see her in the dress before the wedding. It's bad luck.'

'Not for us, Mamma,' Maria had said blissfully.

'Not for us,' Lucio had agreed, taking her in his arms.

'We love each other too much. We will never have bad luck.'

How tragically ironic those words had become only a week later, when Maria had crashed the car she was driving, and died from her injuries. She'd lingered for two days before finally closing her eyes. Her funeral had been held in the church where the wedding should have taken place. Lucio and her parents had attended it together, bleak-eyed, devastated.

Roberto never recovered. A year later his heart gave out and he died within hours.

'He didn't want to live after we lost Maria,' Fiorella said as they sat together late into the night. 'Everything he did was a preparation for his death.' She placed a gentle hand over Lucio's. 'Including rewriting his will.'

'Mamma, I'm so sorry about that. I didn't know he meant to leave me the estate—'

'But I knew. We talked about it first and I told him I agreed. This place needs you. He's left me money and the right to live here, so there's no need for you to worry about me.'

He'd plunged into running the estate, making such a success that the profits soared and he was able to expand magnificently. Soon he owned several more vineyards and began to spend time travelling between them. The money increased even more. His life expanded into a routine of glamour.

Sometimes he felt like two people. There was the man who gladly returned home to where Fiorella, the mother of his heart, would care for him. And there was the other man who fled the estate with its memories, so achingly sweet, so beautiful, so unbearable.

There were plenty of female entanglements in his life, but none touched his heart. He steered clear of emotional

involvement, flirting with women who seemed as sophisticated and cynical as himself. Even so he sometimes blun-
dered, and knew he'd inflicted much pain before he came
to realise that the part of him that loved had died with
Maria.

It was lucky that he'd met Charlotte, who seemed like
himself, taking life as it came, ready to make the best of
a situation. He could be honest with her. He wouldn't fall
in love but neither would she. Apart from the child they
would give each other strength, safety, comfortable affection, but no unrealistic dreams on either side.

The future was hopeful.

Next morning Charlotte was awoken by Elizabetta, with
coffee.

'Breakfast will be served downstairs when you are
ready,' she said respectfully.

'I won't keep them waiting.'

She bathed and dressed quickly. Her thoughts of the
previous night had shown her where the road led—developing love with Lucio and a future based on the certain-
ties of that love. A child. A family. A secure home. It was
a pity he hadn't come to her the night before. There was so
much they could have said. But she suppressed her disappointment. Time was on her side. She was singing as she
got out of the shower.

She chose a blue dress that was stylish, elegant, but
modest. Today was about making a good impression.

There was a knock on the door, and Lucio was standing there, smiling.

'You look wonderful,' he said.

'Thank you, kind sir,' she said, taking his arm.

'Fiorella has cooked a splendid breakfast for you,'

he said, leading her downstairs. 'She's the best cook in Tuscany.'

In fact, the meal was more elaborate that she normally chose, but she appreciated that Fiorella had gone to a lot of trouble to make her welcome, and expressed much appreciation.

'Your room is comfortable?' Fiorella asked. 'If the mattress is too hard or too soft it can be changed.'

'No, it's perfect. I slept so well.'

'Good. You need to build up your strength to prepare for what lies ahead. Pregnancy is exhausting. If there is anything you want, you simply tell me.'

Lucio regarded them with a pleased smile. This must be just what he'd hoped for, Charlotte thought. She returned his smile. Just looking at his handsome appearance was a pleasure.

He was dressed as she hadn't seen him before, not expensively fashionable as on the first night, nor in workman's clothes, as she'd seen him in the vineyard.

Had that only been yesterday? she wondered. The world had changed since then.

Today he looked like a businessman, plain and efficient.

'Got a meeting this afternoon,' he explained. 'Could be a big deal at stake. But we'll have this morning to ourselves and—'

His phone rang. He greeted the caller cheerfully.

'I'm looking forward to this afternoon. There's some interesting— What's that?...Damn! All right, I'm coming now.'

He hung up, scowling. 'He's got some crisis. He didn't go into details but he sounds in a bad way.' He laid a hand on Charlotte's arm. 'Sorry.'

'Don't be,' she said. 'Business comes first.'

'Bless you.'

'You can leave everything to me,' Fiorella said. 'I shall enjoy showing Charlotte around.'

When they were alone Fiorella said, 'Now, tell me how you are feeling. Is your pregnancy going well?'

'Very well.'

'Morning sickness?'

'Mostly no.'

'How lucky you are. But you will need to be registered with a doctor, and I should like to take you to the one we use. He's in Siena, only four miles away.'

She made the call at once, and a few minutes later they were heading down the hill. As the car turned Charlotte took the chance to look back for her first real view of the palace, rearing up against the sky, a magnificent building, but not at all like the farmhouse she'd been expecting.

As they neared Siena, Fiorella explained that the doctor was an old family friend, and very happy to hear her news.

In the surgery he listened to her heart, asked her questions and nodded.

'Excellent. You're in good health. About your diet—'

'You can leave that to me, Doctor,' Fiorella said.

Siena was a beautiful, historic city. As they strolled the short distance to the restaurant Fiorella had booked for lunch, Charlotte looked around her at the ancient buildings.

'I've always wanted to come here,' she murmured.

'You'll have plenty of time now. Soon it will be time for the Palio, which we never miss.'

Charlotte had heard of the Siena Palio, a horse race and pageant that was part of the town's colourful history. She asked Fiorella eager questions until they were settled in the restaurant, where, it was clear, the table had been booked in advance.

'This place is just as beautiful as I've heard,' Charlotte enthused. 'I can't believe that incredible...'

Fiorella let her talk while the food was served, occasionally joining in with an observation.

'You know this land so well,' she said at last. 'And you speak the language fluently. Lucio told me you were taking a long trip to study Italy.'

'This country has always been my passion,' she said. 'I translate for a living, and I thought I should see the reality for myself.'

'You are obviously a very independent young woman, who makes big decisions for herself. Now I am afraid I have offended you.'

'How could you possibly have done that?'

'I practically frog-marched you off to the doctor, I had this restaurant arranged without consulting you—'

'Considering how little I know about Siena restaurants, that's just as well,' Charlotte said cheerfully.

'True, but you might complain that my family had taken you over.'

'Well, perhaps I don't mind being taken over,' Charlotte mused. 'You've welcomed me, and I'm not foolish enough to object to that.'

'Then we are friends?' Fiorella asked.

'Friends,' she said warmly. Isolated from her family back home she was doubly grateful for this welcome.

'But there is still something troubling you,' Fiorella said gently.

'Not trouble exactly. I just wonder how this must be for you. You're very kind to me, but I think how painful it must be for you. Your daughter—Lucio was going to marry her, and she died....'

'And you think I must hate you because of that?'

'I couldn't blame you. I'm having the baby that should have been hers—your grandchild.'

'But it's not the same. Lucio has told me that what has

happened since Rome is a surprise to both of you. He needs the stability that you can give him. Maria was—' she hesitated '—she belonged in another life, lived in another world. Now a new world opens to both of you, and I hope to be part of it, because to me he is my son.'

It was pleasantly said, and there was kindness in the older woman's eyes as she squeezed Charlotte's hand. Charlotte supposed she should be glad, since this meant Fiorella could offer her friendship. But what if she won Lucio's heart—would there be trouble looming? And it was his heart that she was determined to win.

CHAPTER FIVE

ON THE way home Fiorella said, 'I wonder if he's finished with Enrico Miroza yet. That's the man who called this morning.'

'Enrico Miroza?' Charlotte echoed. 'Not *the* Enrico Miroza?'

'You know about him?'

'You hear his name everywhere. They say that where money's concerned he's the "big man", with a finger in every financial pie. I saw him once at a reception and he seemed so forbidding, grim and fearsome, like he ruled the world.'

'Yes, he strikes people like that, but there's another side to him. While his wife was alive he had a life of quite unnerving virtue and respectability. Then, a year after she died, he met Susanna, a greedy little gold-digger who set out to marry him for his money, and managed it. Any other man would have been wary of her, but he had very little experience of women, and he just collapsed.'

'Lucio mentioned a crisis.'

'Yes, and this is a bad time for it. Enrico is an important associate for Lucio. In a few days they'll be hosting a weekend house party in Enrico's home, for a lot of important guests. Bankers, investors, people like that. Also, they're buying a business together, and the owner will be there.'

A few minutes later they reached the palazzo, where they saw Lucio's car parked outside.

'Good.' Fiorella sighed.

Lucio appeared and came to them quickly.

'I've brought Enrico home with me,' he said. 'He's in a bad way, and I didn't like to leave him alone.'

'But what's happened?' Fiorella asked.

'His wife's walked out on him.'

'That terrible woman!' she exclaimed. 'He's better off without her.'

'I agree, but he doesn't see it that way. He's madly in love with her no matter how badly she behaves.'

Fiorella snorted and turned to Charlotte, saying, 'This is always happening. To Susanna he's just money, money, money, and if he doesn't hand over enough she throws a tantrum.'

'This time she set her heart on a lavish set of diamonds,' Lucio said. 'When he hesitated she walked out, and I don't think it's coincidence that she picked this moment, two days before the big "do", so that he'll be humiliated before his guests. But before we go in, tell me how the two of you managed?'

'Wonderfully,' Fiorella said. 'The doctor is very pleased with our Charlotte. Now, I must go and talk to Elizabetta.'

She hurried out of the room, leaving them alone.

'Our Charlotte,' she mused. 'Did you hear that?'

'Of course. You are "our Charlotte". You're mine, but you're also hers. It's all over the estate by now, that you're keeping the family going, so in a sense you're everybody's Charlotte.'

'All over the estate? You mean people already know?'

'Good news travels fast.'

'She's so kind to me.'

'Fiorella is a matriarch in the old-fashioned sense. What

counts is family. You're part of the family now. Both of you.' Smiling, he indicated her stomach.

'Yes, she as good as told me. It's so nice to be wanted and—' She checked herself, fearful of revealing too many of her innermost feelings.

'Did you notice how tactfully she left us alone?' Lucio asked. 'She knows we need time.'

He led her outside to where some seats overlooked the magnificent view down the hillside.

'I knew this was hilly country,' she said, 'but now I see it, it takes my breath away.'

'The slopes give the grapes more direct sunlight, which is one reason this area is so good for wines. At one time this part of the country housed a lot of nobility, but gradually the wine took over.'

'Is that why the house is so grand?'

'Yes, it used to belong to a count.' He grinned. 'But Enrico's home puts it in the shade. It's a real palace.'

'That's why you're having the big "do" there?'

'Right. And I'm not looking forward to it. I'll talk to some contacts and make my escape. How do you feel about coming with me? You don't have to if you think it's too soon to plunge into deep water.'

'I'd like to plunge in. Don't worry, I'll cope alone and not distract you from talking business.'

He grinned. 'Thanks.'

'Tell me about your other vineyards,' she said. 'What made you buy more?'

Lucio hesitated. To tell her that he'd been fleeing the pain of Maria's memory would have been unkind, so he merely said, 'I guess I wanted to prove myself independently, rather than just taking over another man's achievement.'

He began to describe the other estates, lingering over

details to forestall more questions, until the door opened and Fiorella beckoned them.

'Time to return to duty,' Lucio said, taking her hand.

Charlotte recognised Enrico from their brief, previous encounter. Tall, thin, reserved, with a lined face and white hair, he gave the impression of a man who would never yield an inch. But his manners were perfect.

'I do apologise for my intrusion,' he said, holding her hand between both of his and speaking English.

'You don't need to. I'm delighted to meet you.'

She spoke in Italian and saw his eyes brighten with surprise.

'You know my language?'

Now he, too, spoke in Italian, and launched into a speech. At first he spoke slowly, but when she replied, speaking fast, he responded in the same way. Lost in the mental excitement, Charlotte was barely aware of Lucio watching them with a look of astonished pleasure.

'This has been a pleasure,' he said at last. 'I look forward to seeing you at the party. My friends will appreciate you, and you will enjoy yourself.'

'I look forward to it.'

Enrico stayed the night and spent dinner telling her about his home and the planned celebration. It was clear that he knew her status as Lucio's 'official lady' and the mother of his child. As Lucio had prophesied, word had spread fast.

She asked many questions, all guaranteed to show that she was up to the task. Lucio watched in silence, but seemed pleased.

Later, when Enrico had gone to his room, Fiorella surprised Charlotte by saying in a censorious voice, 'Of course, you're not properly equipped for this occasion.'

'I think she's demonstrated that she's very well equipped,' Lucio said, astonished.

'Oh, you men! You never know what's important. So she's intelligent! So what? I'm talking about clothes. She'll need a glamorous wardrobe for this.' She took Charlotte's hand. 'Ignore him, my dear. Tomorrow we'll go into Florence and spend money.'

'Of course,' Lucio agreed. 'You must forgive my male ignorance. That hadn't occurred to me. I leave it in your hands, Mamma.'

When he'd gone Fiorella said, 'We're going to have a wonderful time tomorrow.'

Charlotte was glad, for her travelling wardrobe contained nothing that would suit such an elaborate occasion, but an imp of mischief made her say, 'Suppose I don't need any new clothes.'

'Nonsense! Of course you do!'

Laughing they went along the corridor together, and said an affectionate goodnight.

As Fiorella had prophesied, the following day was a delight. They headed for the Via de' Tornabuoni, lined with fashion boutiques. Fiorella declared that Lucio would pay for everything, and spent an amount of money that made Charlotte stare.

'The more, the better,' Fiorella declared. 'You must do him credit. There will be many such occasions, not just when you go visiting with him, but also when he brings important people home to dinner. Which reminds me that I need a couple of dresses myself for a dinner party next month.'

'Then let's start looking.' Charlotte chuckled.

They returned home in triumph, both sporting new clothes, which they displayed to Elizabetta and the maids. Lucio, attempting to enter the room, was firmly excluded.

Two days later they set off for the Palazzo Vidani, once the home of the Dukes of Vidani, now Enrico's pride and joy.

'What did you think of him?' Lucio asked as they travelled.

'Very interesting. He seems grim and chilly, but obviously there's another side to him.'

'Yes, he's spent his life putting money first. So when he reached sixty and a fortune hunter got him in her sights he was helpless. Now she treats him like dirt, but he can't bear to get rid of her. The closest he's ever come to making a firm stand is about these diamonds which would have cost him millions.'

When they arrived Enrico greeted them at the door and personally escorted them upstairs to the luxurious ducal apartments.

'Duke Renato built this for himself and his wife in the seventeenth century,' he said, showing them around the splendid bedroom. 'She was of royal blood, so he wanted to impress her. Normally I sleep here, but tonight it's yours. I'll be in the dressing room next door.'

It was truly a room from another age. Oak panels lined the walls, which were elaborately decorated with paintings. There was also a huge fireplace, although rendered unnecessary by a discreetly located radiator. Floor-length brocade curtains framed the tall windows, and matching curtains hung around the bed which, Charlotte realised with a slight disturbance, was a double.

Clearly Enrico had assumed they slept together. He would have been aghast to learn that they had separate rooms, and that Lucio came to hers only briefly to say a chaste goodnight.

The bed was large, so they could keep a certain distance, but it was still a slight shock to discover that she had no choice in the matter. She wondered how Lucio felt about it, but when she glanced at him his face revealed nothing.

'I'll leave you to get settled in,' Enrico said. 'Tonight's the big night.'

When she saw the multitude of cars that drew up in the next hour Charlotte knew he had been right. Excitement was rising in her. If she and Lucio were to work out a future she had to be able to fit in with occasions like this, and she was confident that she could do it.

He took the first shower while she unpacked with the help of two maids who gasped with admiration as they discovered her new clothes.

'Hang them in the wardrobe,' Charlotte said. 'I want them to be a secret until the last minute.'

They nodded, understanding perfectly and giggling.

She surveyed them, wondering which one would make Lucio catch his breath. That was the one that really mattered. She didn't try to deny it to herself.

The gown that attracted her most was deep gold silk. It was elegant, sophisticated, and the bosom was just low enough to be enticing without being outrageous. When it was time to dress for the evening she slipped into the bathroom while Lucio attired himself in the bedroom. When she emerged they were both fully dressed.

It was hilarious, she thought wryly, to take such trouble not to see each other in a state of undress, when they already knew each other naked. The memory danced through her brain: Lucio, as he'd been that night, lean, vigorous, delightful.

Tonight he wore a black dinner jacket and bow tie. His hair just touched his collar, and his face was handsome and intriguing. Somehow she must spend the evening with this man without revealing how much he disturbed her. But what about him? Didn't she cause him any disturbance? Surely she must. But if so he concealed it behind perfect control.

She had a partial answer at the astonishment on his face as he approached her, and nodded.

'You'll knock them all flat,' he said. Then he dropped a light kiss on her cheek and said, 'Let's go.'

They entered the great hall down a wide staircase, and Charlotte knew at once that word had gone ahead of her. Everyone here knew what this occasion was about, and who she was.

So many people to meet. So many successful men and beautiful women, and most of those women had eyes for Lucio. The looks they cast him were the same as she'd seen in the hotel in Rome, when almost every female seemed aiming to be first with him. He could have taken any one of them to bed.

And some of them he probably has, she thought. *But he's with me now, so the rest of you can just back off.*

She took a deep breath and raised her head. She was ready for anything.

From the first moment she was a success. As so often the Italians warmed towards a non-Italian who'd taken the trouble to become expert in their language. They were particularly impressed by her knowledge of dialects.

Most regions of Italy had dialects vastly different from Italian. This did not apply in Tuscany, where the dialect was so like standard Italian that it was reputed to be the basis of the main language. But it was certainly true of Venice, where the *lingua Veneto* was less a dialect than an independent language that defeated most non-Venetians.

But Charlotte had been fascinated by it and, during her visit, had managed to master a certain amount. So she was looking forward to meeting Franco Dillani, owner of the shop in Florence that Lucio and Enrico were aiming to buy.

When the moment came Signor Dillani greeted her in English.

'It is a pleasure to meet you, *signorina*.'

Beaming, she took his outstretched hand, saying, *'E mi so veramente contenta de far la vostra conoscensa, sior. Lucio me ge parla tanto de vu.'*

She had the pleasure of seeing both Lucio and Franco Dillani stare in amazement. She had spoken in Venetian, saying: 'And I am delighted to meet you, *signore*. Lucio has told me so much about you.'

'You speak all Italian languages?' he exclaimed, again in Venetian.

'No, I was just very attracted to yours,' she said.

'But that is wonderful. I am honoured.'

He immediately monopolised her, talking Venetian with great vigour until she had to protest, laughing, that he had exceeded her knowledge. Whereupon he proceeded to instruct her in *lingua Veneto*, which he enjoyed even more. By the time Lucio and Enrico converged on him for a business talk he was in the best of moods.

'How's it going?' she murmured to Lucio as the evening drew to an end.

'Wonderfully. A few more details to be settled, but the feeling is positive, thanks to you.'

'It can't be me. It must be a good deal in itself or he wouldn't be interested.'

'But tonight he's been listening as he never did before, and that's because you cast a spell on him.'

'Nonsense,' she protested, but her heart was soaring. This was what she'd hoped for, to find a niche in his life as well as his heart.

'No, it's not nonsense. Now, let's retire for the night. You need rest. I shall want you to do a lot of this kind of thing tomorrow.'

'Your wish is my command,' she said merrily.

'You should be careful. I might take you seriously.'

Laughing they ascended the stairs together, watched by several envious pairs of eyes.

Once in their room he collected his night attire and vanished into the bathroom. Charlotte guessed that this night, however triumphant so far, would end prosaically, however much they might each hope otherwise.

Did he hope so? she wondered wistfully. Was he so much in command of himself that he could resist the temptation that teased her?

Whatever the answer, self-respect demanded that she stay in control. Her thin silk nightdress was too revealing, too obviously enticing. She covered it with a matching wrap.

There was a knock on the door that connected them to Enrico's room, and his voice called, 'May I come in?'

'Yes, of course,' she said, opening the door.

'I just wanted to say goodnight,' Enrico said. 'And to ask if you have everything you want.'

'Everything,' she said. 'It's such a lovely place.'

Lucio emerged from the bathroom and the three of them exchanged friendly goodnights, before Enrico retreated, closing the door again.

'Oh, my goodness!' Charlotte exclaimed. 'Did you see where he's sleeping? That tiny narrow bed, how spare and dismal everything is.'

'It's only meant to be a dressing room. He's making do with it tonight so that we can have his room. Still, I know what you mean.' He yawned. 'It's been a long day. I'm really looking forward to a good night's sleep.'

'So am I,' she said untruthfully.

He laid a gentle hand on her shoulder.

'You did wonderfully tonight. They all admired you.'

The movement of his hand caused the wrap to slip away to the floor. He retrieved it and laid it around her bare shoulders. His fingers barely brushed against her but suddenly Charlotte was intensely aware of every inch of her body. Every day she studied it to see if her pregnancy was becoming noticeable, but for now there was only a slight increase in the voluptuousness of her breasts and hips. It was still the same beautiful body that had entranced Lucio on the night that had changed the world. Perhaps it was even more beautiful.

And he, too, realised that. The sudden rasping sound of his breath told her that he'd become aware of her in another way. This was no longer just the mother of his child. She was the woman who'd made his spirits soar and his body vibrate.

She knew she should try to get control of herself, to subdue the thrilling impulses that invaded her. But they had always been there, she now realised, lurking in the shadows, waiting to spring out and remind her that her freedom was an illusion. Lucio's presence, or even just the sound of his voice, was enough to bring them to life, teasing, troubling, tempting.

Now she couldn't deny that ever since the first incredible night, she had wanted him again. Not just for his body's power but also its subtlety—the instinctive understanding that had told him which caresses would most delight her, the gentleness and skill that he devoted to her.

And he, too, was filled with yearning. She knew it from the way he trembled, standing so close to her. In another moment he would yield to his desires, take her in his arms and claim her in the way they both wanted. She raised her head, searching his face, and finding in it everything she longed to see. She reached up to touch him—

Then he seized her hand, holding it away from him.

'It's late,' he said. 'We both need our sleep.'

She wanted to scream that what she needed wasn't sleep. It was him, his thrilling body, his power, his passion. But that would tell him that her desire for him was greater than anything he felt for her, and her pride revolted at the thought.

'You're right,' she said. 'After all, we're here to work. Which side do you prefer?'

'This one,' he said, walking away and getting into bed on the far side.

He settled on the extreme edge, so that when she'd climbed in on her own side there was still a clear distance between them. She lay still, her face turned towards him, her whole being tense for any movement from him. But there was nothing. Lucio stayed motionless, only a slight unevenness in his breathing revealing that he was less relaxed than he pretended.

At last the sound changed, becoming quieter, more regular, telling her that the impossible had happened. Lucio, lying a few feet from her half-clad body, had fallen asleep.

It was insulting.

Only the fact that she was tired prevented her seething with indignation.

At last she, too, sank into sleep, driven more by desolation than tiredness.

She was awoken by a heavy hand on her shoulder, shaking her. Opening her eyes she saw the face of a furiously angry woman.

'I should have known,' the stranger snapped. 'I haven't been gone five minutes and already he's got another woman in my bed.'

'In your—? Are you Signora Miroza?'

'Yes, I am and you're going to regret this. And he's going to regret it even more.'

She switched on the bedside light, pointing at the far side of the bed.

It was empty.

A light beneath the door of the bathroom showed where Lucio had vanished.

'So that's where he is,' Susanna grated.

'No,' Charlotte said, pushing the woman aside. 'You've got this all wrong.'

To her relief the bathroom door opened and Lucio appeared, seemingly relaxed, smiling.

'Susanna, how nice to see you. I'm sorry that Charlotte and I are in your room, but Enrico thought you wouldn't mind.' He slipped an arm around Charlotte's shoulders, a gesture designed to make matters plain.

It worked. Susanna's jaw dropped.

'Are you two—I mean—?'

'Charlotte and I are a couple,' Lucio said. 'Enrico thought it would be nice for us to be in here.'

'But where is he? No, don't tell me. He's off in some floozy's bed, making the most of my absence.'

Charlotte lost her temper.

'No, I'll tell you where he is,' she snapped. 'And then maybe you'll stop your nonsense. Here!'

In a flash she was at the door of the dressing room, wrenching it open and switching on the light, revealing Enrico, virtuously alone in the narrow little bed.

'Nobody else,' she said firmly. 'There isn't another door into this room and you can see he's completely alone.'

She wrenched open the wardrobe door, revealing clothes but nothing else.

Roused by the commotion Enrico had opened his eyes and was regarding them with sleepy surprise.

'Hallo,' he murmured. 'You're back.'

'I'll go now and leave you to it,' Charlotte said.

She marched out.

Lucio was waiting for her, watching her with a new light in his eyes.

'I'm beginning to realise that I've underestimated you. You can be so proper and serious when it suits you, but your other side is a cheeky imp and a warrior by turns.'

'And which one do you think is the real me?'

Slowly he shook his head.

'I'm not sure there is a real you. I think you produce whichever "you" it's useful for someone to see. You've already shown me several different faces, and I'm curious to know what surprises you still have in store for me.'

She stepped back and looked up at him, eyes bright with teasing humour.

'You'll find out—one day,' she said. 'In the meantime you'll just have to wonder.'

CHAPTER SIX

SHE spoke lightly, watching his reaction, and was pleased to find him regarding her with new interest.

'But how long will I have to wonder?' he mused. 'I'm not a patient man.'

'Well, I know that,' she agreed.

'But it doesn't worry you?'

'Not in the least.'

He grinned. 'Think you can get the better of me, huh?'

She laughed softly. 'Think I can't?'

'I'm not foolish enough to answer that question. Like I said, I don't know how many different personalities you have hiding, ready to pop out and knock me flying.'

'Maybe I don't even know that myself. Perhaps you're the man who'll bring them out. Why don't we just wait and see?'

'I'm up for it if you are.' He nodded. 'I think life is going to become very interesting.'

'Really?' she asked, wide-eyed. 'Whatever makes you think that?'

'Either interesting or alarming. Or both.'

Before she could answer there was a noise from Enrico's dressing room.

'I wonder what's happening in there right now,' she mused.

She had an answer with unexpected speed. The door opened, revealing Susanna and Enrico, arms about each other's waists.

'Goodnight,' Susanna said majestically. 'We shall not disturb you again.'

Heads high, they crossed the room and departed. Enrico, Charlotte was fascinated to notice, looked ecstatic.

'He's got a grandiose suite down the corridor,' Lucio observed. 'They'll head for there and—whatever they feel like doing.'

'He's won this one,' Charlotte said. 'Did you ever see a man look so pleased with himself.' She gave a choke of amusement. 'Oh, goodness! His face when he first saw her.'

Lucio joined in her merriment, placing his hands on her shoulders, and suddenly the laughter died. She was no longer wearing the wrap, and the feel of his fingers against her bare skin filled her with delicious tension. The nightdress seemed flimsier than ever and she realised that his pyjama jacket was no longer respectably buttoned up high, or even buttoned up at all. It had fallen open, showing the smooth, muscular chest that she remembered.

She sensed his tension equalling her own. Also his confusion. He'd dealt with this situation earlier in the evening, but it had refused to stay dealt with. Now it was taunting him again, and he was struggling with himself, with her, but most of all with his own desire.

Good, she thought with a surge of pleasure. It would be an enjoyable battle, the herald of many. And she would always be the victor. It was time he understood that.

She leaned forward, turning her head slightly so that her cheek rested against his chest. She felt the shock go through him and the thunder of his heart, a sensation so intense that she drew back to look at his face. It was haggard, tormented, the face of a man driven by demons, far beyond his own control.

She understood that feeling. It possessed her too, giving her a powerful urge to drive the demons on, cry out to them exultantly to do their worst, because their worst was what she desperately wanted.

His caresses intensified, the fingers slipping behind her head to draw her to him so that his mouth could touch hers softly, tentatively, then urgently. Her warm breath against his face drove him on to put his arms about her, exploring, rejoicing in the feel of her flesh through the thin nightdress. He kissed her repeatedly while his hands roved over her as though this was their first time together.

And perhaps that was true. Their night in Rome had been so different, so impossible to repeat, that now they were like two strangers knowing nothing of each other except that they were flooded with desire.

He took a step towards the bed, moving slowly as though giving her time to refuse. But she was far from refusing, clinging to him frantically. He was breathing heavily, his flesh rising and falling beneath her fingers.

Then they were lying down, he was stripping away her nightdress and tossing aside the rest of his own clothes. His eyes, looking down on her, were full of fervour and his lips were touched by a smile that she had never seen before.

'You're beautiful,' he whispered. 'More beautiful than ever.'

'I don't know what you mean by that,' she said provocatively.

His fingers drifted over her, causing a storm to go through her.

'I mean this,' he said softly. 'And this.' He laid his lips against her, moving them so skilfully that she trembled, holding him closer, whispering 'Yes, yes…'

Her hands seemed to act of their own accord, seeking, begging, demanding. Their only previous lovemaking had burned itself into her consciousness so deeply that she knew what he most enjoyed.

She closed her eyes, holding him tightly against her, desperate to relish every possible moment.

Now she could face the thought that she had never before dared to admit; that if she'd had to live the rest of her life without this man ever making love to her again, she would not have known how to endure it.

Inwardly she pleaded for this to last forever, pleasure unending, happiness without boundaries. Then, it was over, and yet not over. It would never be entirely over, she thought. Now she had everything to look forward to. Not just the sedate companionship of two people who were to have a child, but the blissful closeness of physical harmony, with its promise of a sweeter, more emotional union.

She searched his face, trying to meet his eyes for an exchange of feelings. But he turned away from her and she almost thought he shook his head. Then she saw that his eyes were closed, as though he'd retreated inside himself. With a convulsive movement he wrenched himself away from her, left the bed and strode to the window. Aghast, she followed him.

'Lucio, whatever's the matter.'

'I'm sorry,' he groaned. 'I shouldn't have done that.'

She pulled him around to face her. 'Why not?'

'Because you're carrying our child. Just the sight of you was too much for me…. Forgive me—it'll never happen again, I promise.'

She regarded him tenderly, astonished by his miserable self-blame which roused her protective instincts as nothing else in her life had ever done.

'Lucio, dear, it's all right,' she said. 'There's nothing

wrong in what we've just done. I've got friends who go on enjoying each other practically until the birth. One of them has four children, all perfectly healthy. The doctor says I'm in fine shape, and as long as that's true nothing else has to change.'

'It's not just the baby,' he said sombrely. 'We've got to be careful about you. We never know what might be going to happen.'

She was about to say that he was being overly dramatic when she remembered that Maria had died suddenly, leaving him devastated. Now he went through life alert for danger and heartbreak.

She forced her own feelings to abate. It was sad that he couldn't share her delight at their union, but they had a road to travel. It was too soon to say what awaited them at the end of that road, but to her hopeful eyes it looked increasingly bright and happy.

'Don't worry about me,' she said, touching his face softly. 'I'm strong, and I'm going to give you a healthy baby.'

'Thank you. And in future I'll take better care of you. I promise.'

He spoke fervently and she loved him for his concern. Now they would fall asleep tenderly in each other's arms, the perfect way for passion to end. And there would be other moments. He might mean to keep his distance, but she knew how to change his mind.

'Everything's going to be all right,' she assured him. 'Now, let's get some sleep.'

She took his hand and tried to lead him back to the bed. But he resisted her.

'No,' he said. 'I told you I'm going to care for you, and I meant it.'

'But—'

'I can't trust myself. I've just discovered that. But you must sleep. I've tired you, and I blame myself.'

He took up her nightdress, holding it out to her at a distance and waiting while she slipped into it. Then he pulled back the covers on her side of the bed and helped her in, pushing her gently back against the pillows.

As though I was a weakling, she thought desperately, *when I've never felt so strong as I have tonight.*

But this wasn't the moment to protest, so she lay down and let him draw the covers over her.

She waited for him to go around to his side of the bed. Once he was in he would fall asleep, and she would be able to move quietly across the space between, slide her arms about him, rest her head on his shoulder. When he awoke to find her there he would understand that this was the truth between them. She smiled to herself.

But her smile faded as he turned away from the bed, heading for a sofa on the far side of the room.

'Lucio—' she protested.

He lay down on the sofa, his head on a cushion.

'Goodnight, Charlotte. Sleep well. I won't disturb you.'

And he wouldn't, she thought bitterly.

As she'd feared, he kept to his resolve, breathing steadily until she reckoned he must be asleep. So that was how easily he could shrug off their glorious union, she thought bitterly. That was how little it meant to him. Damn him!

From the sofa, Lucio kept his eyes on the bed where he could just make out her shape in the darkness. She lay very still, he noticed. Was she stunned by what had overtaken them? As stunned as he was himself? Or did she feel triumphant at having exposed his weakness?

When he remembered how easily he'd yielded he groaned inwardly.

He waited a long time before leaving the sofa, crossing

the floor slowly and carefully to stand by the bed, watching her as she slept. At last she moved, turning over, throwing out her arms, then letting them fall back. She was murmuring something, but although he leaned closer he couldn't understand.

He reached out as if to touch her, but stayed his hand at the last minute, holding it still for several seconds before drawing it back.

He stood there for a while before returning to the sofa and lying down in the darkness.

Charlotte awoke to find herself alone. From the bathroom came the sound of Lucio singing cheerfully. After a moment he entered, fully dressed.

'Good, you're awake,' he said. 'I'll see you at breakfast.'

He departed, apparently not having noticed that the nightdress was slipping from her shoulders, revealing the beautiful swell of her breasts.

After a shower she donned a brown linen dress that was one of Fiorella's choices. It suited her perfectly, while projecting the air of sedate respectability that she guessed Fiorella had been aiming for.

She found Lucio deep in talk with Enrico, who immediately broke away to take her hand and speak warmly.

'Thank you so much, my dear Charlotte, for your help last night. I shall not forget your kind friendship.'

'I was glad to be of help. Did you and Susanna sort things out?'

'We've a way to travel yet, but we'll get there. Thanks to you. Excuse me a moment.'

Susanna had appeared, causing Enrico to hurry across to her. She was dressed in high fashion and clearly ready to flaunt herself as the hostess. She reached out to Enrico, accepting his hug as no more than her due.

'There's no fool like an old fool,' said a voice behind Charlotte.

Turning, they saw Piero, a young man-about-town they'd met the night before. He was handsome with the air of a man who would indulge himself at all costs.

'You'd think he'd have seen through her by now,' he added.

'Perhaps he doesn't want to,' Charlotte said.

'That's pretty certain. Like I say, he's a fool. Everyone knows she slept with him the night they met. That should have warned him. If a woman jumps into bed with a man she's only just met, well—we know what kind of woman she is, don't we?'

'Not necessarily,' Lucio said, clenching his hands.

'I suppose she might take you by surprise,' Charlotte mused.

'No way,' Piero declared. 'Sex on the first evening means she's after whatever she can get. Ah, I see someone I need to talk to. Bye!'

He vanished.

'Stop looking like that,' Charlotte muttered. 'Smile.'

'How can I?' Lucio ground out. 'Why aren't you insulted?'

'Why should I be? He wasn't talking about me. Unless of course you'd told him—'

'No!' He stared at her, incredulous and aghast. 'You're enjoying this, aren't you? How *can* you?'

'What I'm enjoying is the sight of your face. When he said it you didn't know where to look.'

'I was concerned for you. Evidently I didn't need to be.'

'That's right. My shoulders are broad. Come on, Lucio, enjoy the joke. Life's too short to get uptight about everything.'

'The sooner I get the serious business sorted out, the better,' Lucio growled. 'Then we can leave.'

'How close are you and Enrico to concluding your deal?'

'I'm not sure. He thinks the price is too high and he's holding out for a reduction.'

'Any chance that he's right?'

'None. It's a bargain because the seller wants to get rid of it quickly, and if we don't settle it now I'm afraid it'll be too late. So if Enrico delays again I'm calling it off.'

He had no need to. An hour later Enrico increased his offer, the seller accepted and the deal was concluded.

'Between you and me,' Enrico said, drawing Charlotte aside, 'I yielded out of gratitude. How could I obstruct Lucio when his wonderful lady has been such a good friend?' He added to Lucio, 'You're a lucky man. You've acquired a real asset. She'll bring you a big increase in profits.'

'That's what I'm there for.' Charlotte chuckled, and both men laughed with her.

'Now I think we'll leave,' Lucio said. 'I don't want Charlotte to get tired.'

'Of course you must look after her,' Enrico agreed.

They packed in record time and were soon on the road. Halfway home they stopped at a little village restaurant and relaxed over coffee and cakes.

'You didn't mind dashing away, did you?' Lucio asked.

'No, I think we needed to get out of there before there were any more dramas. Poor Enrico.'

'Yes, she's got him under her thumb again, and I bet she'll get her diamonds next. I don't understand how it can happen to a man like that, so powerful, so confident. He doesn't need anybody.'

'That's not true,' Charlotte mused. 'In a strange way he needs *her.*'

'How can any man need what she puts him through? You know why she came back, don't you? She was hoping to catch him with another woman, then she could divorce him and get a handsome settlement.'

'Or maybe just threaten divorce and keep him under her thumb. I think he'd pay up rather than lose her.'

'We need to rescue him from her.'

'You won't do that,' Charlotte predicted. 'She matters to him too much. And even if you could do it, it wouldn't be kind.'

'Not kind, to rescue him from a gold-digger?'

'From the only person he has to love. I heard a lot about him from other guests while we were there. He has no close family since his wife died. They had no children. He's alone in a—in a desert. And if you're stranded in a desert you often feel that you'd do anything to escape, even marry someone totally unsuitable and put up with the way they behave.'

'A desert,' he mused. 'You spoke to me of a desert on the night we met. You said you were living in one.'

'And you said it could be a good place to be,' she reminded him. 'A place to recruit your strength, and there was nobody to hurt you.'

'That's right,' he said wryly. 'It's a kind of safety.'

'Fine, if you want to be safe. But Enrico doesn't. He'd rather put up with Susanna than be safe and isolated.'

'Safe and isolated,' he murmured. 'Enrico's a brave man.'

'Yes, sometimes you have to take risks. Like we did, that night. Not that we thought of the consequences. If we had—'

'If we had you'd have run a mile from me,' he said, regarding her intently.

She gave him a faint smile. 'I'll let you know that another time.'

He had certainly never thought of the consequences, he recalled. The Charlotte he'd met in Rome had seemed so sophisticated, so adventurous and confident, that he'd simply assumed she was ready for anything.

Now he knew that what had happened that night had taken her by surprise. He, too, had been surprised, although not by the way the evening ended. That had happened to him before. What was new was the intensity of his enjoyment, not merely pleasure but a feeling of happiness as he lay in her arms.

She was wonderful. He wasn't sure if he'd told her so, although he hoped he hadn't. Safer that way.

But safe was one thing he couldn't feel in her company. She threatened his precious isolation, which he'd valued since everyone he loved had either died or betrayed him—the isolation that gave him strength and which he would cling to forever. In this mood he had fled her next morning.

But from some things there was no escape.

When they were on the road again he told her some more about his business with Enrico.

'It's just the one shop for the moment, but we'll eventually have a whole chain of wine shops in different cities. Now we've taken the first step, thanks to you.'

'Hey, I didn't do much.'

'You pulled a trigger, and it helped. And the fact that he likes you so much will also be useful in the future.'

'I'm going to be good for business, huh?' She chuckled.

'You'd better believe it. Enrico's right. Meeting you was a stroke of luck in more than one way.'

He didn't elaborate and it wasn't the time to press him,

but one day soon Charlotte promised herself that she would make him enlarge on that topic.

'Did you notice that he was delighted to see us leave?' she mused. 'He wants the room back for himself and Susanna.'

'That's very cynical.'

'Sometimes cynical is the right thing to be. Aren't you ever cynical?'

'There are times when you have to be.' After a moment he added, 'And there are times when you can't afford to be.'

'I wonder which we—'

'Hey, look at that idiot!'

He braked sharply to avoid a pedestrian, then continued on the way.

Nothing was said about the night before, and soon they were on the last stretch home.

Once there he told Fiorella about the successful deal, emphasising that Charlotte had helped by winning Enrico's goodwill.

When they were alone Fiorella said triumphantly, 'You see how well you fit in here? I knew it. I'm going to cook you a special meal to celebrate.'

Charlotte couldn't help but think that Fiorella was simply trying to secure her and the child for the family, but even thinking that, it was pleasant to be treated in such a way. When she looked back on the trip she felt she had much to make her glad. If only Lucio hadn't spoiled the memory of their lovemaking by regretting it. But they were still strangers in many ways. Things would get better.

Late that night he looked into her room to say goodnight.

'The deal is set up and I'll be signing papers at the lawyer's office in a couple of days. Care to come with me?'

'I'd love to.'

'Fine. Goodnight. Sleep well.'

He departed without having come anywhere near her.

He was as good as his word, taking her to the lawyer, where they found Franco Dillani, full of good cheer at having sold the shop. With all the papers safely signed he invited them to lunch. Enrico couldn't stay but Lucio and Charlotte accepted with pleasure. Over the meal Franco was open in his admiration of Charlotte, talking Venetian with her while making the occasional apology to Lucio, who waved him aside good-humouredly.

Charlotte leaned back and just enjoyed herself. It was good to feel that she'd established a position for herself in her new life, and actually been of some real use to Lucio.

But sweeter than anything else was the knowledge that Lucio was watching her with a knowing smile on his face. His eyes, too, were full of a message that made her heart beat faster. Pleasure, admiration, satisfaction—they were all there.

But she also sensed something else, something to which she couldn't yet put a name, but which she was determined to pursue and make her very own.

Brooding on the way home, she knew the task she'd set herself wasn't going to be easy. Lucio was passionately attracted to her, yet in a strange way he feared her. What she'd seen in his eyes was a secret that he wasn't ready to disclose. She would have to lure it from him, even against his will.

At the vineyard he immediately immersed himself in work. His manner was kind, gentle, considerate, but he came to her room only for a few moments to say goodnight. He would kiss her cheek when other people were there, but never when they were alone. Nor did he ever take her in his arms. He was a perfectly behaved gentleman, but not a lover.

She guessed that he kept his distance because he was determined not to be tempted again. But it hurt that he could resist so successfully. Within herself temptation raged. At night she would listen for the moment when he put his head around the door, longing for him to come right in, sit on the bed, talk to her, give her the chance to reach out to him. But he would smile and be gone. Recalling what she'd seen in his arms at her moment of triumph she even wondered if she'd imagined it.

No, I didn't imagine it, she told herself fiercely. *I won't believe that.*

Lying in the darkness, she would wonder about the future, and the many different ways it could turn out. Was Lucio restrained only because he dreaded to hurt her? Or was there another reason? Was he avoiding her emotionally? When he'd said that meeting her was a stroke of luck, had he only been talking about business?

Once he'd said she was wonderful.

Would he ever say it again?

CHAPTER SEVEN

Two days later Lucio set off to visit one of his other vineyards, accompanied by Charlotte. The place was fifty miles south, in Umbria, and she looked forward to visiting an area of Italy she hadn't seen before.

She found the trip interesting rather than enjoyable. As Lucio had warned, he would be working morning, noon and night, and there was no time for pleasure. She accompanied him whenever possible, learned all she could about the different varieties of grapes and listened to endless work discussions.

The trip was valuable for the insight it gave her into him. Before her eyes he turned into someone else. She'd known him first as an elegant man-about-town, then a skilful and imaginative lover, and then an efficient manager. Now that final aspect was growing harder, sharper, revealing a man who lived for nothing but business and shrewd, sometimes harsh dealing. For this he had the admiration of his tenants who ran the place, but not their affection. Nor did he apparently want it.

She remembered the night they'd spent in Enrico's palace, when he'd remarked how many different aspects there were to her personality.

'You've already shown me several different faces,' he'd

said, 'and I'm curious to know what surprises you still have in store for me.'

She was beginning to understand what he meant. Her view of him was exactly the same.

As they drove home he asked, 'What did you think?'

Receiving no answer he glanced at her briefly and saw that she was asleep. He nodded. He didn't blame her.

He had two more visits coming up, but she gently declined the chance to go with him. He didn't protest and she had the feeling he was glad of her decision.

At home she concentrated on learning about life there, and fitting in with it. Fiorella took her to meet the neighbours, most of whom were kindly and pleasant. One family surveyed her with suppressed hostility, which Fiorella explained thus.

'Those two daughters had set their sights on Lucio, and they're furious that you've snatched him from under their noses. Good for you. I prefer you to them any day.'

Three times Lucio called her, asking how she was, assuring her that he was thinking of her. But there were always distractions in the background that caused the call to end soon.

When he returned to the Vigneto Constanza he embraced Charlotte, then stood back with his hands on her shoulders and regarded her closely. 'How are you?'

'Doing fine,' she told him.

'That's good because I've brought a couple of guests home with me. We've got a lot of business to do, but they're anxious to meet you.'

The guests took up his attention through the meal and the rest of the evening, but as she was going to bed he came into her room and opened his arms to her. She threw herself in gladly, and felt him enclose her in a fierce hug. Her heart leapt.

'How are you? Are you really all right?'

'Ready for anything,' she said, hoping he would detect her real meaning.

But he only said, 'That's the best news I've had. I drove Fiorella crazy every night demanding to know how you were. But you look fine. Come here.'

He enfolded her in another hug. She held her breath, waiting for the sweet feel of his hands drifting over her, but they never moved until he said, 'Go to bed now. Sleep well.'

He put her to bed, pulled the covers up over her and departed.

She was left staring at the ceiling, coming to terms with the discovery that while he'd called her only three times, he'd checked on her by calling Fiorella every night.

For the next few days he was preoccupied with his guests, and she decided to spend some time looking around the area, especially Florence. Lucio arranged for Aldo, one of the workers to drive her there and wait for her. But when they reached the town she sent Aldo home. He looked uneasy and she guessed Lucio had told him to stay with her if possible.

'Tell your boss I'm all right,' she said, adding firmly, 'Goodbye.'

She had an enjoyable day in Florence. When it was time to get a taxi home she paused, considered, then made her way back to the hotel where she'd stayed when she first arrived here, and where she had hired a car. As she had hoped they willingly hired her another one.

This was better, she thought as she drove back to the estate. She was happy with the welcome she'd received from the family, but she also felt a little swallowed up by it. Now she would have some freedom and independence.

She had to admit that driving across the estate was a

little confusing. The roads were unlit and twice she lost her way. But at last she saw the house, high on the hill, gleaming with lights in the darkness, and heaved a sigh of relief.

As she drew closer she saw Lucio standing there, watching her until she halted, when he strode over and opened her door.

'Where have you been?' he demanded.

'What's the problem? I've spent the past few months finding my own way around Italy and I can manage these few miles. And I called to say I'd be late.'

'Yes, Fiorella told me, but I didn't expect you to be as late as this. Can't you understand that I—?'

He stopped, clearly searching for words and not finding them. The next moment he reached for her and pulled her fiercely against him, holding her in a grip of iron. His breath was hot against her cheek.

'Hours and hours and you didn't come home,' he growled. 'Anything could have happened to you.'

He drew back a little to look at her, and she was shocked at the torment she saw in his face.

'I'm here now,' she whispered. 'It's all right. Lucio, it's all right. *It's all right.*'

'Yes…yes—'

His mouth was fierce on hers, kissing her again and again while his arms grew even tighter.

'Let me breathe,' she gasped, laughing and delighted.

'You think it's funny to put me through the wringer?'

'No, I don't think it's funny. I'm sorry, Lucio, I never imagined you'd be like this.'

'Didn't imagine I'd want to protect you? Don't you understand that I—? I don't know…I can't explain…I can't—'

She was overwhelmed by a feeling of protectiveness. At first she'd thought he was angry, but he was distraught. Gently she took his face in her hands and kissed him.

'It's all right,' she repeated. 'And it's going to stay all right, I promise.'

'But you're not going to drive that old banger,' he said, indicating the hired car.

'Hey, you're not telling me what I can do, are you?'

'No, I'm telling you that I'm going to buy you a decent car. Think you can put up with that?'

'I guess I'll try.'

'I'm sorry, I didn't mean to upset you.'

'And I didn't mean to upset *you*.'

'When you didn't come back… These dark, unfamiliar roads—you could have had an accident. You could have—both of you.'

She nodded, touching her stomach. 'Yes, there are two of us, aren't there? I guess I wasn't thinking straight. I like my freedom, but I should have remembered that when you're pregnant you lose a lot of freedom.' She gave a rueful sigh. 'It's not just me any more. I did get lost, just for a little while.'

'Only because the roads are unfamiliar. When you've driven in and out of Florence a few times you'll know the way and have no more problems. Now come inside and have something to eat. You must be famished.'

He kept his word about the car, escorting her to the showroom next day, watching her reactions to vehicle after vehicle, until he saw her face light up with pleasure.

'That one?' he said.

'That one. Oh, no, look at the price!'

'Let me worry about that.'

The test drive confirmed her best hopes, and within an hour she was the owner.

'Now you can drive me home,' he said.

'But what about the car we came in?'

'Aldo can pick it up. Come on. This time I'm going to be the passenger.'

He did everything in his power to make her forget his agitation of the night before, and all seemed well.

But when she thought how distraught he'd been she knew there was something there that she didn't understand, something that suggested another, deeply mysterious man, tormented and troubled to the point of agony, lurking below the surface.

Who was he? How often did he emerge? And why?

Now her life was contented, even happy. Not only was Fiorella friendly but Elizabetta and all the servants combined to spoil her. They knew about the coming child, were delighted by it and would do anything to make sure she enjoyed living with them.

The only disturbances were tiny things, impossible to predict, such as the time she opened a cupboard door and found a picture of a young girl.

She knew at once that this must be Maria, and gazed, fascinated. Maria had been not merely pretty but glorious, vibrant with youth, seeming to sum up in one delicate person everything that would make life worth living.

She then saw Lucio in the photo, clasping Maria's waist and standing behind her. She couldn't see much of his face, but she could just make out that he was smiling ecstatically, and his attitude was one of triumph, the victor holding the trophy.

She put the picture carefully back and closed the door, guessing that it had been hidden away so that she should not see it. Doubtless it was kindly meant, but she couldn't help thinking that it had the perverse effect of warning her that Maria was still her rival for Lucio's heart: a rival who had no intention of giving up easily.

She lowered her head, her eyes closed, a prey to a sudden feeling of weariness, almost despair. Once again she was on the outside looking in. Her family, Don. They had all made her feel excluded. But recently things had changed. Here in Tuscany, at the vineyard, with Lucio, she had been made welcome. Or so she'd thought.

But the welcome was not complete. Suddenly the door was barred against her again, and the one who stood there, warning her that she would never get past the barrier into Lucio's heart, was Maria.

But she would refuse to yield to the treacherous feelings. Giving in was for weaklings. She was ready for the fight. If only Lucio was here, so that battle could commence.

One evening she came home to find he had arrived a day early. He greeted her cheerfully with a kiss on her cheek.

'Been exploring again?'

'Yes, but mostly the towns, which isn't what I want.'

'Surely towns are interesting. All those delightful fashion shops—'

'Yes, I've visited a few. And the shop that's going to be your wine store. But I haven't seen much of the place that interests me most.'

'And where would that be?'

'It's called the Vigneto Constanza,' she said, her head on one side as she reminded him of his own estate. 'You must have heard of it.'

He scratched his head. 'It seems vaguely familiar.'

'Everyone says it's the biggest and the best. I'd really like to explore it properly.'

He grinned. 'Then I guess I'll have to oblige.'

It was little more than a month since she'd come here to find him, but already she could see a new lushness in the grapes that would one day be Chianti wine. As they strolled down an alley he said, 'Do you remember this place?'

'Yes, this was where I told you I was pregnant. You were standing down there.'

.'Watching you walk towards me from a great distance. I knew even then that you were going to cause an earthquake, but I had no idea how big it was going to be.'

'Neither had I. I knew I was pregnant but this—' She made a flourishing gesture, taking in the view for miles. 'This makes everything different.'

'Do you like it here?'

'Oh, yes, it's lovely. I've been learning as much as I can. I go online, and read books. I know that you'll harvest these grapes in October, and store them for two years before they can be wine. But that's just facts. Standing here amid all this beauty is different. But I suppose you see it more practically.'

'You think I can see only the money, but I can feel the beauty, too. When I first came here I spent a night sleeping under the stars in one of these fields. It was pure magic, and next morning I went to ask for a job because I knew I never wanted to leave. I'm glad it affects you, too.'

They strolled on, both enjoying their shared warmth and contentment. But, as often happened, it died in an argument only a moment later.

'There's been something I've been meaning to tell you,' he said. 'I don't know how you're fixed financially, but I don't want you to have any worries about that. So I've opened a bank account for you. Here.' He handed her a chequebook. 'It's all set up and I'll be making regular payments.'

But instead of eagerly taking the chequebook she stepped back and shook her head.

'No, thank you. I'd rather not.'

He stared. 'What did you say?'

'I've already opened an account for myself. I'm not in need of money, my family are fortunately very wealthy and I've saved quite a bit from my job back in New York. I wouldn't have started this trip if I couldn't finance it without help.'

'But you're carrying my child. It's my job to look after you.'

'And you're doing that. You've given me a home. I don't need any more. I appreciate you thinking of me, and I'm not ungrateful, but I won't take your money, Lucio.'

'But why?' he demanded.

'Why should I? Not all women want to take a man's money. Let's take it easy. There's a lot we still don't agree about.'

'Do we have to agree about everything?'

'Not about everything, but some things matter.'

'All right. Have it your way.' He sighed and thrust the papers back into his pocket, making a wry face. 'After all, why should I object? I can spend the money you've saved me on riotous living.'

'Naturally. That's what I hope you'll do.'

'You're the most maddening woman, do you know that?'

'Of course. I work at it.'

'Why work at it? You have a natural gift for awkwardness.'

'I'm not the only one. That's one of the things we still have to negotiate, whether my awkwardness and yours can live with each other.'

'Would you like to take bets on who'll be the winner?'

'No, that would be boring.'

He grinned. 'That's one thing I'm never afraid of with you. I'll let you win this time.'

'Coward,' she jeered.

'Whatever you say. Come on, there's a lot for you still to see.'

Charlotte wondered at herself. Lucio seemed to have offered her a gesture of acceptance, the very acceptance she was eager to find. Yet was it her he sought to bind to him, or only the child?

With all her heart she longed for him to want her for herself, and until she was certain of that she would retain some independence—however perverse and awkward she might seem, not only in his eyes but in her own.

These days she was often in contact with her family in the States, not just through email but with a video link on her new laptop.

Ellie had much to tell. She had been to see their Calhoun relatives in Larkville, Texas.

'Clay had four children,' she told Charlotte. 'Two daughters, Jess and Megan, and two sons, Holt and Nate. I haven't met all of them yet but that's going to be the next thing. Every year in October Larkville has a festival. This year it's going to include a celebration of Clay Calhoun's life, to mark the first anniversary of his death. His children really want us to be there, so I'm going to stay here for it, especially now I've met Jed, and you must come, too.' Ellie had travelled to Larkville earlier in the year wanting to know the truth about her father and had fallen in love with Larkville's sheriff, Jed Jackson.

'But I can't,' Charlotte said. 'My baby's due about then. I can't take a long flight so close to the birth. Just imagine Lucio's reaction to that idea.'

'And who's Lucio to tell you what you can and can't do?'

'He's the father. That gives him some rights.'

'But he can't tell you whether you can or can't come home.'

Home, she thought. How strange that word now sounded. Wasn't Tuscany her home now?

'What about marriage?' Ellie demanded.

'We haven't talked about it, but we get on well.'

'Charlotte, shouldn't you be facing facts now? Does he actually want to marry you? I mean, if he hasn't asked you—'

'I—'

'He hasn't, has he?'

'No, but that doesn't mean—'

'Doesn't it? Look, I care about you. I know you don't believe that after the trouble recently, but it's true. I want you to be happy, and I don't think you are. You're having his child, he's moved you into his house but he won't make it final. Doesn't that tell you something?'

Charlotte couldn't speak. Conflicting thoughts and emotions stormed through her. Her feelings were greater than Lucio's, but she'd told herself a thousand times that she could cope. Now Ellie was forcing her to face something she wanted to avoid, at least for the moment.

'What about you?' Ellie pursued remorselessly. 'Do *you* want to marry *him*?'

'Don't be so old-fashioned,' Charlotte said quickly. 'People don't have to marry these days.'

'No, but if things are right between them they want to get married. That's how you know. Does he say he loves you?'

'Look—'

'I guess that means he doesn't. For pity's sake, get yourself back here as soon as possible. He thinks he owns you but he won't commit to you. Come home, Charlotte.'

'Ellie, I've got to go. We'll talk again soon. Goodbye.'

She shut the call down and sat with her face buried in her hands, devastated. It was no use telling herself that Ellie didn't understand the situation. The words 'He thinks he owns you but he won't commit to you' rang in her ears despite her frantic attempts to shut them out.

'It's not true,' she whispered. 'He needs time. We're close, even if it's only as friends. I can build on that.'

But in her mind was another voice, saying cruelly, *'You're fooling yourself. He doesn't care for you in the way you want, and you just believe what you want to believe.'*

'But I'm not giving up yet,' she whispered.

As part of her desire to fit in with Lucio's life she asked him to show her the shop in Florence that he had bought with Enrico. It was in the luxurious Via della Vigna Nuova, which translated as the Street of the New Vineyard. Not surprisingly it was to be a wine store.

She met Vincente, who would be in charge, organising the shop, stocking it, arranging the grand opening. She found him pleasant and receptive to the ideas that were beginning to bubble in her mind. She wanted to be involved in this venture.

As they were just about to leave there was a new arrival, the last person they expected to see there.

'Franco,' Charlotte exclaimed, holding out her hands.

'I'm not selling this place back to you,' Lucio said at once.

'Don't worry, it's all yours. But I remember I left some stuff of mine in the cupboard under the stairs.'

They helped him fetch his things, and the three of them had lunch together.

Franco continued to happily talk away in Venetian with Charlotte, until at last he switched back to Italian to say,

'I suppose you'll make a bid for one of the Bantori vine-yards now.'

'I've been thinking of it,' Lucio agreed, 'but why do you say "now"?'

'Because now you have Charlotte, who speaks Venetian, you'll find a lot of things easier.'

'Venetian?' Charlotte exclaimed. 'But surely you can't grow grapes in Venice, with all those canals?'

'Not actually in Venice,' Lucio told her. 'But there are vineyards in the surrounding countryside, and I've been thinking of expanding.'

'I can put you in touch with several useful people,' Franco said.

Charlotte grew very still. An idea was creeping up on her, mischievous, delightful, a bit naughty but all the more fun for that.

Assuming a tone of serious consideration she said, 'I think we should go to Venice as soon as possible. There's important business to be done. The next few days would be a good idea.'

Lucio eyed her curiously. 'What are you up to?'

'Me?' she asked, eyes wide and innocent. 'I'm just try-ing to help you make money. Why would you suspect me of an ulterior motive?'

'Because I'm beginning to know you, and an ulterior motive is the first thing that comes into my head.' He grinned. 'Come on. Own up. What am I being tricked into?'

Franco began to laugh. 'Of course, I should have thought of it. Where was my head?' He beamed at Charlotte. 'I should have known that someone as knowledgeable about Italy as you would have been alert to this.'

'It's something I've always wanted to see,' she said. 'And here's my chance.'

'When you two jokers have finished,' Lucio said ironically. 'Are you going to let me in on the secret?'

'Perhaps we ought to tell him,' Franco asked.

'I reckon we'd better,' she said solemnly. Her eyes met Lucio's, his wary, hers brimming with fun.

'If we go now we'll be in time for the festival. You know—the Festa della Sensa. You must have heard of it.'

'Of course I—is it now? Yes—' He slapped his forehead.

'And you're an Italian,' Charlotte mocked.

'I'm Tuscan not Venetian. I don't keep all their festivals in my head. But I've heard of this one and I agree it would be good to go.'

The Festa della Sensa was a glorious Venetian water pageant, whose peak was the moment when a ring was tossed into the water, symbolising Venice's marriage to the sea. By sheer lucky chance it was due to start in a few days, and they would have time to get there and join in.

'You're a conniving little so-and-so,' he said when they returned to the car.

'Nonsense. I'm doing my bit as your Venetian assistant. Just wait and see how useful I can be.'

'I think I'm going to enjoy this,' he said.

'I hope so. I know I am.'

That night, somewhere in her dreams, Charlotte heard Lucio's softly murmured, 'You're wonderful.' Then she awoke and lay awake listening, longing to hear again the whisper that would bring her to life.

He'd said it to her after their night of passion. Surely one day he would say it again.

Waiting—waiting…

Light was coming in around the gaps at the blinds, and she rose to go to the window, wanting to watch the dawn. Now she felt as though light was dawning in her life. Everything in her yearned towards the trip to Venice that she would take with Lucio, share work with him, and perhaps share even more.

Then she saw something that made her grow still. At a little distance on a hill there was a man, completely still, watching the dawn. As the light slowly engulfed him she could see that it was Lucio.

What had made him go out to that isolated place to stand against the sky, so alone that he might have been the only person alive in the world?

And she remembered what he'd said about a desert that very first night; that it could be a place of safety because there was nobody to hurt you. And he'd meant exactly that. She knew it now.

With all her heart she longed to go to him, open her arms and draw him against her heart, telling him that he didn't need to live in a desert. But at this moment he would turn away from her, because the desert was what he had chosen.

She stood watching him for a long time, hoping to see him move, to return home to her. But he stood there, imprisoned in a terrible, isolated stillness.

At last she returned to bed and lay down in her own desert.

CHAPTER EIGHT

THEY nearly didn't make the trip to Venice. With only two days to the festival every hotel for miles was booked. But a sudden cancellation came just in time.

'We're going to stay in the Tirani Hotel,' Lucio told her.

Charlotte's eyes widened. 'Wow!'

The Tirani was one of the most luxurious hotels in Venice. On her last visit she had stayed in a far more modest establishment, occasionally walking past the Tirani, just close enough to see that it was way out of her price range.

'I hope it lives up to your expectations,' Lucio said, grinning and correctly interpreting her amazement.

They travelled by train, boarding at Florence Station for the two-hour journey.

'I loved Venice when I was there before,' she said as they neared the magical city. 'But it was winter and everywhere was under snow, even the gondolas. I've always wanted to go back and see it in the sun.'

'And you managed it, by manipulating me like a puppet. Well done.'

'Oh, that's how you feel. Well, if the vineyards in the Veneto aren't worth fighting for, why don't we just go back?'

He eyed her with grimly humorous appreciation.

'If you think I'll fall for that, forget it. I know you well enough by now to reckon that you'll have researched the subject and know exactly how good they are.'

'Right! I did just that, and I know that the Bantori vineyards are well known for their white grapes, which are used to make the very best prosecco wine. In Tuscany you grow Sangiovese grapes to make red wine, so you'd probably enjoy branching out into a different area.'

'You really have been doing research,' he observed.

He wished he could have kept the touch of admiration out of his voice. It galled him to discover that he respected her brains, but he couldn't help it.

He'd never sought the company of intellectual women. Nor was that how she'd appeared on the first evening. True, she'd argued like someone whose brain was up to every trick, but soon other aspects of her had risen to distract him. Now he was discovering that to keep one step ahead of her he would need all his wits.

As she gazed out of the window he took the chance to study her, knowing that her combination of beauty and brains was likely to cause him even more trouble in the future than it had already. Pregnancy suited her, causing a glorious flowering. Yet the alertness was always there in her eyes, warning him to take nothing for granted.

He marvelled at the situation in which he found himself. He, not she, was Italian, yet in thirty-two years he had never visited Venice. But she knew the city well and was revealing it to him. Something in the irony of that appealed to his sense of humour.

Not that there had been much humour in his life. Once, briefly, he'd enjoyed a time of vibrant emotion, but when it was snatched from him he'd determined to banish feelings, clinging only to things that could be relied on. Work, money, philanthropy. He was known for his fine actions benefiting his neighbours, raising money for good causes and donating generously. Few could have guessed that this was actually another way of keeping people away. When they praised his noble generosity they did it at a distance, so there was little need to reach out to them.

Eventually he supposed a wife and child might have formed part of his schedule. To have them imposed on him out of the blue had been a shock, but one he had decided to accommodate. It was good to have an heir, and a woman who understood the kind of man he was had seemed ideal. Understanding her in return hadn't entered into his calculations. At least, not at first.

But being with her was like living with one of those legendary beings whose touch changed the world. There was no choice but to follow. Gradually he was getting into her mind, but her ability to catch him off guard was disconcerting. Sometimes even pleasant.

She turned and met his gaze.

'Nearly there,' she said, smiling.

They had reached Venice Mestre, the last railway station on the mainland before the Liberty Bridge, which stretched nearly two miles out across the lagoon to the Santa Lucia Station in Venice itself. As they crossed the water Charlotte gazed, riveted, at the view she had longed to see again ever since she had left the city.

When they got down from the train she almost ran out of the station to where it opened onto the Grand Canal, and stood, breathless with delight at the sight of the boats and the water.

'This was it,' she breathed. 'This was it! Oh, isn't it beautiful?'

Now Lucio found that she could wrong-foot him again. Charlotte the efficient researcher had vanished, replaced by Charlotte the eager child, ready to plunge into a delicious fantasy.

'This is where I have to rely on you,' he said. 'What do we do now?'

In a city where the roads were made of water there was no place for wheeled vehicles. To get to the hotel they must either walk through the multitude of little back alleys, or travel by motorboat.

'We could get onto a *vaporetto*,' she said, indicating a huge water bus that had just docked. 'But a taxi's better. Over there.'

She pointed to where a group of motorboats were moored, ready for passengers. In a moment they were aboard, gliding along the Grand Canal, between the palaces, beneath the great bridges, until they reached the hotel. The receptionist greeted Lucio with the awe due to a man who'd hired the most expensive suite.

The place lived up to all Charlotte's expectations. She had her own bedroom, next to Lucio's, with a view of the canal. Looking out she saw Lucio at his own window, just a few feet away. He nodded.

'I'm glad we came.'

'Hey!'

A cry from below made them look down to see Franco standing up in a boat, hailing them.

'You're here!' he yelled. 'That's wonderful! Tonight you will be my guests for dinner. I have important people for you to meet. I'll collect you in an hour.'

Charlotte sighed as she saw her dream of dinner alone with Lucio vanish. But there was no choice. Doubtless the 'important people' Franco mentioned would have something to do with vineyards. This trip was about business, and she mustn't let herself forget that.

While she was unpacking her cell phone rang. It was Ellie.

'Is he there with you?' she wanted to know.

'Not in the room, but we're in Venice together.'

'Has he mentioned any further commitment?'

'No, but—'

'Charlotte, you've done some pretty mad things in your time, but this is something that affects us all. We think you should come home. You can't cope alone.'

'I'm not alone. I'm living with nice people who are kind to me.'

'But you can't mean to stay there for good. You belong here, with your family.'

'Family? Belong? Ellie, do you know how hollow those words sound to me now?'

She heard her voice sounding sharper than she'd intended and checked herself.

'I can't talk now. I have to go out—'

'Can't it wait? This is important.'

'And my life here is important to me.'

'If we could just talk about—'

Suddenly Charlotte felt her temper rising.

'No. Not now. When I'm ready to talk I'll call you. Goodbye, I've got to go now.'

She hung up, wishing Ellie hadn't chosen this moment to make contact. The last thing she wanted to think about was her old life, not when her new one was so tempting.

For the evening she chose her attire with great care. Something suitable for a business meeting, yet which would attract Lucio. At last she chose a cocktail dress of black velvet. It would be the last time she could fit into it for a while, and she was going to make the best of what it could do for her. Lucio was determined to behave 'properly' as he saw it, making no sexual claims on her for fear of causing harm. But she knew there was no need to fear harm, and while she still had the chance she was going to get him to behave 'improperly,' no matter what it took.

She knew she was on the right track when she saw his face, eyes alight with admiration, a smile that he was trying to keep under control, and not entirely succeeding.

'Do I look like an efficient assistant?' she asked. 'All ready to do my duty?'

'Is that how you're trying to look?'

'Well, this is going to be a working meal, isn't it?'

'Is it?' He sounded baffled.

'Who do you think these "important people" are that Franco wants us to meet? They must be something to do with the vineyards. Obviously they're friends of his and he's helping them find a buyer. That's why he suggested you might want to buy a Veneto vineyard, and why he's bringing you together.' She met his gaze with well-contrived innocence. 'Surely that's obvious?'

'Yes—yes, of course,' he said hastily. He pulled himself together. 'I can see you're going to be an excellent assistant. I'm impressed.'

Franco was waiting downstairs, ready to lead them the short distance to the restaurant.

'There will be ten of us,' he said. 'My son has recently become engaged, and will be joining us with his fiancée, Ginevra. Also Ginevra's parents will be there. You'll have a lot in common with them, Lucio. They own several vineyards around here.'

Charlotte stole a sly glance at Lucio and found him looking right back at her. As their eyes met each knew the other was suppressing a smile.

'I think you must be psychic,' he whispered in her ear.

'You might find that a very useful gift in an assistant.'

'An assistant isn't exactly what I had in mind. Yes, Franco, we're just coming.'

Together they walked on, each wondering exactly what the other was thinking, and each thoroughly enjoying it.

In the restaurant they found the four people Franco had described, also his wife, who greeted them with a beaming smile. Charlotte found herself sitting next to Rico, owner of the vineyard, with Lucio on his other side, confirming her suspicions that this was a work meeting.

She did what was expected of her, speaking Venetian, making the occasional error and leading the laughter at her own expense. As the evening moved on the mood became increasingly friendly. Rico, in particular, was happy to talk to Charlotte. The subject was his vineyard but he seemed unable to take his eyes off her, as Lucio in particular noticed.

There was a brief, awkward moment when her cell phone rang and she answered it to find Alex.

'I've been talking to Ellie,' she said. 'She's worried about you, and we were both think—'

'I can't talk now,' she said hastily. 'I'll call back. Bye.'

She shut the phone down and switched it off, cursing herself for not doing so before. Everyone was looking at her with interest, as though speculating who her caller might be.

She turned her brightest smile on Rico. 'I really look forward to seeing your estate,' she said.

'And I hope you will come very soon, perhaps tomorrow,' he declared fervently.

'That would be excellent,' Lucio said before she could reply. 'May I suggest an early start?'

They all agreed on an early start.

'Then I think we won't stay out too late tonight,' Lucio

said. 'An early start tomorrow means an early night now. Are you ready, my dear?'

'Quite ready,' she said.

'Oh, surely, just a little longer—' Franco protested.

'I look forward to tomorrow,' Lucio interrupted him.

As they strolled back to the hotel she said, 'Were you wise to risk offending him? After all, if you're going to do business—'

'I'm the buyer. I make the terms. And if he rakes you with his eyes like that again I'll—I don't know…'

'Knock a few thousand off the price you offer?' she suggested.

'I had something else in mind,' he growled.

'Nonsense! Money's far more effective. He badly needs to sell that vineyard.'

'He told you that?'

'Not in so many words, but it came through. He's had a lot of "expenses" recently, by which I think he means gambling debts. His wife said the word *casino* in a certain tone that spoke volumes. They're planning a lavish wedding for their daughter and counting on the money from the vineyard. So you've got the advantage.'

'I'd still rather punch his lights out.'

'Only the money matters. Cling to that.'

'Yes, ma'am! You're really getting the hang of this.'

'Right. I think I missed my vocation. I should have gone into big business. Since I've been here I've seen a whole new future opening up, chief of a money-making enterprise, giving orders left, right and centre—' She stopped, glancing up at his face. 'All right, I'm only joking.'

'And I fall for it so easily, don't I?'

'You have your moments.'

'Fine, go ahead. Have fun. My time will come.'

My time will come. She'd said this to herself so often

that hearing it from Lucio caught her by surprise. Suddenly she glimpsed thoughts and feelings inside him that she had never suspected. Was he really holding his breath for what could happen between them? Just like herself?

'I suppose I shouldn't have dragged you away like that,' he mused.

'No, you shouldn't. I was still eating a lovely cake.'

'Then I'll buy you another one.'

'First you bought me a car, now a cake,' she teased. 'What next? You think money buys you out of any situation, don't you?'

'Of course it does. You just taught me that, and I'm learning. Let's go in there.'

He indicated a little café just up ahead, and soon they were sitting at a table, being served with cake and sparkling water.

'You can drink alcohol if you want,' Charlotte said. 'Are you afraid that I'll be tempted if I see a bottle of wine? No need. I'm quite grown up. Honestly.'

He made a face and ordered some wine. 'I was trying to be considerate.'

'Thank you for the thought but there's no need.' She gave a blissful sigh. 'Oh, I did enjoy today.'

'I'm glad to see you in a happier mood.'

'Whatever do you mean? I haven't been grumpy, have I?'

'Not with me, but whoever you were talking to on the phone earlier today. I heard you from the next room. You sounded ready to bite their head off.'

'Oh, that! Yes, I wasn't at my best.'

'This person did something to annoy you?'

She made a wry face. 'You could say she's been annoying me since the day we met, twenty-seven years ago.'

'Family?'

'Sister. Well, half-sister. I've always been fond of her but I can't help resenting her, too. She's so beautiful, so elegant. Men have always pursued her and she has to fend them off. Honestly, sometimes I could have murdered her for being so gorgeous.'

'Don't underestimate your own looks.'

'Oh, come on!' She turned to regard herself in the wall mirror, giving a disparaging flick to her long hair. 'I'm not beautiful.'

'You're striking,' he said, recalling how her hair had looked spread out over the pillow. 'I have no complaints.'

'That's because you're a gentleman with perfect manners.'

'Liar!' He grinned. 'Well, I had to say something. Was that her who called you during the meal?'

'No, that was my other sister Alex.'

'Is she gorgeous, too?'

'She's pretty, but she has something more important than looks. She has charm. And don't you dare tell me I'm charming.'

'I swear it never crossed my mind. I'm much too afraid of you.'

'Good. Keep it that way.'

'So how did Ellie offend you?'

'Nothing special,' she said quickly. 'She was just concerned about how I was managing.'

'But you sounded annoyed.'

'Yes, well—they have their own ideas but it doesn't concern them, and I don't want them interfering.'

'Is this what you hinted at the first night? You mentioned an older brother and sister who were twins and a younger sister. But you said there was a big family secret, and you were the last to know. It made you feel like an outsider.'

'Yes.' She sighed. 'My father is my mother's second husband. Before him she was married to a man called Clay Calhoun, but the marriage broke up, she left him and met Cedric Patterson soon after. They planned to marry, then she discovered that she was pregnant by Clay. But Cedric still wanted her. They married and she had twins, Ellie and Matt, which my father raised as his own.

'But recently we found out that my mother wrote to Clay telling him about her pregnancy. If he'd responded she might never have married my dad. But he didn't because he never got the letter. Sandra, the new woman in his life, kept it from him and then they got married.

'She died a couple of years ago, and Clay died last year. His daughter Jess was going through his things when she found a box belonging to Sandra, and the letter was in it. That's how she learned that her father had two other children.

'I think she had to search for them on the internet. At last she found Ellie and told her. So just a few months ago she and Matt discovered that they were Clay's children, and not our father's. She told Alex first, I guess because she's always been closer to her, but she delayed telling me.'

'Hell!' Lucio exclaimed.

'Yes, that's how I felt. You remember the hotel in Rome where we met?'

'The Hotel Geranno.'

'Right. I'd just been down to their internet café and found an email from Alex telling me all about it. From Alex, not from Ellie. She couldn't even be bothered to email me herself, not about that nor the fact that she seems to have found "Mr Right". I felt I'd come at the end of a long queue.'

Lucio took her hand and squeezed it. 'They shouldn't have done that to you.'

'I felt so unwanted, unnecessary, surplus to requirements, don't call us, we'll call you—or perhaps not.' She
sighed. 'Until then I'd always felt so pleased about having a family—a "real family" as I called it. With a family
you weren't alone. Only then I discovered I was wrong.'

'But Ellie and Matt are still your siblings even if you do
only share one parent now. And Alex is your full sister.'

'Yes.' She sighed.

'But that doesn't help much, does it? Is there no one in
the family who could help you? Your parents?'

'I can't talk to them about this. A while back my father's mind started to go. These days he's very confused
and looking after him is my mother's priority. Nothing else
really matters to her, so when I called her—'

'She wouldn't talk to you about it?' he asked, frowning.

'Not exactly. She confirmed it had happened, but she
said it was all a long time ago, and why should I worry
about it? Obviously it involves Matt and Ellie because
they're Clay's children, but I'm not, and she didn't seem
to think it concerned me.'

'But a family upheaval like that concerns everyone.'

'That's how I think, but my mother doesn't seem to
understand. I used to feel close to her—well, sort of. The
twins were special and Alex is gorgeous. I'm the middle
one and I don't stand out like the others. I've always felt
that, and sometimes I've acted a bit daft, trying to attract
attention, I suppose. Some of them call me the rebel of the
family, some call me the idiot—'

'Stop right there,' he interrupted her. 'You're going to
put yourself down and I won't have it.'

She smiled. 'Well, I can't help remembering what that
man at the party said about women who—'

'*That's enough!* He knows nothing.' Lucio laid his hand
over hers. 'At least, he doesn't know what I know.'

'Thank you,' she choked.

'You'll sort it with your family one day.'

'Will I? I don't know. They've made me feel so shut out. You know that saying, "Home is the place where they have to let you in". Now it's as though they wouldn't let me in.'

'That feeling won't last. You need time to get over it, but it'll happen. After all, you have another home now.'

She studied him curiously, aware of the mysterious sensation that had overcome her before in his company, as though their minds were in harmony. Even Matt, the sibling to whom she'd always felt close, hadn't given her such a feeling.

Had he ever? she mused. His failure to tell her what the others knew had left her feeling distant from him. But even in the past, had she felt as she did now with Lucio, that she'd found a friend to confide in? In time he might be more, but best friend was the least she would settle for.

'Is something funny?' he asked, watching her.

'I was just thinking what a wonderful brother you'd make, which I suppose is a bit funny in the circumstances.'

'Not really. You and I need to be friends, allies, comrades.'

'That's true. We always could read each other's minds, couldn't we?'

'From the first moment,' he agreed. 'Remember that argument we had at that café near the Trevi Fountain? I kept having a weird sensation that I knew exactly what you were going to say next. And you usually did.'

'That must have made me very boring,' she said lightly.

He shook his head. 'No, you're never boring. Don't put yourself down. You were in a bad way that night, and you needed someone. I'm glad it was me.'

He raised her hand and laid his cheek against the back.

'So that's why I got lucky,' he said softly. 'I've always wondered.'

'What do you mean?'

'Well, I could tell that you're not the kind of girl who goes in for one-night stands. Even if you are the rebel of the family, it was the first time your rebellion had ever taken that particular form, wasn't it?'

She nodded.

'But it happened with me. I'm not conceited enough to think you fell for my "looks and charm". You felt sad and lonely and I just happened to be there.'

'It was a bit more than that,' she said huskily. 'You made me feel wanted.'

'I'm glad. And you know what I'm even more glad about? That it was me and nobody else. You were so vulnerable. You could have been hurt.'

'But not by you,' she said, smiling.

'No, not by me. You made me feel wanted, too, and I guess it filled a need, just at the right time. It's almost enough to make you believe in fate. You needed me, I needed you, fate brought us together.'

'You didn't need me,' she said. 'Don't forget I saw you in the hotel, surrounded by admirers. Or do I mean worshipers? There wasn't a woman there who wouldn't gladly have changed places with me.'

'And did you see me inviting them?'

'You wouldn't have had to try very hard,' she said wryly.

'If you mean that I lived a self-indulgent life in those days, I don't deny it.' He pulled a self-mocking face. 'But that's over. I haven't slept with another woman since I found you.'

'You mean since the day I told you about the baby?'

'No, I mean since that night in Rome. Yes, I don't blame you for looking cynical, but it's true.'

'But why should you? I mean, you didn't expect ever to see me again.'

'I know. But somehow you were still with me. There were times I was tempted but you always stepped in and made me back off. I found myself living like a monk.'

He saw her gazing at him in astonishment. 'It's the truth, I swear it. Say you believe me. But only if you mean it.'

For a moment she was lost for words. This was the last thing she'd expected to hear.

He made a wry face, misunderstanding her silence.

'I guess I can't blame you. I probably wouldn't believe me either.'

'But I do,' she murmured. 'I do believe you.'

Incredibly, she really did.

'Do you really mean that?' he persisted. 'Truly?'

'Truly.'

'Thank you. Not many people would, given the way I've lived, dashing around, enjoying a superficial life. But once there was you, something changed.'

'But suppose you hadn't made me pregnant, and I hadn't come to find you?'

'That doesn't bear thinking about.'

She knew a surge of pleasure so intense that she struggled to hide it. She managed by retreating into cynicism.

'Oh, come on!' she jeered lightly. 'If it hadn't been me it would have been one of those willing ladies.'

'Most of those "willing ladies" have husbands or make a career out of being available. And they're all the kind of people that I can't get close to—not as we've grown close. I can talk to you like nobody else. I'm close to Fiorella but there are things I can't confide in her about. She's been hurt too much, I have to protect her.'

'And that's my big advantage?' she teased. 'I don't need protection.'

'Hey! You've missed no opportunity to tell me that you can look after yourself. I've lost count of the number of times you've said it as a way of slapping me down.'

'Some men need slapping down, preferably as often as possible.'

'Duly noted.' He gave a mock salute.

'But I guess in future I'll have to find another way.'

'I'm sure you'll think of something.' He grasped her hand and gave it a squeeze. 'But seriously, of course you need my protection. As though I'd let you of all people run any risks. But I do know that you're strong and independent. If it came to a battle between us I'd back you against me.'

'So would I. Let's agree on that.'

'I guess we should be going,' he said. 'It's late and you should be in bed.'

'I'm not a child to be sent to bed.'

'I'm making sure you're all right. Isn't that what I'm supposed to do?'

'Just be careful not to push your luck.'

'Let's go.'

Together they strolled out. The street was narrow, and above it was a fine strip of sky, glittering with stars. Charlotte gazed up entranced.

'It's as though they're pointing the way home,' she said. 'Just a few yards and then— Whoops!'

'Careful!' he said, grasping her as she stumbled, nearly losing her balance. 'If you don't look where you're going I guess you do need someone to keep an eye on you, after all.'

'Well, perhaps you're right.'

His arm was now firmly around her shoulders, and it was natural to lean her head back against it.

'You're still not looking at the road,' he reproved her.

'With you to guide me I don't need to. I leave everything in your hands.'

'Hm! Why does that submissive act fill me with suspicion?'

'I can't think.'

She slipped her arm about his waist and, like this, laughing and holding on to each other, they drifted on their way.

CHAPTER NINE

EARLY next morning a motorboat collected them from the hotel and drove them to Piazzale Roma, the car park on the edge of town, beyond which no wheeled vehicle was allowed. Here they all loaded into Franco's palatial car to be driven over the Liberty Bridge onto the mainland, and from there another fifty miles to the vineyard.

There Rico met them and gave them a conducted tour through his magnificent fields. What little Charlotte had seen of vineyards was enough to tell her that this was a splendid place, and the greatest favour she could do for Lucio was stay in the shadows.

She could tell that he was impressed by what he saw and heard, although his outward response was muted, as befitted a man with money at stake. Occasionally Rico would address her in Venetian, but only as a courtesy. Serious business was conducted in Italian, and increasingly she sensed that all was going well.

She particularly liked the house; not a palace like the ones she saw in Tuscany, but sprawling with an air of warmth and friendliness. Children could live happily here, she thought, wandering through the rooms.

At last there were handshakes and smiles all round. It was settled, and everyone was pleased.

'Tonight we meet again in Venice, to celebrate,' Rico declared. 'You will all be my guests.'

On the journey back Lucio and Franco continued an animated discussion on the necessary arrangements. Charlotte stayed quiet, but made notes.

Back in the hotel she adjusted her attire a little more than last night, choosing a neckline just an inch lower to take advantage of her generous bosom. Lucio made no comment, but the way he nodded told her something she wanted to know. She was determined to believe that.

The evening was a triumph. There were the same guests as the night before, and everyone involved in the deal felt they had gained.

'I can't thank you enough,' Lucio murmured as he clinked glasses with Charlotte.

'For what? I've kept my mouth firmly shut all day.'

'I could say that a woman who knows when to do that is worth her weight in gold, but you'd probably accuse me of being a sexist beast, so I won't. It was clever of you not to get involved in the negotiations—'

'Since they would have been over my head.'

'Will you stop trying to trap me, you little fiend? And stop laughing.'

'No, why should I?'

'I meant that you made the negotiations happen. Without you I probably wouldn't be here, and I'd have lost a lot.'

'So if it turns into a disaster it'll be all my fault?'

'Of course. What else?'

She began to laugh and he joined in. Glancing at them Franco thought that he had never seen a couple who belonged together so completely. He turned away to make a discreet call on his cell phone.

The rest of the evening was spent discussing the festival next day. At last Franco rose to his feet.

'We shall all meet again tomorrow,' he said, 'to take part in the festival. But now I have something else to say. Work is important, but this is also an evening for couples. My son and his future wife are a couple, my friends Charlotte and Lucio are a couple. My wife and I recently celebrated our wedding anniversary, and you—' he indicated Ginevra's parents '—will celebrate yours next month. So tonight I've arranged something special. Ah, I think it's here now.'

He looked up at a man, dressed as a gondolier, signalling him from the doorway.

'They are waiting for us,' he said. 'Shall we go?'

One of the doors of the restaurant opened on to a little side canal. There they found five gondolas ready to receive them.

'A romantic journey for each of us,' Franco said. 'Goodnight until tomorrow.'

Hardly believing that this was happening, Charlotte took the hand that the gondolier held out to her, and climbed in carefully. When all the boats were full the procession glided away.

Looking around Charlotte saw the other three couples snuggled happily in each other's arms. Franco was clearly a master of show business—a gondola ride in Venice, the very essence of romance.

Cheers and jeers rose from the other three boats when the occupants saw that Lucio and Charlotte were the only couple not embracing.

'Go on, spoilsport!'

'Why don't you kiss her?'

From Rico came words in Venetian which made Charlotte laugh.

'What did he say?' Lucio demanded.

'Something rather rude about you.'

'Tell me.'

'No way.'

'I see. Then I'll just have to put him right.'

He tightened his arm, laying his mouth against hers in a theatrical manner that made their companions cheer even more raucously.

Charlotte restrained her impulse to pull him closer, knowing that this was just more showmanship. If only they could be alone. Then she could do everything she wanted to turn showmanship into reality.

It was the gondolier who came to her rescue, calling in Venetian, *'Dove voi andare?'*

'What was that?' Lucio murmured.

'He asked where we want to go.'

'Canale Grande?' the boatman called. *'Ponte di Rialto?'*

'Do you want to see the Grand Canal and the Rialto Bridge?' she translated.

Lucio shook his head. 'I'd prefer something a little quieter, more private.'

'We'll keep to the little back canals,' she called.

'Sì, signorina.'

Now it was like being in another universe, created from narrow alleys, gleaming water and darkness. The boatman made no intrusive comments and they could imagine they were alone in the whole world.

'Your night of triumph,' he murmured.

'Hardly,' she said, thinking of how much she still had to achieve. 'It doesn't feel like triumph. Not yet.'

His eyes met hers, seeking her true meaning.

'What would make it a triumph?' he asked softly.

'You,' she said, reaching for him. 'Only you.'

This was her kiss. She was the prime mover, and knew that her triumph was beginning. She slipped her arms above his head, determined that this time he would not escape, but he had no thought of escape. She could tell that with every fibre of her being.

She had dreamed of this ever since he'd fled from her at Enrico's home, making love to her and then setting a cruel distance between them. Now everything she longed for was being given back to her. Every movement of his lips was a promise, and she would reclaim that promise with interest. She assured herself that while her sense of triumph soared.

A slight bump announced that the gondola had arrived at the hotel. Dazed, they wandered into the hotel and up to their suite. But there he paused, and a little fear crept over her. To conquer it she drew him close again. He put his arms about her, gentle, almost tentative.

'Charlotte, I—'

'It's all right,' she whispered against his mouth. 'Everything's all right.'

'Is it? Can you be sure? I know myself. I can't be near you without wanting to do something selfish. Just touching you brings me to the edge of control.'

'Good. That's where I want you—until you leap over the edge completely.'

'Or until you lure me over.' He tightened his arms, speaking in a tense voice. 'I've tried to be strong but you're not going to let me, are you?'

'Not for a moment.'

'Charlotte, don't—don't— *Charlotte!*'

And then there was only the feeling of victory as he drew her into his bedroom, pulling at her clothes. She would have helped him but he moved too fast for her, so she ripped his off instead.

No doubts, no hesitation, no false modesty. Just the plain fact that her will was stronger than his.

'Charlotte...'

'Yes, yes...'

His eyes, looking down on her, were mysteriously fierce and tender at the same time. 'You're a wicked woman,' he whispered.

'You'd better get used to it.'

'In a thousand years I'll never get used to you.'

He laid his head down against her breast and she wrapped him lovingly in her arms. There was still a way to go yet, but they would get there. In time she would win everything she wanted. In time he would be all hers.

After a while she felt him move, raise his head and grow still again, looking down on her.

'Are you all right?' he whispered.

'Of course I am.'

'Are you sure?' Now he was backing away, leaving the bed, until she reached out and stopped him.

'Oh, Lucio, please—don't do this again.'

'What do you mean?'

'I mean that last time we made love you ran from me as fast as you could, as though it had been a traumatic experience for you. Am I really so terrible?'

'The terrible one is me, selfishly taking what I want when you—'

'Then you're not the only selfish one, because *I* want it, too.'

He gave a sigh that was part a groan, and sat on the edge of the bed, running his hands through his hair.

'You probably think I'm mad, being so paranoid. Perhaps I am.'

'Lucio, I do understand, honestly I do. But no harm will come to me because of what we've done. Or to our child.'

'But things happen so easily. Just when you think everything's going well it's all snatched away from you. And you start to feel it might be better to have nothing, than to have something precious and lose it.'

'Why don't you tell me everything?' she asked gently. 'I have the feeling that there's so much you're keeping from me. Can't you trust me?'

'I do trust you, but it can be so hard to— Do you remember the night we met, the life I was living then?'

'Yes, you seemed on top of the world. Everyone wanted your attention, everyone was out to attract you.'

'Huh!' He gave a bleak laugh. 'That may be how it looked but it was an empty life. I felt that all the time— bleak, meaningless—but I couldn't live any other way. There was nothing else for me in those days. I had no anchor, and I didn't want one.'

'Didn't want one? As bad as that?' she asked softly.

He nodded.

'Tell me how it happened.'

'It started so long ago that I can barely remember it— the place, the people, everything I once called home.'

'Before you came to Tuscany?'

He nodded.

Now she knew she must tread carefully. Seeking him online she had several times found him described as a man of mystery.

'He appeared from nowhere,' one article had said. 'Nobody seems to know where he came from, or, if they know, something—or someone—has persuaded them to keep silent.'

She sat in silence, refusing to ask any questions. What happened now must be his choice. At last he began to speak.

'Sometimes I feel so far away from that world that it's almost as though it never existed. But when I'm honest with myself I know that it shaped me, created the dark side of me.'

'The dark side?'

'The part of my nature that's capable of revenge, ruthlessness—deliberate cruelty.'

She was about to protest but something held her silent. She'd never seen cruelty in Lucio, but instinct told her it was there. Driven too far he would be capable of the most terrible acts, the most coldly savage indifference.

Somewhere a warning voice whispered, *Leave him. Flee quickly while there's time. He's only using you because he wants the child and one day he'll break your heart. You know that. Don't you?*

Yes, she thought. *I know that. But I won't ever leave him. Because I can't.*

Because I'll never give up hope.

Because I love him.

The words seemed to leap out at her. She hadn't meant to admit the truth, even to herself. But it had crept up on her without warning and now there was no escape.

He was watching her, seemingly troubled by her silence.

'Now you know the worst of me,' he said. 'Don't tell me you never suspected.'

She shook her head. 'You're wrong. I won't know the worst until I discover it for myself. And perhaps I never will. Stop trying to blacken yourself. Just tell me about this "other world". You had to escape it, but you've never really left it behind, have you?'

'No, I guess that's true.'

'The night we met you told me you came from Sicily. Did you have a large family?'

'No, just three of us, my parents and me. My father was a lawyer, but a very particular kind of lawyer, as I came to realise. His clients were rich and powerful. At first all I

saw was that he was powerful, too. I admired him, wanted
to be like him. I'd have done anything for his good opinion, or even just his attention.'

'He ignored you?'

'Not exactly. In his way he was a good father, did everything correctly. But I never felt that I was important
to him. He only really loved one person in the world, and
that was my mother. She was the same. Only he existed.
They had the sort of marriage that most people would say
was charming and idyllic.'

'Not if you were the child looking in from the outside,'
she said.

For a moment he didn't react. Then, very slowly, he
smiled and nodded.

'Yes,' he said. 'Of course you understand. I suppose I
knew you would.'

'If your parents really love each other, you're never
going to come first with either of them.'

'That's true, although to be fair to them they were kind
and affectionate, in their way. As long as things went well.
It was just when it came to a crisis—' He stopped.

'And one day the crisis came?' she asked softly.

He nodded. 'My father wanted me to become a lawyer.
When I'd finished my training he reckoned I could become
his partner. He gave me a job fetching and carrying in his
office, so that I could "get the feel". That's when I started
to realise what his clients were like, what he was like. He
made his living protecting men who used violence and cruelty to get their way. He didn't care what they were like or
what they'd done, as long as they paid him well.

'What really hurt was that he didn't understand why I
minded. He called me a weakling for "making a fuss about
nothing". No son of his would be such a fool. I knew I had
to leave but I stayed for a while, hoping to persuade my

mother to come with me. I couldn't believe she knew the truth about him, and I was sure when she learned it she'd want to flee him, as well.

'But when I told her, all she said was, "I knew you'd find out one day. I told him he should explain carefully". She kept saying my father was a good man who did what he had to for the sake of his family. But I couldn't believe it. He didn't do it for us. He did it because he wanted money at any cost, and he got a kick out of associating with crooks, as long as they were successful crooks. I begged her to come with me, but she wouldn't. She gave me some money and stood at the window as I slipped away one night.

'That was the last time I ever saw her. Three years later they were both dead. Someone killed my father and she died trying to save him. She didn't have to die, but she preferred that to living without him. Then I remembered something she'd said just before we parted, when she was trying to explain why she chose him above everything else, good and bad.'

He fell silent, and there was such pain in his face that Charlotte reached out and touched his cheek.

'Don't talk about it if you can't bear to,' she said.

'No, I want to tell you. I know I can rely on you to—to know...to feel.'

'Yes,' she whispered.

'She said that one day I'd know what it was to love someone beyond reason.'

'That's what we all hope for,' Charlotte murmured.

'Yes. She said I should be glad, for without it life would be empty. And she was right.'

'You found that out yourself?'

He squeezed her hand. From somewhere she found the resolve to say, 'You found it with Maria?'

He nodded.

'Did you fall in love with her at once?'

'No, we used to squabble a lot, but not seriously. Her parents took me in and I just seemed to fit in at once. I loved the life. I belonged. As Maria and I grew up we became closer until at the end it was just what my mother had predicted. Love beyond reason. I began to understand why she'd chosen to die rather than live without my father.'

'That must have been…earth-shattering,' she said softly. 'And beautiful.'

'Yes,' he said in a husky voice. 'Yes.'

From outside came a roar of laughter. She rose quickly and went to close the window, determined to protect Lucio. His memories were tormenting him and the last thing he needed was disturbance from outside. At all costs she would prevent that.

Before returning to him she took a moment to sort out her thoughts, which were confused. She wanted his love, and it might seem unwise to talk with him about Maria, the woman he'd loved. Yet she needed to understand how deep that love had gone, for only then could she guess her own chance of winning his heart.

She turned back to him, then paused at what she saw.

Lucio was sitting with his head sunk so low it almost reached his knees. His whole being radiated pain and despair, and she felt as though her heart would break for him.

He looked up. The sight of her brought a tense smile to his face, and he stretched out his hand in a way that was almost a plea.

'I'm here,' she said, hurrying over and clasping his hand. 'I'll always be here.'

'Will you? *Will you?*'

'Of course. I promise.'

He lifted his head and she gasped at the tragedy and desolation in his eyes.

'It's easy to promise.' He groaned. 'But nobody is always there.'

'Did she promise?' Charlotte asked softly.

'Many times. She vowed she'd never leave me—never in life—and she didn't leave me in life. She left me in death. She was so young. Her death was the one thing we never thought of.'

'How did it happen?'

'She went to Florence one afternoon, to do some shopping. I saw her driving home and waved. The next minute the car swerved, hit a rock by the roadside and overturned. I managed to get her to hospital. She was terribly hurt, there seemed to be no hope, but still I—'

He choked into silence. His eyes were closed again, as though he'd chosen to retreat back into a private world. But his fingers clutched Charlotte's hand convulsively. She laid her other hand over his, sending him comfort in the only way that could reach him.

'She lived for two days,' Lucio said softly. 'Mostly she was unconscious. Sometimes she opened her eyes and seemed to look at me, but even then I'm not sure if she could see me. I begged her not to leave me, to forgive me—'

'Forgive you? Surely she had nothing to forgive?'

'I may have caused her accident, waving when I did. Perhaps I distracted her, perhaps she waved back and took her attention off the road—'

'Lucio, don't—'

'But for me she might not have died.'

'That's just your imagination—how could you be sure?'

'I can't,' he said with soft violence. 'That's what's so terrible. I'll never know but I'll believe it all my days. I did it. *I killed her.* How can I ever have peace?'

'By asking yourself what she would have wanted,'

Charlotte said. 'Maria loved you. Surely you know that, deep in your heart?'

'Yes, I—'

'If you let this idea wreck your life you're being unfair to her, to her memory. Did she manage to say anything to you before she died?'

'Yes, she said she loved me.'

'Of course she did. Her last message to you was love, so that you would always remember it. She was trying to give you peace. Don't refuse her the last thing she wanted.'

He didn't reply, and she wondered if he'd even heard her. But then he leaned towards her, resting his head on her shoulder so that his face was hidden. His clasp on her tightened, sending her a silent message, and she clasped him back.

Would she one day regret what she was doing? Instead of banishing Maria's ghost she was restoring her to him. But nothing mattered but to ease Lucio's suffering and perhaps even give him some happiness. If it meant that she herself was the loser, she would find a way to live with that.

'I'm sorry,' he said. 'I shouldn't really be talking to you about this.'

'Why not? Remember what we said? Friends, allies, comrades? I'm the best friend you have, and you can tell me anything, any time.'

'Thank you,' he said softly. 'You don't know what a comfort that is—what it's like never to be able to talk to anyone.'

'What about Fiorella?'

'I never could. Maria's death caused her such pain— how could I make it worse? And then her husband died only a year later. She's suffered such unbearable pain.'

'So you protected her,' Charlotte said.

He protected everyone, and they had all left him alone,

she thought, her heart aching for him. But he wasn't alone now, and she must let him know that.

'You're exhausted,' she said. 'Lie down and go to sleep.'

Gently she pulled him down onto the bed, drawing him across her so that his head rested on her chest. A mirror in the corner gave her a slight glimpse of his face, enough to show that his eyes were closed. Everything about him radiated contentment.

'That's it,' she whispered. 'Now you can do whatever you like. We can talk if you like, because there's nothing you can't tell me, and I promise never to do anything to make you regret it. Or you can sleep in my arms. And don't worry about anything, because your friend is here.'

He stirred, and she felt the warmth of his breath against her skin. She stroked his face, laying her lips against his hair, whispering, 'She's here, and she'll always be here, as long as you need her.'

CHAPTER TEN

SHE awoke to the sound of music from the canal below. It was the day of the glorious water parade, and the wedding to the sea, and all Venice was alive with pleasure and expectation.

'It's going to be wonderful,' she murmured, reaching for him.

He wasn't there.

In an instant she was back in the nightmare, alone, rejected, unwanted, first by her family, then by Lucio.

'No,' she groaned. 'No, *no, oh, please, no!*'

At once the door was flung open and Lucio hurried in.

'Charlotte, whatever's the matter?'

'Nothing,' she choked, 'nothing—I—'

He sat on the bed, placing his hands on her shoulders.

'Then why are you crying? Why were you calling out? What's upset you?'

'Just a nightmare,' she floundered frantically. 'I can't even remember....'

You vanished and all my demons began shrieking again.

But she couldn't tell him that.

'No time for nightmares,' he said merrily. 'Franco has just called to say he expects us on his boat at nine o'clock. So I've ordered breakfast up here and then we must be off.'

He kissed her cheek and retreated to the bathroom.

Left alone, she took some deep breaths, trying to focus her mind on the day ahead, but it was hard when dazzling memories still lived inside her. Last night they had achieved perfect physical union, and it had been beautiful. But just as beautiful had been the emotional and mental union that followed. He had called her his friend, and she had assured him that was what she would be.

But a friend could be a lover, too, and in time he would understand that. This was her promise to herself.

By nine o'clock a multitude of boats had gathered in the water next to St Mark's Square, and within fifteen minutes they had moved off in a colourful parade across the lagoon to the Lido island. Rowers in medieval costume hauled on the oars as they crossed the glittering water.

Franco had hired a magnificent vessel, big enough for thirty people; he leaned over the side enjoying the procession as it glided over the lagoon to the Lido island. There they were joined by an even more magnificent boat, known as the *Serenissima*.

Once the Doge of Venice had performed the ceremony of tossing a golden ring into the water, intoning in Latin, *'Desponsamus te, Mare, in signum veri perpetique dominii.'*

'I marry you, O sea, as a sign of permanent dominium.'

Now the ceremony was performed by the mayor. Cheers went up as he made the triumphant declaration.

A few feet away Charlotte could see Franco's son and his fiancée, gazing into each other's eyes.

'Presto,' he said joyously. *'Presto mi sposera.'*

'They were going to marry in autumn,' Franco confided. 'But now he's pressing her to marry him quickly. That's the effect this ceremony can have. It makes people long for their own marriage.'

He turned away, calling to his other guests.

'Perhaps he's got a point,' Lucio observed.

'How do you mean?'

'Maybe it's time we were talking about marriage. We agreed that when you'd been here for a while you'd make a decision about staying. I can't believe you want to go away. You've fitted in from the beginning. Everyone likes you and they're all eagerly waiting for the announcement of our forthcoming marriage. Perhaps we should give it to them.'

So that was his idea of a proposal, she thought. After the night they'd shared she'd expected something that at least acknowledged their shared passion. Instead there was reasoned logic and efficiency.

'Only if we actually decide to marry,' she said. 'I don't remember us doing that.'

'Sorry. Where are my manners? Charlotte, I want to marry you. I think we can have a good life together, not just because of our baby, but because you really belong here. You've felt that, too, haven't you?'

'It's true that I like it here. As you say, I've been made welcome and people are kind. But there's more to marriage than that.'

'Of course there is. A man and a woman have to go well together, and we do.'

'Yes, we're good friends,' she said wryly.

'That's important. The strongest couples can be the ones who started out knowing they could rely on each other. You know how deeply I trust you. We spoke of it last night. Surely you remember that?'

'Yes,' she murmured. 'I remember last night.'

'So do I, and there were things about it that mean the world to me. There's such freedom in being able to talk to you. You know things about me that nobody else knows, or ever will, and I'm so glad. And I hope you have the same feeling that you can rely on me.

'Do you think I won't work to make you happy? I promise that I will. Anything you want, if it's humanly possible I'll see that you get it.'

Anything I want, she thought wryly. *Your heart? Your love? But you're telling me they wouldn't be humanly possible.*

How had this happened? Only a little time ago she'd vowed to be satisfied with their close friendship and not ask for more until later. Simple common sense.

Common sense hurt more than she'd suspected, but now she realised sadly that it was all she had. And it wasn't enough.

'Don't rush me, Lucio,' she said. 'I know we've talked about where this road is leading, but I'm not sure yet.'

He looked astounded, and she understood. How could she refuse him after last night? She didn't comprehend it herself. She only knew that she wouldn't be rushed into handing over her life to a man whose feelings fell short of hers.

'We'll talk about it later,' she said.

'All right. When we get home tonight.'

'No, I meant in a few weeks.'

His face grew tense. 'Last night you promised to always to be there for me.'

She wished he hadn't said that. The memory was so painful that she winced. He saw it and misunderstood.

'I see,' he said with a touch of bitterness. 'You regret it already.'

'No, I don't, but we were talking of friendship. As a friend, and the mother of your child, I'll never entirely leave you but I still need some independence. Just how much I need I'm not sure.'

'Come along!' That was Franco, coming towards them

to sweep them back up into the festivities. 'We still have a wonderful day before us.'

'I'm not sure how long we can stay,' Charlotte faltered.

'But you must see the races,' Franco protested.

'And after that we must return,' Lucio said. 'We're grateful for your hospitality, but I have urgent things to attend to at home. I'll arrange matters through my lawyer, and come back soon to sign papers.'

For the rest of the day they smiled and said what was appropriate before travelling back across the lagoon. All around them Venice was enjoying colourful celebrations, but they could take no part. Hurrying back to the hotel they packed and prepared to leave. A motorboat was hired to take them to Piazzale Roma, and there they collected the car and drove across the bridge to the mainland.

As they drove back to Tuscany in the twilight Charlotte gazed out of the window and wondered at herself. She'd been offered so much that she longed for, yet without warning her old rebelliousness had come alive, saying that it wasn't good enough. Perhaps she had devastated the rest of her life. Maybe the day would dawn when she cursed herself for being unrealistic.

But it made no difference. The streak of sheer cussedness that had always intervened at inappropriate moments had cropped up now.

And, most incredible of all, she had no regrets.

For the next few weeks they saw little of each other. Lucio spent much time at distant vineyards and for once it was a relief to Charlotte that he wasn't there.

When he came home he behaved courteously, constantly asking after her health, patting her growing bulge protectively and accompanying her on a check-up visit to the doctor. Wryly she recalled a friend back home whose husband distanced himself from the details of her pregnancy. When she protested at his lack of emotional support he was astounded. He gave her plenty of money, didn't he? The rest was 'women's stuff'.

She would really envy me, Charlotte thought wryly. *Lucio is everything her husband isn't: kind, attentive, interested, concerned.*

And yet—and yet…

She tried to distract herself by going online to talk to her family, and found Matt putting a call through to her. It was good to see his face on the screen. In the past she had often found more comfort in his presence than with her sisters. They were alike in many ways, sharing jokes, standing back and taking the same ironic view of life. She could tell him what had happened, and count on him to be supportive.

But this time his support took a more detached stance than she had expected.

'Ellie told me she was worried that this guy hasn't proposed to you. Now you're telling me that he did propose and you turned him down. Are you nuts?'

'I didn't turn him down. I just said we could talk about it later.'

'Listen, there are ways and ways of rejecting someone, and saying you'll talk later is one of the best known. You're nuts about him, you admit that, yet you're taking the risk of losing him altogether. Why? Because he didn't say all the right words and you want to kick him in the teeth.'

'That wasn't it. Truly, Matt, I wasn't just being awkward—'

'Oh, I reckon you were. As long as I've known you, you've been famous for awkwardness. You could get a medal for it. How many times have I rescued you from your own foolishness?'

'About as often as I've rescued you.'

'OK. Check. But now it's *me* riding to *your* rescue. I don't want to see you break your heart because you're too stubborn to admit you're an idiot.'

'All right, all *right*! I admit it. But what can I do?'

'You'll have to work that out for yourself, but whatever it is, act fast. Time isn't on your side.'

'I know that,' she said, patting her stomach.

'I don't just mean the baby, although it's true your time for playing the seductress is running out.'

'Thanks!'

'I'm talking practicalities. You're not Italian, so if you want to marry in Italy you'll need to produce a mountain of paperwork, starting with your birth certificate.'

'Oh, heavens! I never thought of that.'

'Time to be practical, decide if you really want to marry him and, if so, get things organised.'

'Yes, I guess you're right.'

'Let me know what happens.'

However blunt his words she knew Matt had spoken out of concern for her. *He's right,* she thought. *If I lose Lucio it's all my own fault. I played it so stupidly but I couldn't help it. I gambled on all or nothing and it looks like I'm going to get nothing. It's going to take a miracle to bring us together, and miracles don't seem to happen any more.*

If only Lucio was here now and she could say everything she was feeling. But another two weeks passed while he stayed away. She used the time investigating the other part of Matt's warning, and found it to be alarmingly accurate.

On the day Lucio was expected home he was late. She stood at her window, desperately looking for him, and as soon as she saw him she realised that something was up.

He was driving faster than usual, and when he parked the car he leapt out, looked up at the window and ran inside.

'All right,' he said, coming into her room. 'Enough's enough. I've been doing a lot of thinking on the way home, and you've played too many games with me. I want an answer.'

'I'm not playing games—'

'Then give me an answer and make it yes.' He grasped her arm. 'Charlotte, I mean it. You've driven me to distraction and I can't take any more. I know I made a mess of the proposal. I'm not the kind of man who can go down on one knee, but I asked you because I really want you.'

'Lucio, I—*aargh!*' She broke off in a gasp.

'What is it?' he cried. 'Charlotte what happened? Did I hurt you? I didn't mean to—I barely touched you.'

'No, you didn't hurt me,' she said in a dazed voice. *'Aaah!'* She gasped again.

'What happened?' he demanded, in agony.

'The baby—it's moving. It kicked me. There! It's done it again.'

'You mean—?'

She looked down, running her fingers over her slight bulge. 'Just there. You can feel the movement from the outside.'

Tentatively, almost fearfully, he touched the bulge with his fingertips.

'Can you feel it?' she asked.

'No—yes—I think. But is it all right? Should that be happening?'

'Of course. I've felt movement before but not as much as this. It's good. It means our child is strong and healthy. It'll have a good start in the world.'

With a sigh that was almost a groan he knelt so that he could lay his head against her. He kept it there, not moving for a few moments. Then he raised his face far enough for her to see his closed eyes and gentle, ecstatic smile.

'Yes,' he whispered ecstatically. 'I can feel it—*yes*.'

He opened his eyes to see her looking down at him.

'Yes,' he repeated. 'It's wonderful.'

'Yes,' she agreed, taking his face between her hands.

'Charlotte—please—'

'Yes,' she repeated.

'You don't understand what I'm saying.…'

'But I do.' She held his gaze for a moment. 'And my answer is yes.'

He rose, looking at her intently. 'You mean it?'

'Yes.'

'Marriage?'

'Yes.'

He put his arms around her, drawing her a little closer, but giving her extra room for the bulge.

'We're going to have a child,' he said in a dazed voice. 'I already knew that but…suddenly it's more real.'

That was also how she felt. She'd longed for a miracle, and it had been given to her. Now they had shared this moment no power on earth could have made her refuse him. Filled with contentment she rested her head on his shoulder, then tensed as there was another kick.

'Ah!' she gasped.

'Does it hurt?' he asked, full of tender anxiety for her.

'No, it just means our offspring is establishing a personality already. It's probably a boy. With a kick like that he's going to be a soccer player.'

'Or a politician,' Lucio said with a wry smile. 'He already knows how to get the better of people. Remember I said I couldn't go down on one knee?'

'And he made you do just that,' she said. 'Your first trial of strength and he won.'

He hugged her. 'I'm really looking forward to meeting this lad. Come on, let's tell everyone.'

He led her out of the bedroom and down the stairs, holding her gently but firmly.

'Be careful,' he said.

'Lucio I've used these stairs a hundred times without an accident.'

'I know but…it's different now.'

'Yes, it is,' she said, taking his hand and smiling happily.

Downstairs they told Fiorella, who went into ecstasies.

'We must arrange everything as soon as possible,' she said. 'Charlotte, my dear, have you told your family that you're getting married?'

'No, we wanted to tell you first. I'll email them, and later we'll go online and talk.'

'And then you can introduce us. We will all meet as one big happy family.'

'We can't do it all at once. My family live a long way apart, Ellie in Texas and my parents in New York, Matt in Boston and Alex in Australia. I could tell Matt and Ellie now. We're only five hours ahead of them.'

She fetched her laptop, set it up and connected to the program that provided the video link. A glance at her list of contacts showed that neither Matt nor Ellie was online.

'No problem,' she said. 'I'll email them, tell them the news and say let's talk face to face.'

'But if they live miles apart how can you get them together?' Fiorella asked.

'They won't really be together but I can put them on the screen at the same time,' Charlotte said. 'There, the emails are on their way. If they receive them soon they'll come online without delay.'

After a few moments an email arrived announcing that Alex was away today but would be back by evening.

'Her evening,' Charlotte said. 'We'll all be asleep by then. But I'll find a way to contact her soon. Ah, I think that's Matt.'

Sure enough a flashing light was announcing Matt's arrival on screen.

'Did you really write what I thought you wrote?' he demanded. 'You're getting married?'

'Yes, and this is Lucio, my fiancé,' Charlotte said, speaking quickly in case Matt should say something that would reveal his earlier advice.

But he was tact itself, congratulating them both. Everything went well. Courtesies were exchanged. Lucio introduced his mother. Then a bleep announced that Ellie had made contact and she, too, arrived on screen, smiling and pleasant.

When all the introductions had been made again Ellie said, 'So now you've got to come to Larkville, Charlotte, and of course Lucio will come with you.'

'They're celebrating Clay Calhoun's life in October,' Charlotte explained to Lucio.

'Matt and I are invited because he was our father,' Ellie said, 'but they want you and Alex there so we can all be together.'

'But I told you, I'll be giving birth about then,' Charlotte said. 'I'd love to come, but it won't be possible. Such a shame.'

'You might give birth early,' Ellie protested. 'Promise you'll come if you can.'

'If I can,' Charlotte agreed. She could sense that this conversation troubled Lucio and was eager to bring it to a close.

More smiles, congratulations, good wishes, and the links were closed down.

'It's nice that they want us to go over there,' Charlotte said. 'But I don't think it will be very practical.' She looked down at the bulge.

'It's not just that,' Lucio said. 'If you do go, it'll have to be without me. October is when we harvest the grapes. I couldn't possibly leave here.'

'Of course not,' she said. 'And I couldn't leave either, even if I'd already given birth. It would be too soon. Don't worry, it's not going to arise.'

His brow cleared. 'I hope not. I'd hate to refuse you the first thing you've asked me.'

'So now we have a lot of talking to do,' Fiorella declared. 'You must set the date, send out the invitations. How soon can we make it happen? How about the week after next.'

'I'm afraid not,' Lucio said. 'Because Charlotte wasn't born here we have to get a lot of paperwork—her birth certificate, a sworn declaration that she's free to marry which must be translated, annotated and taken round a load of offices. It can take a few weeks.'

Charlotte stared. This was what she'd been preparing to tell him, but he already knew.

'Oh, what a pity,' Fiorella mourned. 'Well, you'd better get to work on all those papers, and we'll have the wedding as soon as possible.'

She bustled away, full of plans.

'I know what you're thinking.' Lucio sighed. 'How do I know all this? I must have been checking up, which means I took it for granted that you'd say yes. Or I was planning to pressure you, which makes me all sorts of an undesirable character. It's not like that, Charlotte, truly. I just wanted to be ready for anything. Don't be angry with me.'

'Have you finished? Then listen to what I have to say.
I know about all these formalities and how long they can
take, and I've been doing something about it. Matt's already sent me the birth certificate and a sworn statement
that I'd never been married.'

'You've been doing all that?' Lucio breathed.

'Yes. There's still some work left to do....'

'But you did this? So you meant to marry me?'

'I suppose I did. I've got as much ready as I can, but
there's still some—'

She broke off as he seized her in his arms, and after
that there were no more words.

Two days later he drove her into Florence.

'There's something I want to show you,' he said, leading her along the street until they reached a jewellery shop
and pointing to a double-stranded pearl necklace in the
window. 'What do you think of that?'

'It's really beautiful.'

'Would it make a beautiful wedding present?'

'Oh, yes.'

'Let's go in.'

In the shop she tried on the necklace and loved the
way it looked on her. It was a wedding gift to make any
bride happy.

'But what am I going to give you?' she asked as they
left the shop.

He glanced down at her waist.

'You're already giving me the best gift in the world,'
he said. 'I don't need anything else.'

She knew a burst of happiness. Everything was going
to be all right, after all.

CHAPTER ELEVEN

FOR the next two weeks they were seldom out of each other's company, travelling from office to office, presenting documents, signing paperwork.

'So now everything's in order,' she said as they sat in a café, having just left the American consulate in Florence. 'Everything signed, every permission granted. The perfect business deal.'

'I wish I could say you were wrong—' he grinned '—but I've had commercial ventures that were less complex than this.'

'You can't blame them for being careful about foreigners,' she pointed out. 'I might have a dozen ex-husbands back in the States.'

'I'm not even going to ask you about that. I recognise one of your wicked moods. You'd enjoy freezing me with terror.'

'Well, anyway, we made it to the end, and we're all set for the business deal of the century. Shake?'

'Shake.' He took her extended hand.

She often teased him like this these days. It saved her from the embarrassment of making it obvious that her feelings were stronger and deeper than his.

It wasn't the kind of wedding a woman would dream of, especially with a man she loved. But it was better than parting from him. Inwardly she sent a silent message of gratitude to Matt, who had alerted her to danger in good time.

When everything was sorted they opted for a speedy marriage on the first available date. Instead of the huge array of business contacts that would normally have revelled in the public relations, only the very closest friends were invited.

Fiorella helped her choose a wedding gift for Lucio, using her knowledge of him to direct Charlotte to a valuable collection of books about the history of the wine industry. To add a more personal touch she bought a vest with the logo of the local soccer team, and wrote a note saying, 'You can give him this when he's ready.'

It was settled between them now that she was to bear a son who would make his name in some profession where his mighty kick would give him an advantage. When Lucio opened the parcel his delighted grin told her that he understood the joke. His hug was fierce and appreciative.

'We haven't discussed a honeymoon yet,' he reminded her.

'It's not really the right time, is it? Let's wait until after October when the harvest is in.'

He kissed her. 'You're going to be a great vintner's wife. But have a think about the honeymoon, too.'

In fact, she already knew where she wanted to go for their honeymoon, but she would wait for the right time to tell him.

The big disappointment was that none of her family could come to Tuscany for the wedding.

'Your father isn't well enough to make the journey,' her mother said. 'And I can't leave him alone.'

'Oh, I wish I could come,' Alex said.

'But Australia's so far away.' Charlotte sighed.

Ellie and Matt were also too tied up with events in their own lives. There was a triumphant video link during which they toasted Lucio and Charlotte, who raised their glasses in return.

'But it's not the same as seeing them,' Charlotte sighed to Lucio afterwards.

'No, it would have given you the chance to feel part of the family again,' he said. 'But there'll be another chance. There has to be.'

'I don't see how. Going to Larkville in October would have been a good chance because everyone will be there together, but that's out of the question. I'll be giving birth, and even if I'm not, *you'll* be giving birth.'

'*Eh?*'

'To a grape harvest.'

'Oh, I see. Yes, I suppose it is a bit like producing an offspring, being a proud father—'

'Telling the world that your creation is better than the next father's?' she suggested.

'Right. Or letting the world find out for itself.'

'Which it'll do at our wedding reception,' she said lightly.

But he wasn't fooled by her attempt to put a brave face on things.

'I'm really sorry your family can't be there. I wish there was something I could do.'

'But even you can't tell the grapes to wait another couple of weeks,' she said lightly. 'I'll get over it. Thanks anyway. Now get outta here. I'm going to put on my party dress and I don't want you to see it first.'

Although there would be no lavish reception there was a small party three nights before the wedding. Chief among the guests was Franco, who clearly felt he could take some credit for bringing the wedding about, and made a theatrical speech.

'What is life without love?' he demanded. 'There is no more beautiful sight in the world than two people deeply in love, vowing fidelity to each other. Together they will face the challenges that the world will throw at them, and because they are united they will be strong. Because they are one in heart they will achieve victory.

'My friends, a couple in love is an inspiration to us all.' He raised his glass. 'Let us toast them.'

Everybody rose, lifting their glasses and uttering congratulations. Lucio rose also, raising his glass to her. She responded in the same way, managing to look blissfully happy, and refusing to heed the irony in the speech. Lucio was her promised husband, as she was his promised wife. Together they would play the role of devoted lovers.

Somebody struck up on the piano, and there was dancing. The guests roared their appreciation as Lucio led her onto the floor and took her into his arms for a slow, dreamy waltz.

'You look beautiful,' he said. 'That's a lovely dress.'

'Thank you.'

'I'm wearing something special, too.'

'Yes, you look very handsome in that dinner jacket.'

'I don't mean that. I mean underneath. Look.'

He released her hand and slipped his fingers into the front of his shirt, pulling the edges apart just far enough for her to see—

'The soccer vest!' she exclaimed. 'You're wearing it.'

'It's the cleverest gift you could have bought me. I wear it in honour of you, and of him.'

'Oh, you—' She began to laugh. 'Of all the things to—honestly!'

Now he, too, was laughing, drawing her closer so that

she laid her head against him and together they shook with amusement. All around them their guests sighed with pleasure, for surely nobody had ever seen a couple so deeply in love.

'You don't mind if I vanish for a stag night?' Lucio had asked her.

Since he was already attired for an evening out the question was purely rhetorical.

'I'm tempted to say yes I mind a lot, just to see what you'd do,' she teased. 'Don't be silly, of course you must have a stag night. You don't want people to think you're henpecked, do you? Not yet anyway.'

'Yes, we'll wait a decent interval before you crack the whip,' he said, grinning.

'Oh, you think that's a joke, do you?' She pointed to the door and said theatrically, 'Get out of here at once!'

'Yes, ma'am, no, ma'am.' He saluted and hurried out to the car where his friends were waiting. She waved him off, thinking that these were the best moments between them, for now they were most completely in tune.

She was awoken in the early hours by the sound of the car arriving outside, and went hurriedly down to open the door. Having delivered him safely his friends said farewell and drove off.

For a man returning from a stag night he seemed relatively sober, although sleepy, and he regarded the stairs with dismay.

'I'll help you up them,' she said.

Together they managed to reach the top, but there he clutched the railing and murmured, 'I don't think I can go any farther.'

'Never mind. You can sleep in my room. It's just here. Come on.'

She got him as far as the bed where he dropped down with relief.

'Did you enjoy yourself?' she asked.

'Mmm!'

'Good. That's all that matters.'

He turned his head on the pillow. 'You're a very understanding woman.'

'If I'm going to marry you I'll need to be.'

'Mmm!'

'Go to sleep.' She chuckled.

His eyes were already closed, and he was breathing deeply. She watched him tenderly for a moment, then leaned down and kissed him on the mouth.

'Sleep well, and don't worry about anything,' she said.

Still without opening his eyes he moved his arms so that they enfolded her, drawing her close. Happily she snuggled up, her head on his shoulder.

'Mmm!' he said again.

'Mmm!' she agreed.

'I'm sorry,' he murmured.

'No need.'

'The baby.' He sighed. 'I feel guilty.'

'There's nothing to feel guilty about,' she assured him.

His next words came in such a soft whisper that she had to lean closer to hear it. What she heard made her tense, wondering if she'd misheard, for surely it wasn't possible—surely...?

'I wasn't fair,' he murmured. 'You wanted to wait until we were married...I wouldn't listen...forgive me—'

'But back then we weren't—'

'I begged and begged until you gave in...not fair...but when we're married, nobody will know that we...our secret...our secret. Say you forgive me.'

She took a deep breath, summoning her resolve. She

didn't want to do what she was about to, but there was no choice if he was to have peace.

'There's nothing to forgive, my darling,' she assured him. 'I want you as much as you want me. We love each other, and we'll be married soon.'

She had known about the burden he carried, blaming himself for Maria's death. Now she knew there had been another burden all along, one which haunted him, sleeping and waking.

They had been lovers, and Maria had conceived his child. Doubtless her pregnancy had been in the very early days, so nobody else suspected, and the truth could be hidden until after the wedding. But she had died, and the child had died with her. There had been nobody he could tell, and even now he staggered under a terrifying sense of guilt.

'Dead,' he was murmuring, 'my fault.'

'No!' she said fiercely. 'None of it is your fault.'

But she despaired of convincing him. She'd known that he was haunted by the fear that he had inadvertently killed Maria. Now she saw that his feeling of guilt and self-blame extended to the death of his first unborn child. It was wildly unlikely and illogical, but it shed a new light over his protectiveness towards her, his fear of making love.

The thought of his suffering made her weep, and she held him tenderly against her.

He stirred, clasping her more tightly. 'Are you there?'

'Yes, I'm here. Hold on to me, and go to sleep, my darling.'

He sighed and she felt the tension drain out of him. Now he was at peace, and all was well as long as she was there for him. She held him gently until they both fell asleep.

She awoke first, to find that neither of them had moved in two hours. His eyes were still closed, but as she watched they opened slowly. For a moment his expression was vague, but then he smiled as though something had eased his mind.

'So much for a macho stag night,' he said.

'As long as you enjoyed yourself, what else matters?'

He eased himself up, moving carefully.

'I'm sorry,' he said. 'I had no right to bother you while I was in that state.'

'What state? You didn't do anything objectionable. You just couldn't stay awake.'

'I probably talked a lot of nonsense.'

'Not a thing. Stop worrying.'

He made his way to the door, but looked back, seeming troubled.

'I didn't…say anything, did I?'

'Not that I remember. Bye.'

He hesitated a moment. 'Bye.'

He gave her a final look, and quietly departed.

The words were there in his mind, she thought, but he wasn't sure if it was a memory or a dream. Let him think of it as a dream. That would be easier for him.

In the beginning loving him had seemed simple. Now she knew it wasn't going to be simple at all.

But she had made her choice, and nothing was going to make her change it.

Franco was going to give the bride away. He arrived just as Lucio was about to leave for the church, slapped him on the shoulder and told him to be off. Then he ushered the bride out to his chauffeur-driven car, with Fiorella following.

'Have you got the ring?' he asked before they started.

For this marriage ceremony there were two matching rings, which the bride and groom exchanged.

'Here,' Fiorella said, holding it up. 'Everything has been taken care of.'

Everything taken care of, Charlotte mused as the car headed for Siena. But there were still so many questions unanswered, questions that might never be answered because they would never be asked.

As soon as she entered the church she could see down the aisle to where Lucio was waiting for her. Enrico gave her his arm, the organ struck up and she began to advance. As she grew closer to Lucio she could see that his eyes never left her for a moment. There was a contented look in them that filled her with pleasure, and as she neared he reached out to her, taking her hand and drawing her to his side.

The first part of the service was formal, but at last it was time to exchange rings. Slowly Lucio slid the ring on her finger, saying quietly, 'Take this ring as a sign of my love and fidelity.'

Then it was her turn. Raising his hand, she slid the ring onto it, murmuring, 'Take this ring as a sign of my love and fidelity.'

Love and fidelity.

She meant the words with all her heart. Looking up into his face she saw there an intensity of emotion that gave her a surge of joy.

The moment came. She felt his lips on hers, not passionate as she had known them, but firm and gentle. A brief trip to the sacristy to sign the register, then a return to the church where they were proclaimed husband and wife as they began the journey along the aisle, hand in hand.

He is my husband and I am his wife. Now I belong to him and he...perhaps he belongs to me—perhaps—or at least to our son.

The rest of the day was a triumph. To Charlotte it

seemed that almost everything she had wished for was coming true. Acceptance, a home, a new family.

At last it was time to retire to bed, now a shared room with Lucio. She climbed the stairs on his arm, followed him into their room and accepted his help undressing.

'I'm worn out,' she said sleepily. 'Who'd have thought getting married was so exhausting?'

'True,' he said, yawning. 'And I've got to be up early tomorrow to talk to Toni, my head steward. He's got some ideas for next year that we'll have to plan for now.'

'Goodnight,' she said.

His kissed her forehead. 'Goodnight, my dear.'

This was their wedding night.

The months moved on. Now she was glad to live a slower, more relaxed life, her thoughts always focused on the future. Eight weeks until the birth, seven, six—

'Oh, I can't bear this,' Fiorella squealed. 'We want to welcome him into the world and he keeps us waiting.'

'No, he doesn't,' Charlotte said with mock indignation. 'He's not late, it's just us that's impatient.'

'We are all impatient,' Elizabetta chimed in.

Charlotte regarded her fondly. By now she knew Elizabetta's history. As a young woman she had been married, and pregnant. But the child had been born early, at only seven months. Within a few hours it was dead, and Elizabeth, too, had nearly died. Charlotte felt that many a woman in her position would have felt resentful of another woman's luck. But Elizabetta was too generous and warm-hearted to feel bitterness towards her.

As autumn gradually appeared it was a pleasure to sit on the terrace, watching the setting sun, drinking in the warmth.

One evening she was sitting there feeling at one with

life, with the world and everyone in it. In the distance she could see a car that she recognised as Toni's. Doubtless he was on his way to make a report to Lucio. She would go inside and arrange with the kitchen staff to have his favourite coffee ready.

Exactly what happened next she was never sure, but as she passed across the tops of the steps that led down from the terrace to the ground, she felt her foot turn underneath her. She tried to grasp something to save herself but it was too late. She felt a bang as her head hit the stone railings, and the next moment she was tumbling down the stairs.

From somewhere far above she heard a scream. Then she blacked out.

CHAPTER TWELVE

The pain was everywhere, sweeping through her in waves. She had the strange sensation of sleeping while being racked by gusts of agony. She tried to reach out, pleading for help, but it was hard to move.

From a great distance came voices: Fiorella screaming, 'Call an ambulance!' Then Lucio crying, 'Charlotte—oh, my God, what happened? Charlotte, speak to me, please. Charlotte! *Charlotte!*'

She tried to respond but his voice faded as she blacked out. But after a while she managed to open her eyes a little, and see strangers, wearing uniforms. One of them, a woman, was saying, 'Lift her this way—careful, easy now. How did this happen? Did anyone see it?'

'She fell down the steps of the terrace and hit her head.' That was Enrico's voice. 'I saw it from a distance but, oh, heavens! I was too far away to help her.'

'My baby,' she whispered.

The strange woman's voice replied, 'We'll soon have you in the hospital. Hold on.'

She was being carried. From somewhere came the sound of doors opening, then being slammed shut, engines roaring.

'Lucio?' she cried.

'I'm here,' he said, close to her ear. His hand grasped hers. 'Can you feel me?'

'Yes, yes...'

'Can't this ambulance go any faster?' he shouted.

The woman's voice said, 'I've alerted the hospital. They're ready for her. They'll do their best to save the baby.'

'They've got to save *her*.' Lucio's cry was almost a scream. 'Don't you understand? *Her!*'

She tried to open her eyes but the blackness was sweeping over her again. It blended with the roar of the engine to create a world in which there was only fear, pain, uncertainty.

Then she was being hurried along a hospital corridor on a trolley, lifted onto a bed. A doctor and nurse regarded her anxiously, and a fierce pain convulsed her.

'The baby,' she gasped. 'I think it's coming.'

'No,' Lucio groaned. 'Please, Doctor, don't let that happen. She's so weak and hurt, it'll be too much for her.'

'If it's really started,' the doctor said, 'then there's not a lot— Stand back please.'

He leaned over Charlotte, asking her urgent questions, which she found it hard to answer with her consciousness coming and going.

'Save my baby,' she begged. '*Please*—save my baby— *Aaah!*'

Now there was no doubt that her labour had started, nearly six weeks early. The focus of her life, the child that was to unite her and Lucio on the road ahead, was in danger.

Nothing was in her control. The urge to push possessed her and she bore down, struggling against the pain, groaning.

'No,' she whispered. 'No, please—I can't do this....'

'I'm afraid you must,' the doctor said. 'But we'll do everything we can to make it easier.'

'What can *I* do?' Lucio demanded harshly.

'Be here and support her—that is, if you feel you can. Some fathers can't bear to be present during childbirth.'

'Then they ought to be shot,' Lucio snapped. 'Just try to get rid of me.'

He dropped to his knees beside Charlotte so that his face was close to hers.

'Did you hear that? I'm staying here. We're going to do this together—no, that's not really true. You're going to be doing all the hard work, I'm afraid. But I'll be here, cheering you on.'

'And him,' she whispered. 'Our little soccer star?'

'And him. Right into the goal.'

'Always on the winning side. *Aaah!*'

'That's it,' said the doctor. 'Push. Excellent.'

To brace herself against the pain she clenched her hand tighter than ever, so that Lucio gave a sharp groan at the fierceness of her grip.

'Sorry,' she gasped.

'Never mind me,' he said. 'You just worry about yourself—and him.'

Her head was aching badly. A nurse tended it, wiping away a trickle of blood. In her confusion she believed that there could be no way out of this. She was trapped in a desert of agony and dread, and there seemed no escape. She had sworn to help Lucio in every way, and if the child died it would destroy him.

But then she felt Lucio holding her, sending a message of comfort and love that seemed to reach her down the corridors of eternity. She yearned towards him, not with her hands but with her heart and soul, knowing that now he was all she had in the world.

She had no idea how long the birth took. She only knew that nothing else existed in the world. Then, after a while, the pain ceased to attack her and faded to a constant ache. Swamped by exhaustion she vaguely sensed that something was gone from inside her.

'My baby,' she whispered. 'Please—'

Lucio leaned close.

'Our daughter was born safely,' he murmured. 'She's been put into an incubator, and she'll be there for several days.'

'She's…going to live?'

'It's too soon to be certain, but they're hopeful.'

'You said…daughter.'

'Yes,' he told her gently. 'We have a little girl.'

She wanted to say something but the world faded again. Surely Lucio had wanted a son, and she had disappointed him? What would he say? What would he feel?

Now she was on fire. Heat was all around her, inside her, destroying thought and consciousness. Destroying her. Voices again, talking about fever. But one voice dominated them all.

'Charlotte, listen to me. Can you hear me, wherever you are? You must, *you must hear me.*'

'Yes, yes…'

He seemed to become more agitated.

'You've got to hang on. You've got a fever but they're giving you something for it, and you're going to be all right. You understand that? You're going to be all right, but you've got to fight. I'm here. We'll fight together. You can't go off anywhere now, not when you've made me love you so much. That would be really inconsiderate, wouldn't it? And I know you'd never do that.'

His voice grew more gentle.

'Or perhaps you don't know how much I love you. I've

never said it but you're clever enough to understand without words. Mostly I didn't understand it myself. I don't think I really knew until now, but you knew. Sure you did, because you know everything. You saw through me from the start, and let's face it, you've had me dancing to your tune.

'But you can't do that and then just vanish. You can't just abandon me. Charlotte, my love, can you hear me? *Can you hear me?*'

His voice seemed to follow her into the engulfing darkness, holding on to her, never leaving her, so that at last she felt the darkness yield and give her back to him.

'Open your eyes, darling. That's it! Look, everyone, she's awake!' Lucio's face, haggard and unshaven but full of joy, hovered above her. 'Can you see me?'

'Yes, I knew you were there,' she murmured.

'I'm still here. I always will be.'

'Our baby—?'

'She's fine. She's beautiful. The doctors say you're both doing well, but if you knew how scared I've been.'

She could believe it. He looked terrible, like a man who hadn't slept for a year.

Suddenly she remembered him as he'd been at their first meeting in Rome, just over seven months ago; wickedly handsome, vibrant, sophisticated, dominating the company with the power of his looks and personality, alive to every challenge, in control of every situation.

Now, even through several days' growth of beard, she could see lines that hadn't been there before. And his eyes told a story of agony. It was like looking at a totally different man. Who had done this cruel thing to him?

She had.

'There was no need to be scared,' she told him.

'How can you know that? If you could have seen how you looked—as though you'd already gone far ahead to a place where I couldn't reach you.'

'It's all right,' she whispered. 'That was never going to happen.'

'You can't be sure—'

'Yes, I can. I would never have left you.'

Fiorella came forward, her eyes warm and loving.

'Bless you, dearest Charlotte! Oh, it's so good to see you getting better! We were all so worried.'

Lucio had turned away to say something to a nurse. Fiorella lowered her voice.

'I thought he was going to go crazy. He's been here for days, refusing to leave you, except for a moment to see the baby. I had to bring food in to him because he wouldn't even go to the canteen.'

'Poor Lucio. He looks terrible.'

'Yes, but he'll be all right now his mind can be at rest about you.'

'He's seen the baby?'

'Yes, they couldn't bring her in here because she's in an incubator, but she's strong enough to leave it now so they'll bring her to you. If only you could have seen his face when he saw her for the first time. He wanted to take her in his arms but she had to stay in the incubator, and he was so upset. Lucio, tell Charlotte—oh, he's gone.'

While they were talking Lucio had left the room. They discovered why a moment later when he returned carrying a small bundle close to his chest. Fiorella slid out of the way so that he could sit on the bed, and discreetly glided out of the door, leaving them alone.

'Here she is,' he said. 'Our child.'

Gently he laid the tiny being against her mother's bosom, then turned his body, putting his arm behind her shoulders, supporting mother and child. Charlotte gazed down, entranced, at the tiny face. The baby's eyes were closed and she was deeply asleep, blissfully oblivious of the outside world and the anguish that her arrival had caused.

So we meet at last, Charlotte thought. *You're going to make everything different.*

Lucio's arms were keeping her safe. His rough, unshaven face was scratching her cheek. She turned her head to share a smile with him, receiving his answering glow before they both returned their gazes to the baby.

'Thank you,' he murmured. 'Thank you with all my heart.'

'No, thank you,' she whispered. 'You and she have given me something I never thought I'd have. Now I know I'll have it forever.'

Fiorella appeared in the doorway.

'I left because I thought you three would like to be alone for a while,' she said. 'But I must just see her.' She came over to the bed. 'She's so beautiful.'

'All this time,' Charlotte reflected, 'we were wrong about it being a son.'

'Only because we assumed that a strong baby must be male,' Lucio said. 'That was very old-fashioned of us. We forgot that females can be strong, too. The doctor says she's fit and vigorous, and she's come through that premature birth with all flags flying.' He grinned. 'You never know. She might grow up to play soccer yet. Or maybe she'll settle for ruling the world, the way she already rules ours.'

'But didn't you really want a son?'

'I told you, I didn't mind either way.'

'Yes, but I thought—'

'I know what you thought, that I was just being polite about it. You kept telling me I wanted a boy and I just accepted what you said.' He laid a finger against the baby's cheek. 'I guess I'll just have to get used to being bossed around by my womenfolk.' He gave Fiorella a wicked grin. 'After all, I've had lots of practice.'

'It'll come in useful.' Fiorella chuckled. 'And what are you going to call your little girl?'

'We haven't thought about it yet,' Lucio said. He laid a hand on Charlotte's shoulder. 'Do you have any ideas?'

'Yes,' she said. 'I want to call her Maria.'

Fiorella made a sudden movement, pleased but uncertain.

'You will name her after my girl?' she breathed. 'That is wonderful but, Charlotte, are you sure? Why do you do this? If it is kindness for me, I thank you, but please do not force yourself.'

'I'm not forcing myself,' she said. 'It's what I want to do.'

She looked at Lucio, who was watching her in stunned silence. Fiorella also saw his expression, understood it and slipped quietly out of the room.

'Forgive me if I don't know what to say,' he murmured. 'This is the last thing I expected. I don't know why you— but is Fiorella right? Is this an act of generosity because, if it is, you can't think I'd ever ask you to—'

'I know you wouldn't,' she said when he stumbled to a halt. 'This is what I want.'

'But why? Are you afraid of her? Do you think I love her and not you?'

'My darling, you've got it all wrong. I don't fear Maria as a rival. I did once, but now I know that she was one part of your life, and I'm another. Keep her in your heart. Go on loving her. She doesn't threaten me. I don't want to get rid of her, either from your life or mine.'

He was staring at her as though he couldn't believe what

he heard. Far back in his eyes she saw joy warring with something that was almost fear.

'And my love for you,' he stammered, 'tell me you believe in it, I beg you.'

'I didn't believe it for a long time. I knew you wanted to be a father, have the family we can make together.' She touched his face. 'I knew she was pregnant when she died. You told me when you came back from your stag night. You weren't in your right mind and you thought you were talking to her. Gradually I realised what you meant.'

He groaned and hung his head. 'I wondered next day—I couldn't be sure.'

'You could always have told me.'

'I meant to. I just didn't want to have any secrets from you, and I longed to tell you everything, but I was afraid you'd take it the wrong way. You might have felt insulted, or thought I was making you second best.'

'That was true once. There was a time when I felt you were just "making do" with me.'

'And you didn't sock me on the jaw? Why not? I deserved it.'

'I loved you. I didn't feel I had the right to blame you for not being in love with me. You can't love to order. I hoped we'd grow closer in time and then—who knows?'

'Yes, it took me too long to understand my own heart,' he said sombrely. 'It might have taken longer if you hadn't been in danger during the birth. Then it became hideously clear to me that if you died my own life was over. Nothing mattered but you.'

'And our baby,' she said softly.

He met her eyes and shook his head slightly. 'You,' he said. 'Just you.'

Without waiting for her reply he laid his head down on the pillow beside her.

'You make me complete and you keep me safe,' he murmured. 'I never knew before how much I needed that. But now I know, and I'll never let you go. I warn you, I'll be possessive, domineering, practically making a prisoner of you. Don't think I'll ever let you escape me, because I won't. You'll probably get very fed up with my behaviour.'

She enfolded him in her arms and he buried his face against her.

'I think I can just about manage to put up with you,' she whispered.

A week later mother and baby returned home and Charlotte entered a stage of life more beautiful than anything she could have imagined. Her strength returned quickly, her relationship with her child flowered.

She had the pleasure of seeing Lucio completely happy now that both his personal and professional lives were reaching a triumphant peak. Harvest time was approaching, and everyone was studying the grapes intently to pick exactly the right moment. Testing was under way to determine the levels of sugar, acid and tannin.

'At one time there was only one way to find out,' Lucio told her. 'And that was to put the grapes in your mouth. Nowadays there are machines that will do some of it, but there's still no substitute for what your own taste buds tell you. Mine tell me it'll need a few more days, but then I'll unleash my workers on the vines.'

While many vintners used machines for the harvest Lucio still preferred to have his grapes picked by humans. It made him popular in the area where the employment he offered was a godsend to many. Already the temporary workers were appearing on the estate, waiting for the signal to start.

Charlotte's other great pleasure came from the delight

of her family over the birth of their newest member. They squealed with delight when she held up baby Maria so that she could be seen via the video link.

'Oh, I do wish you were coming to Larkville,' Ellie sighed one night. 'You and Lucio and Maria. We're all so miserable at not being able to get over there for your wedding or the christening, and if you all came to Larkville it would really bind the family together.'

'I know,' Charlotte said, supressing a sigh. 'I really wish I could come, Ellie, honestly I do. But the harvest is about to start.'

'But why do you have to be there for the harvest?' Ellie asked. 'Surely they can do it without you?'

'Well, I won't actually be picking grapes,' she agreed. 'But I won't leave Lucio for the first harvest of our marriage. It's a great moment for him, and I must share it with him.'

'Would he really stop you coming here?'

'No, he wouldn't. He's too generous. But I wouldn't be so unfair as to ask him. I want to be here to share the harvest with him. It'll mean the world to me.'

'More than your family?'

'Lucio is my family now.'

'All right, you do what you think right. We'll be able to talk again tomorrow, then I have to be off to the airport.'

Charlotte shut down the link and sat for a moment thinking about what she had just done. It was a final choice, she knew that. Nor did she regret it for a moment. In Lucio she had gained more than she could have hoped for in a thousand years.

Smiling, she raised Maria in her arms and went to find him. Only to discover that he had just left the house.

'I don't know what got into him,' Fiorella said. 'I thought he was home for the day but he suddenly remembered something he had to do, and took off. Look, you can see his car in the distance. Men can be so annoying!'

Lucio returned a couple of hours later, coming upon Charlotte just as she was putting Maria to bed. Despite Maria being only a few weeks old there was no doubt that her eyes brightened at the sight of her father.

'It's lucky I'm not easily jealous,' Charlotte said. 'Or I might object to having to struggle for her attention.'

'Yes, Fiorella does try to come first with her.' Lucio grinned.

'Actually, I meant you. It's supposed to be the mother who gets up to look after her at night.'

'You mean last night? Well, I brought her to you, didn't I?'

'Only because I'm breastfeeding her. That's one thing you haven't been able to take over. It's lucky the harvest will be starting soon, and that will take up your attention.'

'Actually, it won't,' he said slowly. 'I'm going to let Toni take over the harvest, because I won't be here.'

'Won't—? But where will you be?'

He positioned himself to get a good look at her face before saying, 'I'll be in Larkville, with you and Maria.'

'But I—'

'I've checked with the doctor. He says it's OK for both of you to travel. And I know you want to go because I eavesdropped on the video link you had with Ellie yesterday.'

'You what?'

'And I'm glad I did. I learned a lot from listening to you, and it was very clear to me what I had to do. I've spent this afternoon talking to Toni, my overseer, and some of the others, about what to do while I'm away. They're delighted. They're all too experienced to need me.'

'But the harvest—I know what it means to you to be here.'

'And I know what it means to you to reconcile with your family and to meet your other family. There'll never be another chance as perfect as this, and you simply have to take it.'

He grasped her in urgent hands.

'Listen to me, Charlotte. I've told you that I love you, but I haven't proved it. They were just words, easy to say.'

'But I believe them.'

'And you're right. But the time will come when you'll ask yourself what I ever gave up for you, and I don't want the answer to be "nothing". So far all I've done is take. Now it's time for you to take and me to give.'

'Oh, Lucio—Lucio…'

'Come here.'

His mouth on hers was firm and gentle, assertive but pleading—a mixture of the feelings and attitudes around which their love was built.

'Now,' he said when he'd released her, 'get on to the computer and tell them we're coming. All of us. You, me and Maria.'

'Lucio, are you sure?'

'I was never more sure of anything in my life.'

With all her heart she longed to believe that he meant it, but still a little doubt remained. At the last minute he would realise the size of the undertaking he'd committed himself to, and realise that it was impossible.

These thoughts went through her head as they travelled to the Florence airport, to board the plane to Texas, accompanied by Fiorella. Every moment Charlotte expected him to say something, to back off, count on her understanding. But nothing happened.

It's down to me, she thought at last. *I must tell him that there's no need for this. I'll release him. I must.*

As they neared Passport Control she took a deep breath. 'Lucio—'

'Just a minute,' he said. 'There's my cell phone. *Toni!*'

So that was it, she thought. Toni had called to tell him they couldn't manage without him, and he must return at once. She listened to what Lucio was saying.

'Right…. Good…. So that's fine then. Thanks for telling me. Now I can really enjoy myself in the States. See you in a few days.' He hung up. 'Right now, are we ready? Goodbye, Mamma. I'll call you when we get there. Darling, is something the matter? You look strange.'

'No, I—I can hardly believe this is happening.'

'You'd better believe it. Off we go!'

And suddenly all the questions were answered. They were going through Passport Control, down the corridor into the departure lounge and onto the plane. Then it was time for take-off.

Lucio had prepared for the long flight by buying the best seats, and urging Charlotte to sit by the window.

Lying back, her child in her arms, her beloved at her side, Charlotte was able to look out on the clouds that separated her from the earth, and relish the sensation of being in another universe, one where everything was perfect.

'Maria's getting restless,' Lucio said at last. 'I think she wants to be fed.'

He moved, turning his body so that it formed a protective barrier between Charlotte and anyone who might pass down the aisle.

'Thank you,' she said happily. 'And we've got the seats in two rows all to ourselves, haven't we? What a lucky chance that nobody else wanted them. Why are you laughing like that?'

'It's not chance. I bought eight seats.'

'You—you did what? You bought all these seats?'

'So that you'd have privacy when you needed it.'

'You thought of that?' she whispered.

'I think of you every moment. I long for you to ask me for something, so that I can have the pleasure of giving it to you and showing you what you are to me.'

'Well…there is something.'

'Yes?' And the eagerness in his face told her that he spoke truly when he said he wanted to please her.

'That vineyard in Veneto, I loved the house. Now you've bought it, could it be our home? I know you'll still have to spend some time in Tuscany for Fiorella's sake—'

'But that place will be our main home. Yours and mine. You're right. In fact, you've given me an idea.'

'What?'

'Wait and see.'

They sat in silence, watching the child take nourishment from her mother, looking up at her with eyes filled with contentment.

'She feels safe,' Lucio said. 'Everyone who knows you feels safe.'

'But not only safe, surely?' she asked.

'We'll talk about that later, when you've completely recovered.'

She smiled. Lucio's protective side had been in full flood since the birth, for both herself and Maria.

'I still can't believe you let me make this trip,' she said.

'I didn't *let* you do it,' he corrected her gently. 'I *made* you do it, because you needed to. And whatever you need is what I want.'

He was right in everything, she reflected. Because of his sacrifice she could believe in his love as never before.

And he had understood that. It was the final proof of all that she needed to know.

Looking out of the window she saw that the clouds were clearing, and the world was full of sunshine.

Rome: four months later

Against the darkness the lights glittered on the rushing water. Everywhere there was music, people laughing and singing as they crowded around the Trevi Fountain. Coins were spun into the water, and a thousand wishes rose into the air.

'Have you guessed why I wanted to return to Rome for our honeymoon?' Charlotte asked as they made their way into the square.

'I thought it might have something to do with the last time we were here,' Lucio replied. 'Exactly one year ago today.'

'Yes, we sat at that little café over there, and we talked. Oh, how we talked!'

'And then we went to the fountain. You threw in a coin and cried, "Bring me back to Rome".'

'And I got my wish,' she said. 'Because here I am, with you. That was what I wanted then, what I want now, what I'll always want for the rest of our lives.'

'Who could have foreseen what lay ahead of us?' he marvelled. 'We thought we'd know each other for just a few hours. But that night, our whole futures were decided by a kindly fate.'

'Kindly?' she asked with just a hint of teasing. 'Are you sure?'

'You know better than to ask me that.'

She chuckled. 'You weren't so certain when Maria's

milk landed all over your shirt when you'd just got dressed for the evening.'

'She can do anything she likes and it's fine by me. You have to expect the unexpected.'

'And it's certainly been unexpected,' she mused.

'Right. That first night, who'd have thought that a year later you'd have her and me.'

'Not to mention finding myself the owner of a Veneto vineyard,' she mused.

'A man should give his wife a nice wedding present. Like you said, that will always be our real home. I'm glad you like it.'

'If I listed all the things about you that I like we'd be here forever.'

He held out his hand. 'Come on, let's go and tell Oceanus that he got it right.'

There was the stone deity, dominating the fountain, arrogantly accepting all the coins that were tossed at his feet.

'What happens to the coins?' Charlotte wondered.

'They're regularly gathered up and put into a fund for the needy,' Lucio explained. 'So it's a good way of saying thank-you for a thousand blessings.'

From his pocket he pulled out a bag, heavy with high-value coins, which he shared with her. Together they tossed coin after coin into the water.

'Bring us back to Rome,' he cried.

'Next year,' she added, 'and the year after.'

'And again and again,' he called. 'Do you hear that? Bring us back.'

'Bring us back,' she echoed.

Lucio put his arm about her, looking down at her with adoration.

'But it must be together,' he said. 'Because together is what we always want to be.'

Slowly she nodded. 'Yes,' she murmured. 'Yes.'

There was no need to say more. Everything had been said, enough for the rest of their lives. In the shining light of the fountain he laid his lips on hers for a kiss that was a herald of the night to come, and the years to come. Then, arms about each other, they walked away.

* * * * *

THE VILLAGE
NURSE'S
HAPPY-EVER-AFTER

ABIGAIL GORDON

CHAPTER ONE

PHOEBE HOWARD had moved into the apartment above The Tides Medical Practice, in the coastal Devon village of Bluebell Cove, on the first day of January. She'd looked around it sombrely and thought it was adequate in a basic sort of way—it would have to do.

Looking down at the toddler in her arms, she'd said, 'It has one advantage, Marcus. Your mummy won't have to travel far to work as she's based right here. We have Ethan to thank for this—him, and your Aunt Katie and Uncle Rob, who took me in when I was a lost soul. They are the ones who've always been there for me and I will be forever grateful.

'But now Ethan has found the happiness he so much deserves, and is going to live in Paris with his lovely family. At the same time Katie and Rob are moving up north to be near his elderly father, so it's just you and me from now on, little one. Oh, and with a new head of the practice to get used to thrown in for good measure!'

That had been a couple of weeks ago and today Phoebe was at the airport, along with other folk from Bluebell Cove, to say goodbye to the Lomax family as they departed for their new life in France.

In her role as district nurse at the village surgery, she'd arranged her home visits to her patients to leave her free for this moment. Once she'd seen the aircraft take off, it would be time to pick Marcus up from the Tiny Toes Nursery where he was being cared for while she was working.

It had been a wrench, taking him there. They'd spent barely any time apart since the day of his birth. During the months of her maternity leave, she'd lived with her sister Katie and brother-in-law Rob in the bustling market town near Bluebell Cove. On the rare occasions when she'd left Marcus, they had cared for him as lovingly as she did herself, but all the time she'd known it couldn't last. And even though she'd accepted that she had no choice, she still hated leaving him behind every day.

She knew she was fortunate, however, to have such a job. Her sister had seen the vacancy for district nurse in the nearby village of Bluebell Cove advertised on an NHS website. It had become reality from the moment that Ethan Lomax, the likeable head of the practice, had offered her the position. She'd worked there for the last few months of her pregnancy, until she'd started her maternity leave, staying with Katie and Rob.

But as they were moving up north to be near Rob's father it had meant that she'd had to find somewhere else to live. When Ethan had suggested she rent one of the two apartments above the surgery at a nominal rate, she'd been only too eager to accept.

After the noise and bustle of London—and the hurt she'd received there, she was as happy as circumstances permitted in Bluebell Cove. It had seemed strange when she'd first moved there, but it hadn't taken long for the peace and beauty of the place to charm her. She'd soon begun to feel a degree of contentment that she could never have expected so soon in her disrupted life. Now she no longer wept endlessly for what might have been. She was taking control of her life again as best she could, and if she had to hand Marcus over to others to be looked after while she was working, then that was how it would have to be.

As Phoebe watched, the Lomax family waved their last goodbyes and disappeared from sight. Soon the aircraft would be lifting off the runway, leaving yet another vacuum in her life. Suddenly holding back tears, Phoebe went to find her little car and drove off into the cold January afternoon.

At the end of the long flight from Australia, Harry Balfour gazed down sombrely on to the patchwork of towns, motorways and countryside that came into view as the pilot began the descent from the sky.

He was returning to the place of his birth, seeking solace and hoping to find it among the rolling green fields and magical coastline of Devon. It was where he'd always belonged, until five years ago when he'd met a feisty Australian girl. After a whirlwind romance, he'd married her and gone to live in her country with high hopes of happiness and job satisfaction.

The latter had been easy enough to find, but over recent months he'd been in a desolate kind of limbo, as if he didn't belong anywhere or to anyone. It had been a phone call out of the blue that had brought about the decision to return to Devon.

The man who hadn't smiled once during the flight hadn't gone unobserved by some of the female passengers. He was an attractive member of the opposite sex. A big man with a lived-in sort of face, dark russet hair above cool hazel eyes, and a physique that lots of men would die for.

But for any of them who had smiled in his direction, or tried to chat to relieve the tedium of the flight, the verdict had been that he was an unsociable character, and Harry knew they were right. It was what he'd become, and he didn't give a damn.

The last thing he wanted to do was make small talk to strangers. He'd already told the woman who had persuaded him to return to Bluebell Cove that he didn't want to be met at the airport. It wasn't as if he didn't know where he was bound for. He'd lived there for the first thirty-two years of his life.

It was a couple of days after the Lomax family had flown to France and midnight was approaching. Marcus was asleep in his cot in the smaller of the two bedrooms of the apartment, and Phoebe was up a ladder in the sitting room, her long brown hair stuffed inside an old sun hat and wearing a pair of her brother-in-law's cast-off dungarees.

She was painting the ceiling in an attempt to brighten up the place when she heard footsteps on the stairs that led up from the surgery. She became still, with the brush

dangling loosely from her hand. Either there was an
intruder in the building or...

It had only been that morning she'd discovered that
the new head of the practice was going to be living
across the landing from her in the second of the two
apartments above the surgery. For days on end, the departure of the much-loved and respected Ethan Lomax
had dominated every conversation among surgery staff
and villagers alike. In contrast, the arrival of his replacement had been spoken of only rarely, so when the senior
practice nurse had mentioned casually that he would be
moving into the other apartment, it had come as a shock
to her. She'd groaned inwardly at the thought of how
embarrassing it could turn out to be.

Phoebe knew he'd been employed at The Tides
Practice some years ago, so wouldn't be a stranger to
everyone, but he would be to her. Why wasn't he moving
into somewhere more salubrious? she'd thought uncomfortably. The last thing she wanted was to be coming
across him every time she opened her door.

She'd asked if he was bringing a family with him and
had been told that he was a widower without children.
So at least there would only be just the one person living
across from her, which was some slight relief. And now,
if the noise on the stairs *wasn't* an intruder, it would
seem that he'd arrived. But she had to be sure before
she called it a day and went to bed.

Putting the chain on and opening the door a crack,
Phoebe peered out onto the landing. Deciding that the
man in designer jeans and a smart jacket who was entering the opposite apartment fitted the role of new senior

partner rather than burglar, she started to close the door quietly to avoid being observed. He turned suddenly, as if aware that he was being watched, and said, 'Hello, there.'

She opened the door a fraction wider and said through the crack, 'I heard you come up the stairs and was just checking who it was before I went to bed.' Unable to step out and face him in her ghastly get-up, Phoebe closed the door and locked it in one movement. Then, leaning against it limply, she thought she hadn't handled *that* very well.

But she was too tired to dwell on it—her arms ached from the painting and it had been a long day, with some of her calls way out in the countryside. She was in no mood to get excited about the new arrival, even though she had noted when peering through the crack that he was quite something as attractive men went.

But so was Darren, and ever since he'd disappeared from her life she'd agreed that the old saying 'handsome is as handsome does' often applied to good-looking men. Even though she'd survived the hurt *he'd* inflicted on her, if she never saw him again she wouldn't complain.

They'd lived together in London, when he'd been a rising star, determined to get to the top in a big city bank. She'd always been supportive of his career ambitions but had never expected them to come before starting a family. A child to love and care for had been something she'd been looking forward to so much, and she hadn't been prepared for his reaction when she'd fallen pregnant.

They'd discussed starting a family a few times and she'd noted that his interest had been lukewarm, but had assumed that once Darren held his child in his arms, he would be lost in wonderment.

Instead, to her horror and dismay he'd gone berserk at the news, insisting he wanted to get to the top in his profession before lumbering himself with kids. He'd then suggested that she have an abortion. That had been a step too far and, heartbroken, she'd given in her notice at the London medical practice where she'd been employed as a district nurse.

Leaving him unrepentant, she'd moved to be near her sister and brother-in-law, her only relatives, and had filed for divorce. Clearly marriage to a man whose career meant more to him than his unborn child had been a big mistake. She and Darren hadn't spoken since and were not likely to.

She'd written to tell him he had a son when Marcus had been born but had received no response. A phone call from one of the girls at the bank had explained why. He was living with the daughter of the chairman of his bank and soon there would be wedding bells. It was to be hoped that wife number two was aware of his aversion to family life, she'd thought wryly, but was sure that a grandchild for the chairman of the bank would be much more welcome than one whose mother was just a mere nurse.

When she'd taken off the dungarees and freed her hair from under the sun hat, Phoebe went to stand by her baby's cot. Marcus was sleeping in pink and gold perfection, and planting a butterfly kiss on his smooth cheek Phoebe knew that her ex-husband was the loser in all of this.

As he placed the large case he'd humped up the stairs inside a small hallway, and closed the door behind him, Harry thought, *What or who was that?*

The voice had been that of a woman, so had the big brown eyes observing him warily through the narrow opening. But there had been no hair visible, and he'd caught a glimpse of what looked like paint-splashed dungarees.

Not a very good beginning, Harry, he thought. His aunt had abided by his wishes that there should be no fuss on his arrival, but clearly hadn't thought to inform him that he was going to have a strange neighbour.

He'd let himself into the surgery building, which he'd last seen five years ago, with one thought in mind—to get some sleep. The last thing he wanted was to still be under the covers the next morning when he was due to make his first appearance in the practice.

Putting from his mind how the privacy of his arrival had been butted into by some cautious, brown-eyed gremlin, he went to check out the kitchen before having a shower and then going to bed.

There was food in the fridge and the kitchen cupboards—fresh bread, scones, milk, cheese, bacon, eggs, and in pride of place a large carton of the clotted cream so famous in Devon and Cornwall.

He smiled for the first time in hours. His aunt, Barbara Balfour, who had instigated his return to Bluebell Cove, might be less of the woman she had once been, but she would definitely be behind all this, he thought.

Then he explored the bedroom, and came upon the welcome sight of a big double bed made up with fresh linen. When he crossed over to the bedroom window, a winter moon was shining above the village. In the distance, the lights of the house on the headland where his aunt and uncle lived glistened and flickered in the fresh breeze that had been the first thing he'd been aware of as he'd paid off the taxi that had brought him from the airport. As he'd breathed it in, it had been like wine after the dry heat of the country he'd just left.

The next morning, the travel alarm that Harry had brought with him fulfilled its function and he was down in the surgery before eight o'clock, just as the cleaner was leaving. By the time he'd introduced himself to the rosy-cheeked, middle-aged woman called Sarah, who informed him smilingly that her next task was to see her young ones safely off to school, and had renewed his acquaintance with the familiar layout of the surgery, the other staff were arriving.

Dr Leo Fenchurch, his second in command, was the first to arrive, followed by three practice nurses, three receptionists, a practice manager and the local midwife, who was based at the surgery.

As half past eight was approaching, and the surgery would soon be open to the public, Harry called them all together to have a brief chat and introduce himself. Picking up on the atmosphere, which was slightly lukewarm, he thought that Ethan Lomax was going to be a hard act to follow.

The two men had been friends and colleagues in the past, working at The Tides Medical Practice after qualifying. At that time the formidable Barbara Balfour, his aunt, had been senior partner, and no doubt would still have held that position if her health hadn't started to fail.

He had severed his connection with the place when he'd married Cassie, but Ethan had stayed on until recently when he'd given in to his wife's wishes and the family had moved to France.

Following in Ethan's footsteps didn't daunt him. He had no qualms about the job—he knew his own strengths when it came to that. More challenging were the other reasons behind his return. It was a case of hoping that somehow, in Bluebell Cove, he would find some ease from the grief that had been dragging him down during the last six months.

Harry looked over his new staff keenly—after all, they were the nucleus of the practice, so named because of the stretch of golden sand below the cliffs and the surging sea that came and went endlessly into the cove.

As it was his first morning, he was not aware that there was someone missing.

But while he'd been chatting to the cleaner, Phoebe had come down the back staircase that led to the apartments with Marcus in her arms, and had driven off to the nursery where he would be cared for until she'd finished her calls.

His baby buggy was in the boot, where it had been left the day before. In the short time that it took to unload it and pass her little one into the arms of Beth Dryden, who was in charge of Tiny Toes Nursery, Phoebe was acutely aware that she was running late. Marcus, who was teething, hadn't wanted his breakfast or been his usual contented little self while she'd been dressing him, all of which had been time consuming.

But he was smiling now, she thought thankfully. After explaining his earlier teething fretfulness to Beth and receiving her reassurance that she would give him some breakfast and would keep an eye on him, she drove back to the surgery where an explanation for her lateness was due to the new senior partner. After last night's uncomfortable few moments of meeting, she wasn't looking forward to it.

If it had been Ethan she wouldn't have needed to explain. He'd been kindness itself to her ever since she'd joined the practice—even while she'd been on leave after Marcus's birth he'd still kept in touch. Harry Balfour, however, was an unknown quantity.

When she hurried into the surgery he was standing by Reception on the phone. Lucy, the senior practice nurse, said in a low voice, 'Harry's talking to Ethan. What kept you Phoebe, baby's teeth?'

'Yes, he was really fretful this morning, today of all days.'

The elderly nurse nodded and looking towards the newcomer said, 'He's very sombre, not the guy he used to be. Harry was always happy and carefree but, then, he *has* just lost his wife in tragic circumstances. Why don't you go and sort out your calls while he's on the phone and introduce yourself to him afterwards?'

'Harry, it's Ethan here,' the voice at the other end of the line had said when the receptionist handed him the phone. 'Clearly you've arrived safely and are already on the job, so every good wish from all of us here! It gives me a good feeling to know that you are taking up where I left off.'

'It's kind of you to say so,' Harry told him. 'I'd forgotten how lovely it is here. With regard to the practice, I've gathered all the staff together and introduced myself. I'm also very happy with the apartment, it's really smart. Am I right in thinking that my aunt has been involved in the make-over?'

'Yes, you are,' was the reply. 'Have you spoken to Barbara yet?'

'No. I intend to go to Four Winds House this evening if she and Keith don't show up before then.'

'Fine, but prepare yourself for a shock when you see her. Barbara's mobility is very limited and her heart isn't good. She's being treated for that by her new son-in-law, my friend Lucas Devereux, who is a heart surgeon. He and your cousin Jenna were married a year ago and have a baby girl called Lily.'

They'd continued the conversation for a little while longer and by the time Harry was replacing the receiver Phoebe was almost ready to set off on her home visits. First, however, she needed to make herself known to him in a proper manner after the strangeness of their first meeting, if it could be described as that.

He'd turned away from the Reception desk and as she moved towards him, the first thing he observed about her was the pale perfection of her skin. After spending years in a country where women were often very tanned by the sun, it was breathtaking.

Trimly dressed in the dark blue dress of her calling, Phoebe had taken her hair off her face into a neat coil held back by a comb. It wasn't until his gaze met hers that Harry thought there couldn't be two pairs of big brown eyes like that on the surgery premises. But that was the only similarity to the ragamuffin who'd been watching him unlock the door of his new home the night before. He put out a feeler.

'I think we've already met,' he said dryly, before she could explain why she was late. 'Am I right?'

'Yes, you are,' she told him, holding out a smooth, ringless hand for him to shake. 'I'm Phoebe Howard, the district nurse attached to the practice. Last night you caught me in the middle of painting the ceiling—I'm afraid when I heard you coming up the stairs I had to check as it's been rather spooky with just the two of us up there.'

And what was that supposed to mean? he wondered. If she was living with a husband or partner one might expect that they would do the decorating. Yet a vision of Cassie came to mind. She'd been good at that sort of thing, said it kept her occupied when he was working long hours at the hospital where he'd been employed for most of his time in Australia.

She used to have a go at anything, had often been reckless, but it had seemed as if she'd had a charmed life. Until one Saturday morning, when they'd had words because he hadn't been free to do what she'd wanted which was to try out her new car.

He'd been on duty at the hospital, and as far as he'd been concerned, his patients had come first, so Cassie had set off in a huff and while driving along a remote road in the outback, the driver of a large oncoming truck had swerved into her path. The consequences had been disastrous—he'd lost his wife in a matter of seconds.

The accident had been six months ago and coming to terms with it had been grim. Thankfully they'd had no children to be left motherless. They'd both been of a like mind, that there had been plenty of time for that, though for very different reasons.

On Cassie's part, it had been because she hadn't been quite ready to give up what she'd seen as her freedom. But on Harry's part, it had been because he'd had a baby brother who had died from a genetic illness when he had been just a child himself. Yet, he'd been old enough to experience the frightening feeling of loss, and growing up as the remaining child of grief-stricken parents, the fear of bringing a child into the world and then losing it always lurked in the recesses of his mind.

He'd seen his mother weeping and his father's permanently sad expression, and had thought that it was better not to have babies if the angels were going to take them up to heaven.

'I'm sorry I was late arriving,' the young nurse beside him was saying apologetically, and bringing his thoughts back to bear on why he was standing there, Harry said briskly, 'That's OK, just as long as it isn't a habit.'

Hoping that in days to come the new senior partner wouldn't feel that unavoidable came into the same category as a habit, Phoebe managed a strained smile. Then picking up the case that held what she needed for her patients, she went quickly out through the main door of the surgery.

Her first call of the day was to the home of a man who had just been diagnosed with insulin-dependent diabetes. Frank Atkinson was a newly retired forestry worker and she'd explained the procedure of injecting himself the previous day. Now she was on her way to check if he was having any problems.

Always a frightening ordeal at first, most people soon got into a routine and accepted the inevitability of it. Sure enough, when she arrived at a pretty thatched cottage on the coast road she found that he had coped and was less agitated than on the day before.

As was often the case, there was hospitality on offer. His wife Betty, who knew something of the circumstances of the young district nurse, had coffee and shortbread waiting when Phoebe had finished dealing with her husband.

'I won't say no,' she said thankfully. 'My little one is teething and was really out of sorts this morning, so I didn't have time to have any breakfast. I mustn't linger, though. We have a new doctor in charge of the practice and I've already made a poor start by being late, so don't want to transgress any further! He has the look of a man who doesn't suffer fools gladly.'

'Surely he will make allowances for you being a single mother,' Betty protested.

'I suppose he might if he knew, but we only met last night. He doesn't yet know I have a child, and when he does I won't be expecting any favours. It wouldn't be fair to the rest of the staff.'

When she was ready to go, Betty walked to the bottom of the garden path with her. Wistfully she said, 'Under any other circumstances, Frank would have been holding forth about trees this morning—they're his favourite subject—but not any more. I used to weary of it sometimes, but now I'd give anything to hear about the oaks and the elms and the sycamores.'

'I'm sure that you will be hearing about them again soon, Betty,' Phoebe told her consolingly. As she left, she said reassuringly, 'I'll call again tomorrow and for as long as it takes for Frank to be completely confident when injecting the insulin.'

There was another new patient on her list of calls, and as she pulled up in front of a shop across from the harbour that sold fishing tackle, it was clear that its owner had been on the lookout for her. The moment she stepped out of the car, a young blonde guy with a beard came striding out and without wasting a second said, 'I'm Jake Stephenson and the patient is my young nephew Rory. He's staying with me for a while as both his parents are in hospital after a car crash.

'Rory was hurt too, but to a lesser degree. However, he has a nasty leg wound that I've been told he mustn't put any weight on for the time being. The hospital phoned the surgery to ask for a district nurse to come and dress the wound, and keep an eye on it.'

He was leading the way back into the shop and Phoebe followed, not having been able to get a word in so far. But she was used to anxiety creating a non-stop spate of words, and had listened carefully to what he had been saying.

'Here he is,' he said, opening the door of a sitting room at the back of the shop. A young teenage boy, with a bandaged leg resting on a stool in front of him, looked up from the computer game he was playing for a moment and then went back to it.

'Switch that off for a moment, Rory,' the harassed uncle ordered, and the boy obeyed reluctantly.

'Hello, there,' Phoebe said. 'I've come to have a look at your leg, Rory.'

He nodded sullenly but didn't speak, and kneeling beside him she gently removed the dressing.

When the injury was revealed she saw that a deep gash had been stitched, most likely from when he'd first been taken to A and E after the crash. However, the skin around it over quite a large area had been scraped off and was looking sore and weepy, so she hesitated before using more of the cream he'd been given by the hospital.

'It's my dad's fault,' the youngster grumbled as he looked down at his leg. 'He always drives too fast. I hate him. Supposing I can't play footie again!'

'Shush,' she said gently. 'It would have to be much worse than this for that to happen. I'm going to ask one of the doctors from the surgery to come and look at your leg.' Signalling to Jake to go back into the shop so they could talk, she smiled at Rory reassuringly and followed his uncle as he led the way out of the room.

'If only Rory wasn't so difficult,' he said when they were out of his hearing. 'He isn't usually like this.'

'He's feeling frightened and insecure,' she told him. 'The poor boy has been involved in a car crash, which must have been terrifying. Even though from the sound of it his parents were the ones most seriously hurt, all he can see at the moment is what it did to him.'

She was reaching for her mobile phone. 'I'm going to see if Dr Fenchurch is back from his rounds. I need a second opinion before I treat the leg again with the same procedure as before.'

'I'm afraid Leo isn't here,' Millie on Reception told her when she answered the phone. 'His car broke down as he was leaving his last house call, and he's out there waiting for the breakdown services to show up. But Dr Balfour is here, and if you give us the address, he says he'll be right with you.'

Phoebe almost groaned out loud. Since he'd arrived back on his home ground, she'd met the abrupt man twice in the space of twenty-four hours. And each time she *hadn't* come out of it as the epitome of efficiency.

He was bound to think that she should be able to deal with this sort of problem with her eyes shut, she thought rebelliously. But Rory was an injured youngster who was frightened and hurting because of his family's careless-ness, and if he couldn't rely on his father to do the right thing by him, he could rely on her. She knew he needed a second opinion on that leg of his so grudgingly, she gave the address.

When Harry Balfour came striding into the cluttered shop premises ten minutes later, he found Phoebe drinking the coffee that a grateful Jake Stephenson had insisted on offering her, and he frowned. It didn't look much like an emergency at first glance, he thought. But she put the cup down immediately and took him into the sitting room where Rory was, and he had to change his assumption.

As soon as he saw the boy's leg, he knew that the district nurse had been right to send for a doctor.

'How long is it since they sent Rory home from the hospital?' he asked as he scrutinised the wound.

'Last night,' Jake told him.

'How long since the accident?

'A couple of days before. His parents are still in there, both with concussion, broken legs and pelvic injuries. Once they'd seen to Rory's leg, the doctors decided that he would be better out of hospital and sent him to me, his uncle, for the time being.'

So far Phoebe hadn't spoken. Harry Balfour had that effect on her, making her clam up when she should be showing him that she was no pushover. When he turned to her after he'd finished examining the leg, he found himself looking into her wide brown gaze and seeing a defiant kind of wariness there.

Yet not for long. It quickly turned to surprise when he said crisply, 'You were right to send for one of us. I'm of the opinion that Rory is allergic to the antiseptic cream they gave him at the hospital. Although it is highly recommended by most doctors, I have heard of the occasional case where the patient has had an allergic reaction to one of its components, so we will change the ointment and check the condition of the injury once again after twenty-four hours.'

He was writing out a prescription as he spoke and said to Phoebe, 'I see there's a chemist two doors away. If you would like to pop in there and get this made up, perhaps Mr. Stephenson might have another cup of coffee on offer before I depart.'

CHAPTER TWO

So HARRY BALFOUR was human after all, Phoebe thought while the chemist was making up the prescription. Not as approachable as that nice guy Jake maybe, but not quite as scary and abrupt as she'd at first thought. Although, of course, it was early days. He didn't yet know there was a teething infant just across the landing, and his reaction to that might depend on just how much he valued his sleep!

When she returned to the shop, he'd departed, leaving a message to say he'd gone back to the practice to prepare for the second surgery of the day. So once she had put the new antiseptic cream on Rory's leg and placed a clean dressing over the infected area, she bade uncle and nephew goodbye, promising to return the next day to check on the effects of the new cream, and proceeded to the next housebound patient on her list.

She was back at the surgery by half past three. After updating her patients' records, Phoebe was about to depart just after four when Harry came out of his consulting room. Observing that she was dressed for going out into the cold January day once more, he asked, 'Have you had another callout?'

She smiled weakly. 'Er, no. I finish at four. Ethan agreed that I could.'

'I see,' he commented. 'And you didn't think fit to inform me of an arrangement you'd made with my predecessor?'

'It is in my records, Dr Balfour.'

'Maybe, but I only arrived back in Bluebell Cove late last night. Since I presented myself here in the surgery at a very early hour this morning, there have been many things I needed to get to know. As you might imagine, checking staff records is low on my list of priorities at the moment.'

'I'm sorry. It was remiss of me not to mention it,' she said, uncomfortable in the knowledge that he hadn't the slightest idea why she was allowed to finish early, and probably wasn't going to be over the moon when he found out.

Ethan had agreed to her finishing at four each day when she'd started work at the end of her maternity leave, and she'd been most grateful—it had meant she'd been able to collect Marcus from the nursery earlier than she'd expected. The normal finishing time for surgery staff was six-thirty, so the early finish gave her an extra two and a half hours each weekday evening with her baby. It had meant less pay but time with Marcus came first.

'So you'd better be off, then, hadn't you, if that's the arrangement?' Harry said into the middle of the awkward moment. 'We'll have a chat regarding your hours when I've had the chance to settle in properly.'

She nodded and went hurrying off. Watching her go, he wondered what it was about her that brought out the worst in him.

Was it because she was so strangely beautiful...and alive?

When Phoebe arrived at the nursery the report on Marcus was that he'd been a little fretful but otherwise fine. She breathed a sigh of relief. There was no indication that the tooth that was bothering him had come through but at least, from what Beth had said, he hadn't been crying all day.

Teething, walking, talking...they were all natural processes in the normal growth of a child, she thought, but could still prove to be times of anxiety for the parent until they had been safely achieved.

From half past six onwards, after the surgery had closed, Phoebe was listening for the footsteps on the stairs, but all was silent. She wondered if Harry was still down there catching up with more information regarding the running of the surgery, or if he had gone out somewhere.

Marcus had been asleep for hours and she was about to slide under the covers herself when she heard him come upstairs. It was gone ten o'clock, and Phoebe felt herself relaxing. They may not have had the best of introductions, the single mother and the abrupt widower, but it was good to feel that she wasn't on her own above the sprawling surgery complex.

* * *

Barbara Balfour had rung Harry late that morning to pass on a word of welcome, and to enquire if everything had been in order both below and above when he'd arrived the night before.

'Yes,' he'd told her, 'everything is fine.'

'So will you come and dine with us tonight, Harry?' she'd said. 'We are both so pleased to have you back here in Bluebell Cove. It seems a long time since you and Jenna used to take your surfboards down to the beach for hours on end.'

'That's because it *is* a long time, Aunt Barbara,' he'd said with one of his rare smiles. 'It seems strange to think of Jenna married with a baby.'

'Strange or not, it is so,' he'd been assured. 'Her husband Lucas is a cardiac surgeon. I'm one of his patients, as a matter of fact. Our son-in-law is also a great friend of Ethan. He and Francine are godparents to our little Lily.'

'It all sounds very happy and cosy.' he'd said lightly, relieved that she hadn't been able to witness the envy in his expression.

Nonetheless, he'd accepted Barbara's invitation. Having been warned by Ethan about the physical deterioration of his hostess, he had concealed his dismay when he saw her, while at the same time taking note that the razor-sharp mind was still very much in evidence.

After a pleasant evening with his relations, he'd left, promising Barbara that he would keep her informed about what was going on at the practice. At the moment of departure he'd paused and asked, 'Did you know that the other apartment is occupied, Aunt Barbara?'

Her expression had said she hadn't known and her husband Keith said, 'It will be an arrangement that Ethan will have agreed to before he left—probably a member of the staff.'

'That's correct,' Harry had told him. 'Her name is Phoebe Howard, she's the district nurse.'

The retired doctor had shaken her head. 'Although I take a great interest in the practice, I'm afraid I don't know every member of staff, Harry. She must be someone new.'

'Yes, I suppose that could be it,' he'd agreed, and after saying his farewells had disappeared into the winter night.

And now he was back at the apartment and wondering if history would repeat itself, if the door opposite would be opened a crack to observe him. But it remained closed and there was silence all around, which was how he preferred it to be, wasn't it?

It was two o'clock in the morning and there was silence no longer. He'd been awakened by a strange sound and was lying wide eyed against the pillows, trying to identify it. It wasn't a cat yowling out on the tiles, he told himself, or someone who'd had too much to drink breaking into song as they went past the surgery building.

He sat up suddenly. It was the loud cry of a baby that was shattering the peace and he was out of bed in a flash, quickly throwing on a robe.

The door opposite was still closed when he went out onto the landing but he had no doubt about where the cry was coming from. Phoebe had a baby in there and from the noise issuing forth, it was not a happy one. The doctor in him simply couldn't not check if everything was all right.

The crying stopped for a moment and he knocked on the door, but it still remained closed. In case the district nurse had a husband or partner with her who might be bristling at the invasion of their privacy, he called, 'I've no wish to intrude but can I help?'

There was no response and he was in the process of knocking again when the door opened suddenly and he almost fell on top of Phoebe. The baby she was holding observed him with tear-drenched brown eyes as she said apologetically, 'I'm sorry we've disturbed you, Dr Balfour. I'm afraid that Marcus is teething.'

He glanced around the room and still poised on the threshold asked, 'Are you living alone up here with a young baby?'

Phoebe hesitated and as if on cue the infant in her arms began to cry again. She stepped back reluctantly to let him in and said, 'Yes, I'm afraid there are just the two of us. If you want to help, could you possibly hold Marcus for a moment while I make him a bottle? It usually soothes him back to sleep. And, Dr Balfour, the reason I didn't tell you I had a baby was exactly because of nights like this. I didn't want us to disturb your privacy, but I should have known better.'

Harry had stepped inside and was observing her doubtfully as she held out the baby for him to take from her. She smiled and told him, 'He won't bite you. He's only been protesting because he's teething. Look, he's smiling now.' He looked down at the small warm body that he was now holding close to his. Sure enough, there was a little smile coming in his direction from the child with the same pale skin and wide brown gaze as his mother.

She was moving towards the kitchen to make the bottle, and Harry said in a low voice, 'Do I take it that his father isn't around?'

'Yes,' she said quietly, not looking at him. 'We're divorced.'

He nodded, and looking down at the child in his arms said wryly, 'And this is the reason why you finish early? Why on earth didn't you tell me that?'

'Yes, Marcus is the reason,' she said steadily. 'I take him to a nursery in the village before I start at the surgery on weekdays and have to pick him up at four o'clock. I suppose one of the reasons for me not telling you was because I don't want anyone seeing me as disadvantaged. I chose the kind of life I'm living and have no regrets. It was Ethan's suggestion that I finish early and I was hardly going to refuse when it gave me some extra time with my son.'

'So how long have you lived here?'

'Only since New Year. My maternity leave was up at the end of December. I'd lived with my sister and brother-in-law before that,' and with a tired smile. 'So now you have the story of my life.'

'Not entirely, I would imagine,' he said dryly. He looked down at Marcus who was getting ready for another weeping bout. 'If that bottle is ready, now might be the moment to produce it.' With a feeling that he was out of his depth and had served his purpose, he said, 'If you're sure he's going to settle, I'll leave you to it.'

'Yes, we'll be fine,' she said hurriedly. 'I feel that I've been taking advantage of your good nature, Dr Balfour.'

'I haven't got a good nature to take advantage of,' he informed her shortly and then pausing in the doorway, amazed himself by saying, 'Before I go, why don't *I* make *you* a warm drink? Coffee maybe?'

'Er, yes, please, that would be lovely, and do make one for yourself,' Phoebe said meekly, wanting to pinch herself to make sure she wasn't dreaming. She couldn't remember what it felt like to have someone do something for her, and of all people it was the unpredictable new head of the practice who was waiting on her in the middle of the night.

Marcus had been fed and changed, and was now sleeping peacefully in his cot. On the point of finally going back to his own apartment, Harry said, 'Just one thing— if ever you need any help like tonight, feel free to call on me.

'I would rather you did that than me having to lie there imagining you struggling on your own. And by the way, Nurse Howard, why is this place so much less attractive than mine?'

'I'm not sure,' she told him, 'but it isn't going to be like this for long! And I will only ever disturb you if it's an emergency—when we move house we can't choose our neighbours, can we? They come as part of the package.'

Harry wondered if that was in the form of an apology, or letting him know that she wasn't all that keen on having him living so close.

But if she'd been expecting a reply, there was none forthcoming and as tiredness took hold of her, she wished him goodnight and bolted the door behind him.

When she went back to bed exhaustion was there, but not sleep. Her mind kept going over what had turned out to be the strangest of days. It has been full of highs and lows between Harry Balfour and herself, then had ended with him knocking on her door and offering to help with Marcus. She'd been so tired and frayed at the edges she'd welcomed him with open arms and thrust her little one at him.

Yet there was no way she was going to take him up on his offer by using him as a standby in times of stress. The odds were that he wouldn't have taken the apartment across the landing if he'd known that his neighbours were going to be a single mother and her baby.

Despite his offer of help, he hadn't exactly seemed very comfortable around Marcus. Lucy, the elderly practice nurse, had told her on the day he had been due to arrive that he hadn't any family to bring with him, which maybe explained his reluctance to hold Marcus and his eagerness to be off once he had been satisfied that calm had been restored.

Yet he'd lingered long enough to make her the hot drink she'd been gasping for, and had made one for himself, as she'd suggested. But those had been things unconnected with her child... A last thought struck as her eyelids began to droop. Maybe his reaction on discovering there was a baby living only feet away wasn't all that strange, as it clearly wouldn't be every man's idea of heaven.

Across the landing Harry's thoughts were moving along different channels. Seated in a chair by the window, looking out bleakly at a starlit winter sky, he was remembering a time long ago when a baby precious to him and his parents had been lost, and how nothing had ever been the same afterwards.

Only small himself, he'd been left lonely and unloved while they'd tried to cope with their grief by spending all their time in their business, running stables in Bluebell Cove. Ever since, he'd been reluctant to take on the responsibility of bringing a child into a world where nothing was certain and loss could bring with it such pain and loneliness.

So family life wasn't something he was familiar with due to his childhood. Marriage to a woman who had been in no hurry to start a family had also left his wariness of it unchanged.

Yet Phoebe across the landing had opted for it without the support of a husband or partner and seemed content, so which of them had the right idea?

Breakfast and getting Marcus to the nursery went smoothly the next morning, and Phoebe was at the surgery in good time, although with an uncomfortable feeling inside whenever she thought about her nocturnal meeting with Harry.

She shuddered to think what she must have looked like in a crumpled cotton nightdress with an old robe over it and her hair all over the place, yet it didn't really matter. He'd been in her apartment for just one thing and there'd been nothing sensual about it. He'd come to assist in the hope of bringing back the peace that had prevailed before Marcus had begun his tantrum, and she'd do well to remember that!

Leo Fenchurch, the other doctor in the practice, had been out on an early call and appeared while she was making the usual big pot of tea for the staff before the day commenced. He brought a blast of cold air in with him and while warming his hands around a mug of the welcoming brew he said, 'So, what do you think of the new guy, Phoebe?'

He was a fair-haired six-footer with a charm that appealed to most women, but not to her she thought. He was an excellent doctor but a bit lightweight for her to succumb to his charms.

'I'm not sure,' she said in answer to his question. 'I feel that he isn't going to be an easy person to get to know, that he is very much his own man. Yet I'm sure he will be good for the practice, even if he can be somewhat unpredictable on occasion.' *And of that I have on-the-spot experience*, she thought.

'But, Leo, we have to remember that Harry has lost his wife in tragic circumstances. I'm not sure how, but it was an accident of some kind, and for a marriage to end like that must have been horrendous.

'Mine fell apart because of a huge divide in our priorities, but we at least we had a choice, not like Harry.'

'Wow!' he exclaimed. 'That summing-up comes after him having spent just a short time among us? You must have seen more of him than we have.'

She wasn't going to enlighten him on that and almost dropped the mug she was holding when Harry's voice said from behind her in the passage, 'Is there any tea on offer, Nurse Howard?'

As she reached for the teapot, Phoebe was praying that he hadn't heard her discussing him with Leo. It would be just too embarrassing if he had, but his expression was serene enough, and once she'd poured him the tea, he returned to his room without further comment. As the rest of the staff were appearing in varying degrees of haste for their early brew, she tried to put the incident out of her mind.

She wouldn't have been able to if she'd seen Harry's expression as he sat gazing into space behind his desk with the tea untouched. It would seem that little Baby Bunting's mother had him well and truly catalogued, he thought dryly.

Thankfully his visit to her apartment in the middle of the night hadn't been mentioned—it would have gone around the surgery like wildfire! Noting that it was almost time for the day to start, he went out into Reception to have a word with Phoebe before she left.

She was halfway through the main door when he called her back. He saw her shoulders stiffen and almost smiled. What did she think he wanted her for, to tell her that he'd heard what she'd said to Leo?

'Did you manage to get some sleep after I left?' he asked in a low voice.

'Er...yes,' she replied, looking around her quickly to make sure no one was near enough to jump to any wrong conclusions. 'Marcus was fine this morning. It seems as if the tooth might have come through.'

He was smiling and she thought how different he looked when he did, but a second later he was the man in charge as he said, 'You've got young Rory down for a visit, I hope.'

'He's top of my list, Dr Balfour,' she said stiffly. 'If I am still concerned about his leg I will be asking for your presence or that of Dr Fenchurch.'

'Good,' he said briskly, as if he hadn't picked up on the drop in temperature. 'Hope you have a good day after a not-so-good night. I see that the waiting room is filling up so must go.' And off he went, wishing that he hadn't come over as quite so bossy with Phoebe. He wouldn't be surprised if she had him labelled as a control freak!

Conversely, as Phoebe drove the short distance to the fishing-tackle shop she was thinking that the man was only doing his job. So why had she let him get to her like that? He'd been kind and supportive in the middle of the night, even though she could tell that he wasn't used to babies. It was ungrateful of her to take offence at what, to Harry, would just be part of the job.

The infection around the sutures on Rory's leg had improved overnight, and with it the boy's mood. As she changed the dressing, with his uncle looking on anxiously, Phoebe told him, 'Make sure that he takes all the antibiotics he was given when he left the hospital, Jake.

That and the different kind of ointment we're using now should do the trick.'

He breathed a sigh of relief. 'The last thing I would want to tell my sister is that her boy isn't well, so that's good news, Nurse.'

'How are his parents progressing?' she questioned.

'Not bad, but they have a way to go yet before Hunter's Hill will be ready to send them home. So it's just the two of us for a while, isn't it, Rory?' he said to his nephew, who was still in his pyjamas.

'Yes, Uncle Jake,' he chirped. 'And don't forget, as soon as my leg is all right, we're going out in your boat.'

'There's no chance of me forgetting,' was the teasing reply. 'You won't let me!'

Jake turned to Phoebe. 'How about a coffee before you go, Nurse?'

She shook her head. 'No, thanks just the same, I've got a rather long list of patients to see and must be on my way.'

He was smiling. 'If I can't make you a drink, how about letting me take you for a sail when this young fellow is well enough to come along?'

'I don't think so,' she told him gently. 'You wouldn't want a young baby on the boat.'

'So you're married,' he said disappointedly.

'No. I'm a single mother,' she explained, and could tell from his expression that a possible relationship had just gone down the drain. Yet who could blame him? She couldn't help but think it would take a lot for a man to be willing to fill the gap of a father in the life of another man's child, however nice he was.

She'd also only met Jake for the first time the day before. It would take longer than that for her to want to know him better or introduce him to her son. But as a vision of Harry Balfour awkwardly holding Marcus safe and secure in his arms came to mind, she thought that she'd only known *him* for a similar length of time, yet she would trust him with her child.

When she arrived at her next call, pulling up in front of the biggest farmhouse in the area, Phoebe was amazed to see the man who had been in her thoughts getting out of the brand-new red convertible he'd had delivered to the surgery that morning. The question was immediately there in her mind—was he checking up on her?

It seemed that he wasn't. Harry was already ringing the bell and called across to her, 'Well timed. We have an emergency.'

She was out of her car in a flash and hurried to the door, wondering what could be wrong at Wheatlands Farm.

She visited the place every week to put a fresh dressing on a varicose ulcer that was plaguing old George Enderby, the patriarch of the family. As far as she was aware, that was the only thing wrong with the cheerful old guy, but if what Harry was saying was correct...

'Is it George that you're here about?' she asked as footsteps pounded towards them from inside the house.

He shook his head. 'No. A call came through to the

surgery to say his daughter-in-law Pamela had fallen downstairs early this morning and almost knocked herself senseless with a crack to her head. She was soon back working on the farm, until a few minutes ago when suddenly she didn't seem to know where she was.'

The door was being wrenched open as he spoke and George's son Ian was there, his face taut with anxiety.

'Thanks for coming so quickly, Harry,' he said urgently. 'I wasn't expecting us to be renewing our acquaintance so soon. Pamela is upstairs resting with a huge bump on her head and isn't very coherent.'

'So let's have a look, then,' he said briskly, adding to Phoebe, 'Come along, Nurse, you can see to your patient when we've sorted Mrs Enderby out.'

The swelling on Pamela Enderby's head was huge and soft to the touch and her eyes weren't functioning properly. Neither was her mind as Harry gently tried to get her to answer a few simple questions rationally.

Turning to her husband, he said in a low voice, 'There is almost certainly bleeding inside the skull.' He turned to Phoebe. 'Phone for an ambulance, Nurse, and stress the urgency, while I check the patient's heartbeat and pulse.'

She was about to confirm that the emergency services were hastening on their way when he said tightly, 'Pamela's gone into a coma.' He placed his stethoscope against her chest. 'There's no heartbeat! Get ready to resuscitate!'

Together they worked on the patient until the ambulance arrived and paramedics stepped in with a defibrillator and then a faint rising and falling of the injured woman's chest indicated that she was back with them.

Her husband had watched their efforts with tears streaming down his face and as the ambulance was leaving, with him by her side and a paramedic monitoring her heartbeat, he said raggedly, 'Whatever the outcome of this, I will never forget what the two of you did back there.'

Before they could reply, he was gone with flashing lights and sirens wailing to warn other road users that the vehicle was carrying someone seriously ill or injured.

'That was good teamwork, Phoebe,' Harry said with one of his rare smiles when it had disappeared from sight.

It registered that he'd actually said her name, but there was no time for further thought as elderly George, the patient she'd originally come to see, appeared beside them looking distraught and decidedly unsteady on his feet.

'I've kept out of the way,' he said breathing heavily. 'At my age I'm no good in a crisis. So what's the verdict, Harry?'

'Not too good at this moment, George,' the doctor told him gently. 'They will have to operate to control a brain haemorrhage. But she is still with us, so why don't you let me make you a cup of tea while Nurse Howard changes the dressing on your leg? Or would you prefer a brandy under the circumstances?'

'Yes, I would,' he replied. 'My heart isn't too good and the last thing my son needs is me cracking up at a time like this.' He was gazing out at the immaculate farm buildings and the land that belonged to them stretching as far as the eye could see. 'All of this is great, Harry,' he said brokenly, 'but it means nothing when a life is at stake.'

Harry nodded understandingly. The Enderbys were obviously very wealthy, but the old guy had his priorities right.

'Can I leave you to see to George?' he asked Phoebe. 'I left patients waiting to see me when I dashed over here.'

'Yes, of course,' she told him, adding as he turned to go, 'It was great working with you.'

The reluctant smile was back and she thought if he kept it up, he might actually manage a laugh one day. To her amazement he replied, 'It was good to have you assisting me, Nurse Howard.' And then he was gone to face the sighs and fidgets of those awaiting his presence in the surgery.

Having dealt with George's dressing and left him in the charge of the farm's housekeeper, Phoebe continued her home visits. When she arrived back at the surgery late in the afternoon, keen to see if the rapport between herself and Harry was still there or just a momentary thing, she found him closeted with one patient after another and it was still so when she left to pick Marcus up at the nursery.

With the tooth now through, he was back to his usual state of contentment, greeting her with a big smile and a happy gurgle, and in that moment the other part of her life took over. He was all she had, and if that was how it was always going to be, she wasn't going to complain. She'd made her choice when she split up with Darren and had no regrets about *that*.

CHAPTER THREE

WHILE Phoebe was feeding and bathing Marcus before settling him down for sleep, it was the same as the night before—she was listening for footsteps on the stairs to let her know that Harry's day at the practice was also over. This time she didn't have long to wait.

She heard him come up just as her baby's eyelids were closing, his dark lashes sweeping downwards and his small chest rising and falling steadily. Ridiculously, this time she *wanted* Harry to knock on her door so that she could see if the time they'd spent together with Pamela Enderby had really been as satisfying for him as it had been for her. His unexpected presence last night had also shown her another side to him that she wanted to see again.

Disappointed when she heard his door close behind him, she began to clear up after bathtime and was debating whether to get out the paint cans and brushes once more when the sound she'd been hoping for finally came.

While he'd been putting a ready meal in the oven to heat up, Harry had been debating whether it would be pushing it too far if he called on Phoebe again. Yet he felt he had to. It was going to be a frosty night and while her apartment had been warm enough the night before, it definitely was not as warm as his, and there was a spare mobile heater in his hall that he wanted to give her just in case. He wouldn't be able to settle if he hadn't offered it to her on such a cold night.

The last thing he'd expected when he'd told Ethan he'd like to move into one of the apartments had been the presence of a young single mother and child only a few feet away. The solitude that he'd sought wasn't materialising, but for some reason he didn't mind as much as he'd anticipated. As he crossed the landing with the heater, to his enormous surprise he even found himself hoping that he might get a glimpse of the smallest of the other apartment's occupants.

When Phoebe opened the door to him she was smiling, and it hit him again how unusually beautiful she was, with her clear, pale skin and wide hazel gaze that was observing him questioningly.

'Come in,' she said, stepping back while he humped the heavy appliance into her hall. As he straightened up to face her, she asked, 'What is that?'

'It's a heater,' he said in the brisk manner he used when not sure of himself. 'It is going to be a very cold night and I thought it might be welcome.'

'Where has it come from?'

'My place. I don't need it as my heating is excellent, and I noticed last night that yours is not so good. It just needs to be plugged into the electricity. So can I leave it with you?'

'Yes,' she said slowly, completely taken aback that her new boss should take the trouble to make sure that she and Marcus were warm enough on a bitter winter night. There was a lump in her throat and for an awful moment she felt she was going to weep in front of him, but she fought back the tears.

He wasn't to know that his small act of kindness had broken through the armour of self-sufficiency that she wore to protect herself from any more of the hurts that life might have in store for her.

'So where do you want it?' he was asking, observing her curiously.

'Here in the hall, I think,' she told him, desperately scrabbling for some composure. 'When I go to bed I'll leave all the doors open so that the extra heat can circulate.' Hoping that her surprise wasn't making her appear short on gratitude, she asked, 'Can I offer you a drink while you're here Dr Balfour? A glass of wine, perhaps, or something hot?'

'A glass of wine would be nice,' he said smoothly, much preferring a beer but feeling that it wouldn't be quite as suitable to the occasion. 'But I can't stay long. I have a meal in the oven.'

She nodded understandingly as she produced a bottle of white from the fridge, and as she was pouring it asked, 'Have we had any news on Pamela Enderby?'

'Yes,' he said. 'I rang the farm just before I came up and George said that she's in Theatre, having a huge haematoma drained. So far she's coping with it, but it is a serious situation and sadly I feel she will be lucky to come through it.'

Silence fell between them as they drank the wine, both lost in their own thoughts as they contemplated the strain that the Enderby family would be under tonight. In what seemed like no time at all he was getting to his feet and saying, 'I must go, Phoebe. And by the way, when we're not in the surgery it's Harry, OK?'

'Yes,' she said. 'I'll remember. And thanks again for the loan of the heater…er…Harry.'

Her obvious discomfort broke through the sadder thoughts about Pamela, and Harry found himself actually laughing. 'It will become easier as you keep saying it,' he promised. Then, on the point of leaving, he casually asked, 'Is Baby Bunting asleep?'

It was her turn to laugh. 'Need you ask?' she said, and added, amazing herself, 'Do you want to see for yourself?'

'Er…yes,' he replied hesitantly, 'just as long as you don't think it will disturb him.' Phoebe mentally kicked herself. Clearly he didn't want a repetition of last night, or maybe just a repetition of Marcus in general.

'No. Marcus never wakes up during the first few hours after going to sleep,' she informed him stiffly. 'It's in the middle of the night when he sometimes makes his presence felt, and that's only when he's teething. But the tooth that was bothering him is through now, so you should be spared any further nightly disturbances for a while.'

'What a beautiful child,' he said slowly as he turned away from the cherub in the cot, then almost as if he was speaking to himself, 'But they come with a lifetime's responsibility of caring, don't they? Always there is the fear in the mind of the loving parent that they might lose their child to illness or accident.'

Phoebe was observing him in surprise, shocked by his words and the desolation with which he'd uttered them. 'That's a rather downbeat way of looking at family life, isn't it?' she exclaimed. 'Surely you can't be speaking from experience?'

'No, of course not,' he said flatly. 'I was just expressing a point of view that I'm sure you don't agree with.'

His bitterness sparked off Phoebe's anger. 'You're right. I don't. There are always risks in loving someone, whoever it might be. It can end in pain and despair, or it can be the most joyful thing in one's life, giving it a magical sense of purpose. And that is exactly what Marcus has given me.'

She gentled her tone, wondering how to explain to him that love was always worth the risk, no matter how scarred he felt by his past. 'I imagine that you are still hurting at the loss of your wife, Harry, and I can't tell you how sorry I was to hear about her death. But while you may think it's easy for me to talk, I really do believe what I've just said, and I'm sad for you that you don't feel the same.'

'Maybe we could discuss it another time.' he said abruptly. 'I'd better go. I can smell my meal burning from here. Goodnight, Phoebe.' And before she could reply he'd gone.

As he ate his solitary meal Harry was thinking that the woman across the landing must think him pathetic, hovering around her like Social Services and burbling on about the downside of family life.

His marriage to Cassie had been good in parts, but something of a roller-coaster ride. She'd been an extrovert, a risk-taker who'd thrived on excitement. Motherhood had never been high on her agenda, just as fatherhood had been low on his.

Maybe he should make it clear to Phoebe that his concern on her behalf was simply neighbourly, that he would have done the same for anyone he felt the heater would benefit. The fact that she had a child in her not-so-warm apartment had just made it seem the sensible thing to do.

But he'd come back to Bluebell Cove like a wounded animal to its lair, not to fraternise with the locals, and a staff member at that. So maybe he should play it cool with Phoebe from now on, and make sure he avoided bringing up such topics as love and family, which they clearly had wildly different opinions about.

Harry was nice under that brusque exterior, Phoebe thought as she felt the boost that the heater was giving to her very average central heating system. And her heart bled for the grief he'd suffered, and was clearly still struggling with.

Suddenly, instead of wishing that the other apartment was still unoccupied, she felt she was going to enjoy having Harry for a neighbour, but there was no way she would want him to think she saw him as anything other than that.

The responsibility of becoming a single mother had

been frightening while she'd been carrying Marcus and even more so during the first weeks after his birth. But with the help of Katie and Rob, who had been fantastic, and her own determination not to falter in the life she had chosen for herself, she was coping.

Every time she looked at the baby asleep in the next room, she knew she'd done the right thing. If it had been up to Darren, their child wouldn't have existed. The mere thought of that always brought her up with a jolt, especially when she was tired or discouraged at the end of a long day faced with a never-ending list of chores to do once Marcus was asleep.

But she wasn't so wrapped up in her restricted 'mother and child only' existence that she didn't recognise an attractive man when she saw one, and Harry was certainly that!

When she stepped onto the landing the next morning with Marcus in her arms, his door opened simultaneously and with a friendly smile she said, 'We stayed beautifully warm through the night, Harry. Thank you so much.'

There was no answering smile coming her way and she felt the colour rise beneath the smooth pale skin of her face as he said flatly, 'It was there, hanging about doing nothing, so don't feel indebted.'

Chastened, she increased her hold on Marcus and prepared to descend the stairs. In the same flat tone he said, 'Watch your step.'

She'd thought he might offer to carry Marcus down for her, or have a pleasant reply to her greeting, but instead it felt as if she'd entered some sort of cold zone and she didn't know why.

Unaware of his musings of the night before, she thought bleakly that it must be a double-edged warning—to watch her step on the stairs, and at the same time watch her step in her dealings with him, especially if she thought that the offer of the heater the night before had been an invitation to be all chummy. Was Sir Galahad going to turn out to be a Dr-Jekyll–Mr-Hyde sort of person just when she was warming to him?

Automatically reacting to his remote manner she said coolly, 'I've managed to do that so far without mishap,' and began to descend the steep staircase carefully with Marcus gazing around, wide eyed.

Once at the bottom she didn't linger for further downbeat comments. As soon as Marcus was strapped into her car's baby seat, she drove the short distance to the nursery. Handing him over reluctantly to the excellent Beth, she then returned to the surgery complex to sort out her calls for the day.

As usual, she found the staff gathered in the kitchen with their mugs of tea, except for Harry who apparently had taken his into his consulting room. Crossly, she hoped he would stay there until she'd set off on her rounds.

He did, and as she drove along the coast road to the shop by the harbour to check on Rory's injured leg once again, she couldn't help thinking how typical it was. The first man she'd had any social contact with in ages had the kind of looks and the background that appealed to her, but clearly he also had a dual personality!

He'd given her the heater of his own free will. It wasn't as if she'd asked him for it. She wanted favours from no one, was her own woman, and intended to stay that way. Nevertheless, it had given her a nice feeling inside to know that he'd tuned into her needs twice in two days.

So hang onto the memory of it, she warned herself. It isn't going to happen again, and if by some strange chance it should, don't go all gooey-eyed, just be pleasant but aloof.

She had to pass a side turning to the Enderbys' farm on her way to the harbour and stopped off to enquire how Pamela was progressing.

George was there by himself again and informed her that his daughter-in-law had come through the surgery, and had been taken to the high-dependency unit.

'It was a miracle the way you and Harry Balfour saved her life,' the old man said huskily. 'We are fortunate to have him with us again as I'm told that he was doing greater things in Australia than running a village practice.

'But his Aunt Barbara is a great one for getting people to do what she wants and it was she that persuaded him to come home. Though I don't think he needed much coaxing after what happened to him out there. That Cassie was a fiery madam, but it seems as if she took on more than she could handle when she tried to overtake a big truck without warning.

'It's a pity he didn't come back to us in the spring when the bluebells out in their glory, the skies so blue and the sea a joy to behold, instead of on a grey day in January.'

'It won't be long before that happens,' she consoled. 'This month is almost out, then February is the shortest one on the calendar, and when it is gone, Easter won't be far away.' Feeling that she needed to be on her way, and reeling slightly from discovering the awful manner in which Harry's wife had died, she said goodbye to George and drove off in the direction of the fishing-tackle shop.

Rory's leg was definitely on the mend and when she'd changed the dressing once more, Jake said, 'We're going to see his Mum and Dad this afternoon. Knowing that the leg is clear of the infection will be one thing less for them to worry about, thanks to you, Nurse.'

'I'm just doing my job.' she told him as she prepared to leave uncle and nephew to their own devices. Then, given his reaction of the previous day to discovering she was a single mum, she was surprised when Jake said, 'We're going out in the boat on Saturday and the invitation is still there if you can manage to come.'

'What sort is it?' she asked warily. 'Has it got a cabin?'

'Yes, of course,' was the reply. 'It's not the *Queen Mary* but she's a nice little craft.'

'I'll think about it,' she told him to avoid refusing outright. Sailing on the open sea in the middle of winter with Marcus was not something she was going to con-template. Maybe if the invitation was still there in the spring, but not now. Although, if she was honest, she couldn't see herself ever considering going sailing with

Jake—she just wasn't that interested in spending more time with him, however nice he was.

As the day took its course, the man on her mind was not the amiable Jake. It was the cool reception she'd received earlier from a more mature member of the opposite sex that kept intruding into her thoughts.

Had he thought when she'd wished him a friendly good morning up on the landing that his concern on the night before had encouraged her to be over-familiar? She shuddered at the thought. From now on she would be so distant he might want his heater back to cope with the drop in temperature.

Harry had watched her from the window of his consulting room as she'd driven off, clearly offended, and told himself he was crazy. He was the one who'd crossed the divide between stranger and acquaintance. It hadn't been Phoebe who'd made the gestures that he was now halfway to regretting, but neither did he have to upset her by trying to re-establish a sense of distance between them.

Then he reminded himself that he wouldn't have been able to sleep easily with a crying baby so close, and it had been the same with the heater. It was essential that in January's chill mother and child should be warm. Perhaps he should simply embrace being neighbourly?

Sighing, he called in his first patient and let the day ahead take hold of him. Maybe when they were both in their apartments tonight, he would get the chance to make amends. Until then the surgery was full of the coughs and sneezes that spread diseases, along with a few patients with more serious illnesses to keep him on his toes.

One of them was in charge of the information centre on the coast road just above the beach. She'd recently had shingles, which hadn't all come to the surface as they should have. Now the stabbing pains of the illness had flared up again quite seriously and she was in a lot of discomfort.

'Shingles, or herpes zoster, is an odd illness,' he told her. 'For some people it's straightforward. The red rash appears, usually on the upper half of the body, then turns to blisters, and because it is connected with the nerve ends it can be very painful, but once the blisters have gone it usually settles down.

'Though not always. For some the pain is there in the background for a long time, especially as in your case, where the rash didn't all come out. Sometimes other medication that the patient is taking can bring back the pain in those areas. I see that you've recently been prescribed a steroid-based inhaler for asthma. It is possible that the steroids could be the reason for the return of the pain.

'So we will try taking you off that kind of inhaler and put you on one that doesn't contain them. It won't be as effective with regard to the asthma, I'm afraid, so I'll need to keep a close eye on you, but let's see if no longer being involved with steroids reduces the pain.'

When he'd made out the prescription and she was ready to go, the patient asked, 'How are you enjoying being back in Bluebell Cove, Dr Balfour?'

'It's good,' he told her, realising it was the truth. 'It feels strange, of course. I've been gone five years, but there's a sort of agelessness about this place that calms the spirit if you let it.'

When Phoebe arrived back at the practice he was still seeing patients from the late surgery and once she'd updated the notes of those she'd visited, she drove to the nursery to collect Marcus.

He greeted her as he usually did with a wide smile and arms outstretched, and what Harry had said about starting a family came back to her. When it came to the crunch she hadn't thought twice about it, but it was a fact that she was all her little one had to care for him. There was no one else in his life for him to love and if anything happened to her... Banishing the upsetting train of thought from her mind, she was cross with Harry for putting it in her head in the first place.

As she carried Marcus up to the apartments Phoebe was grateful that they had their own entrance. It meant that her comings and goings were not on view to surgery staff—most especially her unpredictable neighbour.

After being given the cold shoulder that morning, she was in no rush to meet him again. In a moment of rebellion she decided that once Marcus was tucked up for the night, she was going to give the decorating a miss and spend a quiet evening in front of the television with a bottle of wine and a box of chocolate. And she just might get dressed up for it as well, even though there would only be herself to see the result!

* * *

When surgery was over Harry didn't go straight up to the apartment. He wanted to make things right with his neighbour, but not to go butting in while she and the baby were having their evening meal or while she was bathing him.

So, not yet having tried the culinary delights on offer in Bluebell Cove, he went for a meal in a restaurant on the coast road where the food was wholesome and delicious and included some of his favourite Devonshire dishes.

When he'd finished what he felt was the best meal he'd had in months, he stopped off once again at Four Winds House on the headland as a follow-up to what Ethan had told him about his uncle's prostate problems.

Keith needed another check up, which would allow Harry to decide whether action was required. A quiet word to his uncle as he was leaving would be a spur to sort out an appointment at the hospital and ensure that Barbara wasn't worried by this news of her husband's health when she was already so busy struggling with her own.

He didn't know if his cousin Jenna knew about her father's problem and was going to sound her out at the first opportunity. She'd been a practice nurse at the surgery until little Lily's birth, and now her only connection with health care was as her husband's receptionist when he saw private patients at the clinic he ran from home.

The older folk were delighted to see him and Barbara's first comment was about the surgery and how was he settling in.

'Fine,' he told her. 'It's good to be back. The days are

lengthening and I'm looking forward to when it's going to be warm enough to swim in the sea.'

'Do you see much of Phoebe and young Marcus in the other apartment?' Keith asked, unknowingly bringing to mind where his last call of the day was going to be.

'We're in contact in the surgery, of course, during her comings and goings,' he replied, 'but that's it. We've met a couple of times upstairs but only briefly. We try not to disturb each other after working hours if we can.' And if that wasn't a distortion of the truth he didn't know what was!

When he was ready to go, Keith came to the door with him as he'd expected, and Harry said in a low voice, 'Ethan has passed on to me your concerns about your rising prostate count, and I feel that it is time you had another check-up at the hospital. Is it all right with you if I make an appointment?'

'Yes, of course,' was the reply, 'but I don't want Barbara to know about it. Time to tell her when, or if, there is something to tell.'

'And Jenna?'

'The same applies there. My daughter is having one of the happiest times of her life with a new husband and daughter that she adores. I don't want to be the one who bursts the bubble if I can help it.'

'She won't like it that you've kept it from her,' he warned.

'It's as I've just said, it will be time to tell when there's something that needs telling.'

The wine and the added warmth in the room were making Phoebe feel drowsy and relaxed for the first time in ages, but when she heard the tap on her door she was jolted out of it.

Surely it wasn't Harry, she thought through the warm haze that had settled on her, not after this morning. Yet he was the only other person who had a key for the entrance to the apartments.

With a half-full wine glass in her hand she glided across to the door and opened it with a sort of queenly grace. Sure enough, he was there, eyes widening in amazement at the vision before him. She was dressed in a long black skirt, a white sequined top and wearing more make-up than he'd ever seen her use before.

'Yes?' she said with the regal mode still on her. If he hadn't been so taken aback he would have laughed.

He could hear a voice in the background and thought, Oh, God! She's got company. I'm going to look a right fool.

'I just want to say I'm sorry if I was rather abrupt this morning. That's it really,' he explained in a low voice.

'Don't give it another thought,' she said smoothly, as if she hadn't been smarting for most of the day. 'Do sleep well.' As he turned to go, she shut the door and went back to what she'd been doing, which wasn't a lot with only the television for company.

So Phoebe of the pale beauty and long brown hair was not the lonely single mother he'd assumed her to be, Harry thought as he cringed from the embarrassment of the last few moments. She'd been entertaining someone all dressed up and waving a wine glass in front of him to make sure he got the message.

So what? Surely he wasn't bothered about that, was he? He was the guy who was wearing a mental badge that said, *Touch me not*. He wasn't going to start yearning after the district nurse! She was the exact opposite of what Cassie had been like, though what was wrong with that?

He poured himself a beer, watched television for a while then went to bed, but not to sleep. His ears were straining for the sound of Phoebe's visitor departing, but it never came. He finally fell asleep just as dawn was breaking.

To his surprise, she had already dropped Marcus off at the nursery and, looking poised for action, was sorting out her home visits when he came downstairs the next morning.

On observing her, his first thought was that she didn't look like someone on the morning after a night of passion. But it had definitely been a man's voice he'd heard coming from her sitting room when she'd opened the door to him and listened graciously while he'd humbled himself outside on the landing.

Whoever it was, she'd certainly dressed up for him, he thought with sudden envy. At that moment she turned, saw him observing her, and said politely, 'Good morning, Dr Balfour.'

'Good morning,' he replied heavily, and went into his consulting room, before coming out again and asking as if some unseen force was putting the words into his mouth, 'Did you have a nice evening with your friend?'

He watched her blink in surprise. 'I'm not quite sure what you mean,' she told him coolly, 'unless you're referring to last night, and you have been jumping to conclusions if you are. I spent the evening alone. What you saw when I opened the door was just me, trying to have a pleasant evening with a bottle of wine and the television.'

Harry felt his jaw go slack as what she was saying registered. Phoebe wasn't wrong about him jumping to conclusions. It was just one more instance of him interfering in her affairs. Yet there was a feeling of relief inside him as well as mortification as he admitted to himself that he hadn't wanted her to be with some other guy all dressed up and drinking wine.

He groaned. 'I am so sorry. If I promise faithfully to mind my own business in future, will you forgive me?'

She wanted to tell him she could forgive him for much more than that.

Despite their recent misunderstandings, he was still the first person who had treated her as a normal woman, with her own needs and reassurances, since she'd had Marcus. The phrase 'single mother' had a kind of stigma to it, as if she'd committed some sort of crime, but he didn't make her feel like that.

She smiled and he thought again how strangely beautiful she was. 'Of course I can forgive you,' she said softly, 'There is no reason why we can't be friends, is there, having found ourselves living in such close proximity?'

'No, none at all,' he replied steadily, as if it was going

to be easy to be just that and nothing else. Then, as Millie went to open the doors to let in the sick and suffering at half past eight, they separated, each to their own functions.

The following day was Saturday and Phoebe intended doing what she usually did at the weekend—going into town to shop. She'd rung Jake to tell him she wouldn't be going sailing with him and Rory, and he hadn't seemed too disappointed, which had been a cause for relief.

She couldn't help but compare Jake with Harry, who, though he had some odd ideas about bringing children into the world, had nevertheless been there for her in the middle of the night, ready and willing to assist her in any way that he could.

It was amazing that someone without, or even with, family ties hadn't made a play for him already. His attractions were many—tall, broad shouldered, with a direct hazel gaze and dark russet thatch of hair to complete the picture.

Yet she'd observed there was a downside to him. He could display an abrupt kind of reserve that spoke of a life she knew nothing about, a life that had contained loneliness and neglect when he'd had no one to turn to for comfort.

All right, she'd had her own pit of despair to climb out of, but from that had come Marcus and everything had suddenly seemed worthwhile. What had happened to Harry to make him so unhappy?

She wondered what his wife had been like. Obviously someone special for him to be ready to leave the

beautiful countryside and coastlines of Devon to move
to her country. Had he ever thought then that one day
he would return without her?

CHAPTER FOUR

PHOEBE was used to the noise and bustle of the town. It was like any other Saturday morning. She was wandering around the excellent outdoor market with Marcus in his baby buggy, gazing around him with interest, when she heard her name called. Turning, she saw Jake and Rory loaded down with shopping.

'I thought you were going sailing,' she said with a smile for her young patient.

'We are,' Jake told her. 'We've just come to get provisions for the weekend and are wondering who else we're going to see from the surgery.'

'Why?'

'We've just seen the doctor that you called out to look at Rory's leg.' She observed him in surprise. 'You know, the new guy.'

'You mean Dr Balfour. Where was he?' she enquired, not sure if she wanted to see Harry again so soon after their conversation the previous day.

'He was coming out of Hunter's Hill Hospital as we drove past.'

'Ah, I see.'

She didn't really, but had no wish to discuss the

comings and goings of her neighbour with Jake and Rory. Yet she was curious to know why Harry had been visiting the hospital.

But she'd come to do some food shopping and as they went on their way she gave her attention to free-range eggs, farm-cured bacon and fresh vegetables, with Marcus looking on.

That was followed by a saunter around a department store and on impulse she bought a pretty sweater and some well-cut jeans, then took Marcus for lunch in the bistro there.

It was as she was making her way back to the car park, pushing the buggy with one hand and carrying what wouldn't fit underneath it with the other, when a voice called from behind, 'Hang on a moment, Phoebe. Let me give you a lift.' And the man who never seemed to be out of her thoughts was by her side in an instant.

'Are y-you all r-right?' she stammered, overcome by nerves at his sudden proximity.

'Yes, of course. Why do you ask?' he wanted to know.

'I met up with Jake and Rory and they'd seen you coming out of Hunter's Hill.'

'Are you referring to the lad with the injured leg and that uncle of his?' he questioned.

'Er, yes.'

'So are you always on such friendly terms with your patients?'

'Not always. It's just that they wanted me to go sailing with them this weekend, but needless to say I refused. I wouldn't take Marcus on that sort of a jaunt in this kind of weather.'

'I'm glad to hear it,' he commented dryly, 'and as to why I was at Hunter's Hill, I'd come into town to shop and thought I'd pop in to see how Pamela Enderby is progressing. Apart from the fact that you and I saved her life, she and I were at school together. I *have* got a past in these parts, you know.'

'Yes, I do, which is more than I have. My past is all wrapped up in the thirst for success and a lack of interest in the things of life that really matter.'

He was observing her thoughtfully. 'And are you going to tell me about how it all went wrong some time?'

'No,' she said flatly. 'It isn't worth telling. So, can we get back to Pamela?'

He nodded. 'According to the registrar I spoke to, she should be home soon. The operation was a success. So it will be up to the neurosurgeon to decide what the hospital does as a follow-up to the nightmare that we walked into that day.

'It was strange, how we barely knew each other, yet in those desperate moments when we worked on her it was as if we were welded into one.'

She nodded. What Harry had just said described exactly how she'd felt.

There'd been an unexpected affinity and it was still there, a closeness that she was uncomfortable about. Although he seemed to be continually at her elbow, she had a feeling that he too had his doubts about it. Another odd thing was that out of all the surgery staff, apart from

Leo, who hadn't been there long, she was the only one Harry hadn't known previously.

At the time he'd left to go to Australia she'd been living in London with Darren as a new bride with not a cloud in her sky. No doubt Harry had been feeling the same, having met the woman of his dreams, but they'd both been brought down to earth since then. And now, as he strode alongside her, carrying the shopping, it felt just as right as it had when they'd resuscitated Pamela Enderby.

As the car park came into sight she put her daydreams to one side and came back to realities by commenting, 'I can't see your car and it isn't one that's easily missed.'

Beside his bright red convertible, her own small run-about felt totally insignificant, but it sufficed for what she wanted it for and that was all that mattered.

'It isn't there,' Harry explained. 'I walked here.' She observed him in surprise. 'Yes, it was a long walk, but I wanted to see some of the places again that once were so familiar. Also, I needed the exercise but now that I've had it, I wouldn't say no to a lift back to the village!'

'Yes, of course,' she agreed. 'Once Marcus is strapped in safely and I've put my shopping in the boot, we'll be off.'

'I'll see to him while you stash the shopping,' he said, and she thought that the offer was a definite improvement on the other night, when he'd held him stiffly in his arms and she'd told him laughingly that Marcus wouldn't bite.

She wasn't to know that Harry wanted to see if the feel of that small warm body against his was as satisfying and wholesome as it had been that first time. As he lifted him out of the buggy Marcus had a smile for him and Harry said, 'He's a happy little guy, isn't he, all considering?'

Phoebe was putting the shopping into the boot of the car and she raised her head sharply. 'Considering? Considering what? That he hasn't got a father?'

'Well, yes.'

'Quality is better than quantity any time. He won't ever feel lonely and lost while I'm around.' And she closed the boot with a resounding slam as if to emphasise the fierce statement..

'That I can well believe,' he said with a smile that took the edge off her irritation. He bent to fasten the harness of the car seat around the baby and then slid into the passenger seat beside her and they were off.

They were silent for most of the journey, but it was clear Phoebe hadn't forgotten what he'd said. As the village came into view, she continued their earlier conversation. 'I suppose your comments earlier were also raising the question of how happy Marcus would be if anything happened to me, and if he was left all alone in the world. That might be a fair comment but, Harry, everything we do in life is a risk. To me, a bigger risk would have been to let Marcus be saddled with a father who didn't want him. I think you might have been down a similar road to that so will understand what I mean.'

When she looked across at him his expression was sombre but he didn't say anything. She wondered if his hurt went too deep to talk about it to someone he'd only just met.

* * *

They were back at the surgery and as Harry was lifting Marcus out of the car, he suddenly said, 'Thanks for the lift, Phoebe. In return, I'll cook dinner tonight if you like.'

Oh, yes, she would 'like' was her immediate reaction to the suggestion, but like many travellers on the sea of life they both had baggage. On her part a hurtful divorce that had not been about infidelity but about rejection and selfishness, and on his a recent bereavement that so far he hadn't spoken of.

So was she going to accept the offer because attached to it was going to be some prime time with him? No, she wasn't. It would be crazy to step any further into each other's lives than they had done already.

She let him down gently. 'No, thanks just the same. I've got our meal already organised for tonight,' and with a final turn of the screw, 'I'll see you on Monday, Harry.' Ashamed that she hadn't had the nerve to tell him the truth—that the more she saw of him, the more time she wanted them to spend together—she took Marcus from him and slowly climbed the stairs to what was left of another lonely weekend.

He was pushing his luck with Phoebe, Harry thought as he followed her some seconds later. Why couldn't he have been satisfied with meeting her in the town and being near her in the car during the lift home? Oh, no, he'd wanted more, and ought to know better.

When he'd left Australia, he'd just been beginning to get over the horror of the accident that had cost Cassie her life. He'd set off for home deciding that those who stay alone are less likely to get hurt, so what was he doing now? Hanging around the first woman he'd come into close contact with like a teenage Romeo, that was what.

If he didn't back off, Phoebe was going to start feeling trapped up there with him continually butting into her life, and there was really only one answer to that. He had to do what he'd intended on coming back to Bluebell Cove—find a permanent place to live.

He had expected his house hunting to be a leisurely thing, with the apartment a base from which to view in his own good time. properties that were on offer. But then again, he hadn't expected to be living in such closeness to a single mother whose solitariness was pulling at his heart strings.

So why not start house hunting today? he thought bleakly. There wasn't anything to stop him. He was sure that Phoebe wouldn't be sorry to see him go.

The village's estate agent was open but doing little business because of the time of year, so the young guy behind the counter had all the time in the world to tell him about an impressive list of properties for sale. That would be much reduced in quantity and greatly increased in price during the summer months.

There was an attractively converted barn, a large period cottage down a wooded lane not far from the village centre, a luxurious apartment in a new complex on the coast road, and even a small manor house that he could probably afford if he pulled out all the stops, but he couldn't see himself rattling around a place like that on his own.

As the estate agent expounded upon their delights and advantages, he found he couldn't work up enthusiasm for any of them because he was seeing a flight of worn uncarpeted stairs, a landing with two old oak doors on it, and behind one of them was…what?

A mother and child that he couldn't stop thinking about, and they were making his longing for solitude go to pot. That was why the brochures of the properties displayed in front of him were not gripping his imagination.

Yet maybe if he viewed a couple of them he might become interested, and if he wasn't there would still be plenty of others to consider. So he made a lukewarm appointment to view the manor house and the converted barn on Sunday morning.

'Guess what I saw when I was out walking my dog yesterday,' Lucy, the senior practice nurse, said first thing on Monday morning, when all the staff—with the exception of Harry—were warming up in the kitchen as usual.

Phoebe had just arrived after depositing Marcus at the nursery and joined in the laughter when Leo suggested jokingly, 'Naturists on the beach?'

'No,' she replied in hushed tones. 'I saw Howard from the estate agent's showing our leader around one of the nicest houses in the area, Glades Manor!'

'Wow!' Leo said, and Phoebe thought miserably wow indeed. So much for their short, thought-provoking acquaintance in the apartments above. She would still see Harry in the surgery, but if he moved out there would no longer be the comforting feeling of having him near when their day's work was done.

Yet she thought she understood his reasoning. Despite his initial awkwardness, he'd been great with her and Marcus. Most likely because he'd found himself in such close proximity and had felt that being neighbourly was the least he could do, but Harry had his own life to lead, as she did. It stood to sense that he wasn't going to want to be living in an average apartment for long if he had the means to purchase something as prestigious as Glades Manor, which stood in several acres among the green meadows of the Devonshire countryside.

Leaving the staff still chatting about the comings and goings of Ethan Lomax's successor, she went into Reception where the list of calls she had to make would be waiting for her. There she found the man on her mind leaning on the counter and chatting to Millie.

Harry was observing her keenly as she approached and deciding that Phoebe wasn't well or something had upset her. Unaware of what was being talked about in the kitchen at the end of the passage, he hoped it wasn't anything to do with him.

'Are you okay?' he asked in a low voice as the phone rang at that moment and Millie was occupied.

'Yes, I'm fine,' she lied. 'I'm just about to sort out my day and then I'm off. Rory doesn't need me any more, but George Enderby's leg needs watching and my patient with the insulin injections is still not feeling too confident about giving them to himself.

'Then there is old Jeremy Davenport, who has developed a bed sore after being confined to bed for so long in hospital with a difficult leg fracture. He's home now but still incapacitated and the bed sore hasn't completely gone, so it's been passed to me.'

He was nodding gravely. 'That sounds enough to keep you occupied but, Phoebe, if you get the chance, take note of snowdrops in cottage gardens. The daffodils and crocus won't be long either. They are some of the things I missed while down under, as well as women with pale unblemished skin that the sun hasn't tanned. It was the first thing I noticed about you.'

Was he paying her a compliment or hinting that she looked wishy-washy? she wondered, and in the next moment thought she had the answer as he went on to say dryly, 'Just as long as you're not anaemic.'

She was picking up her bag and about to head for the door. 'I'm not. My mother's skin was the same.'

'And where is *she* now?'

'She died shortly after I was married. We lost my father when I was small. Luckily my sister and her husband filled the gap when my marriage broke up. Katie and Rob were there for me every step of the way, and it made all the difference. Rejection slowly turned into revival.' As the rest of the staff came filing in from the kitchen, Phoebe wished she hadn't opened up to him about her past so much, and said briskly, 'I'm off, Dr Balfour, and I won't forget about the snowdrops.'

I won't forget that you are house hunting either, she thought glumly as she left the village behind and drove along the coast road to the first of her home visits.

Was it significant that it had happened the morning after she'd been so unapproachable and turned down his offer of dinner? she pondered. Yet surely he hadn't set such store by her acceptance of the offer that he'd decided to move into somewhere more permanent when she'd refused.

One thing was sure, there was no way she was going to mention Glades Manor to Harry. He had no idea that Lucy had seen him viewing it when she'd been out walking her dog, and she felt he would take a dim view of it being surgery gossip that could end up on the village grapevine. If he didn't tell her she wasn't going to ask. It was as simple as that.

As the days went by, the house remained on the market and Harry and Phoebe were polite but distant when they met on the wooden staircase or on the landing.

He didn't knock on her door again as January shivered into February, and, as he'd reminded her they would, daffodils were nodding in golden perfection in small gardens and sheltered glades, with crocus blooming beside them less gracefully but just as beautiful.

Harry *had* been impressed by the small manor house, it had been beautifully restored by the present owner, but every time he thought about it, he felt that it was a house that needed a family. It needed parents with growing children and maybe more to come, not a wifeless, childless, empty vessel like him.

He was staying clear of Phoebe as much as possible in the evenings and at weekends because he felt that he'd been too pushy. Deep down, he knew that finding a permanent place to live *was* the thing to do, but something was holding him back. As he lay sleepless, or at the best tossed and turned restlessly in his solitary bed, the reason why was just a few feet away behind a door that remained steadfastly closed against him.

Phoebe had no intention of attending the Valentine's Day ball that the village's social events committee was organising, until Lucy surprised her by offering to look after Marcus while she went.

'It's time you got out and about more,' she said kindly, 'and if you could bring baby Marcus across to Jenna and Lucas's house, where I've promised to babysit Lily, I can look after them both. So what do you think?' As Phoebe hesitated, she continued, 'There will be a few there from the surgery. Even Harry has bought a ticket, though I doubt he'll make use of it.'

'Yes, all right then,' Phoebe said. 'I'd love to go. Marcus is always asleep by seven o'clock at the latest, so when its time to go I can carry him across wrapped in a warm blanket and settle him on the couch for the evening. Once he's in a really deep sleep he rarely wakes up so you shouldn't have any problems with him.'

When Harry heard Lucy telling Maria, the other practice nurse, that she was going to mind Lily and Marcus on the night of the ball, he stopped Phoebe one morning as she was leaving the practice and wanted to know why she hadn't asked him to take care of Marcus.

He said, 'It seems to me that you're making heavy weather of something that could be so simple if you left me in charge of him.'

'I was told that you've already bought a ticket,' she said, trying to conceal her surprise at his suggestion.

'Yes, I have, but it doesn't say I'll be going, unless you're short of an escort.'

'Do you have to make me sound so needy?' she snapped, irritated.

'I'm not. I just thought you might be going with that Jake person.'

'What?' she cried with increasing indignation. 'Why him?'

'Thought he had the hots for you, that's all.'

'He might have had, but they soon cooled down when he found out about Marcus, and before you ask if I was upset, the answer is no.'

'So you'll let *me* take you to this Valentine's Ball, then?'

'If you intend on going, yes.' Still rattled by him taking her for granted, she went on, 'It will be one step better than standing around the edges of the dance floor like a wallflower.'

Harry was taking in the sarcasm and trying not to smile. He hadn't *intended* doing anything of the sort until he'd discovered that she would be there, but now he was totally tuned in to the thought of dancing the night away with her in his arms.

She went out on the district then, still stunned by his offer to mind Marcus while she went to the ball but glad that Lucy's offer had come first. For the first time she was now looking forward to it, though she had no intention of letting Harry know that. Instead, like most women with a special occasion in view, she was already debating what to wear.

Since splitting up with Darren, the only clothes she'd bought had been maternity wear, plus those in the department store on the Saturday when Harry had seen her on the way to the car park. Unless she could find time for another quick trip in to town before the ball, it would have to be one of the smart outfits she'd worn when she'd been married, which belonged to what she thought of as the days of wine and poses.

There was a new patient on her list that morning. The surgery had sent her to evaluate what kind of care and assistance was needed by the local plumber, who had just been unexpectedly diagnosed with a form of inoperable stomach cancer that was terminal.

Expecting to see a very sick man, she was amazed to see him painting the outside of his bungalow on one of the lanes leading from the village's main street with every appearance of good health. When he assured her that he was fine, she left him to it, knowing that soon he was going to need the special care of a hospice, but for now she was content to leave him to enjoy a task that he might not be able to do for much longer.

Back at the surgery Harry was too busy to think any further about the strange conversation they'd just had, or the outcome of it. It was one of those mornings when one crisis was following another.

The first was parents bringing in their seriously unwell five-year-old daughter. The moment he saw the child Harry realised that she was showing signs of meningitis—the light was hurting her eyes, she was running a temperature, had an inflamed throat and, most worrying of all, the red rash of the illness that was one of its most easy to recognise symptoms.

He was amazed that they hadn't taken their child straight to hospital, yet was aware that where most parents were swift to panic, others were slow to grasp the seriousness of a situation. Within seconds he was phoning for an ambulance and emphasising the extreme seriousness of the little girl's condition.

The response to his call was fast and soon she was on her way to hospital with sirens screeching and paramedics and her stunned parents watching over her.

As he'd watched them go he had prayed they would get there before the infection took its terrible toll. If the child was treated quickly there would be a chance, but modern medicines and the Almighty would be equally responsible for the outcome.

The next person to give grave cause for concern was Lorraine Forrest, who controlled the school crossing as lollipop lady. A pleasant thirty-year-old with twin boys in the juniors section, she'd been knocked down outside the surgery while doing her job by a car driver who had collapsed at the wheel. A member of the public had come rushing inside to inform the doctors.

Harry and Leo were out and running in a flash to find the young mother lying on the crossing with a crowd beginning to gather around her and the local policeman frantically redirecting the traffic.

The driver was still slumped over the wheel and passersby had just managed to get the car door open when the two doctors appeared, so Leo went to check him out while Harry knelt beside Lorraine.

She was semi-conscious, with one of her legs bent awkwardly beneath her and bleeding from the temple where she must have hit the road or come into contact with the car bonnet.

When he checked her heartbeat it was erratic, which was not surprising under the circumstances, and she was beginning to go into shock. She was cold and shaking as if with ague and needed warmth to help ward off the effects. For goodness' sake, where were Lucy and Maria, the practice nurses?

'Has anyone sent for an ambulance?' he bellowed above the noise of the traffic and the voices all around him.

'Yes, I've asked for two,' the policeman said, pausing in his task for a moment.

This is hellish, Harry thought. Where *were* the rest of his staff? He couldn't leave the injured woman but she desperately needed blankets over her and any other kind of heating they could rustle up in the surgery.

He was about to tell one of the onlookers to go and find a nurse when Phoebe's small runabout pulled up at the kerb beside him. Thank God, he thought to himself.

She was out of the car in a second and he cried, 'Blankets and anything else you can find to keep her warm. Lorraine is in shock and we can't move her because she has what looks like a serious leg fracture.'

She turned and was gone, returning seconds later with a pile of blankets and a hot-water bottle that she'd found. As they did their best to wrap the blankets around the injured woman and placed the hot-water bottle at her feet, he gave a tight smile and said, 'Is it history repeating itself, do you think?'

She smiled back. 'It might be. If you are wondering what's happened to Lucy and Maria, Lorraine's mother was in the waiting room and she collapsed when someone came in with the news that her daughter had been hit by a car. She's only just coming round because she banged her head on a radiator as she fell.'

He groaned. 'What a mess! Leo is doing his stuff with the old guy who caused all this. We don't know yet what made him collapse at the wheel but as soon as the ambulances arrive, our two casualties—or perhaps I should say three, including Lorraine's mother—need to be taken to A and E fast.'

Leo came across at that moment and informed them, 'The guy who is responsible for all this appears to have had a heart attack. He's alive and is conscious now, but there would have been nothing he could have done to avoid the accident. He's still in the car. I thought he would be warmer there.' Without waiting for any comments from the senior partner and the district nurse, he hurried back to his patient.

'How do you come to be here, Phoebe?' Harry asked as the church clock struck twelve.

'I came to get something to eat as lunchtime was drawing near and found myself in the middle of this. Do we know who the man in the car is?'

'Yes. I heard someone in the crowd say he's an artist who has only recently moved into Bluebell Cove. His name is Adrian Docherty and he has a history of cardiac problems.'

He was checking Lorraine's heartbeat and pulse again, observing her anxiously. He commented, 'I hope they keep the children inside until the ambulances have been. It would be dreadful if her boys should see their mother like this.'

'Charlotte Templeton is headmistress and she's no fool,' she told him.

'They'll be having their school dinners at the moment and probably be kept inside the big hall afterwards until this catastrophe is sorted.'

She was tucking the blankets more closely around the injured woman and said quietly, with her head bent to the task, 'I dread that one day something like this might happen to me, because apart from Katie and Rob I'm the only family that Marcus has got.'

'There's his father surely.'

'He has forfeited the right to be called that.'

'That sounds a bit strong.'

'Not without just cause.'

'So do you want to tell me about it when we have our three casualties safely on the way to A and E?'

She shook her head. 'No, I don't think so, Harry. Just as you wouldn't want to talk about losing your wife.'

Or would he? she thought when she saw his expression. Having introduced an awkward moment, Phoebe wished she hadn't. Thankfully the emergency services arrived at that moment and all else was put to one side.

CHAPTER FIVE

IT WAS early afternoon and the surgery was back to its normal well-organised routine after the distressing events of the morning. Phoebe had gone to carry out the rest of her house calls and the two doctors were having a quick bite before setting out on *their* home visits, which were going to be much later than usual due to the accident on the crossing.

As Harry drove along the coast road to answer a request for a visit from the husband of a patient with dementia, he was intending to stop off at his aunt and uncle's house on the way back. The results had come through from the hospital for the prostate check-up he'd arranged for Keith and he wanted to pass them on to him as soon as possible.

The day had started on a high, he was thinking, with the promise of taking Phoebe to the Valentine's Ball, but before he'd had the chance to feel any pleasure at the prospect there had been a series of lows. His thoughts went out to the three people whose lives had come unstuck in the surgery area in a matter of minutes.

Thankfully, what he had to tell Keith was not in the same category. The tests had shown that his prostate count hadn't risen any more. It had steadied and for the present there was no cause for alarm. But he would have to pass on the good news in private as Barbara hadn't known that there *was* a problem, so the least said to her the better.

But first he had to see what was wrong at a big detached house overlooking the sea, where the sadness and frustration of dementia ruled the lives of its two occupants.

'Harry!' Peter Drummond exclaimed as the two men shook hands.

'I didn't know you were back with us until I rang the surgery this morning. Deborah and I seem to live such isolated lives these days. We rarely get to the village, or anywhere else for that matter.

'She gets frightened if I want to take her anywhere and only feels safe inside the house, so that is where we spend most of our days. It's hard to believe that she was once the life and soul of every party, but that's how it is.'

The Drummonds had been newly retired from the hotel business when Harry had left Bluebell Cove and they'd been at the centre of every social event for miles around before that. It was only after he'd gone that Deborah had begun to show signs of the deterioration that came with the illness.

'So what's the problem?' he asked as Peter showed him into a large sitting room overlooking the sea, where just as immaculate as she'd always been, his wife was staring into space.

'A chest infection of some sort.' he replied. 'Deborah

has been coughing most of the night and her breathing isn't good.'

Harry sounded her chest and coaxed her to let him look down her throat, and when he'd finished he said, 'You are right about that. I'll drop a prescription off at the chemist and arrange for it to be delivered to you, Peter. What about the flu jab? Has Deborah had that… and the once-only pneumonia injection?'

He nodded. 'Yes. Phoebe, the district nurse, has given her them both.'

'That's good then, and make sure that Deborah takes the full dose of the antibiotics I've prescribed, won't you, Peter?'

As he was on the point of leaving he asked, 'How often does the district nurse visit?'

'Three times a week. She helps with Deborah's bathing, offers feeding suggestions and is generally most helpful. Although my wife doesn't know who she is from one week to the next, she is always more tranquil when Phoebe has been.'

When he arrived back at the practice, after bringing light into his uncle's life when he'd gone to the door with him to say goodbye, there was news from the hospital regarding the casualties of the morning.

Lorraine was conscious and was waiting for them to operate on her knee, where some of the bones were shattered and would need pinning together. Her husband had been informed about the accident and had taken the children out of school so that they could all be together, and the family was now waiting for her to be taken to theatre.

Her mother was being kept in overnight, but was due to be discharged in the morning, and the artist—the unintentional cause of the disastrous events—was in Coronary Care, where he was in a serious condition.

Phoebe had arrived as Lucy was in the middle of regaling Harry with the bulletin from the hospital. Although he thought she looked cold and tired, she had a smile for him and he had to look away and grip the corner of the desk that he was perched on to control the wave of longing that washed over him.

When he looked up she was gone again, this time to collect Marcus from the nursery, and she hadn't come back by the time he was ready to ascend the wooden staircase at the end of his working day, which was strange.

It was half past six, two hours since she'd gone to pick Marcus up, and he was watching the fingers of the clock like someone hypnotised. Surely nothing else could go wrong, he thought desperately. But she and her little one were out there somewhere in the dark February night and he was pacing around his apartment like an anxious expectant father, a role that he'd never visualised playing.

When he heard her car pull up on the forecourt down below, his relief was swamped by annoyance and he went down the stairs two at a time. 'Where the dickens have you been?' he cried. 'I've imagined all sorts of things having happened to you!'

She was bending inside the car, undoing the straps

on the baby seat, and as she stretched up with Marcus in her arms she said mildly, as if dealing with a fractious child, 'I've been shopping,' making him feel even more frazzled.

'Shopping! What on earth for, after working all day? Surely nothing could have been that important. And what about this little guy's meal? He looks happy enough, but he must be starving.'

Suddenly her calm deserted her. 'I've been shopping for something to wear on Friday night so that I won't show you up,' she said hotly, and as he observed her in mute astonishment she continued, 'So will you please stop shouting so loudly that the whole village can hear you.'

Turning her back on him, she began to march up the stairs with a parting shot over her shoulder to the effect that she and Marcus had already eaten in a little bistro, and all he was going to need was his bedtime bottle.

'I'm sorry,' he said stiffly as he followed her up. 'If you had just said what you intended doing, I wouldn't have been so tensed up.'

'I'm not used to anyone being concerned on our account, except for Ethan when *he* was here,' she said, calming down as he drew level with her. 'Perhaps I ought to have let you know what I had in mind, and as a fitting finale to a dreadful day I didn't find *anything* to wear.'

She was putting her key in the lock with tears threatening. In a second she had the door open and was gone, closing it behind her with a decisive click.

* * *

Would he ever get it right with Phoebe? Harry wondered as he made himself a belated meal. He'd ranted and raved down there on the practice forecourt as if he had the right and in the process had insulted her by presuming that she hadn't put her child's needs first, all because she hadn't told him where she was going.

Of course Phoebe wouldn't let Marcus be hungry while she tried on clothes in some department store. As well as the beautiful mother, he was letting the beautiful child get to him, he thought wryly, remembering his concerns for Marcus when she'd finally put in an appearance, *and* when he'd offered to baby-sit on the night of the ball and been pipped at the post by Lucy's offer.

He should have just been happy to see that no harm had befallen the two of them and left it at that. His face was tender at the thought of her going all that way, at the end of a long and tiring day, to buy something to wear for his sake. Although, if he was to tell her that he didn't care what she wore, that just being with her would be enough, that would probably be the wrong thing to say as well!

Maybe later he would risk another rebuff by doing the thing he'd been trying so hard not to do over past days—knock on her door and try to make amends for his churlishness. But first he had to give her some breathing space, let her see Marcus settled for the night and give her time to unwind before he barged into her life again.

He wasn't to know that Phoebe was fighting the urge to open the door that she'd been so quick to shut in his face and rush across the landing to tell him how sorry she was for causing him so much anxiety, and that she understood his annoyance.

It was true what she'd said about not being used to having anyone so concerned about her, but that didn't mean she'd had to snap at him, especially when it had become clear how worried he'd been.

He was washing up after his scratch meal, with hands deep in warm suds, when he heard her knock. Without drying them, Harry was out of the kitchen, into the hall and opening the door before she had time to change her mind.

She'd changed out of her nurse's uniform and was dressed in the jeans and sweater she'd bought on the day when they'd met up near the open market. Her hair was tied back off her face in a ponytail, and this time, unlike earlier, she'd thrown off her tiredness, wiped away her tears and was about to say her piece.

He stepped back to let her in and as he did so asked, 'Where's Marcus?'

She smiled. 'I would have been disappointed it you hadn't asked, given your recent concern on his behalf. He is asleep in his own little dreamland. I wouldn't have come otherwise.'

He groaned. 'Please don't remind me of my interference. I squirm every time I think about it.'

'You mustn't,' she chided gently. 'It was good of you to care, Harry.' Their glances met. 'I've come to apologise for not telling you that I was going shopping after work. We are such close neighbours it was only fair that I should have let you know.

'My sister and her husband have been the only ones there for me for a long time, so I'm afraid it takes a bit of getting used to when coming from another direction. I have never ever met a man like you before.'

They were only inches away from each other and she could feel a force reaching out between them, a heat that was making her bones melt. She wondered if he could feel it too, yet it didn't seem like it as he was making no attempt to get closer. In fact, it was as if he was rooted to the spot.

But when she reached out and touched his face with gentle fingers, he came alive. In an instant she was in his arms, his mouth was on hers, and the hard strength of his body was telling her without putting it into words how much he wanted her.

But it appeared their magical coming together was not going to go any further. He was loosening his hold and putting her away from him gently as he told her, 'You deserve better than me, Phoebe. I came back to Bluebell Cove intending to steer clear of relationships after losing Cassie. Then I found you almost on my doorstep, and all the vows I'd made to myself were suddenly hard to keep.

'I've always prided myself on my self control but twice this evening I've lost it, the first time in anger, the second in lust, and neither were fair to you. So go back to your child and maybe we can get to know each other all over again at a slower pace.'

So far Phoebe hadn't spoken but now she was finding her voice. It didn't sound like hers because it was cold and clipped, yet it had to be because there was only the two of them there.

'I'm sorry to hear you describe what happened to us a moment ago as lust,' she told him. 'If it had been, we would have been in bed together by now, throwing caution to the wind.

'But you clearly think I might see that as a sign of commitment, and you've just made it clear that you want to keep away from that kind of thing, so fret no further. I was content enough before we met and shall continue to be so without any assistance from you.'

And before he could think of a sensible justification for the further mess he'd just made of everything, she was gone and he made no attempt to follow her.

As Phoebe lay sleepless, the indignation that Harry had aroused in her was disappearing. In the short time that she'd known him she'd grown to care for him, but until now had never realised how much.

She was drawn to his rugged attractiveness and his integrity, and moved at the way he was with Marcus and how he coped with the world of baby care. Those moments in his arms, brief as they had been, had shown her that was where she wanted to be, but if he had his doubts about that kind of closeness, she would have to be patient.

As the fingers of the clock said that it would soon be daylight, she decided that she wouldn't refer again to what had happened between them, that magical moment when, for a few seconds, he'd ignored any reservations he might have and had reached out for her.

She'd known then that he had felt the same heating

of the senses that she had, and the same kind of pull, yet something had made him draw back and she'd been angry and confused. But now all she wanted was to be there for him when he needed her, and maybe one day...

On that thought she turned on her side and slept for what felt like a matter of minutes before Marcus was shaking his cot rails and wanting his breakfast.

Coming down the stairs the next morning, she met Harry returning from an early home visit. When she smiled across at him, she watched his jaw slacken in surprise, but he merely nodded and went to take off his coat in the privacy of his own room, while she began her usual morning routine of driving to the nursery.

Surely Phoebe wasn't going to forgive him for last night's fiasco, he thought as he seated himself behind his desk. He'd been like someone deranged ever since they'd met, behaving totally out of character.

Yet his attraction hadn't exactly been from their *first* meeting. He smiled to himself at the memory of a strange figure peering at him through a crack of the door on his first night in Bluebell Cove.

It had been on the following morning when they'd met officially and he'd seen how beautiful she really was that he'd become entranced. From that moment, he'd gradually come to realise that he wanted Phoebe more than anything he'd ever wanted in his life.

But always there was the downside of his yearning for her—did he want the same things that she wanted, when a happy family for herself and Marcus was at the top of her list?

* * *

The thing uppermost in Phoebe's mind as the week drew to a close was the Valentine's Ball—was Harry still going to take her, and if he was, did she want him to? After all, it was only a few days away, and she still hadn't decided what to wear.

The items of evening wear she'd taken with her when she'd left Darren to his climbing of the ladder of success were all attractive—they'd had to be as the wife of the chairman's protégé. Needless to say, none of them had seen the light of day since, so she supposed there was no harm in giving one of them an airing if she did end up going to the ball.

It was to be held at the Enderbys' luxurious farmhouse, as all special events in Bluebell Cove were, because they had a very large reception room that was just right for those sorts of things. Although Pamela hadn't been home from hospital long after the fall and its consequences, she had insisted that it must still go ahead as the outside caterers that they always used were all geared up to run the whole thing, along with a popular local band.

'I shall just sit at the side and watch,' she'd said to the committee who organised the yearly event, and to her elderly father-in-law George. 'You'll keep me company, won't you, Dad?'

'I will indeed,' he'd replied. 'Neither of us will be getting out our dancing shoes this year, eh, Pammy?'

As one of the members of the events committee, Lucy had been there at the time, and when she'd reported back that conversation, Phoebe had thought that at least Pamela and George had their night mapped out, restricted though it may be. She wished she could say the same for hers.

There'd been little personal contact between Harry and her in the last few days, though they'd been pleasant enough towards each other when they had met. But Phoebe felt like it was the lull before a storm and kept putting off the moment of clearing the air regarding the ball.

If he was going to back out, she was quite prepared to go on her own, but if he didn't say something soon, it was too bad, because she wasn't going to bring up the subject.

'So am I still taking you to the Valentine Ball after upsetting you the other night?' he asked the morning before the event.

'If you still want to,' she said evenly, 'I have every intention of going, so it's up to you what you do.'

'What time shall I call for you?' he asked, as if there was nothing further to discuss.

'About half past eight. I'll be taking Marcus across to Jenna's house as soon as he's asleep, so I should be ready by then.'

'Do you want me to carry him across for you?'

'No, I can manage, I usually do.'

'Fine,' he said levelly, as if the comment hadn't registered. 'So eight-thirty it is. I'm looking forward to it. Are you?'

'Yes, I suppose so.' she said, aware that a truthful reply would be more along the lines of *I was, but now I'm not so sure.*

* * *

When he knocked on her door at exactly half past eight, Harry took a step back when she opened it to him. The dress that had graced a few cocktail parties in its time was of apricot silk and fitted her like a glove.

She'd taken her hair up and piled it in shining brown braids, revealing the slender stem of her neck and the smooth lines of her shoulders. She would be the most beautiful woman there, he thought achingly.

He wasn't the only one to be taken aback. As she took in the vision he presented in the doorway, Phoebe thought that some men looked good in a dinner jacket and black tie, some average, and the appearance of a few was heart-stopping. The man observing her with a cool hazel gaze was one of those and she couldn't believe that he had come to take her to the ball.

'I thought you had nothing to wear,' he teased as she stepped over the threshold and closed the door behind her. 'The dress is amazing and so are you.'

'It belongs to another age, a time that I don't want to be reminded of,' she replied. 'A time of wine and poses.'

'I'm not with you,' Harry said over his shoulder as he preceded her down the stairs.

'It means wining, dining, pretending—things that to some are as natural as breathing, but not me. When the chance came I got out of it, gave birth to my son in a place where he was well away from all of that and safe from psuedos. I'm happy in this new life I've chosen in Bluebell Cove, and hope that you will be too.'

He was holding out his hand to help her down the last step and when they were both on the same level he said, 'I'm working on it. For instance, it is ages since I've been anywhere socially.'

He would have preferred them to have stayed upstairs in her apartment, to give him the chance to hear anything further that Phoebe might want to tell him about her life before Bluebell Cove. But, as he'd just said, it was a social occasion, and *he* wasn't ready to tell her about *his* past, which might be what she would expect in return.

Still holding her hand, he said, 'So let's go, Phoebe. Let's head for Wheatlands Farm and the Valentine Ball.' She nodded and lifted the hem of her dress so that she wouldn't trip over it in the dark, and, with the high heels of her strappy gold sandals clicking on the hard surface of the practice forecourt, they walked hand in hand to where Harry's car was parked.

When they arrived at the farm, Pamela Enderby and her husband were waiting to welcome the partygoers in the spacious panelled hallway of the farmhouse. As they approached, they saw that she had a bouquet of beautiful flowers laid across her knee and Ian was holding a magnum of champagne.

When they stopped in front of them, Pamela presented Phoebe with the flowers and said, 'These are to say thank you for helping to save my life, Phoebe.'

'And our deepest gratitude to you, Harry,' Ian said, passing over the champagne. 'If it hadn't been for the two of you, Pamela might not have been here tonight. We shall always remember what you did for her.'

'We were only doing what we are employed to do,

Ian,' Harry said. 'So much of helping patients is being there at the right time, but thanks for your kind words…' he smiled in Phoebe's direction '…and for the champagne and the flowers.

'My aunt and uncle are here,' Harry said when they'd left the Enderbys greeting the next lot of guests. 'Do you mind if we have a word with them before we start enjoying ourselves?'

'No, not at all,' she told him, hoping that the stories she'd heard about battle-axe Barbara Balfour, as she'd been called in years past when she'd been in charge of the practice, weren't true. Her patients had been her life and the hospital had always jumped to her tune when she had been on the line or visited it in person.

She recalled how Francine, the French wife of Ethan Lomax, had come under her scrutiny, even though Barbara no longer had any say in the running of the practice. When the man that she'd loved like a son had been stressed and very unhappy, it had been Barbara who had brought Harry home from Australia to save Ethan's marriage.

Barbara was normally to be found in a wheelchair due to advanced rheumatoid arthritis, and tonight was no different when the two of them presented themselves to her.

At a first glance Phoebe took an immediate liking to Barbara's husband, but observed Harry's Aunt Barbara warily as she asked him, 'So who is this that you have brought to meet us, Harry?'

He smiled. The days were long gone when Aunt Barbara ruled the roost. 'Phoebe is the district nurse

I told you about, who is based at the surgery,' he explained.

'Ah!' she said, and he thought she had only to hear someone refer to the practice and she was tuned in.

'And so where do you live?' she asked, and listened with raised brows as Phoebe told her, 'I live in the opposite apartment to Harry.'

'And do you have family?' was the next question.

'I have a child, yes.'

'Are you married?'

'No. I'm divorced.'

Phoebe would have been annoyed at the woman's impertinence if it hadn't been for Harry's desperate expression. He was listening tight-lipped, eyes rolling heavenwards, and taking her arm, was ready to move on to the dance floor with a brief goodbye to his relations.

'I'm so sorry about that,' he said as he took her in his arms. 'I'd forgotten just how much my aunt thinks she owns Bluebell Cove.'

'Don't be,' she said. 'She is only looking after your interests, protecting you from the husband-hunting part of the local community—clearly she thinks I might be one of them!'

'And are you?' he asked quizzically, with his good humour restored.

'That's for me to know and you to find out,' she said laughingly, and with the heady excitement of being dressed up and out for the evening with the man that she so easily could fall in love with making her heart beat faster, she gave herself up to the moment.

There was a buffet in the interval decorated with red

hearts and ribbons and a red rose for every lady present. As they were about to eat, Ian Enderby said he had an announcement to make.

When they heard what it was there was much cheering and laughter among those assembled there. It seemed that a young man at the ball had taken the opportunity on such an appropriate occasion to propose to his girlfriend, and she'd accepted. Soon waiters were bringing round glasses of champagne, courtesy of their host, for those present to drink a toast to them.

Phoebe was smiling as she raised her glass, but Harry's expression was sombre and she wondered what was in his mind.

The rest of the evening passed pleasantly enough. They spent some time chatting to Maria, the youngest of the practice nurses, and her boyfriend, and shared a table with Jenna, and her husband Lucas, who was clearly head over heels in love with his bubbly blonde wife. But Phoebe couldn't help feeling that the magic had gone ever since they'd toasted the St Valentine's Day lovers.

'What's wrong?' she asked, as Harry drove them home in the dark night. 'You were enjoying yourself until we drank the toast to the young couple.'

He nodded. 'Yes, I know. I'm sorry for being such poor company. It just hit me that they were so sure, so ready to commit to each other, with no idea of what fate might have in store for them.

'That was how it was with my parents—fate had something dreadful in store for them that they never came to terms with, and I suffered greatly as a result.

'We were all happy and content until they lost my baby brother to a serious illness, and after that I was left out in the cold while they grieved for him evermore.

'So you can see why I'm wary of playing at happy families. I would never do that to a child of mine, and one way of making sure is to stay clear of that kind of thing,' he concluded flatly, gazing straight ahead with his hands tight on the steering-wheel.

'You are wrong to think like that,' she said gravely. 'You would make a wonderful father if you would put those sorts of thoughts out of your mind. Don't let your parents' inability to cope with their grief blight *your* life, Harry.'

He gave a dry laugh. 'Thanks for the vote of confidence, but I'm not ready for playing mothers and fathers yet.'

The practice building was in sight. It was time to pick Marcus up from Jenna's house, hopefully still sleeping, but she didn't want to leave Harry in this sombre frame of mind. Her spirits lifted when he said, 'Let me carry him across this time, Phoebe.'

Was there hope that Harry might change his mind one day because of the protective affection he was beginning to feel for Marcus?

CHAPTER SIX

MARCUS was still asleep as Harry picked him up and cradled him in his arms. Phoebe wrapped him in a blanket while Lucy looked on approvingly and said, 'I haven't heard a sound out of your little one, but Lily has made up for him! She's been the one exercising her lungs tonight.

'Jenna has just phoned to say that they're on their way and then Lucas will take me home. So, how was the ball? Was it up to the usual standard of a combined Enderby and events committee occasion?'

'It was wonderful,' Phoebe told her with her glance on Harry, who didn't respond, and she thought it was incredible that they had disrupted the foundations of each other's lives with their totally different viewpoints.

When Marcus had been tucked up in his own cot once again, Phoebe plucked up her courage to reach out to the clearly still-hurting Harry in the only way she could think of. Taking a deep breath, she said, 'You shouldn't be on your own tonight, Harry, not after that painful reminder of the past. Stay here with me.'

He'd been about to depart, but stopped and asked, 'In what capacity?'

She met his gaze steadily, for once not trying to hide the feelings for him that shone in her eyes. 'Whatever you want it to be.'

Harry dragged in a swift breath then exhaled slowly. 'No, thanks just the same, Phoebe.' He gave her a self-deprecating smile that took the sting out of his gentle rejection. 'I'll be fine if you'll just forgive me for ruining your evening.'

'You didn't. So don't concern yourself about that,' she replied. But she couldn't let him walk out of her door without trying to express her affection and support for him. As he turned to go a second time she caught his arm and pulled him round to face her, cupping his face between her hands. As his arms went around her, she was reminded of the gentle way he held her son, and his heart-breaking childhood loss of his baby brother. She said softly, 'You like holding Marcus, don't you?'

He was smiling. 'Oh, so you've noticed? How could I not? He is delightful, and do you know what, Phoebe? I like holding you too.' Bending, he planted a butterfly kiss on her lips and then with the smile still there said, 'I'm going before I give in to temptation and accept your offer to stay the night.' Closing the door quietly behind him so as not to disturb the sleeping child, he went.

In the silence that followed Phoebe decided that after their bleak conversation in the car on the way home she understood him better, and would expect nothing from him until he was ready to let the past go.

If that never happened, at least she would have known him, admired and respected him, and above all else loved him for being the man he was.

* * *

After the highs and lows of Friday night, the weekend felt like a non-event. Harry didn't appear, though she imagined he was there behind the old oak door. So keeping to her usual routine Phoebe did some chores, put the washer on, and in the early afternoon of Sunday took Marcus out in his baby buggy for some fresh air.

The days were lengthening. The next event in the village would be Easter and she'd heard rumours of an Easter Bonnet Parade, which sounded interesting. But spring had yet to wrap itself around Bluebell Cove, when it did the whole village would come alive. There would be families down on the beach, the cafés and restaurants would raise their shutters, and the farmers would rejoice to see another winter gone. Already there were newborn lambs in the fields, staying close to their mothers, and each time one came near them Marcus squealed with delight.

A turn in the path brought them to the gates of Glades Manor, which Harry had viewed some time ago. She stopped to admire the lovely old house that must have caught his imagination or else he wouldn't have gone there. Yet as far as she was aware, he had made no further ventures into the property market so might have changed his mind.

She'd seen no one on the leafy lane where the manor house stood, so turned quickly when she heard a twig snap behind her. She was taken aback to see Harry there, observing her in surprise and asking, 'So what has brought *you* here?'

'I saw the house advertised in the estate agent's

window,' she told him, improvising quickly. 'That's *my* excuse for dreaming. What's yours?'

He didn't reply. Marcus had seen him and was straining against the harness that was strapping him into the buggy and crowing with excitement. As Harry bent over him, he was struck by how much the little one had grown in the short time he'd known him. A worrying thought suddenly occurred to him. 'He's going to be walking soon, Phoebe, and the apartment above the surgery won't be a safe place for an active toddler. He'll be down the stairs to where cars are arriving on the surgery forecourt if you're not careful, or even darting into the road.'

'I'll have to acquire a gate for the top of the stairs to prevent that, won't I?' she said equably. 'The thought of Marcus being in any kind of danger is not to be contemplated. I know what you say is right, but I am doing my best for him under the circumstances, Harry. I'm sorry that you don't think it is good enough.'

'I don't think anything of the kind,' he protested. 'But the fact remains that Marcus needs to be out of that sort of situation. This would be a fantastic place for a child to grow up in. I could buy it, I suppose, and turn some of the rooms into an apartment for you and him.'

She was observing him as if she hadn't heard right. 'What do you mean?'

'I was thinking it would give him a more stable background.'

'Which is something you don't think I'm capable of,' she said slowly, stunned to discover how far apart their dreams were. Harry would be happy to have her in his life as a tenant, but not as anything more. So it was still there, the backwash from an unloved childhood. He wanted the best of both worlds—she and Marcus in his life but only on the fringe of it, not taking the risk to open his heart to them fully and consider how perfect they might be as a little family.

Bending, she released the brake of the buggy, and when he took hold of her arm in a restraining grip she shrugged it off in fury. With a look that dared him to follow her, Phoebe stalked off into the winter afternoon.

Watching her depart, he couldn't believe that she could have thought there was criticism in what he'd said, when his comments about Marcus's safety had only been prompted by genuine worry. Since meeting Phoebe, he was getting a whole new slant on care and caring. She was the best, the brightest, and coped brilliantly in an undeniably difficult situation. He'd let himself get carried away at the sudden thought of the three of them living in the manor house, but had skirted around the real issue—his deepening affection for her—by babbling on about an apartment for her and Marcus as if he didn't want them to be a real family.

It had been totally tactless, but the idea of buying Glades Manor wasn't going to go away. As he looked around him at the spacious grounds and elegant stone structure of the place, he knew that was what he was going to do. But he would ask the estate agent to keep the sale under wraps until he was ready to move in…if ever.

By the time Phoebe arrived back at the apartment,

she'd cooled down and was admitting to herself that Harry's comments had been right. Pretty soon, the apartment *would* be unsuitable for Marcus, but nothing was going to take away the bitter taste of the insultingly patronising way he'd suggested that she might want to be *his* tenant, as if living on the surgery premises was wilfully putting her precious baby's life in danger.

So much for her dream that one day he would realise what he was missing in the lonely existence he'd committed himself to, but if that was his choice, it wasn't for her to interfere.

Yet it didn't stop her from dreaming about Glades Manor and its surroundings that night, and Phoebe's first thought on waking up next morning was that, on the fringe of her life or not, Harry had been ahead of her in pointing out the dangers that would be present when Marcus became mobile.

As the days went by, she decided sombrely that she'd got avoiding Harry down to a fine art. If she heard him go down the stairs first in the morning, she kept to her usual routine, driving straight to the nursery with Marcus and staying there longer than usual, until it was almost time for the first surgery of the day. That way, she knew he would be occupied by the time she got to the practice. If she was first down the stairs, she left Marcus in the car while she sorted out her calls and then set off for Tiny Toes just as Harry appeared. Afterwards, she went straight onto the district and didn't return until the two doctors were involved with the second surgery of the day. Then it was a matter of inputting her patient reports on the computer and at four o'clock driving off to the nursery again.

Once she returned it was a matter of going straight upstairs and shutting the door behind her. As Harry made no attempt to communicate during the evenings, it seemed as if he was getting the message. If she did have any doubts about it, the sardonic gleam in his eye on the few occasions when they did come face to face was answer enough.

Easter had arrived, and with it the uplifting feeling that winter had finally gone.

There *was* to be an Easter Bonnet Parade through the village on the Monday of the holiday weekend with a prize for the best entry, followed by the traditional cream tea in the village hall.

All the female staff at the surgery had been persuaded to take part by the vicar's wife and, in the week before the event were searching around for something exciting to wear on their heads. Phoebe was among them and wishing she wasn't.

There was so little time to prepare, she thought in frustration. Her evenings were taken up with Marcus, meals and what seemed like endless chores, and since the scales had fallen from her eyes with regard to Harry it was hard to work up any enthusiasm for anything except her child.

But when she went up to her apartment in the late afternoon of the day before Good Friday, there were two carrier bags outside her door. When she investigated their contents her eyes widened.

In the smaller of the two there was a cuddly Easter bunny and a chocolate egg with his name piped across it in icing for Marcus. In the bigger bag was a similar egg with *her* name on it, and incredibly, underneath it, wrapped in folds of soft tissue, was a brightly coloured pillbox hat decorated with a plume of feathers and a dress from the same 1950s period with a nipped-in waist and swing skirt.

The card with them said:

These belonged to my mother and were among some things of hers that Aunt Barbara has kept stored for me. Would they be of any use to you for the parade?

A lump had come up into her throat at the unexpected thoughtfulness of Harry's gesture, and she cringed to think how petty her behaviour must have seemed since the episode outside Glades Manor.

At the bottom of what he'd written was a P.S. that gave some indication of *his* feelings regarding that. It said:

I'm not trying to get back into your good books, though I miss your sunny smiles. It was just a thought, Phoebe, and an opportunity for them to come out of their wrappings for once.

The surgery closed at six-thirty, but it was almost seven o'clock when she heard him coming up the stairs. When he reached the landing she flung open her door and came out to face him wearing the dress and hat.

If he hadn't already been conscious of her enticing curves, he was now as the dress fitted perfectly, and the hat, perched on top of the shining swathe of her hair, completed the picture. In a moment the stresses of his working day were wiped away by the vision she presented.

'Wow!' he breathed. 'You look fantastic! You don't do things by halves, do you?'

She was pirouetting in front of him and smiling. 'No, I don't. I just wanted to say that I would be honoured to wear your mother's lovely clothes, and thank you so much for thinking of me. There must have been some bright days in her life. Did she buy them for a special occasion?'

'I don't know,' he replied, 'but while running the stables my parents mixed with some of the wealthiest folk in Bluebell Cove. I suppose they had to be part of the social round to find their customers.'

'Yes, that would seem possible,' she agreed. 'And now that you've had a viewing, will you step inside for a moment and help me with the zip of the dress? I think that it's caught in the fabric somehow.'

'Yes, of course,' he replied, and followed her into her sitting room. As he bent to free the zip his hands brushed against the smooth skin of her back. He became still as the desire that had risen in him when he'd seen her in the dress and the hat spiralled.

When she swivelled round to face him questioningly, he gave one last pull at the zip and the dress fell to the floor, revealing silky underwear that did little to cover her gently curved figure. Phoebe could feel it again, the heat, the pull of the attraction he had for her, and she for him.

'Where's Marcus?' he asked in a low, strained voice.

'Asleep,' was the breathless answer.

'That's all right, then,' and with a thankful smile, Harry took her face between his hands and kissed her hard on the lips. Then his mouth was caressing her neck and the rise and fall of her breasts in the flimsy underwear.

'Can I take them off?' he murmured.

'Mmm. Yes, please.'

'And the hat?'

'What? Oh, yes, of course, by all means,' she said laughingly, catching a glimpse of herself in the mirror. Then everything else was forgotten—the hurt of what he'd said outside the manor house, the way he'd taken the joy from another occasion like this by calling halt at the height of their desire. For now that same passion was back again, stronger than before.

They were hungry for each other, blending as if they were one, and when their desperate longing for each other had been appeased, Phoebe lay close to his chest between the sheets of her bed and said dreamily, 'You must be starving. I'll make you something to eat.'

He kissed the tip of her nose and sighed as he explained, 'I'm expected at Four Winds House for my evening meal and can't let them down. Their lives are so restricted these days that even something as unexciting as having *me* to dine with them is an event.'

She gave him a gentle push and told him, 'Go on, then. You've just given some meaning to *my* restricted life, so now go and liven up theirs. I've never worked under that formidable woman, but can still appreciate her past worth to the community here. Yet she has got some nerve, grilling me about Marcus and my marriage! Jenna is lovely so she must take after that nice father of hers.'

'Yes, she is. It's only since Barbara had to give up the practice that she's really had any time for her husband and daughter.'

'She'll probably give all the affection that Jenna never had to little Lily.'

'Yes, maybe. Better a generation late than never, I suppose.'

He was getting dressed and she lay watching him, admiring the strong flanks, the broad chest, the arresting face. Harry was some guy, she thought. He was taking her out of the lonely world she'd been simply existing in and bringing her to life. So why did she feel that if it came to any kind of total commitment, he would hesitate?

'What are you thinking about?' he asked, tuning into her change of mood.

'I was wondering if you would ever use me to fill a gap.'

'Is that what you think? That I might take advantage of you, Phoebe?

'Use you for my own desires? You're beautiful and

brave, the kind of woman any man would want to spend the rest of his life with.'

'But not you Harry, because you know I would want commitment. Family life with all its ups and downs, joys and sorrows.'

Clutching the sheet around her she raised herself up against the pillows. 'Sometimes it feels as if you retreat into a desert sort of place that only you know about.'

He sighed. 'We've just been to heaven and back. Can't we live with that for a while?'

She could live with it for ever if she knew he felt the same as she did, she thought, but he was saying apologetically, 'I have to go Phoebe, or the old folks will be thinking I've forgotten.' He stopped in the doorway. 'I'm just going to have a peep at Marcus if that's all right.'

'Yes of course,' she told him, still huddled under the sheet. 'You don't have to ask. When I picked him up from the nursery today he said his first word. He must have heard it from the other children when their fathers have been to collect them.'

'And what was it?'

'*Daddy!* Strange, wasn't it?'

'Hmm, yes,' he agreed, and refrained from telling her that he was one step ahead. He'd been called out to the nursery that morning because one of the little ones had been taken ill, and when Marcus had seen him he'd held out his arms and that was what he'd said.

He'd kept quiet about it, partly because he knew that she had doubts about him and also because he'd already decided that Marcus might have used the word collectively rather than directing it at himself.

If Phoebe knew what had happened, she would be worried about the outcome of that incident. *Yet not now, surely, not after what had just happened. Their coming together had been like paradise on earth; there had been no desert places there.*

When he'd gone, Phoebe showered and dressed. Then, finally coming down to earth, she tried to decide whether to carry on with the painting of the sitting room or tackle a pile of ironing.

Not wanting to be messing with paint cans and having to change into the dungarees and old sun hat that she'd been wearing on the night that Harry had arrived, she chose the ironing, which was the kind of chore where one's thoughts could wander without much chance of a mishap.

It was late when she'd finished and there had been no sound of him returning, so she went to bed and slept with the pillow that his head had rested on held close in her arms.

When she awoke the next morning the first thing she saw was the pillbox hat on the dressing table and she smiled at the memory of how she'd still had it on her head when Harry had removed her underwear.

That was the first thing she *saw*. The first thing she *knew* was that Harry hadn't come back from the Balfours. She didn't know how she knew, but when she went onto the landing there was the feeling that his apartment was empty. When she looked out of the landing window, his car wasn't down below on the forecourt.

Maybe he stayed over at Four Winds House, she reasoned. If they'd been drinking he wouldn't have driven home, and to have got a taxi would have meant being without his car this morning.

But the headland wasn't that far away. If he hadn't wanted to drive, he could have walked back to the apartment in twenty minutes, so where was he?

As she was giving Marcus his breakfast the phone rang, but it wasn't the voice she wanted to hear at the other end. Leo was on the line and her mouth went dry as she listened to what he had to say.

'Harry is in hospital,' he informed her. 'He was admitted late yesterday evening after rescuing a couple of teenagers who'd been larking about down on the beach and been caught by the tide. Apparently they were being swept out to sea when he got there, and he went in after them.

'All three are being kept under observation for twenty-four hours at least,' he explained. 'As residents of Bluebell Cove ourselves, we both know that the sea is very cold and often dangerous at this time of year. They could have drowned if Harry hadn't been driving past along the tops and seen them struggling in the water down below.

'The hospital says that the lads are very subdued this morning as not only are they all suffering from exposure but Harry has a deep gash on his hand from where he was thrown against rocks as he was pulling one of them to safety.

'He's asking if you could go into his apartment and sort out some clothes for him, as at the moment all he has to wear is a hospital robe, and he'll need some decent gear to come out in when he's discharged. Apparently there's a spare key for his place in the drawer of the desk in his consulting room.' He indulged in a moment's curiosity. 'Are the two of you an item?'

'No,' she told him, 'but we are very near neighbours, couldn't possibly live any closer. Of course I'll sort out some clothes for him. I can take them over as soon as I've dropped Marcus off at the nursery if I can be spared for an hour or so.'

'Yes, that would be fine,' he said. 'I won't have the chance to go myself with two surgeries to cope with on my own. Without him the surgery staff will all need to pull out the stops so, yes Phoebe, do that. Have you many calls booked for today?'

'Don't worry. Nothing urgent.' She was trying to sound unfazed but inside she was horrified. While she'd been blissfully cuddling his pillow Harry could have drowned, and the thought of life without him was not bearable.

When she arrived back from the nursery, Phoebe went to find the key that he'd mentioned and once she'd found it went up the stairs to find him something to wear, as he'd requested.

As the door swung back on its hinges, it felt strange to be going into Harry's apartment with him not there. It was tidy, nothing out of place, and as she looked around her she saw that there was just one photograph of the woman he'd been married to, which was odd. A smiling blonde with sun-bleached hair and tanned skin.

Yet when she thought about it there was only the odd snapshot of Darren and herself in her place, so maybe it wasn't that strange. But she was not someone to pry and, opening his wardrobe, picked out a change of clothing for him.

As she locked the door behind her she wondered if Harry had ever done anything about his interest in Glades Manor. She shuddered to think that if the fates had been less kind last night on the seashore, he might never have had the chance to buy the place, even if he'd wanted to.

She found him in a small side ward when she arrived at the hospital gazing morosely into space, but his expression changed to relief when he saw her and his first words were, 'Am I glad to see you, Phoebe! Have you brought me some clothes?'

Nodding she went to sit beside him and took his hand in hers. 'I hope you'll approve of what I've chosen.'

'I don't care what you've brought as long as they cover me up and I can get back to the surgery.'

'Leo said they were keeping you in here for twenty-four hours.'

'I've persuaded them to discharge me as soon as I have something to wear.'

She looked down at his left arm, which was heavily bandaged, and asked, 'So what's the damage to your arm?'

'Severed tendon. They operated on it not long after I arrived.'

'In that case, you do need to stay in a bit longer. I'm amazed that you've talked the doctors into letting you leave! Surely that's quite irresponsible?'

'No more irresponsible than what I did earlier in the evening,' Harry muttered under his breath. Phoebe's suggestion that he might just be using her was crystal clear in his memory, and to his shame it wasn't entirely undeserved.

Shock had her sitting up straighter. 'Meaning?'

Harry took a deep breath and tried to explain his conflicted emotions. 'Making love to you when I don't know my own mind half the time perhaps isn't the most sensible thing to have done.'

Phoebe was horrified at his words. 'Well, any pleasant thoughts I might have regarding it in the future will be soured by what you've just said! We were both consenting adults.' Her voice broke. 'I slept with the pillow you'd had your head on cradled in my arms. I was frantic when I realised that you weren't there when I knocked on your door this morning.'

He was observing her sombrely, thinking that he'd been blessed from the moment of meeting this wonderful woman, so what was the matter with him, why didn't he tell her so? But the scars of his emotionally bleak childhood ran too deep to allow the words to form. If anything, the heavenly experience they'd shared in each others' arms yesterday had made him realise how little he had to offer her.

She deserved someone who could truly appreciate her warmth and caring nature, and he knew he wasn't that man for her or good father material for Marcus.

He was going to have to find the courage to pull away from them soon—it was the only fair thing to do. But right now it seemed too cruel, especially as he was so touched by her evident concern on his behalf.

Instead, he said flatly, 'I stayed very late at Barbara and Keith's. She was unwell and I wasn't prepared to leave her until she felt better. There was a full moon when I was driving home and that was why I saw what was happening down below on the beach.'

'You don't have to explain yourself to me about anything,' she said grandly, getting to her feet.

She picked up the holdall that his clothes were in. 'I'm taking these back until tonight. It is too soon for you to be leaving after being operated on such a short time ago and I'm sure the doctors will agree with me when I tell them there is a change of plan. I'll see you this evening.'

'What about Marcus?' he said as she was leaving the ward.

'What about him? I'll bring him with me, or ask Lucy to mind him. We managed all right before you came on the scene, you know, and will continue to do so now. And here's another little item of news to cheer you up—the nurse at the desk in the big ward said that the press are coming to see you. If you can't manage a smile for me, perhaps you'll be able to dredge up one for them.' With that, she swept out of his room, leaving him gaping at her cutting farewell, and went to find the doctor in charge. He agreed with her that Harry would be better staying there for a few more hours.

'An amazing guy,' he said. 'Couldn't care less about

himself. Those kids were so lucky that it was someone like him who went to their assistance.'

By the time Phoebe reached the car park her righteous indignation was dwindling, but by no means gone. It was true what the other doctor had just said, but it was also true what *she'd* said to Harry. Though he might be attracted to her lack of suntan and smooth, pale skin, he was about to discover that she was no doormat—if he thought he could take her to heaven in his arms one day and then explain it away as a mistake the next, he had another think coming!

Everyone at the surgery was eager to know how he was when she got back in the middle of the morning and Leo asked, 'Did you take him some clothes, Phoebe?'

'Yes, but I brought them back with me,' she explained stiffly. 'He had been operated on in the early hours for a severed tendon and I didn't think he was fit to be discharged yet, although he'd already fixed it up with the doctor in charge. So I went to see him and unfixed it.'

'Harry wouldn't like that,' he said laughingly. 'But what a guy, going into the sea fully clothed to rescue not one, but two crazy kids.'

'He could have been drowned, and those lads as well,' Lucy commented from behind in sepulchral tones. Phoebe thought it was only men who could see something to rave about when distress and danger were the topic of conversation. For a woman it was always fear and dread that filled *her* mind.

Leo was the second member of his sex that she'd

spoken to who'd been impressed by what Harry had done. And to be honest, so was she, and so would a lot of the Bluebell Cove locals. But now he had to be sensible and leaving hospital only hours after an operation was not a good idea. In fact, she might hang onto his clothes until next morning and risk his frustration.

By the time she'd finished her rounds, dealt with the paperwork and picked Marcus up, she'd decided that was what she was going to do. She knew he would be furious with her, but another night under medical supervision would do him no harm.

As the evening wore on she was expecting the phone to ring any second and hear his voice asking why she hadn't kept her promise, but the line remained dead, and as the hours crept by she told herself that Harry's silence was worse than having to put up with his indignation.

She would go to the hospital first thing after she'd dropped Marcus off at the nursery, as she'd done the day before.

When she walked into the ward the next morning he was seated by the window, reading the morning paper, and when he looked up he said, 'You've just got here in time. Another five minutes and I was going to make a run for it in this flimsy dressing gown and risk being arrested at the bus stop.'

'You could have got a taxi.' she told him mildly, wait-ing for the storm to break.

'Yes. I know,' he said dryly, and there was a glint in the dark hazel eyes that had observed her so tenderly a couple of nights ago, 'but I didn't want to be missing when you'd taken the trouble to bring my things. Phoebe, I have to admit that you were right. I did feel rather groggy after you'd left and would have been pretty useless at the surgery if I'd gone there straight from here too soon.' He was getting to his feet. 'But I'm fine this morning so can we get moving once I'm dressed?'

'Yes, of course, that's the idea,' she told him, 'just as long as you've had some breakfast. And by the way, what about those two boys?'

'They're going home today feeling rather stupid. Both of them are local so should have known better, though I was just as crazy at their age.'

While he was getting dressed in the adjoining bathroom, Phoebe thought that he'd mentioned his childhood again, but there was never any direct reference to his parents apart from what he'd said about his mother's dress and the hat, and in the car on the night of the Valentine Ball had mentioned briefly their grief at his brother's death.

Harry knew what had happened to her father and then her mother but they'd never talked about his immediate family. His aunt and uncle, yes, his cousin Jenna, yes, but not his mother and father, not as individual people anyway.

If the opportunity came she would ask him. It might help her to understand him better.

CHAPTER SEVEN

THERE was silence in the car as Phoebe drove them back to the village. She could feel Harry's glance upon her, thoughtful and considering, but he didn't speak until they were almost there, and what he said was the last thing she wanted to hear.

'I could tell yesterday that I upset you, but there isn't much joy in being around someone like me.'

She didn't reply, just gripped the steering-wheel more tightly, and he went on to scatter her dreams even further. 'The last thing I would ever want would be to hurt you, so maybe we should cool our relationship.'

Without agreeing or disagreeing, she said, 'And how do we do that with us both working at the surgery and living on top of each other as we do?'

'If you remember, I thought of buying the manor house a short time ago but didn't proceed for various reasons.' *He wasn't going to mention that moment that he would soon be the owner.* 'Well, it's still on the market so I might have a rethink.

'Otherwise it means keeping our doors shut as much as possible when we're in the apartments. Maybe that way you won't find me so interfering. With regard to the surgery it shouldn't be too difficult as we only see each other briefly. Most of the time you're out on the district.'

Her thoughts were in chaos. Although she wasn't interested in being used, now Harry was coolly giving her the brush-off, it hurt more that she could ever have imagined. But if that was how he wanted to play it, he was welcome.

'Yes, whatever you say.' she told him with a casual shrug of the shoulders and fighting back tears. 'Fortunately Marcus hasn't known you long enough to get too attached to you.'

As he nodded in sombre agreement, Harry was thinking of the 'Daddy' episode, of the pleasure he'd gained in those few seconds when the little one had called him that.

And yet he was still going to deny himself what could be the follow-up to that *and* the love he sensed Phoebe had for him, because he wasn't sure that he was right for them, not sure that in the long term he would make them happy. And making Phoebe and Marcus unhappy was the most unthinkable emotional crime he could think of to commit.

The practice building was finally in sight, thank God. He was back on his own patch, with a gammy arm covered in bandages and a feeling that he'd just shot himself in the foot.

'I'm going upstairs to shave and have a shower,' he told her as he eased himself out of her small car. 'I'll be down as soon as I can.'

When he came down Phoebe was nowhere to be seen, but the rest of the staff were happy to see him back safe and almost sound. When he had a moment to spare he rang the estate agents to check progress.

As Phoebe climbed the stairs at the end of the day with Marcus in her arms, there was no joy in her until she arrived at the top and saw a bouquet of spring flowers outside her door.

Her first thought on seeing them was that they wouldn't be from Harry, not after that morning's dumping ceremony.

She was wrong. As she picked them up, with the heady fragrance of daffodils, narcissus and freesia all around her, the card with them read, 'These are just to say thanks for being there for me during the last two days. It was much appreciated, Harry.'

Much appreciated! she thought wearily. It was a wonder he hadn't enclosed a shopping voucher to complete the formal gesture. But he wouldn't have had time to arrange that, whereas a phone call to the florist in the village would have been enough to have the flowers delivered.

Was the man blind? She'd been there for him because she loved him, and did *not* want to be patronised for it.

With the spare key for his apartment that she was still carrying around she opened his door a fraction, placed them inside, and wrote across the card, *Thanks, but no thanks!*

* * *

As Harry came up the stairs at the end of the day he too was in low spirits, physically and mentally. Physically because his arm was hurting—it felt as if all the nerves where he'd had surgery on the damaged tendon were tied in knot—and mentally because with regard to Phoebe, it was as if he couldn't think straight.

It was as if he was punishing her for his inner hurts, the hurts that she'd had no part in. She'd had enough of her own from the little she'd told him, and it seemed that she wasn't to blame for them either. So why couldn't he just give in to the joy of being with her?

His mood took an upward curve when he reached the landing. There was no sign of the flowers he'd ordered, so she must have taken them in. When he'd placed the order he'd been promised immediate delivery, so if all had gone to plan they should have been waiting for her when she came home with Marcus.

The lifting of his spirits lasted until he opened his door and almost fell over the flowers. When he read what she'd written on the card he slumped down onto the nearest chair and stared into space.

She was the loveliest thing he'd ever seen, he thought, and he was so hurt and angry inside he was driving her away instead of making the most of what the fates had deemed him worthy of. But the trouble was, he didn't feel worthy of anything at the moment.

Hanging over him was the thought of the inquest into Cassie's death in just a few weeks' time. He would be going back to Australia for it and was not looking forward to the proceedings at all. Luckily there had been no mention of suspicious circumstances when the autopsy had taken place, and once the inquest was over he was hoping to return in a more positive frame of mind.

When she opened her door the next morning Phoebe's eyes widened at the sight of her flowers on the landing. He doesn't give up, does he? she thought. Can't bear to be in the wrong. But when she read the message on the back of the original card that said, *It was just to say thanks, nothing more*, it seemed as if that was exactly what Harry had done. He'd given up on her, and another empty day stretched ahead of her.

There was a new patient down on her list for a visit that morning and as she drove to the outskirts of the village, she had to pass Glades Manor. The 'For Sale' sign was still there, but she reasoned it would be. It had only been yesterday that Harry had said he might still be interested, and if he went ahead it would be the first time any man had bought a house to get away from her. So much for her sex appeal.

Whereas *he* had it all—the looks, the charisma, the captivating personality and, remembering what he'd done for the two drowning lads, a fearlessness and courage that was amazing. All of that added together came to the total of every woman's dream man and she'd had the nerve to think he wanted to be hers.

Hannah Trescott had been in hospital having intense treatment for gangrene in her foot. She'd been discharged the previous day with a recommended healing regime that was going to require regular after-care from a district nurse.

It would consist of changing the dressing every day, including weekends, keeping a progress report and making sure that the patient took the large doses of antibiotics required to keep the dreaded infection at bay.

When Phoebe arrived at Hannah's cottage down by the harbour she didn't have to knock. The door was ajar and when she stepped inside she found Hannah sitting with her foot raised in front of the log fire that was burning in the grate.

She was a hardy old woman who'd lived in Bluebell Cove all her life and had spent a lot of her adulthood fishing out in the bay and beyond. Until a stab in the sole of her foot from a sharp piece of driftwood had started an infection that just wouldn't go away and had ended up gangrenous.

'Come in, Nurse,' she called. 'I've just had a visit from Harry Balfour. Seems strange having him in Ethan's place, but me and Harry go back a long way. I used to take him fishing with me weekends and school holidays when he was a kid because his parents were always either moping or too busy.'

'Why was that?' Phoebe asked casually as she laid out a fresh dressing for Hannah's foot before removing the present one.

'They had stables just outside the village. Lived and breathed horses until his ma died after being thrown by one of 'em, and a couple of years later his pa followed her. Had a heart attack from the stress of trying to run the stables single-handed. Harry was at college at that time and found out that all he'd inherited from the two of 'em was a bankrupt business.'

While she'd been talking Phoebe had been gently removing the dressing and breathing a sigh of relief to find that there was no evidence of the infection when Hannah's foot was revealed.

'That seems to be healing nicely,' she said with a smile for the elderly stoic, 'but take care not to be on your foot too much and try not to knock it. Also, wear loose shoes so that there is no undue pressure on it.'

As Phoebe was packing up to go she asked, 'Did you request a visit from Dr Balfour, or was he just passing?'

'I didn't ask him to come,' was the reply. 'He came because he was keen to know all about the trouble I've been having with my foot, said he was sorry he hadn't managed to get to see me before for old times' sake, and I understood. Losing his wife over there and then taking over from Ethan here can't have been easy, and I believe he fished two kids out of the sea the other night, which sounds like him.'

'Yes, it does,' Phoebe agreed, not knowing what else to say. It was simultaneous torture and heaven discussing Harry like this.

'It's time something good happened to Harry,' Hannah went on to say, 'I was never sure about that wife of his, but I only saw her once when he brought her over to meet his aunt and uncle and Jenna.'

She sighed and unwittingly brought more gloom into Phoebe's day by saying, 'He might be one of those folk who never meet the right one.'

Or meets the right one and is too blind to see it, Phoebe thought as she left Hannah to her day with the promise to call again the next morning.

It was Easter Monday at the end of what had been an empty holiday weekend with nowhere to go and no one to go with, so Phoebe was looking forward to the Easter Bonnet Parade through the village and the socialising afterwards.

There were twelve contestants and she'd been told that she was number six. She was hoping that Harry would be there, if only to see her wearing his mother's hat and the dress that she'd worn on the evening when she'd needed help with the zip.

What had happened afterwards was locked away at the back of her mind, to be taken out and cherished then put back with haste because the hurt of the rejection that had followed was too great to dwell upon for long.

The vicar's wife had offered to look after Marcus while the parade was on so that she didn't have to worry about him when it was her turn. When she took him to the vicarage, the older woman said, 'I've asked Dr Balfour to judge the contestants. He is well liked and well known in the village. I felt that it would be a good way of showing our pleasure at having him back among us.'

Having Harry back is not *all* pleasure, not for some of us anyway, Phoebe thought as she went back to the apartment to get changed.

The morning had dawned bright and clear, to the relief of the organisers. She'd been really looking forward to the event until she'd heard that item of news, and now she was thinking how embarrassing that Harry should be judging while she was wearing his mother's hat.

The only in-depth conversations they'd had since the day she'd brought him home from the hospital had been about surgery matters. She'd heard him coming and going as the days went by, and a couple of times had looked out of the window of her apartment and seen him pulling off the surgery forecourt in the red car, and that was all.

There was much laughter among the twelve contestants lined up in the village square as they waited for the parade to begin. Jenna Devereux was in modern dress with a large brimmed hat trimmed with lots of roses. Lucy from the surgery had found a crinoline from somewhere with a pokey bonnet to match and looked as if she'd stepped out of the Victorian era, while Charlotte Templeton, headmistress of the village school, had a mortar board on her head, tied under the chin with ribbons.

Meredith, who spent her days chained to the huge cooking range in the kitchen of her guest house on the coast road, was sporting a chef's hat bedecked with corn stalks, and the rest of those competing were in pretty outfits with suitable headgear.

Harry, in a chunky Arran sweater and jeans, was already in place on a small platform that had been erected for the judging, and the contestants were milling around him, waiting for the parade to commence.

When his glance locked with Phoebe's for a moment

he asked in a low voice, 'What have you done with Marcus?'

'He's with the vicar's wife,' she replied smoothly, and he nodded approvingly. What did he think she'd done with him? she thought tightly. Given him to gypsies? Left him making sandcastles on the beach or locked him in the apartment?

The village band had just struck up and the commentator, a retired milliner from the village, was about to introduce the first competitor. With a swing of the hips and a bright smile, Jenna began to walk around the flagged square to display her headwear.

Then it was Lucy in the crinoline, followed by Charlotte with the mortar board then a couple of teenage girls with saucy little numbers perched on their long blonde tresses. In what seemed like no time at all number six was being called.

As Phoebe did her tour of the square with Harry's gaze on her, she was wishing that it was the vicar's wife doing the judging and the man on the podium minding Marcus.

That way she could be her natural self. Her heartbeat wouldn't be pounding in her ears and the rest of her wilting with longing. But she was the only one aware of that and so strolled calmly past those gathered to watch.

No doubt when this event was over there would be a general exodus to the beach, Harry had been thinking while waiting for the event to start. Bluebell Cove came into its own on beautiful spring days such as this.

Phoebe had been thinking the same, that she and Marcus could go to the beach or maybe even to the woods. There, the bluebells that the village got its name from flowered everywhere in bright blue abundance, straight-stemmed and slender. Whatever she did, it would be better than sitting around the apartment, moping.

It was over and the winner had been announced. Lucy in her stiff crinoline and pokey bonnet had been chosen by the man on the platform and had gone up to receive a bouquet of Easter lilies and a ticket to a famous hat museum not far away.

Then everyone was transferring to the community hall for the cream tea that a band of helpers had prepared. While that was taking place, Phoebe went to find Marcus in the care of the vicar's wife.

She had to pass Harry to get to them, however, and he said, 'It's rather a crush in here, but this table has been reserved for me especially, so why don't you and Marcus join me? I haven't seen much of him lately.'

And whose fault is that? she almost said, but refrained in case her sarcasm made the situation worse that it already was.

As she was carrying him through the crowd to where Harry was waiting, her little one saw him and the smile on his face made her heart twist. That wasn't all, however. As they drew level Marcus held out his arms, Harry got to his feet, and to her dismay as he reached out for him the little tot said, 'Daddy.' Now she understood why it had been his first word.

Slumping down on to the nearest chair, she asked bleakly, 'Where has that come from?'

He was observing her sombrely above her son's curly

chestnut mop. 'Not from me, in case that is what you're thinking. I have no idea where Marcus has picked it up from, except that he said it the other day when Beth called me out to the nursery because a child had been taken ill.

'I arrived at the same time as some of the parents, mothers *and* fathers, and as some of the kids started shouting "Daddy" he joined in, but I didn't think it was directed at me.'

Any further discussion was prevented by the arrival of the food, brought over by a member of the events committee especially for the guest of honour and his friends.

As they enjoyed the cream tea, with Marcus biting on a scone with obvious enjoyment, Harry said casually, 'So what have you planned for the rest of the day?'

'Nothing special,' was the reply. 'We might go down to the beach or go to see the bluebells in the woods.'

'But of course!' he exclaimed. 'I'd forgotten this was bluebell time, so why don't we do both?'

'We?' she questioned, and he had no reply.

He was desperate to be with her, like a starving man for food, yet was aware that he was the one who'd set the guidelines and made the conditions. Short of telling Phoebe once again about his dread of the responsibilities and what he saw as the pitfalls of family life, he was going to have to abide by his own rules.

But he'd reckoned without *her* longing to be with *him* and, as if she hadn't questioned what he'd said, she asked, 'So where first, the woods or the beach?'

'Er…the woods, I think,' was the reply, 'then down

to the beach.' As they prepared to leave the community centre, he asked, 'Where's the baby buggy?'

'Across at the vicarage, and we'll have to go back to the apartments to pick up towels and change into our costumes.'

'Yes, okay. Let's go, then,' he said quickly, before she changed her mind.

It was quiet in the woods, with again only birdsong breaking the silence. Marcus had fallen asleep on the way and as Harry pushed the buggy with Phoebe by his side, an onlooker would never have guessed that they weren't the serene couple that they might be mistaken for, out walking among the bluebells.

Yet they'd been happy enough until a few moments ago, when Harry had said out of the blue, 'I'm going to be away from the practice for a few days at the end of the month.' As she'd observed him enquiringly, he'd explained, 'I'm going back to Australia for the inquest on Cassie's death. You can imagine just how much I'm looking forward to that, but needs be. I won't be able to settle to anything until it's over. The only thing in my life that I'm sure of at present is Bluebell Cove and the practice. Everything else is a blur.'

You could have been sure of *me*, she wanted to tell him, if you hadn't pushed me out into the cold. Instead, she asked, 'Us included?' with her glance on the sleeping child.

'Yes, I suppose so,' he replied.

There seemed no point in telling her that her face was always before him, that the memory of them making love was something he would treasure always, and that he wished that these precious moments amongst the bluebells could last for ever.

Down on the beach it was just the opposite from the peace of the woods. There was plenty of noise and laughter, with lots of people milling around either in the sea or playing on the sand. As she watched Harry making a sand castle for Marcus, Phoebe felt like weeping.

He looked up and caught her expression.

'What?' he asked, and with a quirky smile. 'Are you upset that I didn't choose you as the winner in the Easter Bonnet Parade?'

'No, of course not,' she protested. 'Winning meant far more to Lucy than it would have done to me. I thought you were very fair with regard to that.'

'But not fair in everything perhaps. Is that what you're thinking?'

'It might be,' she told him, adding as she picked Marcus up in her arms, 'We're going for a paddle.'

It was really warm for the time of year and picking up on Phoebe's need for a little space from him he spread out a towel on the sand and said, 'I'll join you shortly. I'm just going to try to catch the sun for a little while before it goes down.'

'There's no rush,' she replied. 'We'll be fine on our own.' As he closed his eyes against the glare Harry thought that was one for him again—a reminder that they'd managed very well before he'd come on the scene and no doubt would continue to do so.

It was his last thought before the effect of an

accumulation of restless nights took hold of him and he slept.

It was chilly when he awoke and the beach was almost deserted. He could see a lifeboat ploughing through the waves out at sea and thought that someone was in distress out there.

In the same second he realised that Phoebe and Marcus were nowhere to be seen and he was on his feet in an instant. The buggy was still there but it was empty.

He'd said he would join them soon and what had he done? Wasted precious time with them both by falling asleep. He was pathetic. It was the first time in weeks he'd been near either of them away from the surgery and he'd dozed off.

Maybe she'd gone home in disgust, he thought, and couldn't blame her if she had. 'Have you seen a woman with a toddler in the last hour?' he asked the few people who were hanging on to get every last ray of the sun and a few more breaths of sea air in their lungs.

'No,' was the only answer he received, and now he was thinking surely Phoebe wasn't so disenchanted with him that she *had* gone home, as he'd at first thought.

His mind was in chaos. No one seemed to have seen them and none knew better than him the joys and perils of this beach, unless it was Ronnie the lifeguard, or his cousin Jenna.

The two of them had spent hours on it during their growing years and knew all about the rip tides with their treacherous currents that could sweep the unsuspecting out to sea in a matter of seconds.

There was also the risk of being trapped in the caves or on the rocks when an incoming tide took them by surprise, as had been the situation before the two lads he'd saved had ended up in the outgoing tide.

His glimpse of the bright orange of the lifeboat a few moments ago was also adding to his unease, even though he knew that it wasn't always an emergency when it put out to sea. It could be on a training run for the benefit of new crew members or on a trial run after repairs.

He flung the towels into the buggy and as his glance raked over the rock-strewn beach again, he finally saw Phoebe coming slowly towards him, silhouetted against the last rays of the setting sun. With one hand she was supporting a small figure as he took wobbly steps beside her and with the other she was holding a beach ball.

Thank God! he thought as he ran towards them. 'Where on earth have you been?' he cried when he drew level. 'You've been gone ages. I was getting so worried about you!'

'We came looking for you when you didn't come to join us,' she protested, taken aback by his greeting. 'Didn't you notice that I'd covered you with the dry towels? It was getting chilly and you were so soundly asleep it seemed a shame to disturb you.

'Then Marcus saw some children with a beach ball and wanted it, so I took him to buy his own from the shop on the road above. As he is getting more keen to be on his feet every day it was slow progress. I'm sorry to have caused you anxiety once again on our behalf, Harry, but remember we are not your responsibility!'

Feeling that he'd just made a fool of himself, he

said grittily, 'If I had known that Marcus was walking by hanging onto you, I wouldn't have been thrown by seeing the buggy still here. That was why it never occurred to me that you might have gone up to the top. So maybe I'm the one who should be apologising.'

'Let's forget it, shall we?' she said gently, bemused again by the extent of his concern.

He didn't reply. Just lifted Marcus into the buggy, fastened the straps, and not another word passed between them as they left the beach behind and proceeded up the coast road to the surgery building.

He was insane to have let Phoebe take such a hold of his feelings, his heart, his life, Harry thought as they walked along in the spring dusk. She was kind and loving; everything about her took his breath away. If it had been Cassie who'd found him asleep in the chilly afternoon, she would have found a bucket of water from somewhere, thrown it over him and laughed as he'd shivered and spluttered beneath it. Phoebe's gentleness, covering him with towels to protect him against the cold, would have been completely foreign to her.

They were at the top of the stairs now and Phoebe couldn't stand the thought of them separating with a brooding silence between them. As their glances locked she reached out and touched his face gently, but to her dismay he recoiled, took a step back and said harshly, 'Play fair, will you, Phoebe?'

Turning his key in the lock, he flung the door back and almost in the same movement closed it behind him, knowing that if he'd let another second go by she would have been in his arms. It would have progressed from there, and she would still have wondered if he was using her.

It had been a lovely day until he'd woken up on the beach and found them gone, he thought wretchedly. After that it had gradually lost its charm, especially when she'd reminded him that she and Marcus were not his responsibility.

Not so long ago he would have agreed with that, been relieved to hear it, yet not so much now. His panic on the beach had woken him up to his true emotions concerning the Howard family. He knew now that he didn't want to be on the outside of their lives any more—he desperately wanted to take care of them and be surrounded by the warmth of their love. But first he had to get the ordeal of the inquest over, and until he had closure from that he couldn't ask Phoebe to marry him.

CHAPTER EIGHT

THAT settles it, she decided in the quietness of the apart-ment after Marcus was asleep. She was going to have to leave The Tides Medical Practice, look for a district nurse's position somewhere else.

Bluebell Cove was enchanting. She would have loved Marcus to grow up there like Harry and Jenna had, but she could not endure living so close to the man who had turned her life upside down. She loved him with all her heart, but he was constantly letting her know that she wasn't the woman of his dreams.

She wasn't sure where she would go, maybe some-where up north, not too far away from Katie and Rob. Certainly not to London—that would always be first on her list of places she never wanted to see again because Darren lived there.

This village was different, she loved the place. But she loved the man in charge of the practice more, and Harry was here for life. He hadn't actually said so, but she could tell that being back in the place where he'd grown up was his only comfort after losing his wife.

Where she, Phoebe, fitted into the jigsaw of his life she didn't know. But one thing was clear: she was just a small insignificant part of it. If that was how it was going to be, it was a good enough reason for her and Marcus to move on.

She could still see him recoiling from her and telling her harshly to be fair as if she'd stepped out of line and he objected to the familiarity.

Put it out of your mind, she told herself firmly. Go to bed, get a good night's sleep so that you are bright-eyed and on the ball at the surgery in the morning, and at the first opportunity start job hunting.

It had sounded very positive put like that, but the moment her head touched the pillow the tears came and wouldn't stop.

Yet the next morning the determination was still with her until a wave of nausea had her dashing to the bathroom in the middle of giving Marcus his breakfast. When the retching had subsided Phoebe walked slowly to where she kept a calendar on the wall and her heart began to thump in her chest.

Her period was late. It should have been three weeks ago. How could she not have picked up on that? she thought frantically. Yet the answer was simple.

There had never been the necessity to check on monthly cycles since she'd had Marcus. She'd never slept with any other man since she'd left Darren. Hadn't had the time, the inclination or the opportunity until Harry had come into her life. Ever since their untimely meeting on the landing on the night of his arrival in Bluebell Cove, she'd been living in a different world where she'd fallen in love with a real man.

A man of honour and integrity, who was growing to

love her son and had seemed to feel the same way about her. But there was a lot of hurt inside him and he clearly didn't trust her not to make it worse, so what did she do now?

Marcus was objecting to having his breakfast interrupted by banging his spoon on his plate and switching her thoughts back to the present she made sure he was fed, then, still in a daze, prepared to face the day ahead.

In the late morning she bought a pregnancy testing kit. Returning quickly to the apartment in her lunchbreak, she used it and it was positive. She was going to have another child.

Panic was gripping her. *Harry had to know, but when?* Last night she'd had every intention of leaving Bluebell Cove but what now? Surely he wouldn't leave her to cope alone, but would he offer marriage? Of one thing she was sure—despite her love for him, she wasn't going to marry him just for the child's sake, so where did that leave her?

By the end of the day her mind was clear of the debris of confused thinking. She was still going to move on. She simply couldn't bear his hot and cold treatment of her, it was too painful given how deeply she cared for him. When she was settled, she would tell him she was pregnant and hopefully they would be able to come to some amicable arrangement.

Amicable, she thought miserably. Not joyful, tender or loving, just *amicable*.

Situations she would never agree to were a marriage, or a liaison of convenience, or him having sole custody of their child, and with those sombre thoughts in mind she resumed the duties of the day.

Phoebe was avoiding him, Harry thought as he climbed the stairs at half past six that evening, and could he blame her? He'd seen her three times during the day and on each occasion they hadn't exchanged more than a couple of words.

She'd been home in the lunch-hour, which wasn't usual. He'd seen her whizzing up the stairs as if she hadn't a moment to spare and had intended following her to apologise for the way he'd acted when they'd arrived back from the beach, but he'd been thwarted by Leo wanting a word in private and by the time he'd been free, she'd gone.

It had been the same situation in the afternoon. When she'd returned to the practice to update her patient records, he'd just started afternoon surgery. But now he was free and as he knocked on her door wished he knew what he was going to say to heal the breach between them. She must be weary of his changing moods

When he'd left her the night before, after bellowing at her when she'd touched him, he'd stood behind his closed door and shaken his head in disbelief. All day he'd been aching to hold her close, to kiss her, make love to her, yet had kept a tight hold on his feelings. But when she'd reached out and caressed his cheek, he'd felt himself weakening, and what had he done but behave like a prudish virgin! If Phoebe hadn't already got him labelled as a head case he would be surprised. But there was no way he could have been with Phoebe and felt completely at ease, not with Cassie's inquest looming.

He hadn't told anyone how he was dreading going back to Australia for the inquest, except her. It would bring the memory of all the horror and grief of Cassie's death back again, but he was also hoping for a feeling of closure. He knew he needed that if he was going to put his doubts and uncertainties to one side and ask Phoebe to marry him and make a new life together.

There was no welcoming flinging wide of the door in answer to his knock, just a few inches with her observing him warily. It reminded him of the night of his arrival, and although they'd become much closer since then, tonight it was still just a crack that she was observing him through. He wondered grimly if they were so far apart that she was actually afraid of him.

It would seem not. She was dredging up a pale smile and asking, 'What is it, Harry? I'm just about to bath Marcus.'

'And I'm not allowed over the threshold, is that it?' he questioned dryly.

'Yes, but only because it seems the sensible thing to do,' was the reply. And because she couldn't bear to see the look on Marcus's face when he saw Harry. 'He will only get too excited if you're involved in his bath time.'

He shrugged broad shoulders inside the business suit he wore for the surgery. 'Okay. Fair enough. I just came to say sorry for being so edgy last night. It was unpardonable. Can you forgive me?'

'Yes, I can, so just forget it,' she told him. 'I know you're still traumatised by what happened to your wife.' And thought there was more trauma to come that he didn't yet know about. Would Harry feel that apologies were due on a much wider scale when he knew she was pregnant?

'Yes, I am, to a degree,' he said, 'but even so that is no excuse for my...'

'Like I said, it's bathtime,' she reminded him.

'Yes, I know that's what you said,' he agreed, accepting her obvious reluctance to talk to him. 'Goodnight Phoebe.'

'Goodnight,' she said tonelessly as he turned away.

The 'bathtime' that she'd been hammering home was over. Marcus's eyelids were drooping, and as she wandered restlessly around the apartment, Phoebe was desperate to talk to someone she could trust. Who better than her sister who had already been her rock once before?

'So who is this guy?' Katie croaked in surprise when she'd finished explaining.

'Harry has taken Ethan's place at the practice, and for the first time in my life I'm so in love I can't think straight,' she told her. 'He's everything I've ever wanted in a man.'

'So do you think you're going to get married, then?'

'Er...no. The attraction is mutual, but the love is all on my side. He is a widower who lost his wife in a dreadful accident in Australia and doesn't want to tread that path again.

'Obviously he will have to know that I'm pregnant and that I will expect some support from him, but wedding bells are not on the agenda. It would be for the wrong reason, however much I love him. I'm leaving Bluebell Cove and am looking for a job elsewhere, so if you hear of anything…'

'Will you have to work out your notice?'

'Yes, unless they find someone to replace me immediately.'

'So come and stay with us when you've finished there. You know we love having you, and I'm longing to see how much Marcus has grown.'

'Thanks for the offer, Katie,' she told her. 'I'll bear it in mind, and give my love to Rob.'

'My sister wants me to go and live with her and her husband up north,' she told Janet Crosbie, the middle-aged practice manager, the next morning, when Harry was ensconced with his first patient of the day. The rest of the staff had dispersed after their early morning tea, leaving just the two of them in the kitchen.

'I'm undecided what to do, but did wonder how much notice I would have to work if I took her up on the offer. I suppose it would depend on how quickly a replacement could be found, wouldn't it?'

Janet was smiling. 'Yes, it would normally,' she replied, 'but not in this instance. I know someone who is looking for a position of district nurse locally and would fit in here very nicely…my daughter!

'Bethany and her husband have just moved into the area and that was her job where they lived before. Their two young ones have been accepted into the village school and they are all eager to settle permanently in Bluebell Cove. So you could go whenever you wish, but Phoebe please don't feel as if I'm pushing you!'

'I don't,' she told her, 'but what you've just told me simplifies things, although I haven't yet decided what to do. It is very important that I don't make the wrong decision, and, Janet, please don't say anything to Harry or the rest of the staff about me leaving, will you? You'll be the first to know when I've made up my mind. Now, I suppose I should get moving or he will be thinking that no one requires my services and that would be a first!'

It would be helpful if she could leave without any fuss or palaver while Harry was in Australia, she thought as she drove towards Hannah Trescott's cottage. But how she wished it hadn't come to this!

She'd told Janet she was undecided what to do, but it wasn't strictly true. From the moment of discovering she was carrying Harry's child, she'd known she had to leave the village. When she went, she would leave him a letter explaining about her pregnancy and making it clear that there would be no denying him an active part in the life of their child, but not as the family that he had no taste for.

For the next two weeks she was going to keep a low profile where he was concerned, making sure he didn't pick up on her condition or get too close so that all her resolve flew out of the window by just being near him.

Then it would be a case of facing up to the future as a single mother with two children.

She *was* going to accept Katie's invitation to stay with her and Rob, but only until she'd found a job and a place to live, and that was as far as she could think for now.

There was no knock on the door that evening. Harry had gone to dine with the Balfours at the close of the surgery, and if he hadn't already arranged to do that, the tepid reception he'd received the night before would have made him think twice.

Yet he had actually managed to have a conversation with Phoebe in the late afternoon, though it *was* work related. She'd sought him out to tell him that she was almost sure she'd seen a young boy with rickets while on her rounds.

'Rickets!' he'd exclaimed. 'It's an illness from a bygone age, or at least it used to be. But I do remember seeing a piece in one of the medical journals about it becoming prevalent among youngsters who spend hours in front of the television in one position. Due to their obsession with it, they don't get enough fresh air and sunlight.'

'It's a vitamin D deficiency, isn't it?' she'd said.

'Yes, basically caused by a lack of it in the foods they eat, plus not enough sun and too little exercise. So where did you come across this child? It wasn't him that you'd gone to visit, was it?'

'No. I'd gone to see his grandmother. She has a regular injection every month and is too old and frail to get to the surgery for it.'

'So who is it that we're discussing?'

'The child is Oscar, Jasmine Jackson's eldest.'

He groaned. 'Oh, no, not one of Jasmine's brood. I remember her well from before I went away. How many little Jacksons do we have now?'

'Six. Three girls, three boys.'

'Did you mention rickets to her?

'Yes.'

'And?'

'She said she'd heard that you were back and maybe you'd call round to see Oscar and have a chat about old times. Does she have a husband?'

'Yes, he's a farmhand with fists like sledgehammers,' he said laughingly. 'If she wants to see me, she can bring her child to the surgery and I'll want witnesses present, but what made you think of rickets when you saw the youngster?'

'There was bowing of the legs and enlarged wrists and ankles. Whenever I go to give the old lady her injection Oscar is always huddled in a chair, watching television.'

'Yes, but surely he's of school age. Why is he not there? Don't tell me that Jasmine lets him play truant.'

'I don't know about that, you would have to ask her, but it is my last call of the day when I see him, so he might have already been to school. From what I can see, all Jasmine's children watch TV quite a lot but, then, so do most children. Oscar is the only one showing signs of rickets, though.'

'Yes, well, we'll have a look at young Oscar and see what is going on. Ask one of the receptionists to give

Jasmine a call and make an appointment for her to bring the boy to see me, will you, Phoebe?'

'Yes,' she said, her mind elsewhere.

He was observing her thoughtfully. 'You're miles away. What's wrong?'

As if he didn't know, she thought. *Everything was wrong,* and what on earth had possessed her to ask if the woman they'd been discussing had a husband?

He was waiting for an answer so she gave him one, but again she was avoiding the truth. 'Nothing is wrong. I'm fine,' she told him, and made a speedy exit from his consulting room before he found any more awkward questions to confront her with.

When she'd gone, Harry's thoughts switched to the coming ordeal. He would be flying out to Australia in ten days' time and returning one week later. As well as the inquest, there were a few loose ends that he needed to tie up while he was there.

Yet he didn't like the idea of Leo being the only doctor at the practice while he was away, but the other man was emphatic that they would be able to manage without him for that short space of time.

Leo had spoken to him the other day regarding his apartment if he moved to Glades Manor. 'I've been very comfortable at Meredith's guest house,' he'd said, 'but I'm ready to move into something more permanent when the opportunity arises.'

'Who told you I'm thinking of buying the place?' he'd asked, and the fair-haired six-footer who always seemed to hit the right note with the opposite sex—which was more than he could say for himself these days!—had explained that Lucy had seen the estate agent showing him round when she'd been out walking her dog.

'I see,' he'd said. 'I wondered if it was Phoebe who had told you as she knows about my interest in Glades Manor. She once came across me up there while she was pushing Marcus out in his buggy, yet I can't imagine her being into surgery gossip.'

'She isn't,' Leo had assured him. 'Phoebe is a very private person; we don't see that much of her here. She no sooner appears than she's gone.'

Tell me about it, he'd thought groaning inwardly, I'm to blame for that. As he had patients waiting, he'd told Leo, 'If I buy the manor house, you can have my apartment with pleasure. I would expect that it's the only one of the two likely to become vacant. I'll make sure that Janet, as practice manager, gives you first choice, but nothing has been settled about Glades Manor as yet.'

He was in the process of buying the property but hadn't yet exchanged contracts on it. That would happen around the time he got back from Australia and it would have been a marvellous moment if Phoebe and Marcus had still been part of his life. But he knew who was to blame for that, and it wasn't them.

After the way he'd treated her he was going to be rattling around the place with his dreams shattered. He'd imagined Marcus playing in the gardens and the fields around it, sleeping safe and sound in one of the sun-washed bedrooms, with Phoebe close beside *him* when he went to sleep, and there when he awoke in what would have no longer been his lonely bed. But all of that would have meant commitment, relying on others and them relying on him. He'd given Phoebe reason to believe he wasn't able to offer that, and had been paying the emotional price ever since.

Jasmine and young Oscar came to see him the following morning after Phoebe had roused his interest in a possible rickets situation. When he'd examined the boy, his expression was grave. 'Nurse Howard was right, Jasmine,' he said. 'Your boy lacks vitamin D, which can affect healthy growth in a child.

'He's got rickets. I'm going to send him for X-rays to confirm my findings, and in the meantime increase his intake of the vitamin, make sure he has plenty of oily fish and foods that contain animal fats in his diet. Also see to it that he gets out in the sun more as sunshine can help his intake of vitamin D, and for goodness' sake limit his television watching! He should be getting exercise at his age, out kicking a ball around.'

'All right!' she cried. '*You* want to try coping with six of them on a farmhand's wage and with only twenty-four hours in a day.'

'What I'm suggesting is for Oscar's own good,' he told her. 'Sunlight and exercise cost nothing, and if you give all the family the same food it shouldn't cost any more. Also I'm going to give you a vitamin D supplement for him to take.'

She sighed. 'I suppose you're right.'

'I *am* right. I'm a doctor, Jasmine, and what your son has got was almost unheard of until recently. It belonged to past generations living in hard times. With regard to the X-rays, you should receive an appointment in the next few days and once the results have come through I'll want to see Oscar again.'

'Yes, okay,' she replied, and paused in the doorway. 'You were fun in the old days, Harry. Who's taken the joy out of you?'

He didn't reply, just rolled his eyes heavenwards and called in his next patient. Yet what the sassy Jasmine had said had gone home. If Phoebe was going to continue keeping him on the fringes of her life, joyless was how he was going to stay.

Jasmine's visit had one redeeming feature: it provided him with a reason to talk to Phoebe again when she came back at four o'clock. As soon as she appeared, he called her into his consulting room.

'I've had young Oscar and his mother here,' he said when she'd closed the door behind her. 'And you weren't wrong about the rickets. I'm sending him for X-rays, of course, but have no doubt in my mind about what the results will be.

'She was angry at the inference of neglect on her part, and wanted to know how I would like six kids to look after. I refrained from telling her that I would need a lot of practice. When she'd gone, after telling me what a joyless creature I have become, it crossed my mind that you might want to second her on that.'

'So that's what this is about, is it? Why you've brought me in here,' she said wearily as exhaustion washed over her. 'To find out what is going on in *my* mind? I'm wondering what you think gives you the right to ask. Now, if you'll excuse me, I have to pick Marcus up or Beth will think I've got lost.'

He was observing her pallor. She was white, gaunt almost, with dark shadows beneath her eyes. The pale perfection of her skin that had been the first thing he'd noticed about her was submerged beneath weariness and he said, 'I've just one patient to see. If you can hang on for a few moments longer, *I'll* go and get him.'

'No, thanks just the same,' she told him. 'Marcus is my responsibility.'

'You are still punishing me for pushing you away, aren't you?'

'Yes, if that is what you choose to think,' was her parting shot as she went to collect her child. It had been on the tip of her tongue to tell Harry that when it came to punishment she knew what it was all about. She was giving up her job, a life in this idyllic village, and about to take on twice as much responsibility as she had now, all because he wasn't ready to open his heart to love and family, and *that* was hard enough to cope with on its own.

In a sick sort of way, she was counting the days to him going to Australia so that she could depart, quietly and without fuss, for the next stage of her existence.

She rang Katie when Marcus was asleep to let her know what she was planning to do and explained that she was going to accept the invitation to stay with them until she'd found a job and a place of her own, and then she would move on.

'I can't imagine how you are feeling about all this,' her sister said, 'but whether this guy loves you or not, don't you think you should tell him now that you're having his baby? Every day that goes by without him knowing will make it more hurtful for him when he does find out. If he's already beginning to bond with Marcus, as you say, he might be over the moon when he hears about this one.'

'Yes, I know,' she protested, 'but there is one thing you're forgetting—he isn't in love with me. I thought he was but he isn't, and would only be interested in taking me on as part of the package for the baby's sake. I am not prepared to let that happen.

'I'll be leaving Bluebell Cove in ten days' time, the day after Harry has gone to Australia for the inquest into his wife's death. The move shouldn't be too hectic as the apartment is kept fully furnished by the practice. It will just be a matter of packing clothes and toys belonging to Marcus, getting into the car and driving off early in the morning before the village is awake or in the evening when the light has gone.'

'And you say you're going to leave him a letter telling him about the baby?

'Yes.'

'Will it explain where you can be found?'

'No. I will tell him where I am in a few weeks' time when I feel ready to face up to it. If I see Harry too soon after I've made the break, I might lose the determination to go through with it. He only needs to touch me and I melt, but it would seem that I don't have the same effect on him. I have to keep telling myself this—I am *not* going to marry any man who doesn't love me as much as he loves my children.'

'One of them will be his as well, don't forget,' Katie reminded her.

'As if I could.' The thought was engraved on her mind in a mixture of joy and dismay. 'A friend from the London bank phoned me the other night to inform me that Darren *has* married the chairman's daughter. They are expecting their first child and he is over the moon. It's a strange world, isn't it?' And with her glance on Marcus, playing happily with his toys on the carpet beside her. 'I have no regrets. If I hadn't left Darren I would never have met Harry. Meeting him has turned my life upside down, but I won't ever forget him.

'The problem with us is that when we met, we both had hurtful pasts. But where I've coped with mine, difficult as it was, there are unhappy areas of his childhood that still haunt him. Several times he has made it clear that he wouldn't want to risk any child of his having to experience what he did.

'So how Harry is going to feel when he knows he's made me pregnant I can't imagine, but one thing is sure—we can't go on as we are. I haven't been able to convince him that all families aren't like his, neglecting the one child that they've still got because they've lost another younger one. I couldn't see you or I doing that in those circumstances, could you?'

'Definitely not,' was the immediate reply. 'We would have been even more loving and protective of the remaining child.'

But that hadn't been Harry's experience, and that was why Phoebe knew she had to leave—because he had no happy memories of family life.

CHAPTER NINE

SPRING was everywhere in Bluebell Cove as Harry prepared to fly to Australia and Phoebe made ready to move up north. Blossom was on the trees, surfers were in the sea, which was now blue instead of winter's cold grey, and on the beach families picnicked and frolicked with their children to an even greater degree as each day came and went. Every time Phoebe looked around her, the ache inside increased.

She hadn't done anything about antenatal care as yet, there seemed no point. Better to wait until she'd moved and could register at a clinic near where Katie and Rob lived.

Harry and herself were both counting the days to misery, she thought, him having to present himself at the inquest in Australia and her rootless and forlorn, moving on into an exile that Harry had given her no choice but to impose on herself.

Her vitality was low as her body adjusted to the demands of the pregnancy, and as she coped with her workload and looked after Marcus, her concern for Harry was always at the back of her mind, especially because of what she was planning to do. Would he be relieved to discover that she was dealing with it in her own way, accepting that family ties were not his thing? Or would he be dismayed that he'd been shelved in the process of coping with her pregnancy? She wished she knew.

Yet, even so, there was comfort to be had in small doses, such as seeing young Oscar playing on the beach on a warm spring day, doing what boys did, with the rest of his family, and Jasmine calling across for her to tell Harry that she was knitting them both a jumper as thanks for sorting out her eldest. The X-rays had shown that rickets were present in the child, but had been diagnosed early enough for natural growth to be restored.

When she'd passed the message on to Harry he'd said he hoped the garment wouldn't be pink as that was Jasmine's favourite colour. She'd replied that whatever colour it was he would have to wear it as it was a very kind thought on her part, and as they'd smiled at the prospect, it had been a brief moment of togetherness.

Another time of tranquillity between them had been on a day when she'd been driving along the coast road on her way to one of her calls and had seen his car parked at the side of the road. When she'd pulled up alongside, she'd found him gazing down at the beach below where Beth and her helpers had taken the children from the nursery for a picnic.

When she'd gone to stand beside him Harry had said, 'There's Marcus at the water's edge with one of Beth's girls holding tightly to his hand. He just needs to take that one step on his own, doesn't he? It's nearly always like that—once they've done it they're off. It's just a matter of them having the confidence to attempt it. Or being attracted to something so much that they forget about holding onto a support.'

As they'd reluctantly turned away from the scene below, Harry had said, 'You do realise that once he's taken the plunge you will need eyes in the back of your head? You will definitely require a gate of some kind at the top of those stairs back at the apartments. I'll sort that out for you if you like, either make one or buy one.

'And by the way, what about the lecture for nursing staff regarding new procedures that the NHS is giving the night after next at the hospital? All of you will be expected to attend. Have you given it any thought?'

'Yes, and that is far as I've got,' she told him. 'Lucy won't be able to babysit as she'll be attending the lecture herself, and even if she wasn't I don't want to be continually taking advantage of her good nature.'

'So why don't I keep an eye on Marcus? If you remember, I once told you I haven't got any good nature to put upon, and I'm sure you don't find that hard to believe. We could leave both our doors open and I could pop in and out all the time to check on him. It's the obvious solution to the problem.'

'Yes. I suppose it is,' she said, wishing that a much bigger problem than that had such a simple remedy and not wanting to seem too eager to accept his suggestion. 'Yet it will be too early for him to be asleep when I have to leave, though I can have him bathed and in his pyjamas ready for bed before I go.'

'Fine. It will give us the chance for a little playtime before he goes to sleep, and you a chance to be with people on your own wavelength for a change, as I never seem to be on it.'

When he'd driven off she'd felt tears pricking. In those few moments Harry had sorted out two of her problems, a babysitter and a gate, but unless Marcus decided to step out on his own before they left Bluebell Cove they might not need a gate, not for the apartment anyway.

Yet they couldn't leave it behind. It would be a labour of love where Harry was concerned, not for her but for her little boy. A reminder of how much he was drawn to him, and as she looked down at her still trim waistline, it was as if they would both be taking something with them to cherish that Harry had given them.

On the night of the lecture, and with only minutes to spare, she called across that she was ready to leave and Harry came striding out of his room and took Marcus from her.

She was looking subdued and he asked, 'What's wrong? Are you thinking you've drawn the short straw?'

'If I have, it won't be the first time,' she said, noting that Marcus was content to be left now he'd seen Harry. She wondered if it was wise to let them get any closer, yet she reasoned it would only be for a few hours and her little one would be asleep for part of the time.

'I've left his bedtime bottle ready,' she told him, and

with a long last glance at the smiling pair she went quickly down the stairs into the April night.

Phoebe isn't happy about leaving me in charge of her child, he thought wryly when she'd gone. What does she think I'm going to do? Offer him a game of poker?

'But, then, she doesn't know what I'm planning when I come back from the inquest. If she doesn't turn me down after the way I've treated her, the three of us are going have lots of fun and be very happy in a house called Glades Manor. So what do you think about that, Marcus?'

In reply his small charge said the only word in his as yet restricted vocabulary…'Daddy…' and Harry wondered chokingly how he ever could have been wary of moments like this.

When Phoebe returned, he was seated beside the cot reading a book, with Marcus sleeping contentedly. He said casually, 'So how was it?' he asked casually, raising his eyes from the page. 'That sort of thing can go on a bit.'

'It was all right,' she told him. 'Lots of information about new procedures and regulations. How was Marcus? Was he good for you?'

He smiled. 'Of course. He and I are great friends.'

If he'd expected that to bring relief to her expression he was wrong, but, then, he didn't know what she did, that his days were numbered with her and her child.

It was only a short time after him looking after Marcus, and on his last day at the surgery before setting off on his grim journey, that his comments about the safety measures that would be required when he started walking came into being.

He'd been on his way upstairs to consult a medical journal he'd been reading that had information about a new drug that might benefit a patient he'd just seen. But he wanted to know more about it before he prescribed it, and on the bottom step had found the Easter bunny that he'd bought for Marcus, which he must have dropped as Phoebe had been carrying him up at the end of the day. When he picked it up, he was smiling. It gave him an excuse to knock on her door.

When she opened it wide, he held out the toy and said, 'I've just found this on the stairs.'

Marcus was behind her, standing upright but holding onto the sofa, and the moment he heard Harry's voice and saw him framed in the doorway he forgot the need for something to cling to and took a step towards him.

On the point of saying thanks for bringing the toy up, Phoebe had her back to him and Harry said in a low voice, 'Stay still, Phoebe. Marcus has seen me and is on the move. He's right behind you—one more little step and I'll have him.'

Then Marcus wobbled past her and into the arms of the man on the landing, and as Harry carried him inside she was weeping tears of regret as she closed the door behind them.

'What?' he asked, putting Marcus back onto his feet. 'What's wrong Phoebe? Are you upset that he came to me with his first steps instead of you?'

'No, of course not,' she told him, wishing that she could do the same as Marcus and walk into his arms. 'It was such an emotional moment, that's all.'

He was smiling. 'Yes, it was, and it's happened just as I'm off to Australia. I've got the wood for the gate and am working on it, but it's not quite finished, so take care until I get back.'

She couldn't stand much more of this, she thought. She'd be gone when he came back, but would have been glad to have had the gate as a reminder of how loving Harry was with Marcus.

Instead, she told him, 'Don't worry. I won't let anything happen to him. And, Harry, I hope that your ordeal will soon be over when you get there, and you can return to this place that means so much to you.'

She watched a shadow cross his face and felt she'd said the wrong thing, but didn't know why. Unless it was because she hadn't mentioned him coming back to *her* especially, but he was the one who'd set the boundaries, not her.

'I'll remember what you've said,' he replied, 'and now I must get back to my patients.' He smiled tightly. 'I'll see you in a week's time, Phoebe.'

And that was that, she thought when he'd gone. No tender goodbyes or loving words. If she'd had any last-minute doubts about what she was planning to do, they'd disappeared.

He was crazy, Harry thought when he came up at the end of the day and cast a glance at her closed door. Why hadn't he taken Phoebe into his arms when they'd been together and explained that the hang-ups and hurts that family life had brought for him had now disappeared?

She'd wept after Marcus had walked his first steps in his direction and he'd wanted to hold her close then, but she'd passed the tears off as the emotion of the moment and the opportunity had passed.

As for their cold goodbye, he couldn't wait to tell her that his future lay with her. That she was his second chance of love and tenderness. The first one hadn't been quite what he'd hoped it would be, and since meeting her he'd realised just what he had been missing,

She already had a child so might not want any more, but he could accept Marcus as his own if she would let him and be content. But his mind was leaping ahead. It was just eight hours to him leaving for the airport and in that time he had to pack, make a meal and finish the gate for the top of the stairs.

Phoebe was standing by the window when he drove off at half past two the following morning, and when he looked up, she shrank back out of sight.

His journey would be long, hers much shorter, but they would both be travelling towards trauma, and today would be the first of the rest of her restricted life.

She intended driving up north in the evening when the surgery was closed to avoid awkward questions. During the day she would be making her usual calls to the sick and infirm.

The only people who knew she was leaving were Janet and Leo. They'd had to be told because she wouldn't be working out her notice. Janet knew because her daughter was ready and willing to step into the vacancy that it would create, and Leo had to be told so that he could make some arrangements of his own.

She'd left the letter she'd written to Harry in Janet's safekeeping and the practice manager hadn't asked any questions. Clearly she was expecting it to be a formal resignation from the practice from a courtesy point of view, because her departure had taken place during his absence.

It had been the hardest thing she'd ever had to do, writing to tell him that she'd left because she was carrying their child, and that, loving him as she did, she couldn't bear the thought of him reluctantly accepting the responsibility of a family that he didn't want. She'd explained with stark simplicity, every word a knife thrust in her heart.

I'm pregnant. And any delay in the telling is because of our closeness in the apartments and us being employed in the practice. I don't want to be involved in a scandal.

My wish is to move away from Bluebell Cove, and when our child is born, we can talk about its future. You can have as big a part in its upbringing as you want, except for one thing—this new brother or sister for Marcus will live with me. I know you'll want to talk this through, Harry, but could we please leave it until after the birth?

Hoping you will understand and not be too angry. Phoebe.

When she'd handed the letter to Janet, she'd felt sick inside, but now it was time for action. Harry had gone and her last day in Bluebell Cove was about to commence.

As she stepped out onto the landing her eyes widened. The gate was finished. Propped up against the wall opposite, it was made out of pale wood and well crafted. Attached to it was a brief note that said, 'I've been in touch with a joiner who will come and fix it in position for you, Phoebe. This is his number. Give him a call when you're ready, regards, Harry.

Little did he know that the joiner wouldn't be required, she thought as the ache inside her increased. The gate was too big to go in the boot of the car but there was a roof rack above that she could tie it to. No way was she going to leave behind Harry's gift to them.

Then it was off to the nursery for Marcus's last attendance and another wretched moment as they said goodbye to Beth and her helpers.

Her final visits to her patients followed and it was difficult not to say goodbye to *them* under the circumstances. But as her departure would not be made public for a little while, it was advisable, just as it would be with the staff at the surgery.

When she arrived at a smart semi-detached house on a busy road in Manchester, where Katie and Rob had taken up residence to be near his father in care just a short distance away, Marcus was asleep, as he had been for most of the journey.

It was almost midnight and Katie came rushing out

when she heard the car pull up outside. 'Phoebe, you look exhausted,' she said anxiously. 'You go in and I'll bring Marcus.'

She nodded and told her wearily, 'He's been bathed, fed and is in his pyjamas, so you can pop him straight into bed, Katie, if you would.'

'Yes,' she agreed. 'Rob is making hot drinks and we've got Eccles cakes for a night-time snack, so come on in.'

'What are those?' she asked with a wan smile, 'A local treat?'

'You guess right,' Rob called from the kitchen as they walked down the hallway. 'They're all curranty and puff-pastryish, and the place they're named after is just down the road.'

'Sounds lovely', she said gratefully, thankful for these two caring people who were always there for her in times of need, and wondered what Harry was doing at that moment and where he was.

The inquest was in two days' time and if he'd asked her, she would have gone with him for moral support. But there had been no such request and she'd got the message, just as she had when he'd told her to back off.

Phoebe wept long and silently that first night in Katie and Rob's house. She loved them both. They were kindness itself, but the feeling that she didn't belong anywhere was threatening her resolve to make a fresh life for herself, and it was the dawn of another spring day before she drifted off to sleep.

When she awoke, the cot that Katie had found for

Marcus was empty, and as she pulled herself up against the pillows it all came back. The long journey, the dreadful playacting of her last day among people she liked and respected, and Harry far away in a foreign land with no inkling of what awaited him on his return to the village. It was a nightmare that she would never want to repeat.

But they were safe with Katie and Rob for the time being. It would be almost a week before Harry returned to Bluebell Cove and by that time she hoped to be feeling calmer. He wouldn't know where she was and when he'd read her letter he probably wouldn't want to.

When she went downstairs Katie was giving Marcus his breakfast.

Rob had gone to work and her sister said, 'I advise complete rest for a few days, Phoebe. I'll look after Marcus. Don't even think of finding somewhere to live or looking for a job. You've got to think of your baby. Things can so easily go wrong in these early months and you don't want to lose it, do you?'

'No, I don't,' she said bleakly. 'Whatever the future holds, I would never want that to happen, so I'll follow your advice.'

'I hope this guy realises what he's missing out on,' was Katie's reply to that.

When Harry's plane touched down in Australia, he was surprised to see his lawyer among those waiting to greet arrivals from the UK. As they shook hands he asked, 'To what do I owe this honour, Jonas?'

'To me feeling that you might need some moral

support at the inquest, Harry,' was the reply. 'They can be depressing occasions, so let's go and find somewhere to eat and then I'll drive you to the hotel that I've booked you into.'

When they were seated in a restaurant on the concourse, the sun-bronzed, smart-suited lawyer, who looked more like a playboy than a lawyer, said, 'So how's it going in the UK? Have you settled back into your familiar surroundings?'

'Yes and no,' he replied. 'It's great to be home, or at least it would be if *all* my previous memories of it were good.' Harry debated with himself how much more to say then decided to open his heart—Jonas was a friend as well as his lawyer, and he desperately wanted to talk about Phoebe anyway. 'I've been dragging my feet with this wonderful woman I've fallen in love with.'

'In what way?'

'She has a child from a previous marriage, but in spite of that is very much drawn to family life, which I'm not—or haven't been, I should say. But I adore Phoebe and her little one, and I'm going to do something about it when I get back.'

'Good for you. Will I get an invite to the wedding?'

'Yes, if it materialises,' he promised, and could feel his palms getting moist and his shirt collar too tight at the thought of what he would do if Phoebe didn't want him, even though he would have deserved it.

The verdict at the inquest had been one of accidental death and Harry had breathed a sigh of relief when it had ended. He'd flown straight home afterwards, two days early due to the brevity of the proceedings, and also because he couldn't wait to get back to Bluebell Cove. Now he could go forward into the new life that he was planning, with Phoebe and Marcus to show him what real love and caring was all about.

A taxi dropped him off outside the surgery buildings in the quietness of a Sunday morning. He ran up the stairs to the apartments two at a time, noticing as he did so that the gate hadn't been fixed in place. That was strange, but not so strange that he was prepared for Leo opening the door of Phoebe's apartment dressed only in boxer shorts.

'What are *you* doing here?' he asked with ominous calm, and his second-in-command stared at him.

'I've taken over from Phoebe. She's gone to live elsewhere, so I'm renting the place with Janet's permission. You remember I asked about one of these if there was ever a vacancy? As it turned out, Phoebe decided to up sticks before you did. Come on in, I've just brewed up. Do you want a cuppa?'

'No, thanks,' he said as he tried to take in what he'd just been told.

He was to blame for Phoebe leaving the village, he thought numbly. Now that he'd got his priorities sorted out and rushed home to her, she wasn't here.

'I'm assuming that you have a forwarding address for her,' he said levelly.

'No, I haven't, as a matter of fact,' Leo replied. 'She was reluctant to tell me where she was going and I don't think she gave Janet one either. In any case our practice manager is away for the weekend. I imagine that Phoebe has gone to her sister's, but it's only a guess.'

'And do you know where her sister lives?'

'I have a rough idea. She's moved to Manchester since Phoebe came to live here. As you know, that's where I come from and she knew that. One day when we were chatting she said what part of Manchester her sister lived in, and surprisingly it was the same area where I was brought up.'

'Do you know their name?' he asked, still with that false calm on him.

''Fraid not, but what I do know is that they went to be near his father, who is in a care home just a few doors away from them. My mother was in there for a short time before my sister took her to live abroad with her. And Harry, if you don't mind, I'd like to put some clothes on now.'

'Yes, of course,' he said apologetically. 'If you'll write down the directions to get to this place, I'll be off immediately.'

'Yes, sure,' he agreed, 'though what's the rush?'

'Can't stop now—tell you later,' he said as Leo scribbled down the name and address of the nursing home. 'I don't see me being back in time for tomorrow's surgeries. Can I impose on you for one more day, Leo?'

'Yes, of course,' he said easily. 'You have no idea how many times Ethan filled in for me last year when my mother was ill and I had to keep going back to Manchester to look after her.'

* * *

It was early evening and Harry had found the road where Katie and Rob lived quite easily due to Leo's mention of the nursing home. The fact that Phoebe's car was parked outside a house a couple of doors away from it also helped.

The curtains were drawn upstairs so it would seem that Marcus was sleeping up there, but of the woman he'd come to see there was no sign. Though he was longing to talk to her, he decided to restrain himself until morning and went and booked himself into a nearby hotel for the night.

Now that he knew where she was, he was calming down. To discover Phoebe had packed up and left during his short absence had wiped every other thought from his mind. He'd intended sweeping her off her feet when she opened the door to him and asking her to marry him on the spot.

Instead, he'd been confronted by a bewildered Leo, and didn't want to contemplate what he would have done if the amiable man hadn't come up with a suggestion that had helped him to find her.

He was appalled that he could have upset her so much that she'd left Bluebell Cove without a word, *and* planned the move for a time when he wasn't around. He prayed that, come morning, she would have some answers for him, if only he could get to speak to her. His only consolation so far was that her car was still outside the house.

It was half past nine next morning when he arrived back at the road where Phoebe's sister lived. He'd parked his car down a side street with the feeling that if Phoebe saw the red sports car, she would be forewarned of his presence and might refuse to see him.

He would have been round there at first light, so desperate was he to speak to her, but this wasn't like knocking on the door of her apartment. It was her sister's home where he was going to be intruding.

As he was approaching the house, he stepped back out of sight. Someone who had to be Katie had come out of the house with Marcus in his buggy and set off in the opposite direction.

He breathed a sigh of relief. That left just Rob, Phoebe's brother-in-law, to get past, and with a bit of luck he would have gone to wherever he was employed.

The trauma of leaving Bluebell Cove and the long drive to Manchester was still there, Phoebe thought, but the rest that she'd promised Katie she would have was bringing some of her strength back, though not her sense of purpose. She felt as if she'd lost that somewhere along the way.

Her sister had taken Marcus to the park and Rob was away on business for a few days, so she had the house to herself as she came downstairs from the shower, intending to do something with her hair, which had been fastened back with a rubber band ever since she'd arrived.

She'd just had a bout of morning sickness and was feeling anything but lively when the doorbell rang, and still wearing a robe and slippers she went to answer it.

When she opened the door and saw Harry standing

there, she clutched the robe more tightly around her with one hand and held onto the door post with the other.

'Hello, Phoebe,' he said gently. 'Will you marry me?'

She shook her head. 'No.'

'Why not?' he asked with the gentleness still there.

'You know why not!' she cried as the shock waves that had hit her on seeing him began to recede. 'I've explained in the letter that I don't want you marrying me out of kindness or duty.'

'Do you think I might step inside for a moment?'

'Yes, of course.' She led him into the sitting room.

Still keeping his calm, he asked, 'And what letter might that be?'

'The one I asked Janet to give you.'

'I see. I got back from Australia yesterday morning, made the disturbing discovery that Leo was living in your apartment, and learned from him that you might have gone to your sister's. He remembered a conversation he'd had with you about where she lived, and that is how I come to be here.'

'So you don't know?' she breathed. 'You haven't asked me to marry you because of what was in the letter?'

'No, whatever it might be.' He brushed it to one side. 'I've loved you from the moment of our second meeting. If you remember, the first one on the night of my arrival in Bluebell Cove was rather odd! But, getting back to why I'm here, I've hesitated to tell you how much I love you because for a long time my unhappy childhood cast a shadow over the thought of a family of my own. It has taken you, a single mother, to show me how wrong I've been, and I want to take care of you and Marcus for the rest of my life…if you'll let me.'

'You crazy man,' she said softly. 'You made me unhappy by trying to *avoid* making me unhappy! I adore you, but I left the village because I thought you didn't want me. And there was another reason as well…'

'And what's that?' he asked gently, drawing her into his arms, complete with rubber band.

'I'm pregnant, Harry. That's why I said no when you asked me to marry you. It was what I'd been dreading— that you might offer to marry me because I'm pregnant, and for no other reason. And at the back of my mind was always my ex-husband Darren's response when I told him I was pregnant with Marcus. He wanted me to get an abortion, which is why we got divorced, and I just couldn't bear to think of what I'd do if you weren't interested in being a father. I didn't know you hadn't read my letter and that you were asking me because you really do love me.'

He had become very still, had neither moved or spoken while she'd been explaining. Easing herself out of his arms, she looked up at him questioningly.

'Say something, please,' she begged.

'How about wonderful, marvellous, you amazing woman?' he cried joyfully. 'Not only do you love me but you are going to give me children, and not just one but two, because I love Marcus as if he was my own. I'm so sorry to hear the reasons why your first marriage broke up, but reassure yourself that you've just made me the happiest man in the world! Can I propose to you again?'

'Yes, please do.'

'Will you marry me, Phoebe?'

'Yes, Harry,' she said softly. 'I would love to be your wife.'

'So can I take you back with me to where you belong?'

'Yes, but remember I have nowhere to live. Can I share your apartment?'

'Just for a short time, yes.'

'And what then?'

'We'll be moving.'

'Where to?'

'With hope in my heart, I've bought Glades Manor for us and our children, my beautiful bride-to-be. I'm signing the contract tomorrow, the sale will be finalised soon afterwards. And now can we please spend a few moments making up for lost time?'

'Yes,' she breathed, 'and just think, Harry, we have the rest of our lives to do that!'

He placed his hand gently below her waistline, where his child lay safe and snug, and when their glances locked she saw something that hadn't been there before. The tranquillity that came with contentment.

When Katie returned some time later with Marcus, the scene before her was what she'd prayed for. One glance at the man who had come for his bride was enough to tell her that Phoebe had found her heart's desire at last.

'Harry is taking us back to Bluebell Cove, Katie,'

she said. 'We're going to be married as soon as we can. Thank you so much for your kindness, and we'd love you to be my bridesmaid if you will.'

'Of course,' she said, and with a smile for the man who was going to give Phoebe the love she so much deserved, 'Rob will be so sorry to have missed meeting you, Harry.'

'We'll make up for it at the wedding, Katie,' he promised.

They were ready to leave, with Marcus strapped firmly into his car seat and Phoebe on the point of saying goodbye to Katie, but one thing was missing.

'I brought something with me and don't want to forget it,' she told Harry.

'It's in the garage.'

'Okay,' he replied. 'I'll go and get it. What is it?'

'A gate,' she said laughingly. 'Your first gift to me was a gate and I will treasure it for ever.'

CHAPTER TEN

THEY'D stopped off a couple of times on the way back for refreshment and for Marcus to have a little play. Every time Phoebe saw the two of them together, it was as if all the dreams she'd ever dreamed were coming true because Harry loved her. And in the autumn, when grain was being harvested and leaves were turning to bronze and gold, there would be another child to cherish, born of the love he had for her.

She was going to suggest to him that if it was a girl they should call her Cassie, just so his bubbly and fiery first wife would never be forgotten.

When Leo stepped out of his new accommodation the following morning, he was amazed. If he'd had any doubts about whether Harry's search for Phoebe had been successful, proof was there in the sturdy gate fitted at the top of the stairs. That explained the sound of drilling at a late hour!

They'd slept in each other's arms with the contentment of lovers reunited after a long absence, as that was what the weeks of hurt and misunderstanding had felt like to both of them. Marcus was safely tucked up on the sofa beside them and once the day was under way, they would go out to buy a cot.

When they'd made love before sleeping, there had been none of the doubts and uncertainties of before to trouble them. The way ahead was clear, the past was over, they loved each other totally, and what could be more wonderful than that?

On the way home they'd made plans for the following day in the form of a visit to the solicitor on the main street during Harry's lunch-break at the surgery. There he would sign the contracts for his purchase of Glades Manor and would request an early completion of the sale.

At the weekend they would shop for furniture and fittings to grace the elegant house where they were going to bring up their children and at the same time plan a wedding.

'There are going to be some raised eyebrows when the surgery staff find out that I'm back and living with you in your apartment,' Phoebe said the next morning as they ate their first breakfast together.

'So why don't we put up a notice announcing our forthcoming marriage and inviting them to be our guests when we've fixed a date?' Harry suggested.

On the way to the solicitor at lunchtime he said, 'Janet gave me the letter first thing and, after reading it, I love you more than ever, Phoebe.'

'It was my darkest hour when I wrote that,' she told him, 'and my brightest when I opened the door of Katie and Rob's house to find you on the doorstep.

'I'd been so sure of how I was going to plan the rest

of my life without you, yet putting it into practice felt like a knife in my heart. I was weak and wilting without you, but not any more, Harry, because you love me. I'm not just part of the package that comes with Marcus.'

'You never were,' he said softly, pulling up at the roadside. 'You were yourself, beautiful and kind, loyal and understanding, and I'm going to spend the rest of my life making you happy.' Oblivious of passers-by, he reached across and traced her lips with a gentle finger and then he kissed them.

The legal business had been completed and they were driving back to the practice when Phoebe said, 'When you mentioned Janet earlier, I intended telling you that her daughter is the new district nurse. Have you met her at all?'

'Yes, briefly, and she seemed fine. So was that part of your plan when you decided to move to Manchester, fitting Janet's daughter up with a position here?' he asked quizzically.

'Well, yes, I couldn't just pack up and go leaving the surgery short-staffed, could I? It would have made life difficult for you and that was the last thing I wanted.'

'Life would have been more than difficult without you Phoebe, it would have been hell on earth,' he told her. 'Why don't we call in at the vicarage on our way back and fix a date for the wedding?'

'How about May Day if the vicar is free?' she suggested. 'Saturday the first of May. We could erect a maypole in the garden at the house and after the wedding all dance around it with me wearing the Easter

Bonnet clothes! It will be as if your parents are there with us then, giving us their blessing.'

The church was in sight and everything else was forgotten in the need to get things moving in time for the first of May.

The vicar was able to grant their request for a wedding on that date. The solicitor had already promised a quick completion, and, unbelievably, when Barbara Balfour had phoned Ethan to tell him that Harry was marrying Phoebe, the young district nurse that he'd been so protective of while *he'd* been in charge of the surgery, he'd offered them his house in Bluebell Cove for the wedding reception and accepted Harry's invitation to be his best man. When the decision had been made to go to live in the place where Francine had been brought up they had decided to keep the house in Bluebell Cove for visiting the village whenever the urge came over them, and now it would be serving its purpose.

It also meant that the whole family would be coming over from France for the occasion, Ethan himself, Francine and their children, Kirstie and Ben.

Katie, as arranged on the day that Harry had proposed to her sister, was to be Phoebe's maid of honour, and Lucy had offered to look after Marcus on the great day, and so the arrangements proceeded.

Barbara Balfour was delighted at the prospect of seeing Ethan again and completely overwhelmed at the thought of having the two men that she loved like sons together again in Bluebell Cove.

Leo, whose love life was a flourishing but fleeting thing, was taking stock and wondering whether he was missing out on something every time he saw Harry's contentment.

And, in the midst of everything, Phoebe had been for her first antenatal appointment at a birthing centre that had recently been opened adjoining Hunter's Hill Hospital in the town and been told that her pregnancy was coming along fine.

Glades Manor became legally theirs just before the wedding and while Harry was at the practice, Phoebe supervised the delivery and arranging of the furnishings they had bought. At the same time she watched two men from the village erect a maypole with bright ribbons streaming from it in the centre of one of the lawns adjacent to the house.

When Harry saw it he said, 'You aren't really going to wear my mother's things when you dance around it, are you? You looked wonderful in them, but they are quite old-fashioned!'

'But of course—just watch me,' she teased.

'Watching you is my delight,' he told her softly as she moved into his waiting arms.

All the village had turned out for the wedding of the district nurse and their GP, and as the bells rang out over Bluebell Cove, the small church was filling up rapidly.

Harry had kept his promise to his lawyer and Jonas had just arrived straight from the airport. Ethan and his family had appeared a couple of days ago and those who knew them best thought how well and happy they all looked after their traumas of the year before. It was good to know that moving across the Channel had been the right decision for them.

On a clear May morning, Katie's husband Rob walked Phoebe down the aisle to take her place beside Harry. In a wedding dress of heavy cream brocade that was stunning in its simplicity, and with a coronet of pearls on her head, she walked sedately down the aisle, linking one arm through her brother-in-law's and in the other carrying an arrangement of bluebells and lilies of the valley.

The man of her dreams was waiting and as their glances held, it was there in his eyes how much he loved her, and how much he was looking forward to their life together. But it was down to little Marcus, sitting in the front pew on Lucy's knee, to make their day truly perfect, as he spoke his favourite new words, 'Mummy' *and* 'Daddy'!

THE BABY WHO
SAVED DR CYNICAL

CONNIE COX

This book is dedicated to Sonia, sister of my heart, who always believes in me and to Amy and Winnie who follow their bliss and inspire me to do the same.

CHAPTER ONE

SHE'D done it. She'd sold Dr. Jason Drake's reputation for three million dollars and a closed case.

As Director of Diagnostics, Dr. Stephanie Montclair had agreed to pay off the family's wrongful death claim, with Dr. Jason Drake's name on the line as the attending physician and no fault levied against Sheffield Memorial Hospital.

"We all tried our best to keep that precious little boy alive. Dr. Drake stayed up here three days straight trying to save little Isaac," Stephanie offered in token protest to the ring of lawyers that surrounded her desk.

"You're doing the right thing," the chief legal counselor reassured her. "A good prosecuting attorney would have a judge and jury in tears inside three minutes flat. Even if we were to win the suit in the end, Sheffield Memorial can't risk the prolonged negative publicity. And if Dr. Drake is called to the stand, with his brash manner, we can't predict how he'll come across."

Reluctantly, Stephanie agreed. Jason was a great doctor— one of the best—but he'd never seen the need to sugarcoat his words.

"There has to be a better way. Sanction me instead."

"Not an option, Dr. Montclair. The board would never approve it, and rightly so," one of the lawyers said. "That move could put the whole department in jeopardy."

The case had been heartbreaking. In conjunction with Diagnostics, Sheffield's Neonatal Unit had tried scores of unorthodox methods to keep the premature infant alive, many of them beyond the edge of convention, only to have the grieving parents lash out at the hospital to try to ease their pain.

That little Isaac's parents were high-profile celebrities hadn't helped. The grief-stricken couple had threatened to call in every publicity connection they had if Sheffield Memorial didn't take action against the culprit who'd killed their baby.

Stephanie could understand the parents' anguish. Although she'd only known about her own baby a few short weeks, the thought of losing that tiny life inside her sent heavy waves of dread through her heart.

Still, she and the lawyers couldn't make them understand there was nothing Jason or anyone else could have done better.

And now the hospital's reputation was in danger. As a small, private research and teaching hospital, Sheffield Memorial kept its doors open only through grants and goodwill.

Dr. Wilkins chimed in. "Stephanie, the board recommendation to name Dr. Drake in the lawsuit is the least harmful action we can take for the greater good. Dr. Drake might have his shortcomings, but he's one of the top diagnostic physicians in the world. His stellar professional standing can take the hit with no lasting, detrimental effect. That's why we shell out the big bucks for his malpractice insurance."

Not only was Wilkins the board's treasurer, he was a family friend who had attended her christening. He knew her Achilles' heel.

"We've already seen a drop in patient referrals. A messy court case along with a star-studded media circus would call our accreditations into question and jeopardize critical funding. We would have to turn away sick children who need us."

Before she could waver, she signed on the dotted line. Each of the hospital's team of lawyers stood and shook her hand, sealing the deal. She would be washing that hand as soon as possible.

As they left her office, Dr. Wilkins hung back from the others. "The board and I were worried you'd let your personal relationship with Dr. Drake influence your decision. They will be pleased to learn you had no qualms about putting Sheffield Memorial first."

Stephanie clearly heard the unspoken threat behind his words, despite the fact the hospital was named after her maternal great-grandfather.

Doctors ran on both sides of the family. Her mother was a cardiologist. Her father an endocrinologist. Both sat on the hospital board. Although if a newcomer had suggested Stephanie had been appointed to her current position of Director of Pediatric Diagnostics because of who she was, instead of what she did, she hoped any of the hospital personnel would be quick to disabuse them. Stephanie worked day and night to be twice as competent as any other department head and prove she'd earned her position.

Then again, those who knew her staff didn't envy her. She was the only department head who could handle Jason Drake.

"Tell them not to worry. I would never put the hospital at risk for personal reasons." She hesitated to add more, but everyone on the Diagnostics floor already knew anyway. "Dr. Drake and I aren't together anymore."

"The board will be glad to hear it." Whether that was a comment on her loyalty to the hospital or her relationship with Dr. Drake or both, Stephanie didn't know. She only knew that, even though she'd effectively besmirched and betrayed Jason, she had made the right decision. So why did it feel so wrong?

Her stomach lurched, as if her baby were protesting Mommy's ill treatment of Daddy. Yes, the deal she'd finagled left a very sour taste in her mouth.

Outside the patient's open door, Stephanie stopped to gather her thoughts. She could see that Jason was already inside the room.

In accordance with the terms of the settlement, Stephanie would sit in on this case and every other case Jason picked up for the next six months. It was a mixed blessing that the bad publicity they'd already received had resulted in fewer patients checking into Sheffield Memorial. She wasn't sure how she would have handled the extra duties along with her normal responsibilities. But at least the morning sickness was letting up now.

Her involvement in his cases hadn't been an issue in the past. In fact, even though her administrative duties had limited her patient load, Jason had always invited her in on cases he'd thought would interest her. Hopefully he would continue to welcome her after he learned of the lawsuit.

As he paid little attention to any hospital business outside of medicine, she was counting on him shrugging off the deal as a necessary evil and continuing on as normal.

Only with the compromises she'd had to make it wouldn't be quite as normal as she would have liked, though she would try to make it as painless as possible for both of them.

As usual, Jason wore scrubs, although the other diagnosticians wore business attire and lab coats. On his six-feet-four frame the drawstring pants and boxy shirt took nothing away from his lean build, kept hard with hiking and white-water rafting.

He needed a haircut. His spiky dark blond hair went out of control almost as fast as his mouth did. How many times had she finger-combed those strands into place after making love?

One too many, apparently.

Originally they had agreed to keep it casual. She had avoided relationships in the past, not wanting to take her focus off her climb up the medical ladder, but Jason Drake had seemed perfect. Remote. Stoic. Yet highly sensual and with no strings attached. Perfect for her first intentionally cavalier relationship.

When Jason had seemed reluctant to talk about himself, his roots, his past, his reticence had only helped her stay detached— at least that was what she'd told herself. She had gotten exactly what she'd thought she wanted. But now she couldn't stop herself from wanting more.

She'd thought something special was developing between them, but now she understood she'd mistaken sexual attraction for an emotional connection.

No, she'd never meant to fall for him. He certainly hadn't made the same mistake with her. Jason didn't do emotions.

Now she was certain they had no future together. Not even for the sake of the baby. They might have if he'd bothered to show up for dinner that night, but she'd not been important enough to derail his plans—again.

At three and a half months, she would be showing soon. She should try again to tell Jason about the baby. He had a right to know, even if she didn't expect anything from him.

If only he were daddy material.

Damn. He hated these cases.

The little dark-haired girl wasn't quite four yet. She had big brown eyes that looked up to him to make her feel better.

He flipped through her chart, noting all the tests she'd gone through. The kid had been poked by more needles than a porcupine had. She couldn't understand.

Stay objective. Sympathy doesn't fix anyone.

First the baby boy, Isaac, and now this little girl was really getting to him. He was going soft. It didn't help that this was the anniversary of his brother's death—which should be the perfect reminder to keep his emotions out of the equation.

He needed a stress-reliever.

One good night in Stephanie's bed would fix him right up. Her, too.

Medicine wasn't the only thing he took pride in.

He still didn't understand what had happened. It was only a missed dinner date, and they'd both agreed at the beginning to keep things casual. Their careers were too important for anything more serious, which suited Jason perfectly. He had vowed on his brother's grave that he would never, ever lose himself in a relationship again.

Even if Stephanie didn't want to be intimate they could share a meal, talk, enjoy each other's company. Although he'd never been lonely before, since their breakup his evenings stretched into long, empty, sleepless hours to be endured before morning, when he could get back to his work.

He gave a tight nod to the girl's mother. "The test results are in. It's not multiple sclerosis."

Her mother gave him a protective version of her daughter's smile. "That's good. What's next?"

Automatically he compared the mother's features to her daughter's, looking for clues to an inheritable condition.

The father wasn't in the picture. How could any man look at himself in the mirror after deserting his own child? And a developmentally disabled child at that?

"We're still ruling out various forms of muscular dystrophy. We're testing muscular DNA samples, which may tell us something and may not. I'm not going to do a nerve conduction velocity test until I have to. It's rather uncomfortable and I don't think Maggie will understand." He should really run the test and get it over with, but Maggie had been through a lot lately and he might get his answer in a less invasive way.

Yes, he was definitely getting soft, and it was affecting his logic. Not good. For him or his patients.

His attention was diverted by Stephanie coming up behind them.

Jason would recognize that walk anywhere. Steady, confident and competent. In her customary high heels, she reached his chin. He only had to dip his head to meet her, mouth-to-mouth.

She walked with purpose. She did everything with purpose.

Directness was one of the qualities he admired about her— along with her body, her hair, her smell. He admired everything about her except her decision to break it off with him.

Her long, straight mink-brown hair was gathered into a low ponytail today.

It had been four weeks and two days since he'd freed it from its bindings and wrapped it around him like a waterfall in the privacy of her bedroom.

"I'll be joining you on this case, Dr. Drake."

"You're the boss." Not that he answered to any man—or

woman. He knew his purpose in life. Grabbing people back from the abyss of death had nothing to do with administrative rules or regulations.

Still, she was good at what she did: juggling patient care, internal politics and financial budgets. He had to admit his life ran much more smoothly with her in charge.

What was different about her lately?

Did her eyes look deeper? Her face rounder? Was she glowing? She might have put on a few pounds. He couldn't be certain with her open lab coat covering her button-down shirt and straight fitted skirt. If so, they looked good on her.

"I'm Dr. Montclair." Stephanie introduced herself, giving equal attention to daughter and mother.

"Please call me Anne, and this is Maggie." Maggie's mom stood and shook hands.

Stephanie crouched down to Maggie's eye level as the child sat in her bed. "How are you today, Maggie?"

Maggie looked past Stephanie and stuffed her doll's hand into her mouth.

"I'm going to listen to your heart, okay?" She unwrapped her stethoscope from her lab coat pocket and hung it around her neck.

At Sheffield Memorial it was policy that each doctor on a case would check vitals and make independent assessments. Attention to such details was one of the key factors that made Sheffield Memorial such a renowned teaching and research hospital, even if it was much smaller than most public institutions.

Despite Stephanie's cheerful tone and slow movements, Maggie whimpered and drew back.

Anne spoke up. "She only lets Dr. Drake do that."

Jason frowned. He hadn't realized. Maggie had no reason to like him or trust him. He hadn't asked for that. He only wanted to assess her symptoms, identify the problem and fix it.

Stephanie stepped back. "What if I listen to Mom's heart first?"

Maggie shook her head. An emphatic no.

Anne stroked her daughter's hair to calm her. "Could Dr. Montclair listen to Dr. Drake's heart, then?"

The child grinned around the doll in her mouth.

He and Stephanie hadn't touched, even to brush hands, since their break-up. The anticipation of her hands on him made his skin quiver.

He took a step back. "If we need to forgo this I can debrief you with all Maggie's vitals as well as her current condition before the diagnostics meeting, Dr. Montclair."

"I appreciate that. Now, let's set a good example for Maggie and try the stethoscope." Stephanie fitted the earpieces and waggled her finger at Jason to come closer. "Stand still and take a deep breath, Dr. Drake."

When she placed her hand on his chest, the single layer of material between them did nothing to stop a spark arcing between her hand and his heart. He concentrated on keeping his heart-rate steady but failed miserably. He could feel the pounding in his ears. What kind of example would he set for Maggie if he grabbed Stephanie and bolted from the room with her at her very proper touch?

Stephanie was having no problem being steady, cool and in control.

Using great discipline, he controlled his breathing, steadily in and out. His professional reputation was at stake.

Stephanie gave him a worried look but said nothing.

Finally, she dropped her hands and turned to Maggie. "Your turn?"

Aside from a grimace, the girl didn't protest this time.

"Now let me take your pulse, Dr. Drake." She held out her hand for his wrist.

No sense in fighting the inevitable. When she asked, he could deny her nothing.

Her warm, open palm held him as captive as a set of handcuffs. The pad of her fingers rocked back and forth until she found the throbbing in his wrist.

Would she notice if his heart skipped a beat or two?

"Thank you, Dr. Drake." She turned back to Maggie, who appeared to be avidly looking to the left of their little charade. "Your turn, Maggie. May I hold your arm?"

To Jason's amazement, Maggie held out her wrist. This was the first response she'd made to anyone's request since she'd been hospitalized. From the sudden alertness in her mother's eyes, this was unexpected for Anne, too.

Stephanie found the girl's pulse and counted.

"Thank you, Maggie." The moment Stephanie released her arm Maggie put it under the covers.

"Perfect," she told the girl. "Now, let's check ears and eyes. Dr. Drake, if you'll sit, please?" She pointed to the visitor's chair beside the bed.

Maggie scrambled to turn herself onto her side and peer through the railings to watch. Observing and analyzing Maggie's movements helped distract Jason from the intimacy of his own examination. If Maggie could so easily pull her legs under her and twist sideways, why couldn't she walk? She had once been able to run around the house without hesitation. How did her late ambulatory development factor in?

"Ears first." Stephanie leaned over him, her breasts inches from his mouth. He swallowed hard to keep from drooling.

Her featherlight touch tickled the rim of his ear.

As Stephanie leaned close to look, her sweet breath warmed his neck.

Every primal cell in his body screamed for him to pick her up, throw her over his shoulder and take her back to his lair. For Maggie's sake he kept himself still and unresponsive, although his clenched palms had begun to sweat.

"That didn't bother you a bit, did it, Dr. Drake?"

"No, not at all." He forced the lie past his gritted teeth.

"Now, let's take a look at your eyes."

There was no way Jason could hide the dilation of his pupils—a physiological reaction to his desire. To distract himself, he silently listed the noble gasses from the periodic table while congratulating himself on his own noble restraint.

Stephanie's intense scrutiny made him want to wince away, but her hand on his shoulder held him still. Once she was satisfied with what she saw she released him. He sank back into the chair, so tense every nerve-ending twanged like over-tightened guitar strings.

Stephanie showed no signs of being affected at all. As if they were nothing but colleagues and had never been lovers. As if he'd never made her scream his name into the night, or washed breakfast dishes beside her in the morning.

What had he done besides miss a dinner date or two? Duty had called. She'd grown up in a doctors' household. Surely she understood? It had to be something more.

"Your turn, Maggie." Stephanie moved from chair to bedside.

Maggie began to protest by grunting, and waving the hand that didn't hold her doll, but when Jason enfolded her fluttering hand in his she settled down and let Stephanie shine a light into her eyes as she stared at the wall past her mother.

"All done." Stephanie stuck the small light into her lab coat pocket. "You're a very brave girl, Maggie."

At her name, Maggie slid her glance past Stephanie to rest slightly to the right. She held out her doll in an obvious invitation to be friends.

Careful to avoid the doll's wet chewed hand, Stephanie took the ratty-haired toy and cradled it in her arms, giving the honor proper tribute. She gave the doll a pat and reverently tucked it into bed beside Maggie. "Thank you, Maggie. I'll come back and visit soon."

Stephanie would be a good mother. Jason's thoughts startled him so much he stood abruptly. He'd never thought of motherhood and Stephanie Montclair in the same breath before.

She had a demanding job and a busy social schedule. How could she add motherhood to the mix, even if she wanted to? And then there was the little issue of who would father her child.

He had the strangest urge to volunteer.

First his disturbing emotional reaction to his patients and

now this? No, he was not cut out to be a family man, much as he might daydream about it. He had enough past history to prove he did more harm than good in that role. He really needed to make arrangements for a few days off soon...

"Diagnostics meeting starts in five minutes." He walked to the door to get Stephanie moving in that direction.

"If there's anything I or my staff can do to make your stay more comfortable, let me know," Stephanie said to Maggie's mother, sounding like the concierge of an expensive hotel. Was she really that worried about the fall-off of patients?

She probably was. Sheffield Memorial was her family's legacy—something she took very seriously. There was nothing she wouldn't do to make it thrive. Next thing he knew she would be sending in staff to put mints on the patients' pillows.

Drake couldn't fault her. If he'd had a legacy of any sort he might feel the same. But mongrels like him had no birthright to speak of. And the heritage he *did* have was better off left unspoken.

As soon as the door latched behind him, she stopped him with a hand to his arm, sending tingles to the soles of his feet. "Before we talk about the girl, I want you to get a physical. Your heart rate is too fast and your blood pressure is elevated."

"I'm fine."

"That's a direct order. Got it?"

Protesting wouldn't get him back on her good side. "Fine. I'll get it checked out. I didn't know you cared."

"Of course I care. This hospital is in enough trouble with the media without one of our physicians dropping dead in the hallway because he neglected his own health."

"Your concern is touching." He put distance between them, but his arm still tingled where her hand had been.

Stephanie used all her will-power to keep from reaching out and pulling him back to her.

She craved the vibrations he sent through her when he touched her, the deep-seated sense of wellbeing and protection he gave her whenever he was near. But he had proved to her too many times that it was a false sense of security.

She couldn't count on him to keep a dinner date, much less a vow of happily-ever-after.

Stephanie picked up her pace, putting even more distance between them. She didn't need him, and neither did her baby.

A wave of exhaustion tinged with queasiness hit her, pressing on her shoulders and dragging at her heels. Normal, her obstetrician had promised her. It should pass soon.

Like a good Montclair, Stephanie soldiered on.

She would need to tell her parents soon.

They were so conservative. Telling them about her unplanned baby would disappoint them at first. Not only was she unwed, she was a *doctor*, for heaven's sake. She should know how to prevent pregnancy.

Where once she would have whole-heartedly agreed with them, she now had a more sympathetic view. Accidents happened—even to medical professionals.

And this was a happy accident. She already loved her unborn child beyond measure.

Her parents and grandparents would support her in the end, even if they weren't totally happy to do so.

The Montclairs and the Sheffields stuck together, putting on a united front. They always had. In fact, Stephanie felt confident that once they were over the shock of their dateless daughter being pregnant they would be thrilled at having a successor to carry on the family name—something her father perpetually worried about.

Her child would grow up knowing only respect and her unconditional love, no matter what anyone thought about his or her parentage. She would make sure of it.

Her child would be the center of her universe.

Yes, Stephanie was positive her child would lack for nothing except a father.

"Stephanie, are you all right?" Jason asked.

They had paused outside the conference room. When had

they stopped walking? Preoccupation and distraction seemed to be another symptom of her pregnancy lately.

"I'm fine. Just fine," she snapped at him.

"You're pale." He ran a finger down her cheek—way too intimate for their present circumstances. "And clammy. And you have a faraway look in your eyes."

"I've got a lot on my mind."

"The lawsuit?"

"That's an issue I can't discuss with you right now." Not until the board signed off on her decision. That would probably happen sometime this evening, during the Montclair-Sheffield fundraiser, with board members discreetly disappearing into a private alcove to affix their signatures to the document that would blemish Jason's reputation.

But it was too late for second thoughts.

Soldier on, Stephanie.

Through the partially open blinds of the conference room she could see her diagnostic staff assembled. "They're waiting on us."

"Stephanie, if there's anything I can do to help—"

His offer surprised her.

Too soon she would have the unfortunate duty of telling him how the hospital he had devoted his whole life to was selling him out.

Yes, he would be well compensated for his involuntary sacrifice, but the board didn't understand. Jason didn't do what he did for money. He did it out of passion.

Stephanie knew she was the only one who understood the passion Jason hid beneath his cynically stoic exterior.

All he had to do was brush against her to remind her.

"After you." He held the door open for her, briefly trailing his fingertips on the small of her back to guide her through.

His gray eyes smoldered before he banked the fire, but she'd seen the desire that flickered there. And had felt a responding spark in herself—a spark that could all too easily be fanned into a full-blown inferno.

All vestiges of nausea and lethargy fled at his touch.
They were so good together. Maybe if…
No, it was too late for second thoughts.

CHAPTER TWO

JASON saw that Dr. Riser and Dr. Phillips had already seated themselves at the table with a cup of coffee each.

He turned to the kitchenette that housed a small microwave and refrigerator along with a pair of electric burners. One burner held a pot of brewed coffee, but Stephanie preferred tea.

Filling the extra pot with water, he put it on the burner to boil.

"It's rather warm in here, isn't it?" Stephanie began to peel off her lab coat.

Her skin was now flushed with healthy color instead of holding that pallor her worry had caused her. She really needed to get away—with him. A little time in his mountain cabin on his faux fur rug would fix her right up.

"Let me help you." Jason stepped toward her to help—out of politeness, but mostly out of the desire to touch her again. He yearned for that zing they created between them whenever they made contact, and couldn't keep himself from trying to recreate it whenever he had the chance.

But she shrugged away his outstretched hand as she hung the lab coat on the rack near the door.

Yes, her curves were definitely curvier.

As she slid into her office chair she picked up her glasses, anchored them low on the bridge of her nose and looked over the top at him. Did she know how that prim and proper look set him on fire? Was she teasing him on purpose?

He hoped so, but doubted it.

Since that fateful night two weeks ago, when he'd got caught up in his work and had to cancel their dinner date, she had rebuffed every move he'd made. He set the steeping cup of tea in front of her.

"No, thank you. I'm cutting down on caffeine." She shoved it back to him. "Now, tell me what's going on with little Maggie."

Jason took a sip of the tea himself, although it was too sweet for his taste. Then he stood and pointed to the whiteboard that listed symptoms and possible diagnoses and drew a line through multiple sclerosis. "The child is average in both weight and height. Reduced muscle tone, delayed development, lack of speech, yet good appetite and no fever. These symptoms aren't new. But after walking for a year and a half she now seems to have forgotten how. Dr. Montclair, what are your observations?"

Stephanie traced an invisible circle on the table. Her hands always moved as she processed. "Her vitals are good, all within the normal range. Her palm is warm. Not clammy or cold. Her grip is weak. Her fingernails are thin and flaky. And she has the longest eyelashes for a child of her age I've ever seen."

Fingernails and eyelashes. Only Stephanie had noticed the obvious. Added to the clues he'd already put together, a suspicion began to form in his mind.

Damn it, she looked different. Was she dating someone else?

Focus, Drake, he told himself. Mentally, he considered and discarded possible diagnoses.

"Anyone else have something to add?" he challenged his diagnostics team.

"She's obsessed with that doll," Dr. Phillips said. Dr. Phillips was the youngest and the chattiest, but her expertise in toxicology made her invaluable.

Like a parrot on her shoulder, Dr. Riser nodded in concurrence.

Dr. Riser had been doing a lot of that lately, instead of presenting his own ideas. Jason's team had been picked with great care, but even the best partnerships became stale after a while. And Jason hadn't picked Riser. The board had.

Dr. Riser was a neurosurgeon the hospital had brought in for an undisclosed salary. He regularly moonlighted for the neurology department.

The respiratory/pulmonary member of the group was missing today. Personal business, he'd said. Job interview, the rumor mill said. He was looking for a position with a higher success rate than their department.

Diagnostics was a last-ditch effort after all the other medical personnel had given up. Often the diagnosis came too late, or the patient couldn't be treated. Pediatric diagnostics was hard on the ego as well as the soul if a doctor valued his success rate over saving individual lives.

Stephanie answered Dr. Phillips. "Wouldn't you be fixated on your favorite toy, too? Surrounded by strangers, you'd be clinging to the few constants in your life."

He could always count on her to bring in the human aspect of a case. His team was becoming too narrowly focused, echoing his weaknesses as well as his strengths. Stephanie was exactly who he needed on this case. *And in his bed.*

No. He did *not* need Stephanie Montclair in his bed. He *wanted* her in his bed, but he didn't *need* her there.

What he needed was focus. Stephanie made that damned hard. He was fascinated by this strong, sexy, intelligent woman.

He looked around at the assembled doctors, his gaze deliberately sliding past Stephanie.

Turning Dr. Phillips' observation on its side, he challenged, "Did anyone notice Maggie also chewed the sleeve of her nightgown and the edge of her blanket? Is it that she wants the doll, or does she just want to put something in her mouth?"

Drs Phillips and Riser easily nodded their agreement. Jason scowled, exasperated. He didn't need any yes-men. Or yes-women. He needed independent thinkers. Loyal accord didn't diagnose patients.

He added 'obsessive chewing' to the list, then pointed to the word *'autistic.'* "Anyone get a better read on this?"

Dr. Phillips shrugged. "The girl *is* non-verbal, and she won't look at anyone straight on. That indicates autism."

"She screamed like a banshee the first time I went near her," Jason added. "Did that happen to anyone else?"

"Maybe she just doesn't like you, Drake. You know that old wives' tale—children and dogs instinctively know the good guys from the bad guys," Dr. Riser quipped.

Both Phillips and Riser laughed on cue.

Definitely too much group-think. He would need to change a team member soon.

"Actually, she's opposed to all people touching her—except for Dr. Drake, right?" Stephanie said. Was she taking up the case for him, or just pointing out the fallacy in the other doctors' observations?

In answer to her probing look, both Drs. Riser and Phillips nodded affirmation.

Stephanie drummed her fingers on the table. "Being non-verbal is also an indicator of a hearing deficiency. That could explain why she doesn't look at the person speaking. She may be partially deaf and can't figure out where the sound is coming from."

Dr. Phillips smirked. "Dr. Drake checked her hearing and her reflex reaction at the same time."

Stephanie would end up with a wrinkled forehead if she kept frowning like that. "What did you do?"

Dr. Riser answered for him. "Drake sneaked up behind the girl and dropped a food tray. The child jumped and turned around to look in the direction of the noise."

Riser leaned back in his chair. "I thought the mother was going to take a swing at him. You may be a lot of things, Drake, but daddy material isn't one of them. I wouldn't have been surprised if she had lodged a complaint. That's all we need with the lawsuit ongoing right now."

Jason saw a look of pain cross Stephanie's face. Was the department's legal problems causing her that much heartache?

Dr. Phillips nodded. "The lawyers need to settle it soon. The hospital's credibility is suffering."

Jason couldn't help but agree. His own caseload was the lightest he'd seen since he'd been at Sheffield Memorial. Normally he had to turn down more cases than he accepted.

"Not the whole hospital. Just our department," Riser clarified. "I hear you're helping out in the E.R. now, Drake. I could put in a good word for you with one of the specialties, if you want."

Jason brushed off Riser's offer, along with his condescending tone. "No need. I've already turned them all down."

Being certified in pediatrics, internal medicine and surgery, Jason had been asked to assist on every floor of the hospital—by the same staff who registered complaints when he overstepped their bureaucracy to save their patients.

Instead, since his residency in an inner-city free clinic had more than prepared him for the E.R., he'd agreed to help out his friend and department head Dr. Mike Tyler. While the pace was frantic at times, the cases had been fairly routine so far, and once his shift was over he was done. No getting lost in late nights, researching until he was too exhausted to think.

The lack of complex problems to solve made getting over the infant's loss more difficult. His modus operandi was to throw himself into his work. Or, for a while there, into Stephanie's arms.

Now that option was gone, too. Hopefully, like the shortfall of patients, it would be a temporary problem.

It wasn't just the sex.

They fit together mentally as well as physically. They laughed at the same obscure jokes, watched the same TV shows, liked the same food, and best of all they communicated on the same wavelength. Stephanie *got* him. She really got him. And he got her, too.

He'd never experienced that kind of compatibility before. He'd bet a back-rub, followed by a front-rub would fix them both right up without either of them having to say a word between them. If she'd just give their relationship a chance.

Relationship? That was a pretty strong word.

"Let's get back to Maggie."

Relationship. Put *intimate* in front of that and Jason could live with it. In fact he could live with it a lot better than he could live without it.

"Anyone have anything further to add?"

Stephanie shrugged her shoulders, as if shrugging off her worries.

"Macular degeneration," she said. "Have you tested Maggie's sight? Having only peripheral vision would explain the child's lack of eye contact."

"Possible." Jason agreed.

Stephanie was so brilliant. He loved being around her. Love? Another strong word. This time purely used as a figure of speech. Love wasn't in his scope of training.

"I'll order the test. Anything else?"

Dr. Phillips' phone vibrated.

He scowled, letting her know how he felt about the interruption.

She checked the display, then rose. "I can't stay."

Dr. Riser's phone buzzed, too. He grimaced an apology as he glanced at his watch. "An appointment."

At noon? Both of them?

Jason would bet his lunch they'd preplanned this mutiny so they wouldn't have to skip another noon break.

Yes, he worked his team hard. Anyone who partnered with him needed to show unflagging dedication, and a missed meal on occasion was part of the package.

Riser and Phillips headed for the door.

Stephanie stood, too. But she didn't make a move to leave. "Dr. Drake, could I speak privately with you for a moment?"

Dr. Drake? She only addressed him so formally in front of patients, or on occasion in bed.

"Of course." He closed the door to the conference room.

So she was finally ready to forgive him for missing dinner the weekend before last. It was about time. She'd ignored him for two whole weeks. Though, to be fair, she'd been away for one of them for a directors' conference.

"We both know how quickly rumors spread in this hospital. I need this to be kept confidential between you and me."

Jason's expectations crashed. Stephanie had been worried that their relationship might cause problems with their work. If she suggested they carry on covertly he would refuse. He wouldn't be anyone's dirty little secret.

"Stephanie, we're two consenting adults. What goes on between the two of us—"

"This is strictly business, Dr. Drake." A fleeting expression of something—sorrow?—crossed her eyes before she blinked it away. "We now have an open position in Diagnostics. I would like your opinion on several of our prospects before I contact them for discussion."

She thought about the pulmonary doctor's resignation, locked away in her desk drawer. Now, with Sheffield Memorial's name on the verge of making the gossip rags and tabloids, was not a good time to be enticing new doctors into the hospital. Hopefully Jason's involuntary sacrifice would put a stop to the talk.

But that was a problem for tomorrow.

"Absolutely." Jason's lips twisted into a cynical grimace. "Let's eliminate the candidates that might claim to have sham appointments during consultation meetings first. We've already got two doctors like that."

"Drs. Phillips and Riser's fake pages were rather immature, weren't they? I've talked to both of them about being firm and telling you they aren't at their best when they work through lunch, but they're intimidated by you."

"Intimidated? Why?"

"You're so intense."

"I'm focused."

"Yes, you are." *Too focused—to the exclusion of everything and everyone else.* "No one can refute your dedication to medicine, Dr. Drake."

He used his work as a shield, to keep everyone at a distance. While she had glimpsed the deep sensitivity Jason covered with sarcastic scowls and a cutting wit, she needed more than an occasional lapse in cynicism. She needed a man with a whole heart as well as an exceptional brain and outstanding body.

"*You're* not intimidated by me."

She laughed, but it came out bitter. "Remember who my father is. Dr. William Montclair is known the world over for his intensity of purpose. And my mother isn't a slouch in that department, either."

Jason waved away the mention of the formidable Dr. William Montclair and his spouse, Dr. Clarice Sheffield-Montclair.

"We're good together, Stephanie."

Yes, they were. She could smell his cologne, feel his body heat. His tone made her quiver to the core. Instinctively she felt herself leaning toward him.

She licked her lips.

His eyes followed her movement, like a cat ready to pounce. Intense didn't begin to cover it.

She missed him so desperately, even if he was bad medicine. Being in a room alone with him was not a good thing for her. He was like an addiction. A quick high when they were wrapped arm-in-arm, followed by a debilitating low when he detached and became solitary again.

Which he'd done as soon as she'd tried to take their relationship to a deeper level.

"Jason, I'd prefer to keep things professional at the hospital." Staying firm in her decision to stay apart took all her willpower—especially when he made no secret of the fact he wanted her.

That would end as soon as he found out about the baby.

"And impersonal outside the hospital. I got that from the phone message you left me. Did I say something to offend you?" He looked into her eyes as if he were trying to look into her head—or her heart. Without question, he had immense intensity.

"No, it wasn't anything you said."

While he'd certainly offended everyone else who'd ever walked through the hospital doors, he'd never offended her. He was egotistical, stubborn, overbearing and totally without tact, but she understood him. She could handle all his bad qualities, but she couldn't handle his inability to open himself up to her, his inability to put her first at least on occasion.

"Is this about the missed dinner date? I explained that I needed to read through the lab results so I would know if I needed to order additional tests. Did I do something wrong?" he challenged, certain that another medically related reason would excuse him.

"Other than all those other missed dinner dates and all those refusals to accompany me to social functions? No, you did nothing wrong." Nothing but be himself. But then he'd done nothing right—outside the bedroom.

The night he'd missed their dinner—the dinner during which she had planned to tell him about their baby—had been the breaking point. As she had scraped the congealed gourmet meal into the trash, blown out the candles and exchanged her negligee for her favorite oversized T-shirt and gym shorts, she'd known she couldn't fool herself any longer.

Swathed in her flannel robe, she'd settled in on the couch, hoping. Yet she'd known he wouldn't show. This was how her baby's life would be if she married him. Always waiting for Daddy to come home. She'd lived it with both her parents, feeling guilty all the while for resenting the time they spent with sick children while she'd been well and healthy. And alone.

I'll not do that to you, little one. I'll be here for you, any time you need me.

She wasn't quite sure how she would accomplish that yet, but there had to be a way to balance home life with hospital life.

She took a long look at Jason. He just wasn't the home-and-hearth type. Anything that couldn't be analyzed under a microscope had no place in his life.

Jason raised a sardonic eyebrow. "I really see no reason for you to kick me out of your personal life just because I turned down a gala or two, choosing the art of medicine over the act of socializing. Faux fawning is *not* what I majored in during med school."

He hid his hurt behind his bristling posture.

She had thought they were beyond that. That he had stopped using the mask with her. Maybe they had been before she'd called it quits between them.

"This isn't about the parties."

He'd said more than once that he didn't do emotions, but he'd lied. He'd shown her plenty of passion. And for a while there she had thought he'd also shown her caring and concern and an occasional glimpse of vulnerability. Maybe it had only been in her imagination to start with.

Now it didn't matter. He'd known she'd needed to talk. She'd told him it was important. Standing her up for dinner had been a non-verbal response louder than a shout. She just wasn't enough for him to step outside his comfort zone.

If he wouldn't risk his emotions for her then he wouldn't for his child, either.

"But you just said—" He dropped the attitude. "I don't understand, Stephanie."

This was a huge admission when he prided himself on his intellect. He really *didn't* understand.

"Jason, I want more." She reached out to him, then pulled her hand back before she could make contact. "It's not you. It's me."

Jason rolled his eyes at the platitude.

It *was* her. They'd both agreed from the beginning that neither wanted a serious relationship. Jason would readily admit that his work was his mistress.

She had breached her part of the bargain and taken this much further than an informal friendship with bedroom benefits.

Then, that night at his cabin in the mountains, when they'd lain on his porch looking into the black sky at the pinpoints of stars above, he'd reached for her hand and she'd known. His touch had made more than her skin tingle. It had made her soul vibrate in accord with his. Life and love had flowed through their clasped hands, intertwining their hearts.

That was when she'd known, Jason filled a place inside her that no one else ever could—a place in her heart made just for him from the moment she was born.

Being honest with herself, she'd known their relationship had been destined to become more from the start—at least for her. She didn't do casual sex—and, as guarded as Jason had always been about his dating life, she was sure he didn't either.

But then neither did he do commitment. And raising a child took more commitment than a dozen medical degrees.

Destiny didn't guarantee happily-ever-after, and now she had a child to think about.

That was why she'd had to break it off with him, even though it had broken her heart. *She* might be able to suffer through a casual come-and-go relationship, but she would never subject her child to that kind of pain and uncertainty.

She needed to create a stable environment that would surround and protect her child with love. She was prepared to do that. She had the financial means, the emotional capacity, and by the time her child was born she would have her work-life in perspective, too.

Now was the time. Before she burst into hormonal tears she needed to tell him about the baby and then walk away.

Now. She should tell him now, while she had his undivided attention. "Jason, I need—"

His phone vibrated. He held up a finger to wait.

"Drake here," he answered. Not a word wasted on social niceties. "No, Doctor, I can take your call. We've played tag trying to communicate long enough."

His eyes clouded as he looked through her. Another medical matter taking precedence over her. Was it too much to ask to be first? To know that their child would be first in Jason's life if only for a second?

Yes. It *was* too much to ask. While Jason was devoted to the practice of medicine, extending such devotion to a personal relationship was beyond his capabilities. She had to resign herself to that.

She reached for her lab coat, flailing to find the armhole. He'd been so eager to help her off with it, but he didn't even notice her struggle now.

Nor did he notice when she slipped out, silently shutting the consultation room door behind her.

CHAPTER THREE

JASON kept his hand tightly wrapped around his phone to keep from reaching out and holding Stephanie back—pulling her close to him and never letting her go.

He used all his discipline to concentrate on the question the doctor at the Mayo Clinic was asking. "Dr. Drake, do we have a bad connection?"

"No, I hear you. I'm thinking." He reviewed the question he'd been asked. "Have you considered a gluten sensitivity? They disguise themselves in a multitude of ways, and many of your patient's symptoms match, even though the test results might not indicate a full-blown allergic reaction. I suggest a gluten-free diet for the next fourteen days. Be sure to record behavioral changes as well as antibody levels."

"*I need*—" she'd said. Jason wanted to fulfill that need, whatever it was. But he was pretty sure her need was emotional, and he knew his limitations. He was good at understanding bodies, not emotions. If anyone knew that about him she did. She knew him better than he knew himself most of the time.

How could he give her something he didn't understand?

"I'll give it a try."

Jason was vaguely aware the phone line had gone dead at the other end.

It had begun so simply. A late night of research after the rest of his team had left for their family obligations.

Stephanie had gotten comfortable, kicked off her shoes and replaced her contacts with glasses.

Then she'd noticed his stiff neck, from hours spent hunched over the computer terminal, and offered to massage the ache away.

But the massage had backfired. Instead of relieving his tension, her hands had set him on fire.

Unable to concentrate on the case any longer, they'd called it a night.

But fate had intervened. In the parking lot she'd pulled up next to his motorcycle as he'd been about to strap on his helmet. The light mist of early evening had been turning into a heavy drizzle.

"Want a ride?" she asked.

"Sure." He thought—hoped—she offered more than transportation, but he wasn't sure until he climbed into her red low-slung sports car and she gave him the choice. "My place or yours?"

The whole moment felt like a clichéd scene from a nineteen-fifties *film noir*, but it was effective nonetheless.

Stephanie cooked a meal—of sorts. She shoved a frozen foil tray of lasagna into the oven, set the temperature, and handed him a bottle of Chianti and a corkscrew.

After popping the cork, he stripped off Stephanie's high heels, one by one, letting his fingers do a slow examination from her toes to the arches of her feet to her very sensitive ankles. As he ran his thumb along the arch of her foot, she moaned and arched her back, emphasizing the peaks of her magnificent breasts.

He explored the erogenous and sensitive anklebone, circling his finger until her breath came in short wisps. Her passion brought out the hero in him. He wanted to find a dragon to slay to keep her eyes shining in admiration.

Her hands fluttered to his chest and along his shoulders. A low, deep growl started deep inside him as his hunger for her built.

Her usually graceful fingers fumbled at the edge of her sweater as she tried to pull if off. He helped, covering her hands with his own. His own breath caught as he revealed her silky skin hidden underneath.

As if she were shy, she held back as long as she could, but by the time he reached the band of her thong she was ripping off his shirt and tugging at his belt.

They'd ended up overcooking the lasagna and washing it down with too much wine. And he'd never slept so peacefully as that night in her arms.

He and Stephanie had been of one mind: they were the perfect high-stress couple. They enjoyed each other's company, enjoyed the mutual benefits of an exciting sex-life and understood neither of them had room for more than a series of one-night stands.

That had been at first, but he'd soon figured out that Stephanie wasn't the kind of woman that a man could treat casually. He'd tried his best to treat her as well as she deserved. She was a prize, a hidden treasure.

And he'd prized knowing that she wore a kinky thong under her skirts and tailored trousers. He'd prized even more the fact that he was the only one who knew.

Or at least he *had* been the only one.

Obviously his best hadn't been good enough.

Who was that soft glow for? Was she dating someone already?

No. As fast as word traveled throughout the hospital, he would have heard. Wouldn't he?

And why was he still dwelling on it? He'd broken off relationships before, quickly and cleanly with no regrets.

That their break-up bothered him at all was a clue that their relationship had mutated into more than he had intended. He probably would have insisted they take a step or two backward himself if she hadn't called it off between them. Probably.

But a total severance of the relationship was a bit extreme.

Stephanie didn't need to amputate the head to cure the headache, did she? What was wrong with the "two aspirin and call me in the morning" approach?

He knew she'd been under severe pressure ever since their department had been hit with the big lawsuit. He could understand how she could be overwhelmed. But lawsuits settled down eventually. She would come back to him in due course if only he could find the patience to wait. Right?

And she was definitely worth the wait.

Until then he would bury himself in his work.

He smiled in anticipation as he cranked up his music. Pulling up a half-dozen resources on his computer screen, he reviewed Maggie's list of symptoms.

Exhilaration coursed through his veins as he lost himself in the hunt for the elusive answer. Yes, unraveling the mysteries of medicine was what he'd been born for.

Everything else was secondary.

Why, then, did memories of Stephanie naked in his bed keep distracting him from his purpose in life?

Once safely behind her office door, Stephanie let her shoulders sag. That was twice she'd tried to tell him about the baby and twice he'd let duty distract him.

Maybe she should send him a text message.

Or maybe she should say nothing at all. He'd notice soon enough anyway.

He was one of the topmost recognized diagnosticians in the country. She was surprised he hadn't already guessed. Maybe he didn't want to know.

If he asked, she'd tell the truth. Otherwise it wasn't as if she wanted or needed anything from him. She had the monetary capacity to take care of her child herself. And she was determined to have the nurturing capacity, too. Unlike Jason Drake.

After her rallying self-talk she expected to feel strong. Instead she just felt lonely.

She pushed the button on the intercom. "Marcy, has my dress been delivered yet?"

"Yes, I'll bring it in."

"Thanks."

Marcy gave a perfunctory knock on the door before coming in, carrying the dress covered by a garment bag. "The seamstress sends apologies but she wasn't able to let the dress out at all."

"I was worried about that. I'll just have to wear it as is." She should have checked her wardrobe sooner, but hadn't realized how much her body was changing until last night, when trying on her formal wear.

"Could I see it?" asked Marcy.

"Sure." Stephanie unzipped the bag.

Cocktail-length, red, sequined, halter-topped and backless. She'd originally bought the dress for an Independence Day gala. Now it was the only one that still fit her swollen breasts. It stretched much tighter across her torso and her derriere, too, giving her a vintage Marilyn Monroe look that she'd never had before.

"Wow! That will make a statement."

Since the dress was so much glitzier than the pale, elegant chiffons she usually wore, it was sure to raise eyebrows among those who knew her. Being dateless, she would have to stand up to the scrutiny all by herself—a test of her self-confidence and poise.

She might as well get used to her single state. She would *not* be dating *anyone* for a long while.

She did *not* need another complication in her life, and she'd never been the kind of woman who had to appear on a man's arm to make herself feel confident.

Although she had to admit she'd had her fantasies about Jason Drake.

"I bought it two months ago for the big Independence Day celebration and ended up not going. But tonight, with our supermodel and her friends in attendance, I thought it might be appropriate."

When Stephanie had originally tried it on she'd indulged in a bit of daydreaming, imagining the look of desire in Jason's eyes as she took off her evening stole.

She had intended to invite him to a white tie evening of fine dining, a full-scale orchestra and fireworks viewed from the rooftop of a prominent hotel to celebrate Independence Day.

Of course imagining Jason even accompanying her had been a fantasy. Every formal function she'd asked him to attend he'd cancelled on her, or flat-out turned her down.

"Dr. Drake is going to drag you back to his cave when he sees you in this," Marcy said.

"Why would you think I was going with Dr. Drake?"

Marcy looked puzzled, then embarrassed. "I thought that break-up thing was just a rumor to throw off everyone at the hospital. He bought a ticket at the head table next to you as soon as I put out the invitation list two weeks ago."

"He did?" Stephanie couldn't imagine why. "Marcy, are you sure? Attending galas and balls is not on Dr. Drake's list of favorite pastimes. He's probably never put on a tux in his life."

"Not that he needs one." Marcy grinned. "Scrubs suit him just fine."

Yes, they did. More than that, they defined him. He was a medical professional inside and out. She should know. She'd seen him both ways.

Stephanie turned away to hide her reaction to memories of Jason both in and out of his scrubs.

"Thanks, Marcy, for bringing in my dress." As she rezipped the garment bag she couldn't stop herself from imagining how Jason's hand on her back would feel as he unzipped the dress for her.

What would he look like in a tux, tie hanging loose around his neck, pearl buttons undone enough to show the firmness of his well-defined pecs?

Of course she would enjoy removing *any* type of clothing he wore. She had loved peeling off his scrub shirt that first time.

And the feel of his well-washed T-shirt, still warm from his body, wrapped around her own body... It gave her quivers just thinking about it.

Jason wore casual clothes with the charismatic attitude of

the ultimate bad boy. The aged jeans and T-shirts he wore after work and on weekends molded to his rebellious personality as well as his athletic shape.

All those hours he spent scaling mountains and fighting white-water rapids made for sure-footed grace and iron-hard muscles.

In a moment of passion, she'd asked to go with him one weekend. When he suggested an Independence Day campout instead of the gala she'd traded in high heels for hiking boots, eaten charbroiled burgers to the music of night birds, then watched the stars pop against a velvet sky. She'd never seen anything so spectacular.

That was the weekend the baby had been conceived.

With great self-control, Stephanie turned her thoughts from fantasy to reality.

There would be no happy little traditional family for her child. But Stephanie knew from first-hand experience that the traditional two-parent family didn't automatically equal a happy childhood. Not when the parents couldn't find time for their child.

Without thinking, her hand drifted to her round belly. Her child would never suffer for lack of parental attention. She would make sure of it.

After an hour of distraction when he should have been researching, Jason headed downstairs to the E.R. for some advice. His friend Mike had had a similar dilemma only a year ago. Apparently he'd figured things out, since he was now married with a new baby.

He and Mike Tyler had been roommates after Mike had answered his ad for a roommate to share expenses during pre-med. Although neither of them were big conversationalists, after years of rooming, which had lasted through pre-med, medical school and residency, Mike was the closest friend Jason had. Mike had introduced Jason to hiking and rafting all those years ago, giv-

ing him an effective outlet for letting off steam and finding an
occasional glimpse of inner peace.

Now Mike worked the E.R. at Sheffield Memorial, thriving
on the excitement, while Jason preferred the details and intrigue
of diagnostics and research.

Both he and Mike had come a long way since they'd had to
share one winter coat between the two of them in their younger
days.

Last year Mike had married into an instant family of two girls
and a boy, along with a beautiful, witty wife who'd just given
birth to their son eight weeks ago.

Somehow Mike made it work.

Jason waited while Mike examined a chef's gashed forefinger and ordered a tetanus shot along with a couple of stitches.

When Mike was finally free, Jason asked, "You up for a hike
this weekend? I've got some relationship questions to ask you."

A good, hard climb in the crisp mountain air would clear his
head.

"Can't. I've got to take the five-year-old to a birthday party.
Tea party theme. The birthday girl's father has promised grown-
up drinks for the parents while we wait." He sighed, but his eyes
sparkled with happiness. "The sacrifices of fatherhood."

Jason couldn't imagine himself at a little girl's birthday party,
making small talk with other parents. Even the thought of being
so domestically entrapped made him fidget.

"We've got the waiting room cleared out. Ask me now."

Jason shifted from foot to foot, then just blurted it out. "When
a woman says she needs more, what does she mean?"

"More, huh? That's a tricky one." Mike rubbed his chin. "Are
we talking about Dr. Montclair?"

Jason chose to ignore the smirk Mike didn't bother to hide.
"Yes. Who else would it be?"

"She strikes me as a straightforward woman. Why don't you
ask her for specifics?"

Jason thought that one over. By his evaluation, their latest
conversation hadn't been too straightforward.

"You're not much help."

"Guys generally aren't when it comes to women. Why don't you come by the house on Sunday and ask Caroline? She's good at this sort of thing."

"Caroline doesn't like me."

"She's forgiven you." Mike clapped him on the shoulder. "Never tell a pregnant woman she should cut back on the chocolate, even if she should. The closer they get to their due dates, the testier they get."

"Lesson learned."

A nurse peeked into the lounge. "Dr. Tyler, we've got a patient for you."

Jason took the stairs two at a time, but the dank, enclosed staircase didn't give him what he needed.

He needed to work off some excess energy in the fresh air and sunshine. Wide open spaces normally cleared his cramped brain.

For safety reasons Jason never hiked alone. But he was tempted to risk it. That was what women did—made men do foolish things.

No, he wouldn't risk going it alone with no one to call on for help. No woman was worth being stuck stranded on a mountain with a broken leg. *Or a broken heart.*

No. Not a broken heart. He would have to love Stephanie for that to happen, and he'd promised long ago to never be that foolish again.

Stephanie's phone rang, showing Jason's office number. He never called. He was a face-to-face kind of guy. Warily, she picked it up. "Hello?"

"Stephanie, when you said you needed…" He paused, giving Stephanie time to catch up with his one-sided conversation. "What is it you need?"

What should she answer? *I need you to show me your heart? I need you to love me? I need you to put me first in your life?* "I need you to attend a sensitivity training class."

"A what?"

"A sensitivity class."

"Why?"

"You've got another complaint filed against you, I'm afraid."
Yes, that sounded nice and businesslike. Stephanie was rather
proud of her control.

"So?"

"So the hospital is being very careful about these things nowadays, particularly because of the lawsuit. The class is mandatory."

"Or what? You'll fire me?"

At the thought of never seeing Jason again Stephanie felt her
stomach drop. "No, Jason. Of course not—not you, anyway. But
showing that we insist upon a consistent policy will help with
the lawsuit and our malpractice insurance. I need you to coop-
erate with me."

"What's the complaint?"

"Mrs. Canover said you were rude to her."

"Remembering Mrs. Canover, I would have to agree with
her."

"Jason, we've discussed this before. A large part of patient
care is attitude. We treat the whole patient and the family, not
just the illness."

"No, that's not in my job description. My job is to find the
problem and fix it. Has Mrs. Canover's son had a relapse?
Difficulty breathing? Rash? Fever? Sore throat?"

"No. None of that. Her son is recovering nicely."

"Then what's her complaint?"

"Did you really tell her she should stick with growing African
Violets instead of children?"

"The woman demanded that I give her three-year-old son
allergy shots twice a week rather than getting rid of her house-
plants. What would *you* have said?" Jason had been staggered
when the woman had refused to give up the prize-winning
African Violets that had been passed down through genera-

tions for the health of her son, and hadn't hesitated to give his opinion.

Frankly, Stephanie agreed. But, as her grandmother insisted, there was a polite way to say everything. "I'm not sure, but I probably wouldn't have implied she was as dumb as the dirt in her violet pots."

"Who will take care of my patients while I'm stuck in a class-room being lectured to by an idiot who has never diagnosed an illness in his life?"

"You will. I've scheduled the class for your off hours this weekend."

"I've already got plans."

An unexpected spike of jealousy shot through Stephanie. The thought of Jason with another woman sent her temples to pounding.

Not good for the baby, she reminded herself. She took a deep breath. "Cancel them. I'm sure your date will understand. After all, you're a doctor. Any woman who makes plans with you should expect to be flexible."

"Just because we agreed to see other people doesn't mean I am." He lowered his voice a half-octave, probably because he knew how she liked that. "I was hoping you might want to get away this weekend. We could go to my cabin. We haven't been up there since Independence Day. I could make lasagna."

"Our personal relationship is over, remember?"

"Stephanie, just because our sexual liaison is over it doesn't mean—" He swallowed hard enough for her to hear him. "Doesn't mean we can't still be friends."

His voice sounded strained. As honest and forthright as he was, he wasn't good at voicing what others wanted to hear.

She narrowed her eyes. "You're just saying that to get me back into your bed, aren't you?"

"Busted." He sounded awkward, sheepish. "You've got to admit we're awesome together."

She looked up, as if searching for an answer in the ceiling tiles. "Jason—"

"I know you have a lot going right now, Stephanie. We could both use a little fun to put things into perspective." He sounded serious. "No strings. No commitments. Just a weekend away. A glass of wine under the stars and a few laughs between friends."

That had been more than enough for her only a few short months ago.

They had shared some fun times. His quirky sense of humor was right in line with hers. Together they had snickered and chortled at things the rest of the world didn't get. It had felt good to be understood.

"There's more to life than grins and giggles, Jason."

She took off her glasses to wipe her eyes with the back of her hand. "I'll email you the details on the class."

Stephanie spent the rest of the afternoon familiarizing herself with Jason's patient files, all the while marveling at his brilliance. His reports made for fascinating reading. They were thorough and detailed—and, best of all, unbiased. He didn't slant the facts to support his hypotheses, and he included details of wrong assumptions as readily as right ones.

While all doctors were supposed to be this objective, Stephanie had never found one whose ego didn't shade the facts at least a little bit until Jason.

Lost in work, she didn't realize the time until Marcy buzzed her over the intercom. "Just letting you know I'm leaving for the day. Should I bring in your messages?"

"Yes, please." Stephanie glanced at her watch. Where had the time gone?

Marcy brought in a fistful of messages and notes to be returned and laid them in the in-box on Stephanie's desk.

Stephanie gave them a casual glance. "Anything urgent?"

"Just the usual. Dr. Sim in Obstetrics wants you to set up an appointment with her. She didn't mention the topic of discussion. Do I need to get information on the meeting agenda?"

"No, Dr. Sim and I have talked previously." Soon everyone

would know why she had appointments with the obstetrician. But not tonight. Tonight her baby was still her little secret.

Stephanie folded that particular note and slipped it into her lab coat's pocket. "Anything else?"

"Another in-house complaint against Dr. Drake."

"Can it wait until tomorrow?"

"Yes, I'm sure it can. And your mother's personal assistant called. Should she send the car here for you tonight?"

Stephanie thought of answering no, saying she would drive herself. But she suddenly drooped with exhaustion—mentally as well as physically. She didn't know how late it would be before she could gracefully exit the Baby Isaac Benefit.

While she had intended to run home to do make-up and hair, the drive would steal minutes from her day. She could pin her ponytail into a ballerina bun, and she had sufficient cosmetics to do an acceptable make-up job here at the office. That way she could squeeze in a much-needed rest first.

While she didn't have a lot of time for a nap, she didn't need a lot. Just a few minutes to prop up her feet and close her eyes.

As a resident, she had perfected the art of napping. Fifteen minutes had always been enough to restore her flagging energy and weary mind.

"Tell her yes. I would appreciate having the car sent here. And keep my office phone on hold."

As soon as Marcy left Stephanie dimmed the lights, kicked off her shoes and settled onto her couch.

When she heard the *bing* from her computer that let her know she'd received an email, she ignored it. Unlike her parents and her ex-lover, she knew how to manage her priorities, and right now a quick nap was at the top of her list.

Only six o'clock and she felt as if she could sleep through to the morning. Too many late nights, early mornings, and busy days in between were taking their toll. She needed to take a long look at her schedule and eliminate non-essential functions for the next several months. Possibly longer. It was time to take care of herself.

At least for fifteen minutes.

Just as she was drifting off to sleep, her office door burst open, slamming back on its hinges.

"When were you going to tell me?" Jason demanded, more emotion in his face than she had ever seen. Unfortunately that emotion was anger—at her.

Sitting up too quickly made her light-headed. She blinked through the spots as she tried to gather her thoughts.

Caught off-guard, she thought fast before leading with her most calming reassurance. "I'll take care of everything. There's nothing you need to do."

He waved a computer printout in front of her. "You've already done enough, don't you think? How much was my reputation worth?"

"What?" Stephanie scrunched her toes, feeling vulnerable in her bare feet. Reaching up from the couch, she grabbed the emailed page from his hand and scanned enough to see the hospital's law firm was informing all named parties of their agreement. "Oh."

"Oh?" He grabbed the back of a chair, his knuckles white. "Do you believe I did anything negligent to cause that baby's death?"

"No. Of course not."

Was that relief she saw in his eyes as they settled into a less turbulent gray?

"Then why, Stephanie? Why make me the scapegoat?"

"To protect the hospital." She stood, feeling vulnerable again with him standing over her as she sat on the couch. Still, shoeless, her standing didn't make much difference. "Sheffield Memorial would have been gravely injured in the media circus they were threatening. Our lawyers felt that even if we won the lawsuit—which was unlikely—we would still lose in public opinion, which means funding and research grants and patients.

We've already seen some of that come true. Instead Isaac's parents settled for an internal investigation, with the doctor responsible for Isaac's death being officially sanctioned."

"Sanctioned? How so?"

"I oversee all your cases personally."

"I've got a standing invitation to join the Mayo Clinic. Maybe it's time I accepted their offer."

"Why haven't you already?"

Wasn't that what she wanted? Jason out of her life?

"I thought I had everything I wanted here."

Did that mean her? Or only Sheffield Memorial.

Sheffield needed him. It was her duty to try to keep him.

What about the baby? She pushed away that intrusive thought. She would never use her child to bind Jason in any way.

"It's only for a while. Six months or so." She tried to placate him. Then she would be on maternity leave and someone else would supervise his work for the next six months. But she would save that for later.

"Anything else? Does this settlement come with other repercussions you haven't seen fit to reveal to me? Or should I wait for the email?"

"We've agreed to invest a significant amount of money into neonatal improvements." She gestured to her dress on the coat rack. "My parents are holding a fundraiser tonight for the Baby Isaac Commemorative Endowment Fund."

"But this party has been planned for weeks."

"Yes, this is the annual Sheffield-Montclair hospital fundraiser, with a twist. During the first round of negotiations my father and mother readily agreed to donate the proceeds to kick off the endowment."

"Then what took so long to settle?"

"I had to do a lot of soul-searching to give you up as a sacrifice."

"Good to know I wasn't just a casual snap of the fingers. But the end result is the same, isn't it?" He turned from her to look out her window. "My reputation is sullied and I work under your orders."

"I had to. For the sake of the hospital." Her decision had seemed the only right one to make at the time. Why was she now sure she had committed a major mistake? Although she could still think of no better way. "I'm sorry I've hurt you."

"*Hurt* me? I've always known where I stood with you, Stephanie." He pinned her with a hard, cold stare. "You've only proved me right where I wished I was wrong."

He left as abruptly as he had come.

Stephanie had wanted more emotion from him. She had gotten what she wished for.

Now she feared she would have a difficult time living with the flood of disappointment and pain he'd shown her.

Jason strapped on his helmet, fastened his leather jacket and straddled his motorcycle. As he wove in and out of traffic for the freedom of the highway he laughed at his own arrogance. He'd thought he'd meant more to her than that.

She'd meant more to him.

Wait. She'd meant—*what* to him?

He didn't want to think about it. Not now. Not ever.

He had the strongest urge to ride to his cabin in the mountains, his retreat from the world. Safety partner or not, he would run the footpaths until he was exhausted, then drop into bed, too tired to think. But the five-hour round trip wasn't practical when he wanted to be back in his office early tomorrow to check Maggie's latest test results.

Instead he settled for exchanging scrubs for running shoes and attempted to sweat out his angst with a good run around his neighborhood.

As he pounded the pavement he let his thoughts freefall.

He was a good doctor—one of the best.

Yes, he had the highest mortality rate at Sheffield Memorial. But everyone from the hospital board down to the janitors understood why. He was the doctor of last resort. Too often, when all else failed, the patient was sent to Dr. Drake.

The challenge invigorated him. The frustration he could deal with.

This wasn't the first time he'd been named in a lawsuit and it wouldn't be the last. Only in the past the hospital had fought for him, defended him, believed in him.

Stephanie had believed in him.

She said she still did. Even so she'd betrayed him—sold his reputation to keep Sheffield Memorial's name squeaky-clean.

But the practice wasn't uncommon. This was one of the many reasons why malpractice insurance was so high—and the hospital paid his insurance premiums

So, was it Stephanie's divided loyalties and betrayal, or was it his own ego that had him so angry?

The hospital was her great-grandparents' legacy—a trust passed from generation to generation. With Stephanie being the last of the line, she'd been raised with the duty to keep Sheffield Memorial alive. Some day she would take her father's place as president of the board. Family reputation coupled with career ambitions ran much deeper than loyalty to nonchalantly discarded lovers.

He had to admit Stephanie had been a distraction to his work. Maybe he should thank her for reminding him what was important—saving lives.

Maybe in a hundred years he'd be able to.

His mind drifted to the open invitation he had to join the ranks of doctors at the Mayo Clinic.

Why had he stayed at Sheffield Memorial?

The answer was there in his head, too loud to ignore. Stephanie. He was fascinated by her. *Had been* fascinated by her.

Could he continue to work for her?

He wasn't sure. He didn't think so.

Could he leave and never see her again?

Same answers.

He slowed to a walk as he headed up the steps into his duplex. A quick shower and a call for take-out, then maybe he'd finish that spy thriller novel he'd started reading last night.

But he wasn't in the mood for pizza or Chinese, or any other food in a box that could be delivered to his door.

Hell, what was he doing? Last month he'd paid over fifteen hundred dollars to sit at the Montclairs' table and eat their lobster and steak.

Jason reached for the tuxedo he'd had tailored for the occasion. He was going to get his money's worth tonight—if not in food, then in squirm factor.

CHAPTER FOUR

STEPHANIE crowded Dr. Wilkins behind a potted palm. Her height and her heels gave her the advantage of towering over him. Good for intimidation—except that now his nose was aligned with her cleavage...a cleavage that was much more ample than it had ever been before.

She refused to hunch. Instead she deliberately pulled her shoulders into military straightness. The man was a doctor. He'd seen breasts before.

"An email? You sent him an *email*?" She fought hard to keep her voice to a whisper. Yes, this would be better done in the privacy of an office, but she couldn't wait that long to vent her anger. "I didn't even know it was official yet. What happened to common courtesy? A little warning so I would have time to break the news in person?"

"I tried to call, but your assistant said you didn't want to be bothered."

"So you had to rush out and send an email to everyone and his brother?"

"With the celebrity couple attending tonight, I thought it would be better to let them know ahead of time that we'd made progress."

"Better? Or easier on you?" She pointed her celery stick at him. "Does it feel any easier to you now? What about Dr. Drake? Did you stop and think how *he* might feel?"

"Drake? Feel?" Wilkins dared to grin.

Stephanie used all her will-power to keep herself from wiping that grin off his face.

"If it bothers him that much, we can throw some money at it." Wilkins smiled. "Money fixes most of the world's problems."

Stephanie glanced across the room to the supermodel and her producer husband, huddled together, strain showing on their faces. "I doubt our celebrity couple would agree."

And neither would Jason Drake. She took a deep breath, trying to get her emotions under control.

Was that a licentious smirk on Wilkins's face? Did the man know she had eyes in addition to breasts? He was old enough to be her father, for heaven's sake.

She shook the celery stick at him again. "Never let it be said that I discourage monetary compensation for my staff. By all means have the board give Jason a raise if that soothes their consciences about what we've done. May I suggest thirty pieces of silver as recompense?"

The room fell silent around her. Had she shouted when she had intended to whisper? Or was it one of those odd moments that occurred naturally at large affairs.

She looked around and saw everyone's attention drawn to the entrance stairs.

Dr. Jason Drake.

Could this day get any worse?

Jason stood on the top step at the entrance to the banquet hall, looking down at all the elegant people milling around on the marble ballroom floor below. The way the room was designed, he might have been stepping into Cinderella's ballroom scene.

The politely hushed conversation sounded like a political rally on mute, underscored by chamber music. Which, when he thought about it, was exactly what this gala was.

The wealthiest couples in the city had come tonight to help out the Montclair-Sheffield family. Politicians, business-owners, doctors from all over the city—all with their spouses either at their elbows or working the room nearby.

The room was languidly awhirl with black tuxedoes identical to the one he wore and conservatively tasteful pastel evening gowns. He caught an occasional glimpse of a trophy wife's enhanced cleavage visible through the glitter of diamonds hung around her neck.

A sprinkling of B-list celebrities dotted the crowd, identifiable by their flashier colors, gaudy faux jewelry and short bursts of loud laughter—all designed to draw the attention of any attending media.

"Dr. Jason Drake," the major-domo bellowed, breaking through the sibilant conversation.

Everyone turned toward the entrance, assessing and judging him.

A gaggle of the hospital's lawyers stood near a brightly-lit potted plant as if they were eavesdropping on it. They stared at him while they whispered behind their drink-filled hands.

The stares were quickly averted, but he still caught expressions of disbelief and, in general, unwelcome.

Maybe he should have settled for take-out instead.

Instead he stood taller, lifted his chin and dared anyone to question his presence. He had a very expensive gala ticket in his pocket, should anyone confront him. He'd paid for the right to attend just like everyone else.

He recognized several doctors and a scattering of board members. One of them raised his glass in salute.

Jason acknowledged it with a slight nod.

From his vantage point he scanned the room, looking for the open bar. He would *not* look for Stephanie tonight. He didn't need her to smooth his way. He was Dr. Jason Drake, a brilliant doctor in his own right.

Still, a bright sparkling ruby caught his eye in the midst of all the wilting pastel flowers.

Stephanie. Even though she was turned away from him he recognized her.

Her dress had no back. He could imagine tracing his fingers down her spine, hearing her moan for him. Feeling her own fingers tickle across his chest, hearing her whisper in his ear for more. She would smell of meadows and waterfalls and that special scent that was all her own.

And she would transport him to a bliss he'd known only in her arms.

Before he could stop himself, he found his feet moving in her direction. Standing next to her, Wilkins broke off their conversation and grimaced in his direction.

Stephanie turned, shock on her face.

Jason had the presence of mind to give her an expressionless nod before walking past her to the bar.

"What will you have, sir?" The bartender stood ready to serve, the only person in the room who wasn't sending stunned looks his way.

Jason had bartended plenty while working his way through school, but never at a private party. No tip jar. He slipped the boy a twenty.

"Whiskey." He rarely drank. To drink was to give up a modicum of control. In fact he would probably hold this single glass without even sipping until they were called in to dinner. But he liked the smell and the color. Most importantly, the glass gave him a distraction and kept his hands occupied.

"Straight, sir?"

"Sure. Why not?"

Dr. William Montclair approached, and Jason stuck his hand in his pocket to pull out his ticket.

Before he could do so Montclair put his hand on Jason's shoulder, clamping down firmly. Jason took a step away, breaking the connection and tamping down his old fight-or-flight instinct. Taking a swing at a distinguished fellow doctor, the host of the party, would do a lot to deteriorate the respect the lawsuit settlement had already tried to erode.

"I want to personally thank you, Jason, for taking one for the team." If William Montclair noticed Jason's shocked surprise, he overlooked it. "We all know you're one of the best—not just here in Denver, but worldwide—and we're lucky to have you at

Sheffield Memorial. The board is grateful to you for submitting to such poor treatment—from us and from them." He nodded toward the lawyers who were now ogling a twenty-something starlet who had just appeared upon the entrance stairs.

"Dr. Montclair—"

"William. Please, call me William." Montclair handed his empty class to the bartender for a refill. "I also want to thank you as a father. You've made this whole ordeal smoother for my daughter. For that you will always have my undying gratitude and respect. You're a good man, Jason. Just treat her gently, won't you, son?"

He shouldn't need it. He was a grown man, a successful doctor. But the validation and the compliments filled an empty place deep inside him.

Jason felt like a sponge in the desert after rainfall at being called anyone's son, even if it was only an expression. But he couldn't claim it.

"About Stephanie and me—we're not—"

Montclair looked past Jason's shoulder. "I see someone else intent on speaking to you. If you'll excuse me…"

The hairs on the back of Jason's neck prickled before she glided into his peripheral vision.

Then she was next to him.

He breathed her in like a man too long without oxygen.

"Jason. You came."

Did she sound displeased, or simply surprised?

"Could we talk?" She put her hand on his arm to guide him away.

He thought about resisting, finding an excuse to avoid the talk. He didn't need to discuss his inadequacies in relationships again, but evidently she did. According to Mike, women had a need for closure. Jason had always thought they just needed to have the last word.

Either way, if Stephanie needed to talk that much he would suffer through it. Maybe she'd even changed her mind about ending their love-life. *And maybe pigs would fly.*

He studied the worried strain in her eyes.

"Please, Jason."

He couldn't resist. He followed her into the curtained-off alcove where the band would play after dinner.

Following her had advantages. He didn't know what kind of underwear she could possibly wear under that dress, but the style was certainly making the most of her assets. He would love to ease that zipper down and see. He clenched his fist to keep from reaching out to touch her.

She stopped in the middle of the band's dais. "Why did you come?" Her question caught him by surprise.

"I caught a glimpse of that dress and wanted to see more."

"You didn't seem to care when you saw me earlier."

"I was angry."

"And you're not anymore?"

"Not so much angry as turned on." He went with his impulse and ran his fingertips from her shoulder to her elbow.

He was rewarded when her eyes grew large and dark at his touch.

She took a step back and rubbed her arm, as if to rub off his touch. "You shouldn't be here."

"After all these months trying to get me to attend one of these things with you that's the attitude you take?"

"You didn't attend with me, Jason. You came on your own."

"Did you come with someone else?"

"That's not your concern."

He grinned, hearing her answer in her tone of voice. "You came solo, too." To keep from touching her again, he twirled his whiskey glass in both hands.

"What part of taking a break from our relationship don't you understand, Jason?"

"The part where you forgot to tell me you're pregnant."

The words were out before even he realized what he was saying. Although why it had taken him so long to recognize, he had no idea. Denial, maybe?

For a moment the world stopped turning. Stephanie froze as

still as if she were encased in ice. The loudest sound Jason could hear was his own heartbeat in his ears.

Then Stephanie stood straighter, but redirected her glare from his eyes to his shoulder. "Why do you think I'm pregnant?"

He couldn't hold back his snort any better than he had held back his spontaneous diagnosis. "I don't have to be a doctor to read the signs." He leaned forward, studying her closely. "Your breasts are larger, much larger. Round and full. Do they ache?"

"Why, you—why—that's none of your business."

He gave her a wan smile. "How long?"

Her shoulders fell. "You should know. You were there. 'A little condom slippage,' you said. Not a big deal. 'It probably won't matter,' you said. Well, it mattered."

"Abstinence is the only infallible method of birth control."

"That or a well-placed snip." She scissored her fingers at him with such enthusiasm he couldn't keep from wincing.

"Remind me to hide all the scalpels from you."

"You've got to sleep some time."

He set his whiskey glass down on the harpist's chair before he drained it. He needed all his wits around Stephanie right now.

She began to pace, her high heels clicking on the dais floor. The slit up the back of her dress revealed quite a bit of her incredibly long thighs.

He hated to say it, but as a doctor it was his duty. "You should probably start wearing flats. Heels put too much pressure on the spine as the fetus grows."

She stopped right in front of him, inches from his chest. "It's not a fetus. It's a baby."

"Actually—"

"For once, can you drop the medical jargon and be human? It's a little boy or girl—a child—not just a clump of cells that decided to start multiplying when your sperm ran into my ovum." She dared him to negate her. "Baby. Say it. *Baby.*"

He might be insensitive, but he wasn't stupid. He said it. "Baby."

She whirled around, took a step away, then stopped, putting

the microphone stand between them. Should he go to her? Stay still? Come back later?

He cleared his throat and offered, "If you want to do it this weekend, I'm free."

"*Do it*, Jason? I have proof that we've already *done it*." Stephanie pointed to her stomach, which definitely had a bit more fullness to it. That was one of the things he admired about her. She had curves, not just bones and angles.

"No, not that kind of *do it*—although I'm not averse." He leered at her before he got serious again. "I meant discuss the baby. Make plans. We could go up to my cabin, open a bottle of—" no, wine was not on the pregnancy diet "—milk and look at the stars." So much change to take in.

"I am not going anywhere with you. We broke up, remember? There is no need to change that." Her color was more blotchy red right now than glowing.

"No, *you* broke up. I was fine with our relationship."

"Just friends. We were just convenient friends. Isn't that all you wanted to be, Jason?"

"Now we're obviously more." He gestured to her stomach. "We're good together, Stephanie. We need to work this out."

"I tried, remember?" She gave him a bittersweet smile. "It's too little, too late, Jason."

"Because I missed a dinner date with you?"

"Because you missed *many* dinner dates and gala events and movies and simple suppers and cuddle time on the couch in front of the TV, and all the other things we'd planned while we dated. The only thing you never missed was an opportunity to share my bed." Her eyes reflected anger as well as hurt. "I can't be with you because I can't count on you."

"I'm a doctor, Stephanie. You know what that means. Not only are you a doctor yourself, you grew up with doctors for parents. Patients don't get ill only during business hours."

"Yes, I know the drill. Patients always come first." Her eyes glittered with tears. "You're right. I've lived with that all my life. One of my earliest memories was my first day of school. Mom and Dad and I were all going to eat breakfast together, then they would both drive me to kindergarten. We were all going shopping together for my first backpack, my first lunchbox, and a notebook with my favorite cartoon character on the front." She swiped her dry cheek with the back of her hand. "Do you want to know what happened?"

Jason could guess.

Stephanie confirmed it when she said, "First Mom's beeper went off. Then Dad's. Patients. I knew even then that some person needed them more than I did, and that I was being terribly selfish for resenting that."

Although her eyes brimmed, Stephanie didn't cry. Jason had never seen her cry.

"Then there was my ballet recital, and my first date, and my high school graduation. Even if they did come, I lived in fear of one or the other walking out in the middle, just when I needed them there the most, to go and be hero to some stranger who needed them more. There's always someone...."

He retrieved his glass and took a sip of the potent whiskey so he didn't have to look at the accusation in her eyes. Finally he said what was on the tip of his tongue. "But that's what doctors do. That's who we are."

"Does that mean we can't be more?"

"More?" Jason felt a pang. He still didn't know what *more* was. He walked toward her even though she took two steps back. Only the cello on the stand at her back kept her from putting more distance between them. "Stephanie," he forced out, soft and low. "I know the pain of growing up without a father. I won't doom my child to that same fate."

Stephanie drew back as if she'd just been slapped. "But you'd let your child go through life feeling second-best?"

Jason didn't know how to respond. He felt so helpless. Stephanie's anguish cut him deeply, but emotional pain wasn't his area of expertise. He didn't know how to fix this. He knew of no pill nor procedure to make the pain go away—neither for her nor him.

Still, he couldn't look away. Couldn't dismiss all that raw emotion she'd let him see. Couldn't keep from racking his brain, trying to think of what he could do to make this all better.

He had nothing.

Stephanie broke eye contact first, looking beyond him. Her face cleared of all expression. "Jason, you should go."

Behind him, a shrill, theatrical voice said, "You—"

He whipped around to come face-to-face with the supermodel who was responsible for tonight's whole shindig.

Her silver-sequined dress hung on her skeletal frame. She'd already shed the little baby fat she'd put on, regaining the gaunt, sunken cheeks that photographed so well.

Behind her stood her husband, looking as if he wanted to turn and run the other way, but tethered by the bright red manicured talons she had dug into his arm.

"How *dare* you show your face at my benefit? You're responsible for the death of my baby."

Jason kept himself impassive in the face of her over-acting. If he hadn't seen her sans make-up, in tears, arms wrapped around herself as she rocked back and forth in her hospital room, he would have been hard pressed to take her melodrama seriously.

For the first time ever, he uttered one of the stock phrases he'd been forced to memorize during one of Sheffield Memorial's never-ending continuing education seminars. "I'm sorry for your loss."

He actually meant the sentiment. Another baby wasn't in this couple's future, no matter how much money they could throw at the problem.

"Sorry for my loss? Is that all you've got to say?"

Jason thought he'd done rather well.

She didn't give him time to search around for another platitude. "You killed my baby."

Stephanie pushed her way between him and the woman. Good. He could use a bit of her diplomacy right now.

He waited for her magic words to make everything all right.

"Dr. Drake did *not* kill your baby." Her tone was fierce, almost snarling. Stephanie studied the woman from head to toe. "Poor prenatal care, undernourishment, and hiding the fact that you'd given birth before killed your baby. If we'd known early on we might have been able to use preventative measures to counteract the negative Rhesus factor. And sufficient maternal weight gain and bed-rest as your obstetrician recommended would have given your infant a better chance at survival. Even then your pregnancy would have been high risk. I explained all this when I first met with you and your team of lawyers, remember?"

Her husband looked confused. "Why didn't you tell *me* any of this?"

"You had to leave, remember? To get back on set before production costs went over-budget." The bitterness in her voice needed no theatrics to carry emotion.

Jason glared at the man. No husband should treat his wife so callously. The loss of a baby had psychological effects as well as physical effects. He'd read all the data that confirmed it.

The man shrugged off her explanation. "Is it true? Our baby wasn't your first?"

His wife's scrawny shoulders slumped. "I was young. It was a long time ago."

Jason knew he shouldn't get involved. "Cut her a break, man. Can't you see she's still grieving?"

All three of them looked at him as if he'd just grown another head.

The bartender pushed his way behind the curtain, catching Jason's attention.

He pointed to the microphone between them. "Dude. That thing's on."

CHAPTER FIVE

PANIC overwhelmed Stephanie. She had just revealed her inner-most, closely held angst to a room full of people who thought she had the perfect family—who thought she was the perfect daughter. And now they knew she resented every bite her nanny had ever fed to her from her silver spoon.

"Easy, there." Jason put his arm around her.

She should pull back, but she was none too stable on her feet.

"Get me out of here."

"Will do." He looked to the bartender. "Is there a back way out?"

The bartender pointed to a door behind them. "That leads to the parking lot."

In a mental fog, Stephanie was barely aware that Jason had picked her up and was carrying her out. The celebrity couple trailed behind them, making a quick getaway as well.

"I didn't realize Isaac's mother would be here. My attending probably wasn't such a great idea."

"I'd have to admit sensitivity isn't your middle name. Still, nothing like airing your dirty laundry over a loudspeaker."

Vaguely Stephanie worried about the hostessing dilemma their defection would cause the Montclairs and the Sheffields. She should be concerned about the heartache she had inadvertently caused her parents as well, but that damage was too deep to ponder.

When Jason held her tighter and murmured in her ear, "It will all eventually blow over," she realized she'd been whimpering.

As they looked out over an acre of luxury vehicles, Jason asked, "Where's your car?"

"Mother sent her car and driver for me." She was suddenly conscious of her weight in Jason's arms. "You can put me down now."

"You're not that heavy." He signaled for the attendant who had just arrived with the celebrities' limousine.

"Yes, sir?" The boy tried to look as if he saw women in red-spangled dresses being carried by tuxedoed men all the time. But the crack in his voice betrayed him.

"I need Dr. Montclair's driver."

The boy shuffled his feet. "I'm afraid he's not here, sir. He left to run a quick errand and bring us all supper."

Jason turned so quickly Stephanie's already woozy head swam. "I guess that means you ride with me."

He started across the parking lot, his long, strong legs putting distance between her and her disgrace.

"Really, Jason, I can walk."

"We're almost there." He skirted a shiny black sports car, then stopped in front of his motorcycle. "Steady?"

"Yes. Put me down."

Slowly he lowered her feet, but held her tight against his chest. She should protest, but she didn't.

"Think you can hold on to me?"

Making her escape on the back of his low-slung motorcycle seemed absurdly funny. The giggle she couldn't hold back was tinged with hysteria. "I'm cold."

He whipped off his jacket and pushed her arms through the sleeves. "You're in shock."

He unstrapped his spare helmet and held it out to her.

"I can't. My hair." Stephanie tried to think of a solution but her brain was too muddled.

"Be still." He picked the pins from her hair, gently worked

the band from her ponytail, then braided the long length faster than she could have done it herself.

"You're pretty good at that."

"Practice."

Jealousy broke through her fog. "You do this for women often?"

He grinned, smug and knowing. No sense in explaining that he'd braided three heads of hair every morning in one of the many foster homes he'd lived in. Instead of answering, he pushed the helmet onto her head.

"Chin up." With a finger, he lifted her chin, then fastened the strap.

Putting on his own helmet, he straddled the bike. Before he cranked it, he stopped. "Can you climb on by yourself?"

In answer, she hiked up her dress and swung her leg over the bike while he held it steady.

"Keep your legs away from the pipes." He pointed to the chrome exhaust pipes, well out of her way. "And hang on tight."

With that, he pulled out of the parking lot and onto the street.

Stephanie had never been on a motorcycle before. The power throbbed beneath her as Jason shifted gears, going faster and faster. The wind was both reviving and exhilarating. The night-time lights blurred as they rushed by.

And, best of all, Jason felt warm and secure as she held him tight. If anyone were to ask, she would swear she could feel his own personal vibration revving through her.

All too soon he pulled into the parking garage at her apartment building. When he killed the motor her world became quiet—too quiet. And she could no longer block out the echo of her own words in her ears.

She had spouted all her childhood disappointments and fears to the entire ballroom, and she hadn't even gotten to the root of them. Up until her teens she'd had recurring nightmares that both her parents would rush to the hospital, leaving her alone for days on end in their big empty mansion with no one to care for her, having forgotten all about her while they were so deeply focused on their vocations.

As she'd got older she had rationalized away her fear, realizing that even if her bad dreams came true she could take care of herself.

But obviously her head had forgotten to tell her heart.

Now she had lashed out like the six-year-old she had been when she hadn't had the words to define how desolate she felt.

And now everyone thought…

She would have to borrow a leaf from Jason's book and not worry about what everyone thought.

She didn't protest as he rode with her up in the elevator and then used his own key to open her door. By the time she stepped over the threshold she had her wits back.

She stopped him from entering. "It's been a long day."

"You're in shock," he said again.

"No. I'm fine now." She peeled off his coat, warm enough without it.

"Stephanie, we need to talk."

"I never thought to hear those words come out of *your* mouth, Jason Drake." She held up her hand to stop anything further he might add. "I only need two things from you. Get that physical and attend the sensitivity training class tomorrow, so I can add it to your personnel record."

Before he could protest she stepped back to close the door, but her world shifted under her as red spots floated in her vision.

Vertigo.

"Jason." She reached out. "Dizzy."

She felt his strong arms hold her, then let go, falling, falling into a bottomless black vortex.

As soon as Jason lay Stephanie on the floor she blinked back to consciousness.

Her skin felt clammy to his touch. Her face was pale, her eyes dilated. Her pulse had been thready, but now picked up the beat.

His own heartbeat settled back from his throat. He wished for water to wash the metallic taste of panic from his tongue but didn't dare leave her side.

He settled for licking his lips.

Brushing wispy strands from her loose braid back from her face, he said, "Hey," wanting to hear her voice in reply.

"Hey, back." She sounded fragile. Vulnerable. Very un-Stephanie-like. He wanted to gather her in his arms, but she didn't need jostling right now.

"What happened?" Her question carried strength, and a demand for answers. She struggled to sit as she attempted to focus past the confusion in her eyes.

He put his hand on her shoulder to keep her lying down, then took in a deep breath to break the tightness in his chest.

He'd done this to her. He'd let his passion get in the way of his common sense and he'd gotten her pregnant. He'd taken the responsibility for birth control and he had failed. This was all his fault.

He didn't have to know his father to know the apple hadn't fallen far from the tree. Rotten to the core—like father, like son.

He clamped down on his own visceral reactions and focused on Stephanie.

"Be still." His hand on her bare shoulder looked so dark compared to her pallor. "You fainted."

Stephanie relaxed back. "You caught me before I fell?"

He nodded then affirmed with, "Yes."

Was she aware that her hand had covered his, trapping it firmly in place against her breast? Her other hand drifted to her belly, where their baby lay.

Jason watched the delicate lines of her throat as she swallowed, then said, "Thank you."

"How do you feel?"

Her focus went inward even as she met his eyes. "The dizziness is receding. No spots in my vision anymore. I don't feel as shaky as I did."

"Aside from the emotional turmoil, any other reasons for your fainting?"

"It's been a long day." Her stomach growled. "And I skipped lunch."

"Not a good idea."

"I had a consultation meeting with a demanding doctor."

She gave him a good-natured smirk by way of exoneration. Still, guilt burned through Jason's veins.

He pushed it out of the way. There was no place for emotions in emergencies.

He pulled his hand from hers and wrapped his fingers around her wrist to recheck her pulse. "Have you had problems with low blood sugar before?"

"How do you do that?" She lifted her arm to break the connection. "How do you make your eyes turn from the depths of the sky to the flatness of slate in only seconds?"

Her question struck like an arrowhead, finding a chink in his armor. He brushed away the pain.

"Speaking as your doctor, have you had any other incidents of syncope? Blood pressure problems? Shakiness?" His fingertips searched for the pulse in her throat. He found it gratifyingly steady and strong.

"Jason, you're not my doctor. I have a doctor."

He shouldn't upset a patient, but he had to ask. "Then who am I, Stephanie?"

Under his forefinger, her heart-rate picked up speed and intensity while her eyes searched his. "Who do you want to be, Jason?"

Easy question. "I want to be your lover."

"Lover? You'll need to clarify for me." She held his gaze. "The man who makes love to me, or the man who loves me?"

Not so easy.

Make love? Yes. He wanted to make love to Stephanie—day and night.

When Stephanie stimulated his pleasure center his brain chemistry soaked up the dopamine which made his world better and brighter. That temporary high he got when his synapses and neurons popped always made him think clearer and faster and bigger—outside the box. Exactly the way a good diagnostician should do.

But love her? No, he could never love a woman—not even Stephanie. He'd tried that once in his foolish youth. Loving a woman made him reckless. Illogical. Ineffective. All traits that led to bad decisions. And a doctor who made bad decisions inadvertently killed people.

If his brother were still alive he would attest to that.

Despite his best effort, his eyes shifted from hers.

She blew out her breath. "Help me up. Lying flat like this, my back is starting to ache."

Grateful Stephanie had let him off the hook instead of demanding an answer, Jason helped her sit.

When she tried to stand, he stopped her. "Let me take off those shoes before you fall off them."

Holding her foot in his hand, he slipped off one spiked heel, then the other. His hands lingered on her ankles with enough of a caress that she would know he desired her. He was rewarded by the quickening of her breath, telling him the same.

"I'm going to miss these for the next several months." He rubbed his thumb along the arch of her foot and her eyes glazed with pleasure. As he had anticipated, she couldn't hold back her moan.

The way her body responded to him made his own blood rush through his veins.

She roused herself enough to protest. "I'll dress myself as I see best—like I've always done."

She pulled her feet from his grasp and started to stand.

He helped her up with more strength than grace. She ended up plastered to him, with her dress bunched up tight around her hips. His body couldn't help but respond as he breathed in the scent of her.

"Let me unzip you like I've wanted to do all night," he whispered in her ear.

She purred, and his desire for her hit him in the gut. Then her stomach growled again.

Food. He needed to get her blood sugar up before she fainted again. He had to think of her pregnancy.

A child—his child. In his head, he couldn't solidify the abstract concept into concrete reality.

"I think I need to stay the night to watch over you." He held her away from him. "It's the practical thing to do."

Stephanie blinked and saw the coldly sensible doctor in place of her blazing hot lover. Just like that, Jason could stuff all his passion back into its box. As if she didn't matter to him at all.

She stiffened and took a step away. Her head swam, but she refused to reach out to him and steady herself. How could she so easily confuse sex for something more? Jason would never wholly give himself to anyone, not even her—not in an emotional way.

"Just for tonight," she agreed.

It *was* the practical thing to do since she wasn't feeling that stable. Not that she could find her balance with Jason anymore. Her emotions for him kept her constantly off-center. She needed to get herself in check. To push her vulnerabilities to the side and be as in command as he was.

She turned her back to him. "Unzip me."

Yes, it was a taunt, but she needed to know. Needed to challenge herself and prove that her control over her physical attraction was as great as Jason's. Needed to prove that she could turn on and off her yearning for him as he could his for her.

He worked the zipper down, his warm fingers barely touching her skin, and she knew she'd lost the challenge.

Then she turned. With a great deal of satisfaction she saw it in his eyes. Desire. So he had lost the challenge, too.

Good to know that he ached for her as much as she ached for him.

"I'm hungry." She let all the implications of her hunger come through the huskiness in her voice. "You promised to feed me." For added effect she ran her tongue along her lip.

Jason's Adam's apple bobbled twice before he growled out, "Go change clothes while I make supper."

She looked down, saw his hands spasmodically clench and unclench, and smiled, making sure he knew that she knew.

"Stephanie..." It was a warning with an edge.

She pushed her own limits as she trailed her hand along the pearl buttons on his shirt. "Something spicy, please."

Then she turned on her heel and walked away, feeling his eyes bore through her, but she resisted turning back.

Score one for Stephanie.

CHAPTER SIX

As soon as she was out of Jason's sight exhaustion overpowered her. He felt only sexual attraction—a very powerful sexual attraction—but it was only skin-deep between them.

A woman needed more than good sex to sustain a relationship. She needed to know she was cherished as well as desired. And a child needed total, absolute, unconditional love to thrive.

Claiming responsibility for a child wasn't enough, but that was all Jason had to offer. Or at least all he was willing to offer.

Stephanie dredged up the will to wash off her make-up and replace contacts with glasses. Without thought she reached for her favorite T-shirt and gym shorts. She didn't bother to hang up her dress. She planned to burn it in the morning.

Jason made kitchen noises followed by delicious aromas. As empty as her pantry was, she wondered what he had found to cook. But he was a whiz at that sort of thing.

"About done in there?" Jason called from the kitchen.

Her pride urged her to tell him to leave. But her heart begged to let him stay.

Maybe she could find resignation to the fact that there could be no deep relationship between them?

"I'm on my way."

Jason had set her tiny kitchen table with a linen tablecloth and matching napkins, and full place-settings of china, silverware, and crystal goblets inherited from her great-grandmother. As a centerpiece a pristine white taper from her den's fireplace mantel flickered in a silver candleholder, next to her ceramic everyday salt and pepper shakers, incongruous among the unaccustomed finery.

That was how she felt in her worn oversized sleep shirt and gym shorts. Incongruous. But a negligee would have been playing with a fire she didn't have the energy to contain.

What did it matter in the end? There could be nothing between them. Her life would be made simpler by making a clean cut from Jason and raising her baby alone.

She ignored the wave of sadness that rode in on that lonesome thought and straightened her spine with Montclair independence.

Very properly, she said, "Everything looks nice. And it smells delicious. Thank you, Jason."

He smiled with a hint of strain at the corners of his mouth. "I thought we'd celebrate our happy occasion."

"*Are* you, Jason? Are you happy?" She took a long look into those guarded eyes, at those too-stiff shoulders, that rigid stillness. He looked like a man standing on the rim of a volcano, ready to fling himself over the edge as a sacrifice for the greater good.

"I take care of my own. It's my responsibility and my right." He said it as if he dared her to dispute it.

Not tonight. She'd fought too many battles for one day. She broke their stare first, looking down at the meal he had prepared for her.

On her plate sat a fluffy yellow omelet, filled with tiny white and orange-hued shrimp and seasoned with flecks of green herbs. On a side plate rested toast spread with cream cheese and orange marmalade—her favorite. The crystal flutes were filled with a clear liquid that fizzed.

"Ginger ale," Jason answered before she could ask. "Breakfast for supper. It's all I could find."

"It's perfect."

He lifted a glass.

It would have been churlish not to follow suit.

"To our child," he said.

If she hadn't known him so intimately she wouldn't have noticed that small hesitation in his voice before he said the word *child*. Her throat thickened, but she saluted with her glass and swallowed nevertheless.

They ate in silence. Only two weeks ago the room would have felt light and tranquil without unnecessary small talk between them. Tonight it was heavy with the weightiness of unspoken and unacknowledged feelings.

If the meal hadn't been so delicious Stephanie wouldn't have been able to eat a single bite. For the sake of her baby—and her baby's father—she tried.

As Jason finished his last bit of toast she counted to ten out of politeness—before bolting from the table.

"You cooked. I'll clean," she said. They had fallen into that arrangement the first time they'd shared a meal—the night they'd first made love.

"I'll take care of it." He rose, plates in hand.

She tried to lighten the mood. "That's not very fair, is it?"

"What's not fair is giving you an unplanned baby."

She looked away from the regret in his eyes.

She had no regrets. "I'm pregnant, not an invalid."

"You lost consciousness."

He knelt at her feet and looked into her eyes. She looked for warmth. All she saw was determination.

"I'll take care of you, Stephanie. You and the baby."

Out of obligation. But obligation wouldn't provide the loving environment she was determined to create for her child.

His cell phone on the counter vibrated. For a split second he glanced toward it, the desire to answer that call clearly in his eyes, before he turned back to her. But the intensity of his focus was now diluted as his thoughts drifted to the beep that signaled a voicemail message.

"Jason, there's no need. I'm fully capable of taking care of both myself and my baby. Now, go answer your phone."

"I won't be but a second." He was standing and turning away before he'd even completed his sentence.

While he took the call Stephanie washed and dried the dishes, folded the tablecloth and napkins for the laundry and blew out the candle.

By the time he was finished she was sitting on her couch, pretending to read a magazine and wishing he would just go.

Urgent call finished, Jason laid his cell phone on the coffee table and joined Stephanie on the couch.

She really should tell him to walk away now, before he could tell her that duty called and he had to leave. It was a dignity thing.

Then he slid his arm around her shoulders, pulling her tight into his side. The heat of his body warmed the cold place deep inside her chest.

"So you're staying?"

"I said I would. I won't leave you by yourself tonight." He frowned. "That was Dr. Phillips calling for you. When she couldn't reach you, she called me."

"Couldn't reach me?" That was when Stephanie remembered her red-sequined clutch with her cell phone in it lay on the back seat of her mother's car. "So she assumed you would be here with me? How fast has word spread?"

"At Sheffield? Faster than a virus in a daycare center. But Phillips didn't say anything personal. Just that she'd been calling you and finally reached a point where her request was critical, so she called me." He hugged her to him. "Not to worry. It was just an administrative problem. Dr. Phillips wanted authority to order an MRI on her patient before she recommended surgery. As Senior Fellow for the department, I gave her permission and took care of the problem for you."

If she didn't know better, she would believe that his arm around her could protect her from the world.

But she was made of sterner stuff. "I can take care of my own problems. I'm a Montclair, Jason. I stand firmly on my own two feet."

"I seem to remember a recent fainting episode...." He raised an eyebrow.

She couldn't stop the corner of her mouth from twitching. "Figuratively, if not always literally. And that was an aberration."

No one but Jason had ever teased her before. From the beginning he'd seen beneath her reserved exterior to the hidden part of her that longed to share a laugh with her colleagues but didn't know how.

One of the things that had most attracted her to him was the fact that Jason brought out her lighter side and let her feel comfortable with it.

Stephanie snuggled more securely into him before she realized what she had done, so she made her tone harsh, showing him she meant business. "I was right here, Jason. You could have handed the phone to me."

He responded by tickling her neck with the ends of her own hair. "Then you don't mind everyone at the hospital knowing we're back together?"

"We're not back together." Trapped firmly in his embrace, with no will to move away, she knew her declaration didn't ring as true as it might have.

Jason did the moving away. But only far enough to look her in the eyes. "Stephanie, you're carrying my child. That binds us together—forever. We really need to stop denying what's between us and be adults about our relationship."

"Relationship. New word in your vocabulary?"

He smiled. "Yes. It is."

But his smile didn't reach his eyes. Instead, worry creased his forehead. He cocooned her hand in both of his. "Stephanie, how do you feel about this baby?"

As if she'd been waiting for him to ask, answers she hadn't even put into words bubbled up. "At first I panicked. The idea of having a baby totally overwhelmed me."

How did she explain?

"My time with you was supposed to be a summer fling—an

experience I've never indulged in before." She felt her cheeks
heat up at that confession. But she wanted complete honesty
between them. "You were a reward for my finally achieving a
place in my profession where…"

"Where what, Stephanie?"

Where she felt worthy of her parents' pride. But honesty
didn't stretch to revealing *all* her insecurities. "Before you, I
had been so career-focused. I decided it was time to have a little
fun." Aside from the mandatory escort to various social events,
she'd never really dated that much—another thing he didn't need
to know.

"So I was just supposed to be your boy toy?"

"No!" *Honesty, Stephanie.* She ducked her head. "Yes."

Jason twirled a lock of her hair around his finger and grinned.
"I can live with that." Then he looked down, clenching and un-
clenching his free fist. "No, I can't. That night at the cabin, I
should have—"

"No, Jason. We both should have. Shared act, shared account-
ability." Stephanie covered his tense hand. "I've thought about
this. I'm a reasonably intelligent woman, wouldn't you say?"

He gave her a quirky smile. "More than reasonably."

"I know all the ways to prevent pregnancy, including the
morning-after pill, but I chose not to go that route. Maybe not
consciously, but certainly subconsciously."

"What are you saying, Stephanie?"

"A baby hadn't been in my plans. But now I have new plans.
Better plans. Plans for a future full of nurturing and love."
Instinctively she covered her belly with her hand. Now, with
the world knowing about her pregnancy, she wouldn't have to
remember to hide her intuitive gesture. "I can't imagine my life
without my child in it."

"*Our* child, Stephanie. Our child." The set of his jaw brooked
no argument. "This is shared parenthood. My responsibility as
much as yours. I know you don't need my money, but I fully intend to contribute to our child's upbringing."

"A child needs more than money. The best nanny money can

buy isn't enough. A child needs a parent she can count on to always be there."

"How are you going to manage that? Give up your career to hover over a crib twenty-four-seven? What about the times you're on call?"

Stephanie had been mulling over that issue ever since she'd seen the positive sign on the pregnancy test stick. There had to be a way. "Things have to change. My child will always be first in my life. I'm not going to run out the door every time the phone rings."

"Are you saying I will?"

"Your past record strongly indicates yes, Jason." She felt a deep-seated anger growing inside her. "How many times have I finished dinner alone while you caught a cab from the restaurant? How many movies have you seen through to the end with me? I didn't even suggest attending a play or a concert because of the disruption you'd make threading through the theater seats during the performance. Even when we have good, reliable staff on call, any time your cell phone rings you're gone."

She searched for Jason's reaction, looking for an indication that he understood. All she saw was his stony lack of emotion. As an adult, she knew he was only guarding his own vulnerability. But would a child understand? Or would their baby think he truly didn't care? It was a look she never wanted her child to have to live with.

"You were wrong about the phone call earlier," he said, and his eyes reflected a cold challenge. "That one was for you. What would you have done if it had been your patient in a life-or-death situation?"

She still had five and a half months to figure it out, but so far she had no solution.

Before she could come up with a suitable retort, Jason wrapped his fingers around her wrist.

"Jason—"

"Shh!" He counted her pulse. "Your blood pressure's up. We'll change the subject."

"Or you could leave."

"Not tonight." He stood and moved away to the recliner, grabbed the television remote from the side table and surfed channels until he found a documentary on white-water rapids.

As if they had never exchanged heated words between them, he asked, "This okay with you?"

How could he do that? How could he box up his emotions so tightly and put them behind him? Or maybe she was wrong. Maybe he truly felt nothing after all—except for sexual desire.

She could make him go. If she insisted, he would respect her wishes. If she weren't so tired she would evict him. Wouldn't she?

But, truth be told, her syncope really worried her. Blood pressure problems seemed to be plaguing her pregnancy.

As Stephanie glanced at Jason, firmly ensconced in her armchair, his attention focused on the television, she couldn't deny the false sense of security having him around gave her.

She picked up the magazine she'd laid down earlier, determined to demonstrate how much she didn't need him.

The words in the article swam together as eye-strain took its toll. She would close her eyes for a second, let them rest and refocus. Her eyelids drifted downward. The darkness was soothing, relaxing. She didn't even try to hold back her yawn.

Her next thought was that Jason must have stayed the night.

His sleepy, musky scent wafted from the pillow she hugged so tightly.

Vaguely she remembered stirring when he carried her to bed, and again when he held her close to take away her shivers.

The sun beamed in at her window—proof she'd slept until almost noon. She hadn't slept so long or so well, hadn't felt so rested, since—since the three-week cruise her parents had given her as a medical school graduation present. Even then she'd felt the constant edge of being a single in a couples' environment.

For a while Jason had made that lonely sensation go away.

But this morning he was gone and it was back.

She picked up her glasses on the bedside table to read his note.

Breakfast in the fridge.

How did she reconcile his acts of kindness and thoughtfulness with his display of unyielding stoicism?

Her stomach gave a happy rumble at the sight of fresh strawberries and blackberries in a bowl, next to a cup of yogurt topped with granola—evidence that he'd taken an early-morning walk to the organic food store down the block. Wearing last night's tuxedo, how many eyebrows had he raised?

Not as many as she had raised last night, she'd bet.

She forced herself to eat, hoping the yogurt would help to settle a stomach that revolted at last night's memories. She would need all her strength and sustenance to face the next few days and the consequences of her public confession of the heart.

CHAPTER SEVEN

JASON sat by himself in the back row of the sensitivity training class, earnestly trying to pay attention. But his mind kept wandering.

He prided himself on being flexible, taking whatever life threw at him, but this fatherhood thing had him taken aback.

A baby. Not just any baby but *his* baby.

He had never expected to be a father. He certainly would never have chosen fatherhood, not wanting to subject a child to his lack of family skills. Could character flaws be inherited? He'd never read any definitive research, but then it had never been that important to him until now.

But now, as unworthy as he might be, he would do everything in his power to be the best father he could. He sincerely hoped his best would be good enough.

With renewed determination, he focused on the instructor.

"Class, let's do an exercise to put us more in touch with our feelings." The counselor clicked a new image onto the lecture room screen. "In your notebook you'll see a list of emotions. Quickly, without giving the words much thought, circle the ones that apply to you at this moment."

The list read: "Happy. Angry. Surprised. Fearful. Needy. Hopeful. Anxious. Bored."

Within seconds, Jason had the assignment completed.

He studied the results. He'd drawn thick, bold lines around all but 'Angry' and 'Bored'.

Before last night, those would have been the only two emotions circled.

Amazing how a baby, months away from delivery, had changed his life overnight.

"Everyone think about what you've circled. Is this where you want to be in your life?" The instructor looked smug, as if he had it all figured out. What would this overconfident trained counselor do with Jason's news?

"Now, class, write down three concrete goals—simple sentences will do—on what you'd like to change about your life."

Change? Jason had enough change to deal with without inventing anymore.

How did Stephanie feel about the baby—*their* baby?

He thought through last night's scenario, as he'd done a hundred times since dropping her off at her apartment. Too many things had happened too quickly to sort out her reactions to any of them.

This morning he'd reached for the phone a dozen times, driven past her apartment on his way to the hospital, strolled past her dark, empty office right before class, but he hadn't followed through on making contact.

What did he say? *You've made me the most off-balance, confused, ecstatic, scared stiff—circle all the emotions that apply—that I've been in my whole life?*

Jason bet that even their highly qualified instructor wouldn't have the words for this life-changing occasion.

Life. He and Stephanie had created life—right there inside her womb. The concept overwhelmed him.

"Everyone done?"

No. I'm just getting started, Jason thought. He'd have a child to raise, to nurture, to guide.

Damn. He had no idea how to do any of that. He'd better stop by the bookstore on the way home and pick up some research material.

The instructor called to the class. "Now, let's role-play. Turn to the person next to you and get acquainted."

Jason turned to find Mike seated next to him. When had he slid into class? And why?

Mike should have some of the answers Jason needed.

"What are you doing here?"

They both ignored the instructor, who told them to read from the script in their handouts, finish the incomplete sentences, then take a break.

Mike gave him an awkward smile. "I was just walking by."

Jason didn't believe him for a second. "Yeah, right. Tell me another one."

Mike grinned, ignoring Jason's sarcasm. "Rough night?"

"I've had better." Jason looked down at his list of circled words. "So the rumors are already circulating?"

"I got a text last night from a friend of a friend. Is it true?"

"Is what true?"

"Dr. Stephanie Montclair is pregnant with your baby?"

"Yes, it's true." A sense of pride overcame him, despite knowing their slip-up had put Stephanie in a very awkward position.

Mike slapped him on the shoulder. "Congratulations, Dad. You're going to love parenthood."

An infusion of joy raced through Jason's veins, giving him an ecstatic dizziness as if he'd just scaled a mountain and his head was now in the clouds.

He brought himself back down to earth by thinking of how Stephanie wanted to shut him out of her life and her baby's life—*his* baby's life.

"She doesn't want me—" he had to swallow hard to get out the rest "—involved as the baby's father. She's pretty certain I'll do more harm than good."

"Then you'll have to convince her otherwise."

"What if she's right?"

Mike scanned the room, as if looking for the right words to say. He finally focused back on Jason. "My kids love you. Every kid who comes through your department loves you. They all sense your strength, your constancy, your care for their wellbeing. All those qualities will be intensified the first time you hold your child. Or the kid calls you Daddy. Or you have to clean his first skinned knee."

"Aren't you afraid of screwing it up?"

"Hell, yeah. But my wife tells me that's what makes me a good father. I keep trying to get it right." Mike grinned. "And some days I think I do."

"My track record's not that great."

"You've got other kids?"

"Let's just say I've been in the parental role before. It didn't work out too well."

"I've known you a long time, Jason. Was this during those teenaged years you won't talk about?"

When Jason said nothing in response, Mike jostled him. "All kids deserve a father. This kid deserves *you* for a father. Don't let your child down before it's even born."

The pain of abandonment that Jason had tried to deny all his life crashed in on him.

If his own parents hadn't wanted him, how did he convince Stephanie to want him?

But for the sake of his child he had to try.

The instructor came back in, ready to continue his mind-probing exercises.

Mike leaned over and whispered. "Hey, friend, I've got to go. Need to buy a doll and a pretty gift sack to stick it in before the birthday party. But call me if you want to talk."

"Yeah, sure." What was all this talking stuff? As if *that* would fix anything. Still... "Thanks."

"I'm here for you, Jason."

When had that happened? When had Mike become such a good friend? And how could Jason have missed it?

More proof that he was no good at this relationship stuff.

He turned his attention back to the screen, but held little hope that a two-hour class would teach him how to be good enough for Stephanie and her family.

Once he'd completed the class, he snagged a resident and insisted on a quick physical. This time his blood pressure and heart-rate stayed in the proper range. Stephanie should be pleased—at least that he'd followed orders if not that he was in good health.

After a couple of quick shopping stops he drove home, prepared to spend the rest of the weekend doing hard labor to work out the pent-up energy that made his mind race in endless circles.

Sunday night he dropped into bed, hoping he was finally exhausted enough to sleep. Despite the hours he'd spent pounding on his roof, replacing shingles and tightening gutters, he was no closer to clearing his head.

He lay in the dark, remembering that Stephanie was giving him an easy way out.

The clock blinked as the minutes passed. He put his pillow over his head to block the annoying light but he couldn't block the decisions that plagued him.

Hell. When had he ever done things the easy way?

Stephanie's parents had been more than gracious in accepting her apology. With their bigger-than-life personalities, neither had realized their quiet, studious daughter had felt unimportant and overlooked.

Hearing how much her parents loved her, even when they had never really understood her, had begun to heal a lot of wounds.

After the emotional weekend with her parents, and an emergency meeting with the hospital's lawyers to plan damage control in case the celebrity couple sued for her breach of confidentiality, Stephanie braced herself for the most difficult Monday she'd ever had.

For the hundredth time she wondered what Jason had done with the rest of his weekend. Every time her cell phone had rung her heart had raced at the thought that he might be calling.

But he never had.

For which she was grateful. She had enough problems to juggle. Right?

Running late due to the morning sickness that had reappeared this morning, Stephanie pulled into her assigned slot in the staff parking garage next to Jason's motorcycle.

Dressed in a conservative navy sheath and matching sweater, with classic pearls, she climbed from her car. Her exit wasn't as graceful as she would wish for. The low-slung vehicle would play hell with her dignity as her size increased.

And what was it about telling the world she was pregnant that made her waist grow three inches overnight? The sheath and two other loose-waisted dresses were all that would fit this morning.

As she grabbed her purse, the reality she had been ignoring threatened to overwhelm her. Everyone at the hospital now knew. Those who had only guessed were now positive. She'd had a fling with Jason Drake and now she carried his baby.

They would whisper behind her back. Judge her lack of control, her inability to handle her personal affairs. Wonder if she was competent enough to do her job or if it had been nepotism all along.

Nonsense. She'd earned her sterling reputation through years of hard work. Her personal life had nothing to do with her professionalism at the hospital. If anyone doubted that, she would soon prove them wrong by her actions.

Stephanie raised her chin, pasted on her social smile and went to work, blaming her lapse in confidence on the hormones coursing through her body. Advice from her mother: blame everything on the hormones.

Marcy greeted her with poorly hidden curiosity in her eyes, which Stephanie firmly ignored.

On her desk she found the Certificate of Completion for Jason's sensitivity class, a copy of the findings in his recent physical and a shoebox with a card attached.

"*For the baby*" was scrawled in Jason's outrageous handwriting.

Inside was a lovely pair of ballet-style flats, bright red and butter-soft, with good insole support. They were the right size.

She should give them back. Shoes were too personal for the strictly professional relationship she intended to establish.

For the baby. Was that a challenge? A statement of his parental rights? Or just a thoughtful gift that emphasized his medical advice to stay off the stilettos.

She would give them back and buy her own shoes.

But trying them on wouldn't hurt, would it?

Perfect fit. As she walked around her office the slight nagging twinge in her back went away.

She wiggled her toes.

The thought of squeezing her restrictive dress pumps back onto her slightly swollen feet made her wince. She would wear the red flats around her office this morning, until she had time to run out at lunchtime and buy her own pair. Then back they would go—along with her own note saying "thanks, but no thanks."

Opening her files, she set to work reassigning her patients among Drs. Riser and Phillips. Recruiting a new pulmonary specialist and supervising Jason's workload would be enough.

The solution to the lawsuit that had seemed so perfect at the time seemed so wrong now. She'd thought Jason would just shrug it off. Instead she'd wounded him deeply.

Marcy buzzed the intercom. "Dr. Montclair? You're needed in Maggie Malone's room as soon as possible."

She heard the child's screams as she rounded the corner. Not taking time to knock, she pushed open Maggie's door to the commotion inside.

Stephanie had to squeeze her way into the room past an attending nurse, a new resident she'd recently assigned to Dr. Riser, and Dr. Riser himself to get to Jason.

Like a major general, Jason stood in the middle of the chaos, giving orders to everyone in attendance.

"We need to get her body temperature down. *Now.* Get those layers of clothing off her and wrap her in the thermal blanket," he said, moments before the monitor dinged an alarm.

He spoke with such authority and urgency the nurse and the resident collided rushing for the blanket.

Jason pointed to the nurse. "Don't you understand the word *now*?"

The nurse looked dazed and confused.

Jason lifted Maggie from her mother's lap, pulled off her heavy flannel nightgown, socks and knit cap, took the chilled blanket Stephanie held ready for him and wrapped Maggie without waiting for anyone else's compliance.

Maggie screamed, not happy with her treatment or the pandemonium around her.

"What are you doing?" Dr. Riser grabbed for Maggie.

Like an iceberg in turbulent seas, Jason stood stalwart. "I'm cooling her off." His deep voice undercut the girl's shrieks.

The monitor showed her temperature had spiked to 105 degrees Fahrenheit.

Dr. Riser pointed down to the discarded clothes on the floor. "You're the one who warmed her up."

The blanket was working. The girl's body temperature had already dropped a half-degree.

"Because her mother said she couldn't remember the last time her daughter sweat." He glared at Anne who was wringing her hands together in the corner, obviously distressed.

Stephanie grimaced. Drake's statement sounded like an accusation of neglect to her. Anne had been at her daughter's bedside night and day for over a week, and according to the girl's charts took excellent care of her daughter.

Information about the child's perspiration tendencies might be crucial, but couldn't Jason have used the slightest bit of tact when soliciting it?

She would address that later. Now she had a crisis to manage.

Stephanie put her hand on Dr. Riser's outstretched arm. Deliberately putting quiet steel in her voice, she said, "Stand down, Dr. Riser. This is Dr. Drake's case."

Dr. Riser gave her a curt nod before crossing his arms and moving aside to glare at Jason.

As soon as the monitor registered another half-degree cooler Jason unwrapped Maggie's arms and handed her the doll she'd been holding earlier. She immediately put the doll's hand in her mouth, quieting her cries.

He swept the circle of attendants with a glance, then pointed to the resident. "You—go and get the popsicle I promised her. Make it fast. Then meet me back in the consulting room."

He handed Maggie to her mother and left the room without a backward glance, confident Stephanie and Dr. Riser would follow him out.

Instead, Stephanie stayed behind to smooth ruffled feathers. Her department didn't need another lawsuit right now—especially since she was trying to untangle the one they already had.

"My apologies for Dr. Drake. He comes across rough, but he's one of the best," she said to Anne.

"Dr. Montclair, if this hospital spent less time trying to censor Dr. Drake's bedside manner and more time recognizing his drive and determination we'd all be better off."

Stephanie was taken aback at this mild woman's defense of Jason. It had rarely—make that never—happened before.

Anne put her daughter into the bed, then turned, hands on hips, and squared off. "Dr. Drake is the only professional I've met who hasn't patted us on the head, given us platitudes, then passed us on to someone else because his ego couldn't handle not being able to figure out what was wrong. Why doesn't Dr. Drake's own hospital value him as much as we do?"

"Sheffield Memorial *does* value Dr. Drake."

"Not from what I'm seeing. I heard one of the nurses say everything he does has to be approved by you. And then Dr. Riser comes in and questions his methods in front of that young resident. You've got a problem with your staff, Dr. Montclair, but it's not Dr. Drake. I wouldn't blame him for leaving Sheffield Memorial." She paused, visibly trying to get her emotions under control.

"Dr. Drake isn't leaving." Stephanie's heart skipped a beat. But wasn't that what she wanted? Jason gone so she could raise her child alone?

What would her life be like without Jason Drake in it, for her as well as for her child?

Empty. The word echoed from her heart. Nonsense. *Empty of complications* was what she'd meant to think. *Stable and uncomplicated* also came immediately to mind.

She'd had a life before Jason Drake. She would have an even fuller one after him—thanks to the child she carried.

Jason's child.

She brushed away the wayward thought. Her subconscious was not her friend today. Or maybe it was her hormones making her overly sensitive. But that was her personal life.

She needed to pull herself together. She hadn't worked this hard to become Department Director to let her personal life get in the way now.

"Why would he stay?" Anne gave her a hard stare. "If I were Dr. Drake I would be looking for someone who believed in me, who trusted me, who respected me. But then again, it looks to me like you're trying to push him away before he can leave. Is it because of the baby?"

"The baby?" Instinctively Stephanie put her hand over her stomach. "Of course not."

But she had been. She had been pushing him away ever since that night under the stars—the night the baby had been conceived, the night she'd realized she was falling for him.

Why was she pushing him away?

So he won't leave me first. So I can deal with the loss on my own terms. It made no sense, but then matters of the heart rarely did.

"I've read all about that celebrity baby. Everything I've seen says it's not Dr. Drake's fault."

Oh. That baby. Stephanie slid her hand into the pocket of her lab coat. "Dr. Drake put his heart and soul into trying to save that little life. Without getting into confidentiality issues, all I can say is that sometimes things just happen."

Anne nodded in agreement. "Anyone can see the fire in Dr. Drake's eyes when he's trying to make a child better. He could give up breathing easier than he could give up medicine. How could you chastise a man of such passion and caring?"

Anne had confused caring with obsession. Jason hated to lose a case. It was personal pride. Just as he took personal pride in lovemaking—an obsession Stephanie had certainly benefited from.

"I assure you, Anne, Dr. Drake's passion is one of his most valued traits." An image of Jason naked in her arms, face flushed with passion, invaded Stephanie's mind. "Sheffield holds Dr. Drake in the highest regard."

Anne seemed a bit mollified. "Once Dr. Drake commits, he doesn't abandon. Not ever. He gives his whole heart."

Stephanie thought of the many times Jason had been called heartless by the staff. Yes, doctors had to be stoic to be effective, but Jason carried it to an extreme, claiming emotion had no place in diagnosis.

Anne obviously saw what she wanted to see. It wasn't unusual for a family member to develop a case of hero-worship for their child's healthcare professional. A temporary attachment was generally harmless as long as the healthcare professional stayed remote and professional—a talent Jason excelled at.

Why, then, did Stephanie feel a jealous possessiveness she had no reason to feel? *Because she didn't want anyone else to defend him. That was her job.*

Stephanie took a step toward the door. "Thank you for your endorsement of Dr. Drake. I'll be sure to pass on your compliments."

Anne collapsed into the bedside chair, all the fervor gone from her eyes. "I'm sorry. My psychologist would say I was projecting. This is the anniversary of my divorce and I'm taking out my hurt and anger on you. Raising a child by myself is just so hard sometimes. But then, we're not talking personal relationships, are we? Dr. Drake is probably taking this lawsuit thing in stride. I'm sure professional relationships are handled differently."

"Not so much," Stephanie admitted through stiff lips as a shiver ran down her spine. "If you'll excuse me, I've got duties."

She walked out of Maggie's room with her mind whirling.

Pushing open the consulting room door, she found Jason inside, pouring himself a cup of coffee while waiting for her.

"Dr. Riser and his sidekick have come and gone. They had nothing to add to Maggie's case," he told her. He held up an empty mug. "Tea?"

"Yes, thanks."

Jason put the water on to boil as he stirred cream into his coffee. Digging through the teabags, he pulled out a herbal concoction. "Caffeine-free."

He said it as a statement more than a question, so she didn't bother to answer.

So many issues. Where did she begin?

She thought about taking her usual seat at the conference table. No, dealing with Jason Drake was best done on her feet.

Maybe he wouldn't notice the red shoes she hadn't taken time to change when she'd been summoned to Maggie's room. She should have never put them on. He would read more into her acceptance of the gift than she meant him to.

Of course Jason caught her glance downward to her feet.

She would start there.

"Jason, thank you for the gift, but let's keep our personal lives away from the hospital. I don't intend to broadcast my pregnancy."

"Like you did last Friday night? You're a few days too late for that, little momma." He stared at her baby bump as if he had X-ray vision. "I'll not deny my child, Stephanie."

"I'll not have my authority undermined because people think our past relationship gives you an advantage over them."

His sharp laugh scraped as painful as barbed wire. "Advantage, Stephanie? What advantage would that be? From

Dr. Riser's behavior, it's clear to everyone I'm *persona non grata* around here."

"He shouldn't have questioned you in front of a patient. I'll talk to him." Stephanie would need to do something about Dr. Riser. He was a good doctor, but Jason was the Senior Fellow of Diagnostics and he would stay that way. Dr. Riser's assertive attitude was starting to cross the line from healthy competition to undermining jealousy. Not an unusual powerplay in a hospital setting, and one she'd handled easily enough before. But she'd never been involved with one of the players before.

Was Jason even capable of feeling something deeper for her? Or was she only judging him by the emotionless façade he showed everyone else? Why had she never taken a good long look past his protective shell?

The answer was too obvious to ignore. Because she'd wanted to isolate herself from any potential hurt their relationship might cause her.

"I take care of my own problems." A muscle in Jason's jaw throbbed as if he were forcing the conversation through clenched teeth.

"Jason, you're Senior Fellow, but I'm Department Director. I'll take care of Dr. Riser."

"Like you took care of the lawsuit? No, thanks." He looked as dispassionate as if he were discussing milk or sugar for her tea. But his clenched fist around his coffee cup told a different story.

"I thought…." She dropped into her chair. What had she thought?

Deep down, she'd thought Jason was too arrogant to care what anyone thought of him. Even her.

On some level had she done it to punish him for all those missed dates? For the heartache he'd caused by making her second on his priority scale?

"Stephanie, was it you who gave the hospital labs instructions this morning to hold all my orders for running diagnostic tests? Has the pharmacy been told the same. Have all my privileges been revoked?"

"Not revoked. Just under my signature." She licked her lips, wishing she had the cup of tea to hide behind.

"Not much difference there." As if he read her mind, Jason slid the cup in front of her. Hot tea sloshed over the side, pooling on the clean surface of the consult table. Although his face didn't show it, Jason's lack of precise control stood testament to the magnitude of his anger.

"Sign me off for unrestricted privileges."

"Jason, you know we can't do it that way." She drew an X through the cooling liquid as her conscience pricked once again. Agreeing to that settlement had been a way to gain personal approval from the board—a board that consisted primarily of family and friends.

"We all know the lawsuit is a farce."

"I've signed my name to the agreement. I can't treat it lightly. If I purposely ignore the agreement our whole department could be sanctioned."

He walked to the window, his back to her. "You've taken away the tools of my trade."

She didn't need to hear the flatness of his voice to understand how deeply she had hurt him.

"I made a mistake. I'm sorry. I'll talk to the lawyers and do everything I can to correct it." On the verge of tears, her voice broke. Damned hormones.

She hesitated to add more, but did anyway. "Jason, I might have taken away your hospital privileges, but I could never take away your mind."

"If only that were true." He said it so quietly she almost thought she'd imagined it.

As if nothing had happened between them, he walked over to his whiteboard, picked up the marker and circled 'inability to perspire' on the list that had been marked up and crossed through a dozen times over the last few days. "We can rule out

all forms of muscular dystrophy. Too many symptoms don't fit.
I think we need to look into chromosomal DNA testing."

She needed time to process, to think. For now, she wrapped
herself in the tatters of professionalism and pretended it was
business as usual. "Those tests are expensive. I'll have Marcy
check their insurance coverage."

"So now Marcy has to approve my decisions, too?" He
pointed to a ragged overflowing folder on the table between
them. "Maggie and her mother have a private fund that will
make sure the tests are covered. It's in Maggie's file."

"I only meant…." What had she meant? That she needed that
last fragment of control?

Stephanie was starting to take a long hard look at herself,
and she wasn't liking what she saw at all. "Let me know which
tests and I'll make sure the order goes through." The alarm on
her cell phone buzzed but she ignored it.

Jason didn't. He glanced at his watch. "Lunchtime."

"I ate a big breakfast, if you want to keep working."

"You need to eat regularly, Stephanie. No more skipping
meals. You've got our child to feed."

Our child. Proof that she and Jason would always be tied together. It was time to stop pushing him away and start repair-
ing the damage she had done. "Want to join me?"

Jason stood and walked to the door. "I've got plans."

"Plans?"

"Personal plans. I won't be back today." As he pulled the door
closed behind him the click of the latch sounded loud in the silent conference room.

CHAPTER EIGHT

FOR the first time in memory Jason pulled his motorcycle into his parking slot to see Stephanie's red sports car already in her assigned space.

Making that spur-of-the-moment decision to run in the charity half-marathon yesterday had been a spontaneous choice that was unlike him, but it had produced excellent results. After thirteen miles of pounding the pavement he'd been tired enough to sleep the night through, even past his alarm. No tossing and turning, thinking of a particular woman who thought enough of him to sleep with him but not enough to share parenting with him.

Stuck to the center of his computer monitor was a note in Stephanie's handwriting. He was being summoned—in a polite Montclair way. At his convenience, she'd said.

Nothing about her was convenient.

But then he'd always found convenient to be boring.

He would take Stephanie's request at face value and work her into his schedule. Unapologetically, Maggie came first today.

After forty-five minutes of playing phone tag with doctors across the world, Jason found the chromosomal DNA expert he was looking for in New York, at Mount Sinai Medical Center.

The doctor was in a meeting, so he left a message, feeling one step closer to finding the answer to Maggie's condition.

The hurry-up-and-wait game of diagnostics always tested his patience, but the win in the end made it worth it.

Except when he lost.

Like with Stephanie.

He wasn't sure what he'd wanted to win. But now it didn't matter. Now he understood there was no future for them—only shared custody of their child and medicine. And he'd fight her for his right to practice both of those privileges until his dying breath.

As he sat in her office, waiting for her to emerge from her *en suite* restroom, he braced himself to keep from letting his gut response to Stephanie overrule his logic.

Remembering the flattering offer from the Mayo soothed his ego. Men made long-distance fatherhood work all the time. He'd have to check into how they did it. He would never abandon his child, or his child's mother, no matter how angry she made him, but maybe he could find a way to have it all.

Yes, he was furious with Stephanie. But he also understood. Sheffield Memorial meant everything to her. She'd made the wrong decision for him, but the right one for the hospital. He wasn't sure what he would have decided in the same position. If he took the Mayo Clinic job he would have to make similar tough decisions.

Jason crossed and uncrossed his legs, uncomfortable in the visitor's chair across from Stephanie's empty desk. Despite the closed door, he could still hear the sounds of retching from her small private lavatory.

He winced with sympathy.

Finally he heard sounds of hand-washing and teeth-brushing.

Stephanie walked in to meet him, all poise and grace, as if she *hadn't* been heaving for the last ten minutes. She unwrapped a mint from her cut-crystal bowl, popped it in her mouth and sat, straight-spined and direct-eyed, if a little pale, ready to get on with their meeting.

Despite his best intentions, he felt himself soften around the edges at her bravado. "Stephanie, is this morning sickness or a real illness?"

She gave him a baleful stare. "From where I'm sitting, this morning sickness feels pretty real to me."

"You're past the first trimester. It should be subsiding by now. Shouldn't you do something about it?"

"Do you think I'd be doing it if I could stop it?" She glared at him as if her morning sickness was all his fault.

He guessed in a way it was. Maybe his remarks had been a bit insensitive to a hormonal woman. But then, violently emptying one's stomach every morning would put anyone in a bad mood.

"Sorry." He reached for a mint. "I'm feeling a bit queasy myself."

"Couvade Syndrome." She put on her glasses—the ones that always turned him on. Maybe sex was the reason he couldn't clamp down on his reactions to her.

No, he had to face it. Even with her face pale and smudges under her eyes he felt—he felt tenderness for the mother of his child. The emotion was enough of a distraction that his brain refused to supply him with the particulars of the medical condition Couvade Syndrome.

Just another proof that, for him, medicine and emotion didn't mix.

"This patient has Couvade Syndrome?" He brought the conversation back to business.

"No, you do." Now her eyes twinkled, despite the dark circles under them. "It's a documented psychological condition that some men get when women are pregnant. Most people call them sympathy pains. Expect weight gain, excessive hunger and occasional bouts of morning sickness." She pointed to the pot of hot water boiling in an electric kettle on her credenza. "Why don't you pour both of us a cup of ginger tea?"

Jason's first inclination was to deny any kind of psychophysical reaction to her pregnancy but he swallowed down his protest. Instead, he jumped to comply with her request for tea. Anything to ease the discomfort of carrying his child.

That was when Stephanie caught a glimpse of his clipboard on the floor next to his chair. The coversheet lay askew, and she could just make out the document on top with the Mayo Clinic letterhead. It could be anything—research paper, grant application...employment offer? The little she could see of the document looked very similar to the recruiting documents she was mailing out herself.

But Jason would discuss his future plans with her, wouldn't he?

Why should he? Her conscience nudged. What had she done to encourage that kind of sharing?

Was it too late? She had to try. For her own sake as well as her baby's.

Wanting to feel that electric touch of his, she let her fingertips brush his knuckles as he gave her the cup. Maybe it was hormonal overreaction, but she would swear the spark was hotter than ever between them. "Thank you."

Jason frowned as he took his seat and deliberately looked at his watch.

"The case?" he prompted, his voice as bland as if there had never been anything between them.

To keep her emotions in check, she concentrated on being professional. "Amelia Barker, aged sixteen. She's been diagnosed as being bulimic, but her psychologist wants to rule out any physical problems as part of his rudimentary diagnosis."

"Wouldn't Dr. Phillips be better suited for this one?"

"Dr. Phillips is putting together her first grant package. Her deadline is looming and she's running behind. And before you suggest him, Dr. Riser is spending more time in cardio until our workload picks up. So that leaves you and me."

"I'm a physician—from the word *physical*. I use physical evidence to diagnose problems. Tests—like the DNA samplings for Maggie." He pointed to the clipboard in his lap.

Was that what the paperwork from the Mayo Clinic was? Information on Maggie's case?

Agh! Her moods were swinging faster than she could keep up with them. She had to stay in control here. She had a department to run. *Professionalism*, she told herself. "Amelia's social worker is connected to me through one of the Sheffield-Montclair charity foundations. I said Diagnostics would take care of her exam. It's not like we're overloaded."

"I don't do head-games—especially teenaged girls' head-games."

Stephanie took off her glasses and rubbed circles into her temples. "Jason, I promised."

"Headache? Want me to take care of it? I could take down your hair and massage away the tension."

How could he act so caring, yet so cavalier at the same time? She just knew that when he looked at her with that protective possessiveness in his eyes she felt very, very safe and secure. She had the strongest urge to feel his arms wrapped around her.

That would really blur the line between professional and personal behavior, wouldn't it?

Despite her hormones, she withstood temptation. "There are discrepancies in the diagnosis. Don't you want to take a look?" Stephanie shoved the folder across her desk within his easy reach, knowing he couldn't resist an unresolved case.

Curiosity warred with disinterest in his eyes. "Shouldn't the girl be treated as an outpatient? Why has she been admitted to Pediatrics."

"She's dehydrated. They've got her on fluids. They're talking about a feeding tube soon."

Jason narrowed his eyes. "Will I be the lead on this case or will you?"

They'd never had to define who was in charge before. They had worked together so well it hadn't mattered who was the primary physician. But she had obviously shattered their smoothly working relationship with the lawsuit settlement.

Under Jason's intense scrutiny, she felt as if she'd destroyed a sacred trust. "This is your case if you want it, Jason."

Without commitment, Jason picked up the folder and flipped it open. Within minutes he looked up at her. "This could be interesting."

His brilliance at absorbing and assimilating information always astounded her. Reading the girl's file would have taken her at least twice as long, and she would have had to refer to it several times to glean all the information he had garnered in only a few minutes.

"You don't think she has an eating disorder?"

He shrugged. "At this point I'm unbiased. I'd like to check out a few things before concurring. Let's go take a look."

Outside the observation room, Stephanie stopped Jason with a hand to his arm. "Wait a moment."

The skin-to-skin contact created tingles throughout her central nervous system.

She knew he felt it too when he looked pointedly at the place on his arm where she touched.

She jerked her hand away, as if breaking the connection could stop the sensations she felt standing this close to him, and forced her attention back to the girl. "Being a sixteen-year-old is hard enough, but Amelia is also in the foster care system."

Jason nodded. "I read that in her file."

"There's more beyond her file. The only reason we're seeing her now is because she's just been moved from a group care facility to private care-givers—an older couple. The couple think the social worker, state-appointed psychologist and the pediatrician are all wrong with the diagnosis of bulimia."

"So you think it may be a case of new foster parents wanting a pill to fix the problem instead of welcoming damaged goods into their home?"

"No, that's not what I meant—well, not that harshly, anyway. The couple seem to be very concerned about Amelia. Her foster mother says she has a sixth sense about these things. I don't want to discount her feelings, but...."

"But they're unsubstantiated feelings and not to be trusted? Feelings don't count?"

"That's not...." Stephanie looked to the ceiling for an answer, but found no help in the white tiles. "All I'm saying is you're the best doctor for this job."

"Because I have no feelings. Got it."

Did he say that with pride or with regret? She couldn't be sure, but thought she detected weariness in his voice.

"Jason." She wanted to smooth things over but wasn't sure how. "I'm not at my best with diplomacy today."

"Forget about it. Candy-coated words aren't one of my requirements."

"Thanks." She debated advising him on interview style, not wanting to insult him further by implying he needed her coaching, but then did it anyway. "Jason, teenaged girls are very sensitive—especially foster children with troubled pasts. Try to be more tactful with her than I was with you, okay?"

"I've never been a girl, but I've got experience in the other departments. I can handle this."

On that obscure statement, he turned away from her and pushed through the door, leaving her staring at his very broad back. Stephanie wished she could have seen if the look on his face revealed any more than the flat tone of his voice had. There was so much she didn't know about this man who had shared her bed.

Stephanie followed him in, watching Amelia's shoulders tighten as she braced herself for whatever was to come.

According to Amelia's history, change was the only constant in her life. What would it be like, being shuffled from place to place with no consistency at all?

Holding a grudge because her mother had missed her ballet recital when she was twelve felt rather petty in the face of Amelia's erratic home-life.

Jason took the visitor's chair next to the bed to be at eye level with Amelia. It was a technique he'd recommended to her when he'd first joined the Sheffield. "*No one likes to be talked down to—not even kids,*" he'd told her. She'd never thought about it before.

"I'm Dr. Drake and this is Dr. Montclair."

The girl gave him a fleeting sideways glance through her hair, then turned her attention to her hands, clasped in her lap.

"Why are you here, Amelia?"

"They're worried that I've lost weight," she mumbled.

Amelia had just given them the perfect opening to ask about self-induced vomiting. Stephanie moved closer to probe gently, but Jason sent her a cautionary look with the slightest head-shake.

She bit the inside of her cheek, keeping quiet as he wordlessly warned her off. Everything Jason did, he did for a reason. She trusted his methodology even when she doubted his bedside manner.

Jason took his stethoscope from around his neck. "We check the basics, like heart rate and lungs, ears, eyes, nose and mouth, on everyone who comes into Sheffield Memorial. Because we're a teaching hospital each doctor does his own exam, so Dr. Montclair will check behind me. Just be patient with us, okay?"

Amelia gave Stephanie a hard look. "Is she new?"

"Actually, she's my boss. You've got the top two physicians in the department taking care of you."

Instead of finding that information reassuring, Amelia became alarmed. "Why? What's wrong with me? Is it serious?"

Jason frowned, looking more grave and concerned than he usually did. "I don't know yet. That's why we need to examine you."

Stephanie bit her lip, wishing Jason had said something more reassuring to the girl. This was where she usually jumped in, but Jason's body language was giving her every indication to stand back. This was his case and she would respect that.

"I'll listen to your lungs from your back and then from your chest, okay?" He held up the bell of his stethoscope and waited for permission.

Amelia shrugged. "Okay."

Still, she flinched as soon as he put his hand on her shoulder to steady her.

To the girl, Jason appeared not to notice. But he shot Stephanie a sharp, subtle look, making sure she'd caught Amelia's reaction. She gave him a discreet nod.

Working with Jason was like dancing, and this choreography was proving rather tricky.

No other doctors in her department worked as smoothly together as they did. What would she do if he left her?

"Dr. Montclair, your turn," he said as he jotted notes in his file.

Stephanie listened, hearing a slight wheeze but a strong, steady heartbeat. She stepped back to write her own notes.

Jason held out his otoscope. "Could you hold your hair back, Amelia, so I can check your ears?"

Normally he would simply brush the hair back himself. Reluctantly, Amelia pulled back the limp brown strands to reveal a yellowish bruise fading on her neck—a bruise Jason must have noticed earlier.

This time he was very careful not to touch her as he checked her ears, then her eyes, nose and mouth, treating her cautiously, like a trauma case.

"Dr. Montclair will ask you a few questions while she examines you, okay? If you need me to step out so you can girl-talk, just let me know."

Stephanie picked up on her cue as she unpocketed her own otoscope. She did a cursory inspection of mouth and nose and eyes, then paused. "Amelia, I notice some bruising on your neck. What happened there?"

She bent to continue her inspection of Amelia's left ear, giving the girl a chance to talk without having to look at her. It was a technique that worked well for Stephanie, and one she tried to teach all the interns—another one she had learned from Jason.

She'd never realized until now how much she'd learned about her approach from Jason. Even though he wasn't much of a people person, he was a genius in technique when it came to approaching patients.

Why couldn't he do the same in personal relationships?

"It's not all about you, Stephanie." That was what her last serious boyfriend had said over a decade ago. But then she'd been finishing up medical school and the world had revolved around

studying. She had brushed off his excuse as easily as she had brushed off the break-up, too busy to notice that he'd extricated himself from her life. She hadn't thought about him in years.

Amelia's ear looked clear, although there was some scarring from past infections. Still, she hadn't answered Stephanie's question about the bruising yet.

As Stephanie walked around the exam table to inspect the other ear Jason said, "I'll step outside a moment so you two can talk."

"No!" burst from Amelia. "Stay."

Apparently the girl had formed a bond with Jason. It happened more often than not, but generally with smaller children. They could sense Jason's stability, his strength and safety. That was how she always defended him to the board when she addressed his many complaints.

Stephanie finished her exam of Amelia's ear and stood back, letting Jason have center stage.

"Tell me straight, Amelia. How did those bruises get on your neck? A make-out session that got out of hand?"

At his bluntness, Amelia looked him in the eye, a dare in her glare. "I got into a fight."

"At school?"

"No, at my group home. A few weeks ago. Some new girl wanted the bed by the window, but that's where I was sleeping, so we—" she looked down, her bravado failing her "—we fought."

Fighting over a place to sleep? It was a lifestyle Stephanie couldn't comprehend. "Surely your house mother would have taken care of the problem if you'd gone to her?"

Both Jason and Amelia looked at her as if she had just spoken Martian.

Jason gave her a patronizing smile. "It doesn't always work like that, Dr. Montclair." Turning back to Amelia, he asked, "Do you still have that problem?"

"Not now. Since I've been moved from the group home I have my own bedroom."

"Good for you." Jason sounded as if he were congratulating Amelia on winning the lottery.

Just as the girl showed the slightest signs of relaxing, Jason asked, "Amelia, are you doing anything to purposely make yourself lose weight? Using laxatives? Making yourself throw up?"

So much for diplomacy. Stephanie wanted to bounce her head against his to force tact upon him. But this was Jason's case and she trusted him—even if she had to remind herself she did.

Amelia lifted her head, a defiant spark in her eyes. "No. I've told them all I'm not, but they don't believe me."

"I believe you." Sincerity rang through Jason's answer.

"Why?" Amelia asked the question Stephanie wanted an answer to, also. "Why do you believe me?"

"Because your new foster mother believes you. She's got good instincts."

What was Jason doing? Was he placating the girl to put her at ease? No. That wasn't Jason's way.

"And because your body isn't telling me you're bulimic. There are signs. For instance, when people vomit a lot the bile from their stomachs rots their teeth. Yours look fine. But you *are* too thin for your height."

She shrugged, noncommittal but with no animosity.

"Being too thin will make you more susceptible to illnesses. More colds, more viruses. You've been in the foster care system long enough to know you've got to accept responsibility for taking care of yourself, right?"

She nodded. Another non-verbal response, but still a response.

Stephanie had never thought about that before. At Amelia's age, she hadn't been worried about her own health. Her mother or father had always noticed if she had sniffles, or they'd insisted she get a few extra hours of sleep when she'd been studying too late.

Though she was still determined to find a better balance with her own child, she had to admit, in retrospect, her parents had been much more involved in her life than she'd given them credit for.

Jason flipped open Amelia's chart, even though Stephanie knew he had it memorized.

"I see you play basketball. Dr. Montclair did, too. What position, Amelia?"

"I started off as point guard, but ended up as small forward before the season ended."

"I can see where your height would come in handy at point guard." He glanced at Stephanie and she waited for her cue. "What position did you play, Dr. Montclair?"

Casual conversation to establish a rapport. Jason must be getting ready for some in-depth interview questions since he was trying to get Amelia to open up to both of them.

Specifically, what did Jason want her to bring into the conversation? Playing off his observation about Amelia's height, Stephanie deduced that Jason wanted a comment about positive self-image from her.

When she worked with Jason, there was something metaphysical about their relationship that made Stephanie's blood rush.

She didn't have to search hard for the remark Jason wanted. She had fond memories of her high school basketball days, so making a comment here was easy enough.

"Shooting guard and point guard. I was the tallest girl in school. It was nice to feel that my height gave me an advantage."

He rewarded her with a sincere smile that warmed her to her toes. Why did his approval make her glow like an infatuated teenager?

"And you, Dr. Drake? What did you play?" Amelia asked, drawn out by his charisma, no doubt.

A ghost of sadness crossed his eyes. "I didn't play sports. I transferred schools a lot and didn't stay in one place long enough to be part of a team."

"Too bad. You would have been awesome."

There was the hero-worship his patients usually gave him. If he could only work that magic on their parents, Stephanie's job would be so much easier.

Again, the thought that he might be leaving Sheffield reverberated through her. No. He couldn't leave. He was too good a doctor and Sheffield needed him. *She needed him.*

Before she could talk herself out of that notion, Jason shot another question at Amelia.

From the edge in his voice, he was getting into hunter mode, tracking the signs to identify and obliterate his prey: Amelia's illness.

This was where he needed Stephanie to keep up the rapport while he did his interrogation. Classic good cop-bad cop. They'd run this play many times before. As long as Amelia didn't get alarmed at his intensity, as some of the parents had in the past, they should be successful.

"Amelia, your records indicate you've lost over twenty pounds since you were weighed in for the basketball team. Are these records accurate?"

"Mostly." The girl seemed to take his business tone in stride.

Stephanie smiled encouragingly and exuded acceptance of Amelia's answers while Jason probed deeper. Some day she'd like to switch roles and play the bad cop, but Jason played bad so well she didn't know if she'd ever have that chance. But then if he left the Sheffield she'd have to find another partner to play with anyway.

She found herself frowning—not part of her good cop role.

Her own inner angst had no place in this interview. She vowed to keep her personal life out of the examination and focus on the girl in front of her.

"Mostly?" Jason asked. His eyes were already growing flat as he ran possible diagnoses through his head.

"I lost some weight before that, too."

"When did you first notice?"

"Last summer."

"What did you do last summer? Go hiking? Go camping? Swim in a lake and swallow a gulp of the water?"

"No, none of that."

"Eat strange food from an exotic locale?"

Amelia grimaced. "We had an International Culture Day at this day camp I went to. We had all sorts of strange food there. Some of it was nasty, but nobody got sick."

"Contaminates don't always affect the whole food supply. You could have just gotten the unlucky serving. Or your immune system could have been compromised at the time—one of your frequent sinus infections, maybe?"

"Maybe. I get them so often I don't pay attention to them much."

"You've got to be aware of your own health, Amelia, and ask for help. That's how it works for all of us. We all need to ask for help on occasion."

Stephanie tried to remember the last time Jason had asked for anything, much less help. The doctor could use a dose of his own medicine there.

Jason made a notation, then asked, "Amelia, how's your appetite now?"

"I get hungry, but then I feel sick in my stomach at the same time." Amelia looked as if she expected the doctors to doubt her. "Does that make sense?"

"Yes, it does. Dr. Montclair is pregnant and has morning sickness. I imagine she experiences those same mixed feelings—don't you, Dr. Montclair."

So much for keeping her personal life personal. "Yes, I do, Dr. Drake."

"I'm not pregnant," Amelia said.

"Your urine sample verifies that," Jason concurred. "How about gas?"

Amelia hid herself behind her hair to answer. "Yes, sometimes."

"How often is sometimes?"

"Almost always after I eat."

"And diarrhea?"

Amelia blushed bright red. "Yes," she whispered.

Remembering the sensitivity of her teen years, Stephanie felt for her.

But Jason didn't seem to notice. His eyes glittered with the light that said he was closing in on the problem. "We'll need a fresh stool sample."

Amelia visibly shrank away from him.

"It's important so we can find out how to make you better," Stephanie tried to reassure her. "You'll have plenty of privacy."

"I need to palpate your abdomen, Amelia."

Stephanie interpreted. "If you would please lie down, Dr. Drake is going to press your stomach to see if he feels anything swollen or hard. You must tell him if it feels numb or sore, okay?"

"Okay."

Jason gave Stephanie a grateful smile as he donned a pair of latex gloves.

Yes, they had great synchronicity.

Stephanie helped Amelia lie back, then put on her own gloves so she could follow Jason's probing hands with her own.

After a command to take deep breaths, Jason probed Amelia's abdomen, pausing over her liver. His eyes were unfocused as he used his hands to give him the answers he sought.

"Is this sore, Amelia?"

"A little."

Jason stood back. "Dr. Montclair, your turn."

Stephanie's fingertips found the nodules on Amelia's liver that had made Jason pause.

As soon as she was done Jason caught her eye, and she gave her nod of assent. She had felt an anomaly, too.

"Amelia, Dr. Montclair and I are going to compare notes, probably do a couple more tests, then come up with the best solution for you."

Jason didn't bother with a reassuring smile. That was one of the things the parents complained about. Jason always countered by saying he did what was best for his patients, not their parents.

"Is it bad?"

"I don't know yet." He looked the teen in the eyes. "But, whatever it is, I'll fix it."

"I believe you."

Just like that. In under twenty minutes Jason had engendered trust in a girl who didn't trust anyone.

Amelia wouldn't have believed a forced smile or a placating sentiment. But she believed Jason.

Yes, he was worth the trouble to try to keep.

CHAPTER NINE

"It's not bulimia," Jason said as soon as they were in Stephanie's office.

"I don't think so either."

"Skip the stool sample. I need a colonoscopy and liver biopsy."

"A colonoscopy? You are *not* going to be that girl's favorite doctor." She flipped open Amelia's chart. "You saw in Amelia's file that she has attachment issues. 'Avoids caregiver. Does not seek comfort or advice from caregiver. Unable or unwilling to share thoughts and feelings with others.' Since she's finally reached out for help, I would like to avoid as much discomfiture for her as possible. Why put her through an invasive procedure when a stool sample would do just as well?"

Jason was well aware of the variations of Attachment Theory. His own brother had been diagnosed the same as Amelia. Social Services was fond of labels.

As a child of six, he himself had been labeled with 'Disorganized Attachment,' which meant he'd taken on the parental role for both his little brother and his own mother. That was the summer Social Services had removed him and his brother from his mother for the first time. Not everyone had an easy upbringing.

Jason wavered on the invasive testing, then his saner self prevailed. He couldn't let sympathy stop him from doing what was right. He only had to remember his little brother to know that.

"No. We can't do a thorough assessment without a colonoscopy. We could miss too much."

"Are you thinking giardiasis?"

"Doubtful. Amelia hasn't been near unclean water sources, which is the usual way to encounter giardiasis around here. But she was near food that could have been contaminated. I'm thinking amoebiasis caused by entamoeba histolytica. If it's far enough advanced she could have liver abscesses."

Stephanie bent a paperclip in two as she considered his hypothesis. "Ameobiasis isn't normal for our part of the world."

"Amelia became sick after she ate food at an International Culture Day." He loved the way she double-checked and challenged him. When she questioned him, she made his diagnoses stronger. "The fever usually comes from secondary infections. When I worked at the free clinic I treated a family of missionaries who had been infected. The symptoms presented differently in each family member. In fact one of the missionaries had no symptoms but ended up being a carrier. If this does prove to be amoebiasis, we need to check everyone who ate the food that day."

"Colonoscopies all around. Won't that make for happy campers?"

Jason couldn't help but grin as he reached over and turned a page in Amelia's chart. Nobody could find a way to ease a situation quite like Stephanie. "The broad-spectrum antibiotics the health unit keeps prescribing for Amelia's sinus infections have helped to fight off other secondary infections that her weakened immune system might be susceptible to."

"That makes sense." She drummed her pen. "Our lab may be challenged, evaluating for entamoeba histolytica. I'll make sure they call the right people for advice."

"Page me when the results are in." Jason checked his watch. "I'm heading downstairs to observe Maggie's physical therapy session."

"Problems?"

"Maggie's therapist says Maggie has been reluctant to crawl.

She's already lost walking. I want to see for myself." Jason had a bad feeling that little Maggie wouldn't be one of his success stories.

"You're her best hope, Jason." Stephanie rested her hand on his.

He fought his initial inclination to pull away. This was Stephanie. Instead, he took a deep breath and accepted the warmth of her comfort. "Thanks."

Right now he needed her belief in him to keep going. Amelia's case had brought back too many memories he'd tried to forget a long time ago.

Stephanie put a rush on Amelia's test results, knowing her foster parents wanted her home to finish settling in as soon as possible. The results proved Jason right.

As she often did, Stephanie offered to talk to Amelia's guardians. As usual, Jason accepted her offer.

She enjoyed speaking with Amelia's foster parents, the Davisons. They were an older couple, and had been opening their homes and hearts to foster children for over three decades. They took in older children—the ones that no one else wanted to invest time with.

"All children need love," Amelia's foster mother said.

Stephanie couldn't imagine loving a teen, then watching that teen grow up and leave so quickly. "It takes someone with a special heart to be a foster parent."

"We don't feel complete unless there's a child in our house to care for. We weren't blessed with biological children, and we're sure the reason is because taking in foster children is what we were made to do. It's a calling—like being a doctor. We would be living only half a life if we didn't fulfill our purpose."

Stephanie heard the passion in Mrs. Davison's voice. She'd heard that same passion in many doctors' voices—including Jason's. She was sure it was in hers, too.

After her consultation with the foster parents, she was surprised to find Jason in Amelia's room, explaining her condition to her.

"You're going to feel worse before you feel better, as the protozoa die off and your liver abscess heals," Jason finished up, "but you can handle it. Just take it easy, and in a few weeks you'll be fine. Be sure to let your foster parents know if you notice any of the symptoms we discussed. They're good folks. Give them a chance."

Stephanie knocked on the open doorway. "Amelia, how are you feeling?"

"Very clean inside."

Stephanie laughed. She'd been warned by the technicians that she'd have a very surly teenager on her hands, but it seemed Jason had cajoled Amelia into a better mood.

Jason stood to leave. "Remember what I said."

"I will," Amelia promised.

As Jason's shoulder brushed hers Stephanie had to concentrate on what she was about to say. She had an immediate yearning for a kiss from him. Hormones, no doubt.

"Your foster parents are on their way." Stephanie smiled at the girl. "I've talked to them about your condition and your medication and they are fully prepared to take care of you."

"Jason? Jason Drake?" Mr. Davison said from the hallway.

Stephanie turned in time to see the man clap Jason on the shoulder while his wife gave him a bear hug.

"It's been a long time," she heard Jason say.

"Look at you—a big-time doctor. As smart as you are, that fits. He was always looking after the little ones—remember, Helen?"

"I remember. I know two people who will be so glad we ran into you. Tell us how to contact you."

Stephanie knew she shouldn't be eavesdropping, but she couldn't make herself stop.

Jason pulled a card from his pocket and scribbled on it. "Here's my cell phone number. Call me."

Less than a half-dozen people had Jason's personal cell number. He never gave it to anyone.

"We will, Jason. We will."

"It's so good to see you." This time Mr. Davison hugged him. Jason amazed Stephanie by hugging back.

"We'll be calling you soon."

"I hope so." Without even looking back at Stephanie, he left.

Stephanie stared at the back of the man she knew less and less.

They'd never talked about his life before the hospital. At first she hadn't wanted to. Theirs was supposed to be an uncomplicated arrangement with no strings attached.

When it had become more—at least more to her—she vaguely remembered leading up to asking, but he'd always diverted her. Usually with a slow, deep kiss that had made her forget everything but satisfying her body's craving for him.

She had always thought she had time.

But now she could lose Jason and she would never know the man he was inside. She had to find a way to convince him to stay.

Mrs. Davison lightly touched her on the shoulder. "Dr. Montclair, could we get through the doorway? We'd like to see our girl."

Stephanie used all her will-power to stay professional and refrain from begging the couple to tell her everything they knew about Jason.

She would ask him herself. And she wouldn't let herself be diverted this time—despite her hormone-influenced libido.

After waiting for the perfect opportunity, Stephanie finally realized she would have to force the issue. But how? How did she get Jason to talk to her when for the last few weeks he'd acted as if she was part of the scenery?

The Renovation Committee's budget meeting was running late into the evening and Stephanie's stomach growled.

They had been discussing a bronze of her grandfather for

the remodeled entrance hall for the last forty-five minutes. Remembering her grandfather, Stephanie was sure he would have preferred the money go to a scholarship fund for promising medical students, but one of the committee members had a friend who did bronze sculptures. As she was an ad hoc member of the committee she didn't get a vote, but she would be drafting a letter in the morning.

Tonight all she wanted was pizza. In fact if she didn't get a thin crust pizza with bell peppers and pepperoni she would likely tear someone's head off.

Pizza and Jason, a quiet voice deep inside insisted. Two overpowering needs. The mystery of Jason had been heavy in her thoughts ever since Amelia's exam. His unknown past intrigued her, but his future—their future—made her yearn for him with a hunger that far surpassed pizza.

If she could only discover how to grow their relationship while she grew their baby, maybe they could be a family in some form or fashion.

Understanding and communication was where their relationship broke down. But she would do everything she could to change that. And she was certain that understanding Jason's past was essential to understanding the man he was today.

Stephanie twitched in her seat as Dr. Wilkins blathered on. Tomorrow was a big day: her first ultrasound. She would see her baby. That would make the whole pregnancy real to her in a way it hadn't been before. While reading through some résumés before the meeting she'd felt her baby quicken. Not gas, but the tiniest little flutter. She was sure of it.

She was growing a tiny life inside her. Talking about bronze busts sounded so trivial beside the miracle of life.

She gathered her scattered thoughts and stood. "Gentlemen..." she looked around at the all-male room "...we are now talking in circles. Let's meet again this time next week and see if we can move forward."

After they'd received her letter of recommendation. This was office politics. She'd learned it at her mother's knee. Listen politely and respectfully, then be diplomatic, yet practical.

As she was slated to step into her father's shoes when he retired from the board, she needed to keep her finger on the pulse of the whole hospital, not just her little corner of it in Diagnostics.

Business over with, she called in her pizza order for pick-up, but the thought of eating alone dampened her appetite.

On impulse, she upgraded from a small pizza to a large one. She'd never been to Jason's home, so she looked up his address in her personnel file.

Of course she was working off the hope that he would be there. She didn't really know what Jason did in those rare hours he spent away from work. He'd used to spend them with her, until she broke up with him.

There was so much between them now. The break-up, the lawsuit, the baby.

Would he see the pizza as a peace offering and at least be willing to discuss the baby? Would he even be home?

It was a chance she was willing to take as she drove toward the outskirts of town.

She had caught a glimpse of deep emotion, a crack in his heretofore impenetrable surface, when he'd spoken with Amelia. And then the hugs in the hallway with Amelia's foster parents—a spontaneous show of affection she would have never expected from him.

How much of this man had she never seen before because she'd pushed him away? The passion was still there between them. Could they build on that?

She owed it to herself and to her baby—and to Jason—to try.

Passing through the suburbs, she took a look at the residential houses and wondered about the families inside.

Her own condominium was perfect for one busy doctor, but it didn't have a yard for a flowerbed or a sidewalk for a stroller or a tricycle. Maybe she should think of moving.

Did Jason already have a home perfect for a family—their

family? With a start, she realized she'd worked Jason into her daydreams.

What would Jason's home reveal about him?

Her home said that she had money to hire an expensive decorator who knew how to strategically place heirlooms to their best advantage. The only detail she had insisted upon had been the collection of small framed family portraits on the mantel. She liked seeing all her stalwart ancestors staring down at her, reminding her of the continuity of life.

But what about Jason? She'd never even heard him mention family before. Would he have told her more if she had asked?

Keeping up the illusion of a summer fling, she had acted as if they only lived for the moment. As if their pasts and futures didn't matter. They mattered now.

The closer she got to Jason's house, the older the neighborhood became. His duplex and the two on either side of him looked like daisies among a stand of weeds, with their fresh paint and neatly trimmed yards.

The house was dark. She checked the address. This was the right place but Jason wasn't here.

Was he really leaving Sheffield? Leaving her and their baby? She tried to put that worry from her mind daily, but hadn't managed to stave it off.

Her stomach clenched to the point of pain, but she doubted it was from hunger.

Should she wait for him?

She had always hated waiting. Maybe it was time she learned patience.

She could sit right here, eat her pizza and wait.

She had picked the pepperoni off one piece of pizza, cleaned out all the old voicemail messages on her phone and was flipping through heretofore unexplored channels on her radio when she heard the roar of Jason's motorcycle.

He wheeled in behind her, looking dangerous in jeans and T-shirt, helmet covering his face. She'd always had a thing for men on motorcycles, even in her teens. Her heart raced as she remembered her rescue ride on the back of the bike the night of the fundraiser. It was an experience she would like to repeat— without the humiliating speech preceding it, of course.

Jason parked his bike, took off his helmet and pulled open her car door. "Stephanie?"

"I've brought supper. You haven't eaten yet, have you?"

Jason took the pizza box she held out to him, then offered his other hand to help her out of her car. He looked different here. Vulnerable. Confused.

She liked that. She liked being the woman who could knock the stoic Dr. Drake off-balance. He certainly did the same to her.

"Jason, would you like to eat out here in the driveway or inside your house?"

He blinked, as if he'd just awakened from a dream, then cupped her elbow to guide her into his house. "Is everything all right?"

"No, it's not."

That stopped him in his tracks. "What's wrong?"

She was pleased to note that his voice held the slightest hint of alarm, instead of that flat, unemotional tone he usually employed for emergencies. But she didn't let him worry too long.

"I'm having my first craving, and I'm not going to have it alone. Since you shared in the making of this baby, it's only right you share in its feeding, too."

Right at this particularly euphoric moment Stephanie wasn't sure why she had ever thought to exclude Jason from her life and the life of their child. But what if she had succeeded in pushing him away? Almost as a compulsion, she reached out for him, put her hand on his chest, touched his warmth through his thin T-shirt, felt the pounding of his heart and the rise and fall of his chest.

And knew they were bound together by more than the child she carried.

Now to convince Jason of that.

They might have stood there all night, but a car down the

block backfired. Jason broke contact, putting himself between her and the street, protecting her.

"Let's get inside." He opened the door of his house to a neat, clean and comfortable living room. He had a huge television, two equally huge brown leather recliners, a matching couch and a coffee table. The galley kitchen was barely big enough for one to fit comfortably and it was spotless.

If Stephanie had had to imagine a typical bachelor pad, this would be it. Except for the large pile of parenting books Jason had stacked beside one of the recliners.

"No dining table." He shrugged apologetically. "I usually eat in front of the TV. Have a seat."

He put the pizza down on the coffee table and retrieved two plain white plates from a cabinet.

Stephanie chose the couch. They'd always sat on the couch in her living room, purposely letting their knees bump. Would he sit next to her tonight?

Jason brought two folded paper towels for napkins and two glasses of apple juice.

"Thanks." As soon as she scooped up the first slice of pizza Jason's phone rang.

No, not Jason's phone. The E.R. on-call phone. He munched while he talked, reassuring whoever was on the other end that they had followed the correct procedures and made the right call in admitting a possible heart attack patient for a work-up.

As he finished the call and took a seat on the couch next to her he lifted an eyebrow, half-apologetic, but also half-challenging.

"I'm trying to handle on-call for Mike tonight," he explained. "One of his kids has a school play. The E.R. has a new doctor on duty who's a bit nervous, so we might get interrupted again."

"It's okay," Stephanie reassured him. And it really was. Jason had a calling and he had to answer it.

"That's not what I was expecting from you. Who are you and what did you do with Stephanie?"

"That's who doctors are. That's who you are and that's who

I am." Communication. If she expected him to talk to her, she had to be open with him. She took a deep breath. "What I'm not is a diversion until an intriguing medical challenge comes along. I want to feel wanted, to feel needed—to feel important to your world."

"You always seem so self-sufficient, so sure of yourself. Like you dare anyone to insult you by thinking you might be so inept as to need anyone."

"That stings."

"It wasn't meant to." He gave her a lopsided grin. "I thought you might take it as a compliment."

"I think it was the sting of truth." She leaned back against the couch. "I've spent all my life trying to prove to myself that I don't need anyone. Instead I convinced everyone else."

Communication. It really did go both ways.

Feeling emboldened, she reached for Jason's hand and put his palm on her stomach. "I felt the baby today."

"Really?" His eyes showed a mixture of excitement and concern. His large hand hovered over her rounded abdomen until she gave him a reassuring nod. "Isn't it too early?"

"I might be feeling fetal movement, or I might be feeling normal uterine contractions. Either way, it's because our baby is in there."

"Do you feel anything now?"

"Not now. But I think I did a few minutes ago." She watched his face as he splayed his fingers, trying to ascertain any movement through the material of her dress. "It's so subtle. I have to be very still and quiet."

Reverently he closed his eyes and held his breath.

Then his cell phone rang again.

They both jumped as if they'd been caught kissing behind the barn. Reluctantly Jason removed his hand and grabbed the phone. Stephanie grabbed another piece of pizza.

While Jason was on the phone, his doorbell rang.

"Would you get that for me, please, Stephanie?"

The young man at the door was Jason's next door neighbor

and tenant, who had come over to pay the rent. She learned that Jason owned several well-maintained houses on either side of them. He rented exclusively to struggling medical students. The monthly stipend Jason requested was paltry—and he frequently waived it at the first of each semester, when university fees were due.

His generosity was as great or greater than those who wrote checks for her fundraisers. But Jason gave his time as well as his money, fixing faulty plumbing and holding tutoring sessions before finals.

What else about this man did she not know?

After the phone call Jason finished off three pieces of pizza while she made him laugh at the posturings of the Renovations Committee. She'd missed that rare smile of his.

Impulsively, she said, "I've got my first ultrasound scheduled for tomorrow afternoon. If you want to drop in and take a peek you're welcome to."

She hadn't planned to invite him. It had just happened.

And, being honest with herself, she really wanted someone to share her joy.

Not just someone. Jason.

She wanted to see the look on his face when he heard his baby's heartbeat and saw it move within her.

He sat back on the couch as if he'd just been sucker punched. She watched the muscles in his throat convulse.

"I *would* like that, Stephanie. Thank you." His voice sounded gruff. "When and where?"

"At two in Dr. Sim's office. Can you make it?"

"Yes. I'll be there."

Stephanie didn't let the warm fuzzy feeling spread through her at his words, even though she wanted to. She knew what he meant. *I'll be there if nothing else comes up.* He was a doctor after all.

"Don't make promises you can't keep." Her self-protective words were out before she could call them back. But a lifetime of expectation followed by disappointment couldn't be completely changed in a single day. She softened her response. "I know you'll do your best."

Then the cell phone rang again.

After another bout of instructions Jason returned to the couch, but didn't bother to sit. "I need to go in."

He had that mask on again—the one that hid the hurt. His jawline and shoulders were tight and square—braced for her rebuff, no doubt.

"I understand." She thought of all the times she'd castigated him for leaving. "All I need to know is that I'm not out of sight, out of mind. I'm not asking for you to choose between me and medicine. Just that we find some kind of balance."

"Life would have been a lot easier if you'd had this revelation earlier."

"I think this baby is making me grow up a bit." She laughed to cover her uncomfortable confession. "Some day soon I'd like to know about your upbringing."

He brushed it off. "Not much to tell."

Then his look grew sultry up and down the length of her, pausing on her abundant cleavage. "You look plenty grown up to me." His voice rasped, making her shiver with desire.

That was what he did any time the conversation started to get deeply personal: diverted with a remark that he knew would make her sizzle.

"I really would like to know what's behind the man you are."

He locked up behind them, then walked her to her car, trailing his hand down her spine. "Since your place is on the way, I'll follow you to make sure you get there okay."

"No need." Only a little closer to learning more about her baby's daddy, and now burning for his touch, she covered her frustration with a social smile. "I can find my own way home. See you tomorrow."

"There's that self-sufficiency again." He strapped on his helmet, ending her protests. "I'll follow you."

Knowing he was near *did* make her feel safer. "Thank you. I'd like that."

As she drove home, she couldn't help herself from looking back in her rearview mirror more often than usual to catch a glimpse of him.

That was *not* how her life would be—looking backward, wondering what she'd left behind.

She would fight for him, for herself and her baby.

CHAPTER TEN

STEPHANIE awoke with an energy she hadn't felt in over three months, and made it through the whole morning with no sign of sickness.

Now, almost noon, she was feeling great. She breathed in the scent of Jason's soap as he hovered, looking over her shoulder at the résumés on her desk. She had invited him in as Senior Fellow to make recommendations for their replacement doctor.

Jason sipped strongly caffeinated coffee, looking none the worse for wear after being up most of the night in the E.R., talking the new doctor through his first night jitters. Despite complaints that Jason was cold-hearted and rude, he was the first person anyone at Sheffield called when they wanted a level head. How could they not see the person behind the stoic façade? But, then again, she'd been guilty of the same thing.

Casually, almost absently, Jason rested his hands on her shoulders and began to massage away the tension at the base of her neck with his thumbs. She didn't even try to hold back the rapturous sigh that escaped.

This was how it had all started that first night she'd taken him home.

A cleared throat in the doorway broke the intimate moment. Dr. Phillips said, "Sorry to interrupt, but we have a teleconference at two o'clock on the new procedure you've been wanting to research, Dr. Drake. If we participate we can add our names to the list to be considered for a trial study the Mayo Clinic is sponsoring and our application will be complete. Sorry for the short notice. I'm running a bit behind on this one."

Dr. Phillips thrust documents in front of them that showed the time for the teleconference and the phone number for the sign-up list signatures to be faxed in before the conference began.

"Here's your copies." She handed the papers to Jason.

Stephanie held her breath, bracing herself for the pain that would accompany hearing Jason changing their plans.

Jason shook his head, no. "I'm busy at two, Dr. Phillips."

"But this is our only chance. We can only add a half-dozen names. I've got the Sheffield doctors with the best credentials signed up, but we really need your name on the list, too, Dr. Drake. Your success with last year's study will make us the obvious choice for getting this one if you'll sign up and attend. Tell him, Dr. Montclair—it's for the good of the hospital."

Stephanie could make this easy for him. She could exercise her authority and leave him with no choice but to sign up. She could tell him it didn't matter that he would miss the ultrasound. But it did matter.

"That's up to Dr. Drake."

They both looked to Jason for his answer.

"Not this time, Dr. Phillips. I've got family commitments." Jason took a sip of coffee, rolled the liquid around in his mouth, then set the cup back on Stephanie's desk, each movement deliberate and controlled. "Ask Dr. Riser. He's got good credentials in this area, too."

Dr. Phillips studied him as if he were an unnamed virus strain under the microscope. "Okay, I'll ask him. But you're the right doctor for this project."

"There will be other projects."

"This doesn't have anything to do with that trumped-up lawsuit settlement, does it?"

"No. It's completely personal."

She looked from Jason to Stephanie, then back again to Jason. "It's none of my business, but—"

"You're right. It's not." He pointed to the the hot plate and the coffeepot Stephanie had provided when she'd invited him to her office. "Would you like to stay for a cup, or would you like to track down Dr. Riser before two o'clock? He was on his way to Cardio the last time I saw him."

"I hope you don't regret this later." On those parting words, Dr. Phillips turned and left.

Once she was gone, Stephanie stood, slipping her shoes back onto her feet. "I hope you don't regret it, either."

"I'm going to see my child for the first time. What could compare to that?"

A spark of hope ignited deep inside Stephanie. A spark that in the past she had snuffed out before it could grow. Could this really work? Could they really have a lasting relationship?

She caught a glimpse of longing in Jason's eyes as he read through the documents Dr. Phillips had left.

Cautiously, she banked that spark—not distinguishing it, but not letting it flame any brighter, either.

Jason cut short his phone consultation with Mount Sinai Medical Center's leading expert on chromosomal abnormalities as the clock ticked toward two o'clock. He wanted to ask more about the characteristics associated with the tip of the twenty-second chromosome, but that would have to wait. Still, he was confident he was on the right track with Maggie.

In the hallway, Dr. Riser brushed past him. "Excuse me. I'm in a bit of a rush. I've got a teleconference to get to. Trial study, you know? I would encourage you to attend, but it's by exclusive invitation only."

Jason shrugged. "Maybe next time."

Taking the stairs two at a time, he climbed the six floors from his office in the Diagnostics wing to the Obstetrics floor. He had intended to use the physical activity and private time to think about how to get Dr. Riser out of his department. Instead, all he could think of was how very complex and fragile was the development of a human, and how many things could go wrong.

From gene mutations at conception to *in utero* complications, and plain old bad luck.

Once on the OB floor, he scanned the directory on the wall for the private offices of Dr. Sim. He rarely came up to this floor—had had no reason to until now. Dr. Sim was in the newer section of Montclair Tower, which was connected via a crosswalk between the two buildings.

He glanced at his watch. One minute until two. He'd cut it too close. But the geneticist he'd needed to speak to had been out of the country and unavailable until now, so he'd had to—

He had to start learning to schedule better.

In the crosswalk, he jumped on the moving walkway, weaving past those who leisurely stood and gazed out the glass windows at the traffic below. Why couldn't they all follow directions and stand to the right, to let faster moving traffic like him pass on the left?

Then the automated walkway made a grinding noise and stopped. Not waiting to see if it would start up again, he vaulted over the handrail and took off at a fast lope.

At a near-trot, he almost passed Dr. Sim's office, but rounded the corner just as the minute hand on his watch clicked to two minutes past two.

Skidding to a stop at Dr. Sim's receptionist center, he asked the attendant, "Where's Dr. Montclair?"

"Are you consulting, Dr. Drake?"

"No, I'm here as Dr. Montclair's—" What was he to her? "I'm here for Stephanie Montclair."

"Wait here, please."

"She's expecting me." He tried to push past her.

She put out her hand to stop him. "Privacy laws and respect for the patient. I'll run back and ask permission."

Jason gritted his teeth. It seemed all he did nowadays was ask Stephanie's permission.

He thought about the career possibilities that had been discussed with him at the Mayo clinic. His own research department and staff sounded like a dream come true.

But that would mean moving away from his child. And Stephanie.

Would she care?

Before yesterday evening he would have said no. She wanted more and he didn't have more—didn't even have a clue what more was.

"Dr. Montclair says you may come back, Dr. Drake." The attendant led the way to the ultrasound lab.

He gave a quick knock on the door and faintly heard, "Come in."

Stephanie lay on the examination table, wearing a faded blue-gray hospital gown and draped in a blue paper cloth. He'd seen hundreds of patients in similar situations, and the sight always started his brain on a logical diagnostic path.

But seeing Stephanie like this took all thought away.

She leaned up on her elbows. "You came."

She sounded surprised. Relieved? Maybe.

"Of course I came."

Behind him, the ultrasound technician came in, followed by Dr. Sim. A room full of females. He usually didn't notice things like that.

Dr. Sim acknowledged him with a noncommittal nod of her head. "Dr. Drake."

He definitely felt like the odd man out. As he'd felt all his life before he graduated medical school.

In his own research lab he would never feel that way.

"Now, let's see if we can figure out why you were spotting, Stephanie."

He stepped up next to Stephanie, close enough so she could reach out and hold his hand if she wanted to. "I didn't know that was a problem."

Dr. Sim cocked an eyebrow at Stephanie, looking for her permission to fill him in.

Stephanie gave him a weak smile before she explained, "It's not a problem, but it is outside the norm. So we're checking it out today."

The technician stepped forward and squirted the ultrasound gel on Stephanie's belly, then angled the monitor so they could all see it.

Jason found himself lacing his fingers between Stephanie's. Her grip tightened, locking him in place.

As the technician ran the probe across Stephanie's slightly distended belly a grainy picture emerged on the screen.

Jason had done the minimum in obstetrics years ago as a resident, but hadn't had a case where he'd had to study it further since then—except for the quick cramming he'd done when Stephanie had told him about the ultrasound this morning.

And there it was. His child. A living, breathing part of him.

Stephanie looked up at him. "I didn't expect to feel…." Tears tracked down her face. "Look, Jason. Our baby is so…."

He didn't have the words either. Instead he wiped away her tears with his thumb, then on instinct followed with his lips.

A lump of tenderness rose in his throat, followed by a huge mass of protectiveness in his heart.

It was this kind of emotion that made a doctor miss important signs and symptoms. He worked hard to get himself under control, even though the warmth of Stephanie's hand distracted him.

He swallowed twice before he could speak.

"What are you looking for?" From his perspective, everything looked okay. Or maybe not. What was that shadow by the heart?

Dr. Sim frowned as she studied the monitor. "I don't see anything out of the norm." She used a pen to draw attention to the monitor.

"Phalanges are developed. Organs are all present. Tail is gone. Your baby is being modest. I can't tell the gender, although it's very difficult to determine with any certainty at this stage, anyway. Everything looks good here."

Jason moved as close as he could to the monitor without releasing Stephanie's hand. The shadow was gone—just an artifact on the monitor. In his mind, he ran through the list of tests Dr. Sim had most likely run at this early stage.

"How are her HCG levels?"

"Fine. All her bloodwork looks good."

"Physical examination?"

"Elevated blood pressure, but not dangerously high. At this point it's purely a concern and not an issue."

"Weight gain?"

"Right on schedule." Dr. Sim took another look at the monitor. "I think we've seen everything we need to see. Would you like a print of the ultrasound? Your baby's first photo, right?"

"Yes, I would." Stephanie started crying again. "It's like I've sprung a leak." She dropped Jason's hand to accept the tissue Dr. Sim handed her.

"Is that a problem?" Jason realized he sounded more like a worried layman than an experienced doctor, but he hadn't read anything about excessive crying as he'd skimmed over his research material in the last few days.

If he hadn't had to attend that sensitivity training he would be up-to-date right now.

Dr. Sim smiled at them both. "Extreme emotional swings are perfectly normal at this stage of pregnancy. Your hormone levels are at their highest right now."

Jason patted Stephanie's hand. How hard must it be to manage a chemical reaction in your body so strong that it controlled your emotional state? All the men he knew would need a nice, quiet place to hibernate for nine months. Yet women thought beyond their emotional state, fulfilling all their obligations and in general, living life. Women were so strong that way.

Dr. Sim interrupted his thoughts. "Dr. Drake, if you would accompany me to my office, I'd like to get a family history from you. Dr. Montclair, after you dress I'd like you to join us, too."

Jason nodded. He hadn't even thought about what he'd brought to this pregnancy beyond putting a baby in Stephanie's uterus.

But of course he carried his whole murky gene pool with

him, and now he'd passed it on to their child just like Stephanie had hers.

Their child. One father. One mother. One child.

And together the three of them made up a family. The concept sent a shiver down his spine and raised the hairs on his arms.

Miraculous? Yes.

Scary? Hell, yes.

He pushed his emotional reaction to the side.

To care for his family, Dr. Sim would need to be aware of any inheritable defects.

Once again Jason would fail Stephanie. The information he had was incomplete. But he would do the best he could. It was what a man did for his family.

Maybe, if he hurried, he wouldn't have to confess his family defects in front of Stephanie. She could read about them in the report, but he wouldn't have to look her in the eye as he revealed all.

Stephanie hated that she had to find out about the father of her child from a medical history.

That was one of the many things wrong with this relationship. But holding Jason's hand as they both saw the first image of their baby had felt so right.

Every baby needed a father. *And I need Jason.* She didn't want to think it. She didn't want to mean it. But she couldn't make it go away.

She needed Jason to hold her hand. To wipe her tears. To share their child's life.

To share *her* life.

Forever.

She longed for a future where she would feel Jason's arms around her, his breath on her neck, his whispers in her ear as they lay in bed together, nestled like two spoons in a drawer, night after night. Maybe it was her highly emotional state, but she yearned with an intensity that was painful.

She wanted him in every way a woman could want a man.

Her breasts ached. What would his hands feel like, cupping their newfound fullness? What would his lips feel like, kissing the sensitive tips? What would her womb feel like in joyous orgasm as he told her how beautiful she was and how much he loved her.

Did he love her?

She didn't know. And that was the crux of it.

Would she ever hear those words from him?

Could she ever say them aloud to him?

She wanted him in her heart, as well as in her head and in her body.

But wanting and having were two different things. To have Jason in her life she would have to give of herself. Was she willing to give herself to him? To trust him to be there for her? To forgive him when he failed?

That was if Jason would let her.

"If you don't mind, Dr. Sim, I would really appreciate having a moment with Jason alone."

"Of course. Take your time. I need to consult with my nurses anyway. Feel free to use my office if you'll be more comfortable." Dr. Sim smiled. "Dr. Drake, help yourself to a cup of coffee. I hear you had a long night in the emergency room. Must have been a full moon."

"Jason. Call me Jason." He turned his attention back to Stephanie. "I'll wait for you in Dr. Sim's office."

They started out the door together, leaving her alone. It had taken over five months before Jason had let *her* call him by his first name.

But she'd been a newly promoted department director and hadn't encouraged intimacy back then.

Three years. It had taken three years for her to realize she'd obtained all she'd aspired to and wanted more.

But *more* was supposed to have been a light romantic interest—not a full-blown love affair with a baby thrown into the mix.

Stripping off the frumpy wraparound gown, she reached for her own clothes.

Checking herself in the mirror, she felt pudgy even in an outfit chosen to look classically elegant. A strand of pearls, her new red ballet flats and the simple navy sheath that now only barely disguised her baby bump didn't make up for the bra that had begun to pinch, or the panties that rolled at the waistband.

Another few weeks and there would be no concealing her pregnancy. Not that she wanted to. Seeing her baby had made it more real than ever and she wanted to tell the world about it.

Aware of the sudden mood change over her body image, Stephanie was still unable to control it. She took a few extra seconds to pull her hair into a tight ponytail and to put a subtle coat of color on her lips—more for her own bolstering than for convention's sake.

The door to Dr. Sim's office stood open, with Jason waiting alone inside. He sat in a visitor's chair, reading her chart, learning all her medical secrets—not that she had any, other than her weight. She would have rather kept *that* number private.

Still, she felt naked, despite being fully dressed. Would she feel that way if they were in a committed relationship? Shouldn't she feel completely comfortable with Jason knowing everything about her?

Yet she knew little or nothing about Jason.

Jason was so engrossed in her chart that she slipped into the other visitor's chair before he even noticed her.

"See anything of interest?"

"Everything about you interests me, Stephanie. You're the mother of my child."

And to think that not too long ago she'd thought Jason would have no interest in parenthood. She had really misjudged him.

He was so hard to read. Then again, she was judging a book by its cover when she should be reading between the lines.

Stephanie picked up the clipboard with the questionnaire that sat on the corner of Dr. Sim's desk. "These are the questions Dr.

Sim needs answers to. She wants yes or no answers. I want to hear it all."

"Why?"

"Everything about you interests me, Jason. You're the father of my child," she paraphrased back to him.

Stephanie felt tension radiate from Jason. His hands clasped the arms of his chair and he sat forward, as if awaiting a jolt of electricity. Could his history be that bad?

"Let's get started, shall we?" She tried to keep her voice clinical, hoping that would ease his worry.

They began with the basics.

Jason's middle name was Alexander, and his birthday was a full eight months behind hers.

"I've always been attracted to older women," he quipped.

This was the dry humor Stephanie loved. It had completely disappeared after he'd learned of the baby. She was glad to see it back.

"Are there any inheritable diseases on your mother's or father's side?" She handed him a list with boxes to check. "Any history of high blood pressure? Diabetes? Cancer?"

Without even glancing at the paper, Jason handed it back to her. "I don't know. I've only seen my mother a handful of times in my life, and she wasn't in a state where I could analyze her physical health."

He cast a sideways glance at Stephanie, looked away, then looked at her straight on. "There's mental illness on my mother's side, but it may be due to a chemical imbalance created by illegal drug and alcohol abuse rather than a genetic disposition."

His voice was quiet, steady, monotone—but his knuckles showed white where he gripped the chair-arm.

Those damned tears started to well again. She blinked them back. "Jason, I'm so sorry. Is she institutionalized?"

He shrugged—a casual gesture made so painfully guarded by his tension. "I was eighteen the last time I saw her. She was living on the street then."

Stephanie wanted to cover his hand with hers, but he looked

so untouchable, so remote. She wasn't brave enough to violate that wall he'd erected around himself.

"Were you living with your father?"

"No. On my own."

Gently, Stephanie asked, "Do you know if your father has any health issues?"

"I never knew my father. My mother wasn't sure, either."

Stephanie thought of all the times she'd wished for a father more affectionate, more devoted, more in tune with her wants and needs. And Jason had only wished for a father he could name.

Stephanie wrote "*Unknown*" next to the question, as she had done with so many of them already. "Jason, do you have any siblings?"

"One brother. More than likely he was a half-brother." He said it reluctantly, as if having a brother was a bad thing. Maybe it had been, under the circumstances.

Stephanie had always wanted a brother or sister.

Was her own baby destined to be an only child? She'd never given it much thought, rationalizing that there was always time to worry about that later. But now, out of the blue, she had a longing for children. At least three. Maybe four.

"And his health?"

"He's deceased."

"I'm sorry to hear that." She barely got the words through her tear-clogged throat. "What did he die of?"

"Swelling of the brain from a sports injury. By the time I got him to the hospital he had lapsed into a coma. He never woke up."

Stephanie's heart ached at the pain in Jason's eyes, even while his voice held no emotion at all. "How old were you?"

"Eighteen. That's when I saw my mother. I put the word out on the street and somehow she heard. She came for the funeral."

"But she didn't stay?"

"No. She never stayed." Jason clamped his lips tight, as if he could keep anything else from escaping.

"How old was your brother?"

"Fourteen."

"Do you have anyone else? Any other family?" she asked softly. "Anyone to contact in case of emergency?"

"No one else." Jason blinked, as if awakening from a trance.

No one other than her who cared if Jason lived or died. How lonely that must feel. She couldn't even imagine the depth of it.

Again, Jason did that uncanny thing he did, knowing her thoughts without her speaking them.

"There is one couple. I got their contact information from Amelia's foster parents. They were ministers who took in both my brother and me. We stayed there together for almost thirteen months. It was the longest I was ever in one place."

"Why did it end?"

"They were transferred to a different state. They wanted to adopt us—both of us—and take us with them. I was already fifteen by then, so it was a chance in a million with me being so old. But Social Services needed my mother's consent for release. She wouldn't let us go."

"Even though it would have been better for you?" Stephanie heard the heartache that had never healed despite the flatness of Jason's voice, although his face showed nothing—as if he were reading a case from a medical journal.

"She said she couldn't bear to give up her rights to her children—even though she hadn't seen us once in that whole time we'd been with the ministers. So we had to go back into the system. That's the last time my brother and I lived together until I turned eighteen and took custody of him." Jason took the paper from his pocket, looked at the contact information, then replaced the paper without entering it on the form. "That was years ago. They probably don't even remember me now."

Stephanie wanted to cover his hand, but was afraid she would break down at the slightest touch. Instead, she smiled through her tears. "I don't know about that, Jason Drake. You're pretty unforgettable."

In the doorway, Dr. Sim cleared her throat, drawing their attention. "I have the ultrasound prints."

She handed each of them a handful of black and white images and a couple of small envelopes. "I'll email you the video."

"Thank you." Stephanie slipped hers into the envelope and tucked it inside her purse.

Jason scanned through the images, pausing on each one. His eyes glistened as he finally stacked them, tucked them into their envelope and reverently put them into his breast pocket. "Thanks."

"You're welcome." Dr. Sim retrieved the chart and looked over the scanty information.

"I don't have much of a history to give you, do I, Dr. Sim?"

"We all do the best we can with what we have." She put down her pen. "And may I say you've done very well?"

Jason ducked his head, as if embarrassed by the compliment. Then his chin came up and the familiar glint of cockiness and challenge gleamed in his gray eyes. "Not bad so far."

Now Stephanie understood the intensity of Jason's normally defiant stare. When she looked into Jason's eyes, she looked into the eyes of a survivor.

CHAPTER ELEVEN

SITTING in Dr. Sim's office with Stephanie next to him, hanging on his every word, Jason had never been so uncomfortable in his life. Now that Stephanie knew he carried around so much bad baggage he fully expected her to pull back—for their baby's sake as well as for her own.

Instead, both Stephanie and Dr. Sim were looking at him as if he were some kind of dragon-slayer.

He hadn't done anything special.

Although he had to admit that knowing he had been a part of such a miracle as creating a baby made him feel superhuman.

Seeing that tiny heartbeat had given him a sense of continuity, a feeling of making a difference, that he'd never had before.

He couldn't bear to think of such a fragile life having to experience pain or sadness or disappointment. Seeing his own child had flooded him with responsibility, along with pride and strength and protectiveness.

Immediately a huge sadness overcame him as he thought of his world without his baby in it. Still, his mistake with the condom hadn't given Stephanie a chance to pick her own time, or her own father for her child—their child. And now she knew that having his baby came with so many risks, known and unknown.

He tried to phrase his most urgent worry diplomatically, so as not to infringe into Dr. Sim's territory. The effort was new for him. He'd never bothered with such niceties before.

"Is there anything about Stephanie's case that gives you concern?" he asked. If Dr. Sim was any kind of physician she would say yes.

"There are a few details we need to keep an eye on." Dr. Sim passed his test. "Stephanie, your blood pressure is creeping up. So start moderate exercise, although no yoga right now. We want to keep your uterus as stable as possible. Lots more leafy vegetables, lots less processed foods."

"So no more pizza?" Jason clarified.

"No more pizza," Dr. Sim agreed, while Stephanie groaned. "Stephanie, you'll want to hold off on medication as long as possible. With the right attitude you can do it. I know that telling you to reduce your stress is about as useless as telling you to stop breathing, but try. Do whatever makes you happy. Take long, leisurely walks. Meditate. Knit. Go to movies together. Jason, give her an occasional back-rub. Now's your time to be pampered, Stephanie. Enjoy it and take full advantage of it— for your baby's health as well as your own."

She paused, took a long look at Jason, then looked back to Stephanie. "For conditions like this, I often prescribe frequent sex. It seems to be the most effective solution for many women."

"I can see the benefits there." Jason kept his tone purely professional while his mind raced in purely personal ways. He took a sideways glance at Stephanie. What did she think?

She looked a bit paler than usual, with her hands clasped tightly in her lap.

Sadness and worry layered over a wistful cast said it all. Now that she knew about him, she couldn't bring herself to have him. And she didn't even know the worst of it. She knew why his brother had died, but not how. When she found out, Stephanie would never again want him in her bed.

The idea of never again tracing her spine with his fingertips, leaving butterfly kisses on her neck and between her breasts, of never again feeling her hands on his bare skin, was almost unbearable.

He had to make physical contact—touch her, feel her. He had

to do something—anything—to tell her he would be there for her and for their baby in every way he could. Would she accept him if he reached over and folded her hand in his? Would she welcome his comfort or resent his presumption?

He took the chance and held his hand out to her. For a moment she hesitated and rejection pierced him. Then she put her cold hand into his warm one and folded her fingers around his.

"Are you labeling this a high-risk pregnancy?" she asked. Her voice quivered.

He wanted to reassure her, but given the facts he couldn't. They both knew Dr. Sim's answer.

"You're on the borderline. Let's give it a week or so and we'll check everything again. Cut down on the salt, even the salted crackers in the morning. No caffeine. No carbonated drinks. Plenty of water—at least eight glasses a day. More if you can manage it." She made notations on her chart. "Jason, I need you to take her vitals throughout the day. I'm writing down a maximum heart-rate and blood pressure. If she exceeds this she must immediately stop what she is doing and lie down, feet up. And call me so we can reevaluate the situation." She scribbled numbers on a script pad. "If you consistently exceed these numbers I'll have to order some drastic rest time."

"Bed rest?"

"I try to avoid bed rest for you Type A personalities. The enforced stillness seems to promote a nervous condition that requires medication, and I want to avoid that if possible. But, Stephanie, I am very serious about getting this blood pressure down. I'm worried about your hypertension. Understand?"

"I understand."

"And, Jason, I'm sure you're aware that doctors make the worst patients. I'm counting on you to watch over her. Be a calming influence. Take good care of her."

"Absolutely." He ignored Stephanie's snort of laughter, although he was glad to see her smile. It was the first since she'd put away her ultrasound images. He had never noticed how often she smiled until she didn't.

As they left the office Jason wanted to pick Stephanie up and carry her as carefully, as if she were a porcelain egg. Or at least find her a wheelchair. But Dr. Sim had recommended walking.

Stephanie took off at her normal fast clip, her flats slapping on the tile floor. It was how they all walked in the hospital, regretting the time spent getting from here to there since it took away from patient time.

"Hey, Dr. Montclair, slow down there." He caught up to her, putting a protective hand on her arm. "We've got a few things to discuss before we get back to our offices. We can walk and talk at the same time, right?" He kept his tone low and soothing, overly conscious of her blood pressure.

"I'm not a crying toddler that needs baby-talk to calm me, Jason. I'm already feeling weird, like my body is out of control. Don't make me feel any worse. Just talk in your normal voice, okay?"

Great. His first attempt at being a calming influence and he'd already blown it.

Should fatherhood be this difficult even before the baby was born? He tried again. "Why don't I come over and cook for you? I'd suggest a restaurant, but eating out is not a good way to avoid salt."

"Add a back-rub to that offer and I accept." She reached out and put her hand on his arm. "Sorry I'm so jumpy. I'm a bit anxious."

"About the high blood pressure thing—?"

"How many points does worrying about blood pressure add to my blood pressure?"

They both looked at each other and laughed, appreciating the irony. Jason was glad to see color returning to her face. "Guess I'll have to make that back-rub extra-strength."

"On second thought, I'm not sure your hands on me will lower my numbers." She cast him a wry look.

He could interpret that in so many ways. Instead, he asked the question burning in his conscience. "Are you okay about this baby?"

"What do you mean?"

They stopped at the bank of elevators but neither of them pushed the button.

"I know you weren't ready for all this."

"Jason, if people waited until they were ready to have babies humans would have become extinct eons ago." She'd given this a lot of thought in those first few days of knowing. "The thought of having a baby was overwhelming—at least for me. If I had waited until I was ready—waited until I was sure—I may have missed out on motherhood. And that concept makes me incredibly sad." She stopped walking and turned to face him. "This baby is the best thing that has ever happened to me."

"Me, too," he said. "Me, too."

Stephanie had never heard such tenderness in Jason's voice. She only wished she'd heard joy, too. Without thinking, she touched the back of his hand. The familiar tingle raced up her arm, but this time she felt more than sexual attraction. Or was she just imagining what she wanted to feel?

The elevator dinged and the doors opened, exposing their moment to a dozen staring people.

He shifted away—a subtle movement but enough to break their connection.

After watching floor numbers tick by with the rest of the crowd, they stepped off the elevator in silence, going in opposite directions toward their own offices.

Still shivers raced down Stephanie's spine. She'd bet if she turned around right then she would see Jason watching her walk away. Resisting the temptation to take a backward glance, she worked on her professional demeanor, getting her emotions back under control. She had a department to run.

She couldn't help herself. She looked.

Yes, there he was, watching.

He lifted his hand in acknowledgement while his eyes complimented her. But a ghost of melancholy still hung over him.

Stephanie sighed as she turned away. Jason had never asked for this baby, either. But he was too noble to walk away.

In an ideal world love would bind them together instead of obligation.

She thought back on how different Jason was with her. The way he showed her the wicked sense of humor that he hid from the rest of the world. The way he worried about what she thought, how she felt. His acts of kindness—like the shoes she now wore. The tenderness in his touch and the glistening in his eyes. Surely that was love for both her and their baby? How could she make him realize it?

Tonight. She would connect with him in a way he understood, in the most intimate way a woman could connect with a man.

But she had the rest of the afternoon to get through first, and that included being the Director of Pediatric Diagnostics.

She was strongly reminded of that as she saw that Dr. Phillips waited for her in the anteroom of her office.

"Is everything all right?" Dr. Phillips asked as Stephanie entered her office suite.

"Everything is fine." She gave both Dr. Phillips and Marcy a smile that started as reassuring but turned to joyous as she thought about the tiny life within her.

Marcy gave her a discreet thumbs-up.

"It's good to see you happy, Dr. Montclair," was all Dr. Phillips said. A nice, non-probing acknowledgement that Stephanie appreciated to the fullest.

"Tell me about the teleconference."

Stephanie invited Dr. Phillips in and gestured to a chair. If this went well, it would be Dr. Phillips's first grant-funded project. Stephanie shared her enthusiasm.

"The teleconference went well. Our application for the grant is looking good. We have the facilities to do the study, which was one of my biggest worries, and we have the credentials. But after the conference, as the Mayo Clinic sponsor discussed our application with me via a private phone call, he said something curious. He said he'd expected Dr. Drake's name to be on the application, but perhaps the rumors were true and he would be reserving a space for Dr. Drake in the Mayo Clinic labs instead.

When I asked him to clarify, he said perhaps he'd spoken prematurely. Does that make sense to you?"

Poaching doctors was not unheard of. The best and brightest were promised money, titles, facilities, accolades—whatever their egos needed to entice them. Stephanie had originally acquired Jason from a larger hospital by promising him autonomy, giving him a Senior Fellow position and a team of his own to lead in the Diagnostics Department. Now she'd taken that autonomy away.

After thanking Dr. Phillips for both the work toward the grant and the insider information, she shut her office door.

Could Jason think the Mayo Clinic wanted him more than Sheffield Memorial did? More than she did?

If so, she would have to show him how wrong he was.

From the moment he saw the image on the ultrasound monitor Jason couldn't stop himself from loving his child—no matter how hard he tried to fight it.

He found it reassuring that his child would have a whole family of love—at least from Stephanie's side of the family.

What would life be like, growing up surrounded by love? His child would never know the fear of insecurity *he* had grown up with.

He would be a terrible husband and an even worse full-time father. What did he know about being part of a family?

He was too closed off, too remote. He didn't need the world to tell him. He knew. A child needed to be shown warmth and affection. A child needed to be shown love. All the books said so. But they didn't tell him how to show it. That was something a person was supposed to know instinctively. That was where he failed.

He would not be like his mother. He would let go for the good of his child.

It was the only practical thing to do.

He only wanted one more night for his memories.

Jason had let himself into Stephanie's apartment and was sautéing onions when she walked in.

She came up and sniffed. "Smells great."

"Thanks." He soaked up her approval like a mop soaked up spilled milk.

She glowed with a sense of inner peace and happiness. The radiance made her more beautiful than she'd ever been.

Sexy. He could handle sexy.

He directed his mind to think sexual attraction instead of soulful bonding. Replaying their nights of passion in his mind, he itched to reach up and release the hairband that held back her long, silky waterfall, to bury his nose in the smell, to run his fingers through the strands.

He shifted his weight, trying to find a more comfortable stance.

She pointed to the dishtowel thrown over his shoulder. "You domesticate very well."

"Don't let the sheep's clothing fool you. I'm still a wolf underneath." He leered at her, trying to put the right attitude on the evening.

"I like wolves—especially wolves in faded T-shirts, worn blue jeans and scuffed biker boots." She gave him a come-hither smile like the ones she'd enticed him with this summer. "You look like every woman's fantasy of the boy next door."

He tried to ignore the look of hopefulness in her eyes, the optimism that there might be more between them.

Turning away, he served two plates and set them on the table. "Let's eat."

Stephanie should have expected the pulling back she sensed from Jason. After his revelations in Dr. Sim's office he was probably feeling exposed. And exposed meant unsafe in the world he'd come from.

She would do her best to show him he was safe with her.

But how could she get under that thick skin of his? Sex and medicine were Jason's only acknowledged passions.

A gentle approach wouldn't work with Jason, so she decided on shock treatment. "Totally in the name of medicine, I think we should follow doctor's orders and have sex."

She'd expected a snappy response, but got a probing stare instead.

"Why?"

Stephanie felt as if she was performing microsurgery. Any slip of the scalpel would be disastrous.

"It's what I need, Jason." *And what you need, too,* she wanted to say. But now she understood. Jason couldn't admit need. To need was to be weak, and in the world that formed him the weak didn't survive.

Could she show him he didn't have to live that way any longer?

"Maybe I'm being totally selfish here, Jason, but can't you give me tonight?"

At first she thought he wouldn't answer, but finally he sighed, as if he had been defeated. "Yes, we can have tonight."

Stephanie forced cheerfulness. "I choose not to be insulted by that less than enthusiastic reply. You can make it up to me by giving me a night to remember."

He focused on her mouth, then her eyes. His own eyes darkened with passion. "I want to do that." Then a ghost of hesitation skittered across his face. "Are you sure you're up to it?"

"Absolutely. For health reasons, remember?" she said, making them both grin, although his mouth stayed tight at the corners.

She wouldn't give him a chance to second-guess this.

She led him over to the faux fur rug in front of the fireplace—the rug she'd bought just for the two of them.

She started with his T-shirt, peeling the hem up and over his head. Running her hands along his muscled arms raised chill bumps as his nipples peaked. Hers did the same in response.

He groaned, deep in his throat. It turned into a sexy growl as she put her mouth on the sensitive bend between his neck and shoulder, feeling his pulse beat through her lips as she kissed her way up to his jawline.

"Touch me, Jason."

"Stephanie..." He said it like a whispered prayer. His lips traced her cheek before meeting her lips. His kiss was thorough, possessive, and went on forever. Stephanie leaned against him as her knees started to tremble with the realization of how much she loved this man.

Tonight she was his lover—both the woman who made love to him and the woman who loved him.

His large hands bracketed her shoulders while his eyes stared into hers as if he were memorizing what he saw there.

"My dress..." Stephanie resented the thick material that separated their bodies. "Help me take it off."

Jason was already unfastening the tiny closure in the back as she breathed the words. Then he pulled it over her head and she stood before him in her bra and panties.

She stepped out of her ballet flats as he pushed off one boot, then the other, never breaking eye contact, wordlessly assuring him this was what she wanted.

His hands glided down her body, following her curves.

"So beautiful," he whispered. "So damn beautiful."

His compliment made her blush.

She leaned toward him, pulled in by the passion in his eyes.

Throat too thick to respond, she smiled, feeling beautiful, and reached out to trace the upturned crease of his lips.

"You make me so hot for you when you blush for me." He rubbed her flushed cheekbone with this thumb.

"You're the only one I do it for." It was true. Jason was the only man who could make her lose her composure.

He caught her hand, brought her fingers to his lips and kissed them, one by one, while his other hand stroked her spine.

Then they explored each other's bodies as if they'd never touched each other before. Jason echoed her movements, first the jaw, then the throat, then the collarbone and shoulders.

Impatient, she pulled at the button of his jeans, frustrated when her clumsy fingers couldn't free him.

In a quick move he unbuttoned, unzipped and stepped free of his jeans, taking off his socks with them.

She sucked in her breath. He was so magnificent. All his angles and planes overlaid with muscle.

Slowly and thoroughly he traced her belly and the line of her hips, admiring her lush curves.

His hands grew adventurous, exploring her new silhouette. Suddenly, self-conscious, she feebly pushed at him. "I feel so fat." She wanted to move his palm away when his hand drifted down to explore the roundness of her belly.

"No, you feel so feminine." His voice rumbled deep next to her ear. He dropped to his knees. "Thank you for our child." He covered her abdomen with kisses.

Be well, she told their baby.

Stephanie sensed a contented fullness within her, as if her child were reassuring her.

Her hands threaded through Jason's hair as he pushed down her panties.

He ran his hands along the length of her thighs. "You've got the longest, most gorgeous legs I've ever seen."

She knelt down and guided his hands to the clasp of her bra.

He unsnapped and pulled it free, dropping it before cupping a swollen breast in each hand.

His warm hands gently tested their new weight before his mouth covered one pebbled nipple while his thumb circled the other.

Instinctively she arched back against him as he gave her pleasure. He was so warm, so real, and so very much hers.

His warmth went beyond flesh and blood to penetrate her heart. Yes, there was no doubt she loved him.

As he suckled and rubbed she felt the ripples start, then build, each wave racing over the other one. When she came, she cried out his name in a voice so full of passion she didn't recognize herself.

He held her as she trembled, pressing his hard chest to her throbbing breasts.

Still she wanted him to fill her. "More."

Gently, reverently, he pulled her hair free and spread it around her shoulders. "We've got all night."

"I want you now." She wanted to touch him, to explore every inch of his body. She pushed against his shoulders. "Let me."

In that way he had of knowing her desires, he stretched out on the rug. She followed him down, straddling him. Her hands started at his shoulders, then spread over the breadth of his chest. She walked her fingers down his abdomen, tracing the outline of each muscle. He held himself statue-still, his eyes searching, wanting. She longed to give him what he sought, glorying in the knowledge that she loved him with every cell in her body and every wisp of her soul.

By the time Stephanie got to Jason's pelvic bone they both shook with desire. As she reached lower she marveled at how her long, tapered fingers looked so delicate and graceful against his skin.

"Look at us—how we fit so perfectly together." Ever so slowly she lowered herself, taking in all the sensations making love to Jason created within her.

"Yes, Stephanie, yes." Jason lifted his hips to meet her, restraint evident in every quivering muscle. "You are my bliss."

He ran his hands through her hair, creating a veil around them both. She felt treasured, cherished and revered as he looked into her eyes, his own gray eyes dark with passion.

The rhythm climbed to a crescendo as they shuddered and cried out together. Throbbing pleasure radiated from her womb throughout her body in pulses so strong she lost all control.

Afterward, Jason's breath came gulping and heavy, as if he'd just run five miles, while hers came in quick pants. As they lay together, spent, relaxed, all her pent-up emotions broke free.

"Stephanie?" Jason wrapped his arms around her, pulling her into him, holding her close to him as tears coursed down her cheeks.

"They're good tears," she assured him.

The concern in his eyes turned to cocky pride.

She settled back into his arms, head snuggled against his chest, and basked. The only thing that could make this moment more perfect was an exchange of whispered love words between them.

What they shared between them—the depth, the intensity—meant Jason loved her, too. Didn't it?

Jason had expressed more raw emotion tonight than he had in their whole time put together. Through his hands, through his eyes, through the tenderness and intensity of his mouth.

Still, she needed to hear it. To know it. To be sure they shared that between them. Then she'd know that together they could overcome any obstacles in their relationship.

Maybe she was being unfair, expecting him to say it first. She gathered her courage and drew in a breath, "Jason, I—"

Jason flexed his hard abs to pull himself into a sitting position and held up his hand, stopping her mid-sentence. "I know. You're right. It's getting late."

Being doused with cold water wouldn't have given her a greater shock.

What had happened to the synchronicity they always shared?

Then he pulled his shirt on over his head and rolled to his feet, a perfect coordination of muscle fiber and nerve synapses. Strong. Sleek. Graceful.

After a quick trip to her bathroom he came out looking like a man who hadn't made sweet love only seconds before.

His stance was stiff. His jaw tense. His eyes bland.

No, there was sadness behind that flat gaze of his.

"Walk me to the door so you can lock it behind me."

Suddenly Stephanie felt very naked. A chill erased all the lovely relaxation that had overtaken her body.

As she meekly followed him, she tried to force her befuddled brain to think.

He had almost slipped through the door before she said, "Jason, I love you."

All color drained from his face. His throat convulsed as the muscle in his jaw jumped.

"Thank you." He pulled the door closed behind himself.

CHAPTER TWELVE

THANK YOU? What was that supposed to mean?

Stephanie scrubbed the toilet using Jason's toothbrush. Her cleaning frenzy was the only thing that kept her from giving in to a need to break things. One fragile relationship shattered to pieces had made enough mess for one night.

No matter how much she might want to indulge in a fit of hysterical crying, she had to keep it together for the sake of the baby. It was a good thing Dr. Sim wasn't around with her blood pressure cuff at the moment. Stephanie was certain her numbers would have been sky-high.

She couldn't believe she'd blurted out that she loved him, just like that.

What had she expected? Some kind of fairytale moment where he instantly declared his love for her, too?

Yes. That was what she had hoped for. Instead Jason had acted in character, with an extra dose of politeness added in.

She felt so foolish. And so abandoned.

How was she supposed to face him in the morning?

How had she let her imagination run away with her? In just a few short days she'd gone from feeling confident about raising her child on her own to thinking they could all be a full-fledged family.

She would like to blame her foolish thinking on hormones. Instead she had to blame it on love.

Yes. She loved Jason Drake. But he'd never promised her

anything more than a good time, and then, when he found out about the baby, to be a real father to her child.

So much for her nebulous dreams of mommy, daddy and baby make three.

How would she handle tomorrow? And the day after that and the day after that?

She would act as if tonight had never happened. Business as usual. Professional all the way.

She dropped the toothbrush into the trash, determined to spend the rest of the night re-dreaming her dreams, restructuring her personal life and editing Jason Drake out of the picture.

If her heart didn't break first.

Professionalism. Some days it wasn't all it was cracked up to be. Stephanie faked it, willing herself to keep reading her email even though she could sense Jason standing outside her office door. If she looked up now too much hope, too much desperation would show on her face. First she needed to gather her pride.

After a few seconds, Jason knocked on the doorframe. "Could I interrupt you for a few minutes?"

He looked tired, drained, as if he'd used up the last of his energy. Maybe he had lost a few hours' sleep over her?

He wiped the weary look from his face and squared his shoulders, bracing himself. That was how he faced the world, she realized.

That was what was different about him when he was with her. When they were together the lines that bracketed his mouth and the guarded look that shadowed his eyes disappeared.

That he now lumped her in with the rest of the world made her incredibly sad.

"Stephanie, about last night—"

"Don't mention it, Dr. Drake. I'm pretending that it never happened—that we never happened. I'm hoping you'll do the same."

He gave a single nod and dropped an envelope on her desk. "My resignation. I'm taking a job with Mayo Clinic."

Stephanie felt as if she'd been stabbed through the chest. Only years of professionalism kept her on her feet with a neutral expression plastered on her face. "Mayo Clinic has a lot to offer a brilliant doctor. Sheffield doesn't want to lose you, but you should go where your heart leads you."

"We'll always have a relationship. I'll only be a phone call away if you or our child needs me." He looked away and blew out a great heaving sigh. "I can't love you, Stephanie."

Her throat swelled too thick to reply. She barely got out an acknowledging nod.

"I can give you a month's notice. That should give you sufficient time to find someone else."

She scraped together all her pride to say, "Don't let your obligations here hold you back. I'm certain I'll manage just fine."

Blessed numbness finally overtook her. It felt so unreal—as if it was all happening to someone else.

"I have Maggie's test results back," he said, as if nothing had changed between them. "It's a birth defect." His shoulders slumped in defeat. "I can't undo what nature has done this time."

She was surprised to see his vulnerability show.

The nurturer in her wanted to go to him, comfort him, but that would be a mistake for both of them, wouldn't it? She hoped her heart would catch up with her head soon. Instead she picked up the paper he'd extended and read through the results. "Do you want me to explain it to Anne?"

"No, I'll do it. I just need you to sign off on her case so we can close it out." He glared at her as if he expected her to rebuke him. "I took the liberty of calling her in. She's waiting in a consultation room."

Was that the role she'd been relegated to? Jason's disciplinarian? It broke her heart that they should end this way. "Jason, I'd like to come with you."

"Fine. Let's get this over with."

They made their way to a private consultation room in a united silence.

When Stephanie pushed open the door Anne looked up from

her magazine. She must have read their faces, because she immediately stood.

She glanced at her daughter, to see Maggie so entranced with the purple dinosaur on television that she didn't acknowledge the doctors who had just entered her room. "Dr. Drake, is it bad?"

Jason looked as emotionless as the bronze bust of her grandfather Stephanie had vetoed. "Maggie has Phelan-McDermid Syndrome. From the moment of conception the tip of her twenty-second chromosomes failed to form. Less than five hundred children have been diagnosed, so we don't have a good idea on what to expect."

"So there is no cure?"

Stephanie began to say something comforting before remembering that Anne wanted no sugar-coating.

Jason was the perfect doctor to deliver the news.

"No cure." He glanced down at the printouts he held. "I've talked to colleagues at Mount Sinai Medical Center in New York. Mount Sinai has a team researching the effects of this syndrome. Maggie can join the testing group, if you want her to. She'll get the best medical care and therapy the medical community can provide."

"How much, Dr. Drake? If not for the generous donations to the Maggie Malone Fund and you waiving your personal fee we couldn't have stayed this long."

Stephanie knew Jason had provided a large portion to that fund. His charitable giving was one of the many ways he silently showed he cared. If he could only show that caring more visibly every once in a while he would make everything easier for both of them.

"The study is funded by both government and independent foundations so entering the program is at no cost to you. Since we've identified Maggie's disability, you now qualify for public assistance. And Maggie will have excellent care for a large part of the day, so you'll be able to hold down a job, too."

"What about treatment? Can Maggie get better?"

"No. It's a birth defect, not an illness or disease. There is no antibiotic or surgical procedure that will make Maggie well. All we can offer is therapy. I know this isn't what you'd hoped to hear." He gave her a folder of paperwork.

Anne nodded her acceptance, hugging herself, but otherwise outwardly calm. Still, Maggie picked up on her mother's distress, raising her arms to be held. At four, she was a normal-sized child, and Anne was a slight woman. Anne would soon not be able to hold her like she did now. How would she manage as Maggie grew? What would it be like being all alone, with no one to lean on?

She would find out soon enough.

While Stephanie had her parents and her grandmothers, it wouldn't be the same as sharing the load with her child's father, would it? But then, regretting reality didn't change it. Anne was proof of that, right in front of her.

Anne patted her daughter to comfort her, deriving comfort for herself in the nurturing act, too, no doubt. "Actually, knowing this is a birth defect, I can finally stop chasing a cure while worrying that my daughter's condition will deteriorate. Now I can focus on how to make the most of my daughter's limited abilities."

She smiled despite the devastating news Jason had delivered—proof of her resilience. "I'll be forever grateful for all the care you've taken not only with Maggie but with me, Dr. Drake. You've made this stay as easy for us as you could."

"Thanks. I'm not generally known for my bedside manner." Jason looked down at his vibrating phone. "I'm being paged."

Saying goodbye seemed to be so easy for him. He gave a pat to Maggie, "Take care, little one."

Maggie turned and reached for him with arms that could not be denied.

Jason took the child and held her close. Over Maggie's head, his eyes met Stephanie's, revealing a bleakness and pain that had unfathomable depths.

Then he closed them tight, gave Maggie a little squeeze, and put her back into the chair beside her mother.

"Goodbye and good luck." He held out his hand and gave Anne's a professional shake, then abruptly left the room.

Stephanie stared, nonplussed, at Jason's hasty departure. Normally she would have made an excuse for him. But with Anne she thought she could forgo that.

"Men don't express emotions well, do they?" Impulsively, Anne gave Stephanie a hug.

"Not the ones I know."

"Thank you for all you've done for us, Dr. Montclair. You'll take care of Dr. Drake for us, won't you? He needs you."

Anne had definitely romanticized her daughter's doctor. Stephanie had proof Dr. Drake didn't need her.

For the next several weeks Stephanie moved through her job mechanically. Although she had worked out an agreement with the Mayo Clinic that Sheffield Memorial would keep Dr. Drake until she found a replacement, she was duty-bound to conduct a diligent search.

Since she'd given away all her cases her only distractions were routine paperwork and finding a replacement for Jason. *There can never be a replacement for Jason,* her heart repeated again and again as she sorted through résumés.

But she had no other choice, did she?

At least she'd found a highly competent new cardiologist, so they were fully staffed, even a bit overstaffed, at present.

Even though she and Jason passed in the hallways, his face was a blank mask—as if he was already emotionally gone.

The only reminder she had that he had once cared for her was when Dr. Phillips took her blood pressure three times a day, under Dr. Drake's direct orders.

She picked up the latest official complaint against Dr. Drake. They were coming in fast and furious as he became sharper and sharper to the staff. She had bitten back her own prickly remarks on more than one occasion.

She needed Jason gone so she could move on.

And Jason? It was very apparent he needed nothing from her.

On Wednesday, right in the middle of a very long, tense week, Jason's call came just as Stephanie was getting ready to go home and put her feet up. "Stephanie, I need you in E.R. *Stat*."

He needed her? Even in a purely professional context his words struck her.

He would be flying out on Monday, to sign the contract binding him to the Mayo Clinic. Then she could begin to put him out of her mind. And someday, she might be able to purge him from her heart.

Stephanie passed by Amelia's foster parents in the hallway, their faces pale with worry, their hands intertwined, drawing support from each other.

In the E.R., Jason stood over Amelia, his gray eyes intent and fierce. He acknowledged her with a glance before his gaze darted back to his patient.

"Suspected peritonitis from the rupture of an amoebic liver abscess," he dictated to the nurse recording the case. "We need to do an ultrasound to confirm, and draw blood to see if our patient is septic."

As Stephanie came alongside him she knew just where to stand to keep from crowding him yet be accessible for anything he might need. They had always fit well together in their work-life—and in their sex-life. If only that trait had carried over to their personal life.

A nurse attempted to draw blood, but Amelia struck out, feeble though she was.

"No. Don't touch," she ground through her teeth.

Her blood pressure reflected her distress. They needed to keep her as calm as possible. Amelia had too much stacked against her to add shock to the equation.

"Amelia, look at me," Jason commanded. "Watch my eyes. Keep focused on me and don't move. We have to stick your arm to give you something for the pain."

He locked stares with her while Stephanie held the girl's arm for the nurse to draw her samples.

"You can do this, Amelia," he said. "You *will* do this."

His raw emotion sent shivers down Stephanie's spine.

By sheer strength of will Jason kept Amelia still long enough to insert a catheter and start intravenous pain meds along with fluids and antibiotics.

As the drugs began to take effect, Amelia blinked through hazy eyes. "Where are they?"

"Who, Amelia? Where are who?" Stephanie asked.

But Jason knew the awkwardness of naming people who didn't fit neatly into place yet. "Her foster parents."

"I passed them in the hallway."

"They're here?"

"Yes, Amelia, they're here," Stephanie confirmed.

The brackets around her mouth loosened. "I'm glad. I don't want to die alone."

Jason wanted to reassure her, but he couldn't lie to her. Amelia's condition was critical.

Stephanie stepped into Amelia's line of vision. "You're not alone, Amelia. You have two people in the hallway who are very worried about you. And you have people in here who are going to take very good care of you."

Stephanie always knew the right thing to say. They were so good together. Jason pushed back the regret he had about their broken relationship just as he pushed back his worry for the teenaged girl on the table.

Emotion only got in the way.

Knowing his slightest touch to her swollen abdomen would bring Amelia pain, Jason steeled himself against Amelia's gut-wrenching cries and ran the ultrasound probe over her distended stomach.

"Hang in there, Amelia." Stephanie watched the monitor, assessing the scan. She blanched at the visual confirmation. "Abdominal peritonitis. You're right on the mark, Dr. Drake."

"I need to talk to them," Amelia said through her tears of pain and fear.

"When we're done here." Deliberately Jason schooled his voice to hold no hint of the direness of Amelia's condition.

He had no time to delay. Every second brought Amelia closer to death. He would *not* lose this girl. She would have a chance to grow up, have a career, fall in love, have a family—do all the things his brother had never gotten to do.

He glanced at his staff. "Prep her for percutaneous drainage."

"I need to tell them that I—" Amelia's blood pressure cuff registered hypotension "—I love them. I need to tell them I'm sorry."

"Push more sedative, Dr. Drake?" an attending nurse asked.

Jason glanced up from the ultrasound he was performing. "No. She's too close to shock." He caught Stephanie's attention. At her slight nod, he knew she understood. *Keep Amelia calm and talking.*

"I should have done what you said, Dr. Drake. I should have told them when my side first started to hurt. I just didn't know what to say to ask for help." Her voice was getting fainter and more slurred. "So sorry."

Jason gave her the absolution she sought. "Sometimes those words are hard to find. But they know about people like us. They understand." *People like us?* Damn, he hadn't meant for that to slip out. *Concentrate, Drake!* He directed the attention onto safer ground. "Tell Dr. Montclair and me what happened, Amelia."

"I was playing basketball. I know I was supposed to take it easy, but it was the first time the girls had included me at my new school. I didn't want to..." Her voice drifted away.

"Seem unfriendly?" Stephanie finished for her. She patted Amelia's hand to rouse her. "Stay with me, Amelia. What happened at the basketball game?"

"Elbow to the side. Accident, I think," Amelia mumbled, so thickly Jason could barely understand her explanation. "What's wrong with me?"

Jason moved into Amelia's line of vision. "Your liver abscess ruptured. The infected fluid is invading your peritoneal cavity. I'm going to draw off the fluid, which will relieve the tightness in your abdomen and give you some relief."

"You're going to operate on me?"

Jason was thankful to hear Amelia's coherency. Her vitals were stabilizing with her mental state. "No, I'm going to use a needle to suck the fluid out."

"Is it going to hurt?"

"Not as bad as you hurt right now. Trust me."

"I *do* trust you, Dr. Drake. They told me all about you."

There was that ubiquitous *they* again. Jason knew it could take months, sometimes years, before foster kids were comfortable with their caretakers' place in their lives. He'd only called one set of foster parents by anything more familiar than their surnames.

"We're going to roll you to your side, Amelia. It will hurt, but it has to be done. Then Dr. Montclair is going to hold your hand and keep you still while I do the procedure. Just stay focused on her and I'll be as quick as possible. Ready?"

"Ready."

Guided by the ultrasound scan, Jason began the aspiration and inserted the needle.

"Ow!" Amelia's blood pressure started to drop again.

Stephanie gave her hand a pat to draw her attention. "So, what did your foster parents tell you about Dr. Drake?"

"They said he was the smartest kid they'd ever seen. Like, scary genius smart."

"He still is scary genius smart. Those traits make for an excellent doctor."

"But they don't make you very popular in high school," Amelia successfully deduced.

Jason could feel Stephanie's scrutiny of him. He didn't have the luxury of redirecting the topic of conversation. He needed to keep his attention focused on the job at hand. But he was sure to hear from Stephanie about being "scary genius smart" later.

Then he remembered. There was no *later* for them. He had too much foster kid baggage left in him for a stable family life.

Stephanie was right. A child needed to know he was in a stable family, that he was safe and cared for. Jason had no idea what a stable family was, much less how to show proper care. Tony's death would always weigh heavy on his soul—as it should, since he was to blame.

"What else did they say, Amelia?" Stephanie prompted.

"They said Dr. Drake's brother was very popular. Always laughing and joking around. A complete opposite of Dr. Drake. He was very charming."

As Jason drew off the excess fluid Amelia's pain level receded and the pain meds finally took hold—as proved by her increased chattiness. A good sign, even if the subject at hand made Jason uncomfortable. But what was a little personal discomfort compared to a child saved?

"How about you, Amelia? Any brothers or sisters?" Stephanie asked.

"No. Just me."

"Me, too. I always wanted a brother or sister. Being an only child can be lonely." Stephanie's wistfulness went deep enough to make her voice quaver. "I was so envious of all my friends who had big families."

He checked his progress with another scan. So far, so good. He debated on whether he should leave a drain or not. If Amelia was septic they couldn't afford any more infection, and an open catheter made her more susceptible.

"Are the lab results back yet?" His barked order sounded harsh against the backdrop of Amelia's and Stephanie's poignant conversation.

Totally focused on Stephanie, Amelia ignored him as she asked, "Are you going to have more than one kid, Dr. Montclair?"

"I don't know." The catch in Stephanie's voice threatened Jason's concentration.

A nurse handed him the report and he began interpreting the numbers.

The lab results confirmed Amelia's blood was septic. For the next twenty-four to forty-eight hours antibiotics would be waging a war against infection. Losing the war would mean death. Jason had done all he could do but wait.

CHAPTER THIRTEEN

IN THE ICU, Stephanie peeked in on the sleeping girl. Her fever continued to rage. Odds were against her, but she was a fighter.

Her foster parents sat tensely by her bedside. Generally with patients of her age visitors weren't allowed in the ICU, but Jason had used his incontestable influence and insisted the ICU staff make an exception for Amelia—for the comfort of her foster parents as much as for Amelia.

He obviously knew the fear of waiting alone.

Had he always been alone because foster kids like him and Amelia couldn't find the right words to ask for help?

She might not have had her parents there for her when she'd wanted them, but they'd always been there when she needed them. And she knew in her heart they always would be.

But not Jason. She was the only one who had ever touched his heart. She was sure she had. But then he'd pulled away.

And now he was alone again.

The idea of Jason sitting upstairs all alone haunted her. She'd seen the devastation in his eyes as the orderly had wheeled out Amelia's gurney. He'd looked so lost, so defeated, so heart-wrenchingly sad.

Had he waited by himself the night his brother died?

His brother had died in a sporting accident, he'd said. Had this case exposed old emotional scars? Or had those wounds never healed?

Stephanie ached to comfort him, but she didn't know how.

How would she get through that thick shell he'd built around himself?

Was that what kept everyone else from trying?

Healing was what she did and who she was.

Jason was in need of healing. In need of *her*.

He just didn't know how to ask for help.

She knew him well enough to know he intended to keep solitary vigil in his office. Not this time. This time she would understand without the words. This time she would wait with him.

This time he wouldn't be alone.

Jason's office door was tightly shut, but hard thumping music rocked the shuttered glass walls and door nonetheless. Was he trying to cocoon himself in the music? Wrap the hard rock around him to reinforce that hard shell of his?

A screaming guitar wouldn't stop her.

She knocked out of politeness, not expecting a response.

Dr. Riser came from his own office to warn her. "I wouldn't if I were you."

How many people had walked away from Jason when the going got tough?

"No, Dr. Riser, you wouldn't, would you? Too many people agree with you on that." She turned the knob. "Keep calm and carry on," she said to herself, borrowing one of her grandmother's favorite sayings.

Jason couldn't have heard her over the volume blasting from his desktop speakers. Still, he looked up as she entered, as if he could sense her.

Maybe he could. She always knew whenever he was near her.

I can't love you, he'd said. Not *I don't love you*, but *I can't love you*. Stephanie was determined to find out why.

He cranked the music down and stood. "Do you need something, Stephanie?"

"I need to know about your brother."

A stillness came over Jason as he pulled into himself. "Why?"

Stephanie stood across from his desk, giving him his space.

What would he say if she said he needed to talk and she was willing to listen? Nothing. He would say absolutely nothing.

Not the best approach with Jason. But she knew deep down that he would do anything for their child—including talk to her.

"I want to give our child roots and stability. I need to know what to tell our child about her father's family. If she's outgoing and funny instead of scary genius smart I want to tell her that she inherited her sense of humor from her uncle. I don't even know your brother's name." She went for his Achilles' heel. "Please, Jason. Don't you want your child to know more about her heritage than you do?"

"Tony. Short for Anthony."

"What was he like? Do you have a photo?"

He frowned. "No pictures. As often as we were shuffled around, those kinds of things got lost." He rubbed his eyes. "Nowadays I have a hard time remembering what he looked like. I swore I would never forget, but I have."

Very gently, she asked, "How did he die, Jason?"

"I killed him." The earnestness in his voice would have had anyone else believing he was a murderer. Her heart ached for him and the guilt he carried.

But she knew better than to take Jason's confession at face value. Sympathy wouldn't work here. "How, Jason?"

"I didn't love him enough, didn't take care of him well enough, and he died." Jason rushed the words at her and she heard the unspoken emotion in his tone. He castigated himself with each stark syllable, dared her to refute him, braced himself for her to pull back and leave him alone.

But Stephanie was made of sterner stuff. And if he thought his abrasiveness would make her back off, he had another think coming.

Jason would respond to logic where he would reject coddling. But she couldn't stop herself from moving toward him so there were no barriers between them. "Jason, what was on your brother's medical report?"

"I never saw the report. Swelling of the brain is what the doctor told me. Intracranial pressure sounds accurate for the injury," he said, so flat, so clinical. So excruciatingly in pain, as revealed by the shadows in his eyes.

She couldn't help herself. She reached out to him. "What happened?"

"He played baseball for the high school team." Jason walked past her avoiding her touch, then looked out his window, as if he could see the past if he stared hard enough. "Tony was really good. I wasn't at the game, but I was told he was stealing third base and a wild throw caught him in the temple. He was out unconscious for a few minutes, but then said he was fine. He finished out the game."

"So the coach should have sent him to the emergency room?"

"No. I should have. I was responsible for him." Jason brushed his hand down his face. "He said it was just a headache. It was my girlfriend's twenty-first birthday—a big night for her. So I left him sleeping on the couch in front of the TV. That's where I found him the next morning when I came in. He never woke up."

"I remember you said he was fourteen. You couldn't have been much older yourself."

This time when she put her hand on his arm he didn't shrug it away. Instead, he leaned toward her, ever so slightly, but close enough for her to feel the heat coming off his skin.

"Old enough. I'd just turned eighteen a few months earlier, so I had just been released from the foster care system. I was finishing up my last year in high school during the day and waiting tables at night. I found a couple of guys who would share their apartment, so I petitioned the court and got Tony out of the foster care system." He rubbed his face, then met her eyes, unblinking. "I thought I was saving Tony from a neglectful family. Instead I put him with a worse one—with me. The foster home where he was staying wasn't that great, but I'm fairly sure the foster couple wouldn't have let him die because they had a hot date." He turned from her to stare out the window, shifting to break their connection. "Is that enough family history, or should I dig out more skeletons?"

But Stephanie wouldn't be dismissed so easily. This was too important for both of them. She put her hand on her stomach. For all three of them.

"What happened with your girlfriend?"

Jason was quiet for so long Stephanie thought he hadn't heard her.

As if he'd made a momentous decision, he turned back to face her. "At first I blamed her. Hell, I blamed everybody. But it was all my fault. Lapse of judgment." He drew in a deep breath and let it out. "After Tony came home with the injury I was going to cancel my plans. I was going to do the right thing and stay with him, even though he told me he was fine and I should go. But my girlfriend went on and on about what a big night it was for her. She said if I loved her I'd come with her. I did love her—or thought I did. So against my better judgment I left my brother alone."

"Jason, you were so young. You didn't know any better."

"But I did. The whole time I was undressing her I was thinking I should be taking care of my brother." He laughed—a short, sharp bark full of raw pain. "It's funny how quickly love can turn to hate. I couldn't bear to look at her after that, knowing that we'd been declaring undying love in her frilly bed while my brother was dying on a moth-eaten couch."

He sat down next to her, reached for her hand, then pulled back.

"That's why I can't do it, Stephanie. I can't love you. I can't let emotions get the better of me. I can't get distracted and make mistakes like that."

"So you just pretend you don't feel anything?"

"Not pretend. Control."

"Control? Is that how I should do it? I should control *my* emotions, too? Withhold my care and concern? Carry the burden of my job, my child, all my worries alone?"

"I'll always be there for you, for our child."

"That's right. You're only a phone call away. That's not a relationship. In a relationship, two people share their burdens." She stood and straightened her shoulders. "I'm a strong woman, Jason Drake. I can help you carry your load just like I expect you to help me carry mine."

What could she say to undo the guilt that had eaten at him all these years?

"Jason, do you have the same feelings for me that you had for your long-ago girlfriend? Tell me the truth."

He blinked, then looked into her eyes, all emotions on display in their depths. "No. What I feel for you is so much more."

"And our baby? Will you withhold your love from our child?" As if Tony were whispering in her ear, she knew what to say. "Jason, it sounds like your brother loved you and wanted the best for you. Tony wanted you to find a woman who loves you. That's why he encouraged you to go to your girlfriend. By shutting yourself off you're dishonoring his memory. But you've got a second chance. You've found that woman in me. I love you, Jason Drake. And you love me, too. Denying it won't change it."

Jason didn't know what to say.

Stephanie read his heart. "It's okay if you can't find the words. I've got them for both of us."

For a split second she thought she had broken past his barriers. Then he gave her his stoic doctor gaze and said, "You look tired, Stephanie. You should go home and get a good rest. You've got our baby to think of."

She would *not* give up on him. "I couldn't rest if I were there. I'll do better catching some sleep here, with you." She reached out and took his hand—the hand meant for healing. If only he could allow himself to be healed. "I need you, Jason. Come comfort me and I'll comfort you."

Stephanie led Jason into the conference room and turned off the light. He should insist she go. For her sake and for the baby's sake.

But he was so exhausted. So soul-deep weary.

What would it feel like to rest with Stephanie just for a little while?

What would it hurt to lie with her, take comfort from the feel of her nestled against him? What would it hurt to allow himself the solace of her presence long enough to rest and gather his fortitude?

He guided them both back on the couch barely big enough for one, settling her on top of him. Kicking off her shoes, she laid her head on his chest and threaded her fingers through his. Her breathing was soft and slow and relaxed, the way they'd both learned in med school, so they would drop instantly to sleep, letting go of consciousness to make the most of their short breaks.

But he'd never been good at letting go.

Without reservation, she breathed the trusting breath of sleep.

Stephanie was right. She was the strongest woman he knew.

And she saw into him—saw into the dark places and said she loved him anyway. Unconditional love.

Was that what Tony would have wished for him? It was what *he* would have wanted for his brother. It was what he wanted for Amelia and all the other foster kids out there who needed someone to show them how to love.

In Stephanie he could have that home he'd always wanted. The family he hadn't dared to dream about.

What would it feel like to go to sleep at night, knowing the woman who lay next to him loved him? He couldn't even imagine the feeling. But he would love to give it a try.

Lying with Stephanie like this, he could feel his muscles relax.

He drifted off to sleep, dreaming of the comfort she gave him just by holding his hand.

Some time later—as deeply as he had been sleeping, he had no idea how much later—Jason awakened to the buzz of his phone. He tried to catch it quickly, to keep from disturbing

Stephanie, but she'd had the same training he'd had and came awake and alert instantly.

"Drake, here." He listened as the floor nurse gave him the optimistic news that Amelia's fever had broken and her blood count was improving. Finally her body was responding to all the antibiotics they were pumping into her.

Stephanie put her hand on his arm as he listened, ready to cope with whatever news he broke. Ready to support him however she could.

His heart swelled as he realized that by loving Stephanie he would truly never be alone again. And neither would Stephanie. He could give her that.

"Amelia's going to be fine."

Sunshine broke through Stephanie's drawn features. "You did it, Jason. You saved her."

Then puzzlement followed by pain creased her face and her hand went to her belly.

"Stephanie, what's wrong?"

"I'm not sure. Maybe nothing. I'm a little dizzy— probably from standing up too quickly."

He already had his phone out, scrolling for Dr. Sim's number before Stephanie had finished her self-assessment.

"Dr. Sim just finished delivering twins. She'll see us in her office as soon as we can get upstairs and across the street." Worried about her clammy coloring, he pointed to the couch. "Sit and I'll get you a wheelchair."

"I'm not an invalid, Jason. I can walk."

"You either ride or I carry you."

Her meek nod of acquiescence worried him more than her pallor.

"Wait here while I track down transportation."

"Jason." Her hand shot out to catch his arm. "Don't leave me."

He read the fuller meaning in her eyes—and committed. "No. I won't leave you."

He made another call, arranging for a wheelchair to be

brought to the conference room. While they waited she grabbed his hand and pulled him down on the couch next to her.

"I've missed you."

He swallowed down the lump in his throat. "I've missed you, too."

CHAPTER FOURTEEN

WHILE they waited for Dr. Sim's assessment Jason reached for her hand, although she was already feeling much better now that she knew Jason still cared. From the concern that radiated from his very pores and his fervent promise to stay he cared deeply.

As always, his touch made her body come alive—even in her very maternal state.

He leaned down to brush a kiss on her forehead. "I'll take good care of you." The look in his eyes made her feel very cherished.

"I know." She smiled through her worry.

Ten minutes later, she felt grateful for Jason's hand in hers—and not just for the tingles he sent through her.

Dr. Sim looked stern and uncompromising. "So, while I'm not telling you that you must stay in bed twenty-four hours a day, I *am* ordering you to take the next few days off. With your hypertension, you're now on the edge of pre-eclampsia. I'll check your urine and your blood pressure weekly—daily if you feel it necessary. You're almost at thirty-two weeks. We're not ready to start talking about inducing labor early, but in another few weeks or so it may become a consideration. We'll hold off as long as we can."

Stephanie thought of all the unfinished work on her desk. She had been familiarizing Dr. Phillips for just this circumstance, but now that it was here she was reluctant to leave her duties.

But she would never put her baby at risk. "I'll make arrangements immediately."

"You'll need someone to stay with you," Dr. Sim warned. "Someone to monitor you."

"I will," Jason said.

Stephanie wanted to hope, but— "What about your appointment Monday at the Mayo Clinic?"

Jason rested his hand on her belly. "You're more important to me."

Stephanie let hope bloom, filling that sad, lonely empty hole she'd had since childhood. "Thank you."

The baby kicked and rolled. She couldn't hold back her smile as Jason's eyes went wide.

"I'll make a phone call to Mike to get myself taken out of the E.R. rotation starting now."

Dr. Sim nodded in agreement. "It's best that you aren't left alone too long. And Dr. Drake will be able to monitor your activity level, as well as your blood pressure, and insist on naps a couple of times a day."

Jason let out a deep breath. "I should have insisted you go home last night instead of keeping you with me. If you'd had enough rest—"

"Nonsense." Dr. Sim cut him off. "We all knew from the beginning that this pregnancy was likely to have complications." She stared hard at Jason. "You're a good doctor, Drake, one of the best. But even you can't control everything."

He cast a sideways look at Stephanie. "So I've been told."

Stephanie had never wanted to hug another doctor as much as she wanted to hug her obstetrician at that moment. Dr. Sim had said the perfect thing in the perfect way.

"I've got a few loose ends I need to tie up, then I—*we* will go home."

As efficient as she was, Stephanie was ready to leave the hospital within the hour. A worried Marcy promised Stephanie she would call if an emergency came up, and separately promised

Jason she would call only to give a reassuring report after any emergencies were already over.

By noon they were both bored. Neither of them had ever sat around doing nothing, and they both agreed that they had thrived on the excitement of a hospital setting.

Still, they tried. Television, books, card games, Jason rearranging baby furniture under her direction—nothing held their interest for long.

And they avoided any discussion of their future—Stephanie for the sake of her blood pressure and the baby, Jason because he was Jason.

As they sat on the couch—not cuddled up together, but not hugging opposite ends, either—Stephanie flipped through baby name books while Jason read.

Finally, Stephanie broke the heavy silence. "Jason, sitting around here staring at each other is not going to lower my blood pressure. The only place I've ever been able to sit and do nothing and feel comfortable is your cabin. There I can rock on your back porch, feed the birds, read and nap for hours without getting fidgety."

Jason immediately dismissed the idea. "At the cabin we'd be over two and a half hours away from Dr. Sim. It's too risky."

"Except for my blood pressure, there's no indication of any other complications." Frustrated, Stephanie plopped down the baby name book on the coffee table, sending a cascade of medical journals to the floor. "The weather is perfect. What could be your objection?"

Rationally, Stephanie was right. He just had a feeling—but, researching expectant fathers' psychological profiles online, he'd learned that most of them had overprotective worries and feelings that had no basis in logic.

Stephanie must have sensed he was wavering, because she played her final card. "What if Dr. Sim is okay with it? Please, Jason?"

Jason felt himself weakening. He could deny her nothing.

A quick call to Dr. Sim's office and an affirmative answer saw them on the road by four o'clock.

But at four fifteen Jason turned the car around.

"This is wrong, Stephanie. You can bring in every doctor you know, but this is wrong. Now is not the time to leave town. Let's go home and you can make me rearrange baby furniture again."

Stephanie didn't like it, but the intensity in Jason's voice, in his eyes, his face, his posture, shouted that his nerve-endings were on edge.

"Fine." She pouted all the way home, and had him move the heavy dresser to three different places before she ordered it back into its original spot.

By dusk, Stephanie had started to cramp.

"It's too soon." Hysteria tinged Stephanie's voice. "Jason, I'm scared."

He thought about denying his own fear. But Stephanie deserved better than that. "Me, too."

She rewarded his honesty with a tremulous smile. "Thank you. Sharing our worries makes me feel like we're in this together."

"Together. It was a word I rarely used before I met you."

"It's a nice word, isn't it?"

"With the right person, it's a very nice word."

"Rub my back while we time contractions, okay?"

Jason had never fought so hard in his life to keep calm and analytical. He made slow rhythmic circles on her back, trying to keep his anxiety from being transmitted through his touch.

"Maybe it's Braxton-Hicks contractions," he said as she began to relax under his care. With his free hand he found the pulse point in her neck, reassured by the steady beat.

Then her water broke.

"I'm calling for an ambulance." His hand shook as he called 911.

The disembodied voice of the emergency dispatcher calmly asked, "Sir, do you have any medical training?"

"Yes." Although all his years of experience didn't seem to be doing him or Stephanie any good right now. "I'm a doctor."

Saying the words helped. He *was* a doctor.

"Excellent!" The emergency dispatcher's encouragement soothed him. "The paramedics are on their way. I'll stay on the line with you until they arrive."

Stephanie laid a hand on his arm, giving him a confident smile that turned into a grimace along with an eagle-claw grip as a contraction embraced her.

"Don't push. Just breathe through it. Try to relax."

Stephanie gave him a look as if he had lost his mind. "Relax? How many babies have you delivered, Dr. Drake?"

Before Jason could figure out how to truthfully yet reassuringly admit to no deliveries in his medical history, Stephanie doubled over with pain.

"Let's get you in position."

By the time Jason had positioned her on a blanket on the floor Stephanie couldn't keep herself from pushing. Panic threatened to set in for both of them.

Jason reached for her hand. "You're a strong woman, remember? And I'm here for you."

"Hurts!" Stephanie's voice thickened with tears as her eyes clouded with pain and her hand gripped his. And then she started to bleed.

What if he lost her? No! Not when he'd just realized what he had. He would *not* lose her.

Control, Jason. Control.

'Even you can't control everything,' Dr. Sim had said.

"She's coming, Jason. She's coming. Take care of her."

"I'll take care of both of you." The hardest thing he'd ever done was to prise her fingers loose from his. But he had a job to do. He couldn't let emotion get in the way. "I'm going to gather up the things I'll need to help you. I'll be as quick as I can."

All the things that could go wrong raced through his mind

as he tore through the apartment, assembling makeshift delivery equipment. The sharpest knife. Dental floss for the cord. A entire linen closet's worth of clean towels.

"It's too soon," she repeated again and again as the bleeding increased.

"Breathe, Stephanie. Like this." He leaned down and set the rhythm, but she shook her head, not focusing.

Jason gave up on encouraging her to breathe through the pain. Instead he tried to break her litany with logic. He had to swallow hard to use his sternest, most confident voice, despite the fear that tried to consume him.

"Listen to me. You're almost seven months and your hypertension has helped the baby mature faster." Jason checked her progress. "Baby's crowning. It won't be long now. Really bear down this next time, sweetheart."

"Sweetheart. I like that." Stephanie pushed, her neck muscles straining as Jason braced her back. Then she fell back, panting. The blood was beginning to gush.

Worry for both mother and child shoved his heart up into his throat. He swallowed it down. "Let's put a bit more behind it now."

"I can't."

Jason could see the muscles ripple across Stephanie's belly. He would give anything to take the pain for her. But sympathetic words wouldn't cut it right now.

"You can." He put her feet on his shoulders and braced. "Together. Ready? Now push."

"Together." Stephanie exhaled and pushed as Jason held steady. "Ahhhhh!"

Quicker than expected, Jason saw his daughter's head emerge, then one shoulder, then the other one.

He caught their baby and held her face-down on his forearm to clear her nose and mouth. He was rewarded with a healthy cry.

"She's beautiful, Stephanie." He wanted to examine his child from head to toe, but he needed to take care of Stephanie first. Thankfully, she no longer seemed to be bleeding.

Did he hear buzzing, or was that the blood rushing in his ears?

The buzzing became pounding.

"Paramedics," a man yelled, and he and another medic burst through the door, carrying bags and a stretcher.

The smallest one, a woman, went right past him to Stephanie with a blood pressure cuff, while the other medic broke open an OB kit.

"Looks like we missed all the fun," the woman said as she pumped up the cuff. Her voice was cheerful, but her eyes were worried as she surveyed the blood on the blanket. She called out numbers to the other medic. "BP one-seventy over ninety. A little high, but not dangerously so."

The numbers reassured Jason. He held his daughter close while the other medic clamped and cut the cord. As she flailed her little arms and legs she felt so vibrant in his arms.

"Life, Stephanie. We created life."

As soon as she'd recorded her reading the medic shifted position, crowding Jason. "We've still got to deal with the afterbirth. Why don't you let me take over here?" she asked Jason.

Jason's first inclination was to balk. Letting anyone take over wasn't in his nature.

"Bring me my baby."

Stephanie's demand overrode all Jason's proprietorial instincts.

"I've done this a hundred times," the medic reassured him. "Daddy, don't you want to take your daughter to her mother?"

Daddy? That was who he was. *Daddy.*

It was the best name in the world.

With awe and reverence Jason snuggled his daughter. She was so tiny, so fragile in his big hands. But, by the sound of her cry her lungs were strong.

Jason knelt down next to Stephanie and put his daughter on Stephanie's chest. "Look, Stephanie, our baby. Our little girl."

"She's got her daddy's attitude." Stephanie grinned. "We did it. Together."

Jason felt his eyes well with tears. "Together."

The other medic said, "Mom, I need to assess your baby. May I hold her?"

Stephanie looked as if she was going to refuse.

Jason leaned down and whispered, "He'll give her right back. I'll make sure he does."

Reluctantly, Stephanie agreed.

The medic examined the baby from head to toe, gently cleaning her as he went. "Estimated weight five pounds and a little more. We'll get an exact weight at the hospital. She's an eight on the APGAR. We need to watch her color."

The other medic nodded her agreement.

Stephanie sat up and reached for her daughter. "What's wrong with her?"

Wisely, the medic immediately handed the baby to her. "She's perfect, ma'am. But her skin is a bit mottled. We'll just make extra sure that she keeps pinking up for us."

Stephanie's eyes widened as her second wave of contractions started.

"Jason, hold our daughter, please."

Jason could tell something wasn't quite right when the medic examined the placenta.

She bagged it and looked to the other medic. "Let's roll."

Very gently, the medic knelt down near Stephanie. "Ma'am, your blood pressure is dropping, and you haven't quite expelled all the placenta. Nothing to worry about. We're taking good care of you. But Daddy may want to keep holding the baby since you may continue to have contractions. Stay calm and we'll have you fixed up soon."

Stephanie looked past her shoulder to Jason. "Take care of our daughter, Daddy. She needs you."

And I need you. He wanted to say it out loud, but the words stuck in his throat as all the trauma of the preceding hour crashed down on him. And it wasn't over yet.

All he could do was nod.

The second medic took a silver-sided blanket from the package. "It's a little chilly outside, sir. Skin to skin is best, if you want to put her under your shirt to get her into the ambulance. On the ride, make sure you check her color and she stays alert. If she looks like she's falling asleep thump the bottom of her foot. I'll help you check her."

Jason quickly lifted his T-shirt. "Will do."

The medic wrapped a survival blanket around both Jason and his daughter.

Both medics helped Stephanie onto the stretcher. The smaller medic was stronger than she looked.

On the elevator ride down, Jason held their daughter next to his heart with one hand and put his other hand on his beloved's heart. He wanted to feel the reassuring beat, but couldn't through the vibrations of the elevator. "Hang in there, sweetheart."

"We'll be all right, Jason. I promise." Stephanie made a feeble attempt to comfort him—to comfort *him*!—by patting his hand. "Like you, I don't make promises I don't intend to keep. Trust me?"

He said the three words he'd never said to anyone else in his whole life. "I trust you."

Through her exhaustion she smiled, eyes shining.

Once inside the ambulance Jason held his daughter close, willing his body to give her warmth, to give her life.

Stephanie held onto the baby's foot under his shirt, needing to touch her daughter. "How's our baby doing, Daddy?"

He wanted to lift the blanket and study her, memorize the shape of her eyes, the tilt of her nose, the bow of her mouth. But he made the practical decision and kept her warm and covered.

"I can feel her chest rise and fall with each breath. She's got no ascertainable respiratory distress. Amazing for an infant born this early." Jason felt reassured that Stephanie's coloring was coming back. "Our daughter is very determined. Just like her mother."

Stephanie squeezed his hand at that. "And stubborn like her father, too."

This was his family. The beauty of it all made his breath catch.

"I think I'll rest a while, since you've got everything under control." Stephanie's eyes fluttered closed.

He leaned down close to adjust her blanket.

"I love you," he whispered, dropping a kiss on her forehead. "I'll take good care of our family."

The on-board monitor showed Stephanie's blood pressure coming down steadily. But the ambulance ride to the hospital couldn't be over quickly enough for Jason.

Once there, Dr. Sim took charge of Stephanie, while he was instructed to take the baby up to the neonatal nursery.

The separation felt as if he was leaving part of himself behind.

"You saved them, Jason. Both of them. They would have died without you," Mike said as he accompanied Jason from the E.R. to Neonatal.

"Stephanie is my life," Jason said. "Why has it been so hard to tell her that?"

"You've got another chance." Mike clapped him on the shoulder. "Don't screw it up by holding back."

"I won't."

The next hours went by in a blur for Jason, as he sat in the nursery and rocked his daughter. But finally Stephanie was comfortably settled into her hospital room and Jason joined her, carrying their daughter.

Immediately Stephanie reached for her.

Not wanting to be separated from her, Jason handed over the baby, but continued to stroke her back with his index finger while Dr. Sim debriefed them on Stephanie's condition.

"You had a small tear, probably from the placenta partially separating, but a simple procedure fixed you right up. You'll have no ill effects should you wish to have more children in the future."

Jason watched for Stephanie's reaction. He *would* have a future with Stephanie. He could hardly wait for the right time to ask her—*beg* her, if need be—to marry him.

"That's good news. But let's save talk of more babies for later, after I've gotten used to this one. Jason, what does the pediatrician say about our daughter?"

Our daughter. Frissons of joy raced through Jason every time he heard that. "She's well enough to stay in your room with you, as long as she keeps up her strength. If she'd been full term she would have been a very big baby. As we hoped, your hypertension worked in your favor, giving the baby some extra maturity."

"Look, Jason. She's trying to nurse. Help me with her."

Within minutes their daughter was suckling energetically. Stephanie's face glowed as she watched. "She knows just what to do, despite her small size. It seems she's scary genius smart—like her father."

"And beautifully independent like her mother." Determined to voice his emotions, no matter how exposed it made him feel, Jason said, "I've never seen anything as wondrous as our daughter at her mother's breast. It makes my heart swell."

The brilliance in Stephanie's eyes made his discomfort worth the risk of vulnerability. After all, she had risked her life to bring their daughter into the world. The least he could do was express his appreciation.

Once their daughter was full and fast asleep, Stephanie yawned. "I think I need a nap. Can you put her in the bassinet now?"

"You're all right?" He meant more than in the physical way.

Stephanie understood. She covered Jason's hand which rested on their baby. "More than all right. This is the best moment of my life."

He breathed a sigh of relief. Stephanie was fine. And he was very, very happy.

Now. He should ask her *now*.

But Stephanie already slept.

Putting his daughter down, he stretched. Now he could examine her, trace her nose and her mouth and her ears.

That was when he noticed she'd stopped breathing.

He'd never felt so on the edge of losing control in his life. For a split second he didn't know what to do.

Then his training took over. He pushed aside his panicked emotions, picked her up and thumped her foot.

She took a deep, gasping breath, then snuggled against her daddy's chest, her little chest smoothly rising and falling.

"Apnea and bradycardia," Dr. Rivers, the pediatrician, diagnosed. "It's not unusual for a baby born at thirty-two weeks to forget to breathe and for her heart to forget to beat."

"But this isn't just any baby. This is *my* baby." Now Jason understood all those parents with the worried eyes and sharp tones, demanding answers.

"Yes, Dr. Drake, she's pretty special, and she's already a daddy's girl," Dr. Rivers said diplomatically. "Her heart-rate and breathing seem to stay steady as long as she's lying on her daddy's chest."

Stephanie cradled her daughter's little arm that was threaded through Jason's big hand. "What are our options?"

"We have two. We can hook her up to some equipment to help her breathe, and I can give her drugs to make her heart beat until she matures enough to be weaned from them. Or Jason can hold her until she outgrows the tendency."

"What's it going to be, Jason? Medicine or love?" Stephanie challenged with a knowing look.

"We only have one acceptable option. My daughter isn't starting out life in a cold plastic crib, poked and prodded and drugged for weeks."

She smiled. "I knew you'd say that."

So night after night Jason slept in Neonatal. During the day he caught up on his paperback reading, becoming adept at turning the pages one-handed with his daughter nestled to his chest. The hungry little girl was strong enough to breastfeed, which she did at every opportunity—so long as her daddy was there as well. When Stephanie nursed the baby he had to keep one hand on their child's tiny back, talking to her all the while, or she would quit sucking.

"Jason, we *must* see if she will breathe on her own. You have to put her down sometime," Dr. Rivers insisted. "Consider it an early lesson in parenting. You can't protect them from everything."

"Together, Jason. We can do this together." Stephanie proved what a strong woman she was as she kept a tight hold on his hand while they watched their daughter, giving him strength and courage and helping him hold onto his emotions.

The first time he put her down she turned blue and almost brought him to his knees.

Watching her grow limp then gasp for air broke his heart. And there was no doubt he'd given his heart to her—and to her mother.

When Stephanie's parents came to visit, her mother said, "When are you going to name our granddaughter? We can't keep calling her 'the baby'. I've got monograms to be embroidered."

Jason looked to Stephanie. "That's up to her mother."

He didn't care what his daughter was called as long as she thrived. That was all that mattered to him.

"I've decided on a family name," Stephanie said.

Suddenly it did matter.

Not Clarice, after your mother. Jason silently sent her the message with his eyes.

She grinned up into his worried face. "Antonia. Tonie for short."

"But, Stephanie, there are no Antonias or Tonies on either your father's or my side of the family."

"But there is on her father's side."

Jason was suspiciously quiet. She'd thought he would be pleased.

She cast a look at him—and saw the emotion glitter in his eyes.

"Tonie," he said. "Thank you."

By the end of the third week their pediatrician declared Tonie out of danger.

They wrapped their baby up, and Jason strapped her into the car seat of his new sensible family car for the first time. The short two feet of separation almost made him panic. But Stephanie sensed Jason's turmoil and gave him a tight hug, and Tonie kept on breathing, in and out, as she was supposed to.

"First you save me, and then you save our baby," Stephanie whispered in his ear. "My own personal hero."

Jason had never felt more pride. They needed him. His family needed him.

And he needed them.

Before Jason helped Stephanie into the passenger seat he covered her hand with his. "I was so afraid I might lose you."

"Not a chance. You're stuck with me now." She squeezed his arm. "When I wanted to go to the cabin you told me no. And yet, in the ambulance you said you loved me."

"Stephanie—"

"I'm making a point. Love hasn't distracted you from what's most important."

"That's because you and Tonie are what's most important to me."

She looked up at him. "You might as well say it again. The practice will do you good, because I expect you to say it every day for the rest of our lives."

"I always follow doctor's orders." He could deny her nothing—most of the time. "Stephanie, I love you. Will you marry me?"

"Yes! A hundred times yes!"

His kiss was tender and deep, flooding her with love. Neither of them broke it off until Tonie made a noise from her car seat.

"Stephanie, my love, let's take our family home."

* * * * *

MILLS & BOON

THE HEART OF ROMANCE

A ROMANCE FOR EVERY KIND OF READER

MODERN

Prepare to be swept off your feet by sophisticated, sexy and seductive heroes, in some of the world's most glamourous and romantic locations, where power and passion collide.
8 stories per month.

HISTORICAL

Escape with historical heroes from time gone by. Whether your passion is for wicked Regency Rakes, muscled Vikings or rugged Highlanders, awaken the romance of the past.
6 stories per month.

MEDICAL

Set your pulse racing with dedicated, delectable doctors in the high-pressure world of medicine, where emotions run high and passion, comfort and love are the best medicine.
6 stories per month.

True Love

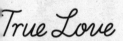

Celebrate true love with tender stories of heartfelt romance, from the rush of falling in love to the joy a new baby can bring, and a focus on the emotional heart of a relationship.
8 stories per month.

Desire

Indulge in secrets and scandal, intense drama and plenty of sizzling hot action with powerful and passionate heroes who have it all: wealth, status, good looks…everything but the right woman.
6 stories per month.

HEROES

Experience all the excitement of a gripping thriller, with an intense romance at its heart. Resourceful, true-to-life women and strong, fearless men face danger and desire - a killer combination!
8 stories per month.

DARE

Sensual love stories featuring smart, sassy heroines you'd want as a best friend, and compelling intense heroes who are worthy of them.
4 stories per month.

To see which titles are coming soon, please visit

millsandboon.co.uk/nextmonth

MILLS & BOON
MEDICAL
Pulse-Racing Passion

Set your pulse racing with dedicated, delectable doctors in the high-pressure world of medicine, where emotions run high and passion, comfort and love are the best medicine.

Eight Medical stories published every month, find them all at

millsandboon.co.uk

MILLS & BOON
True Love
Romance from the Heart

Celebrate true love with tender stories of
heartfelt romance, from the rush of falling
in love to the joy a new baby can bring,
and a focus on the emotional
heart of a relationship.